FIELD OF VISION

A Novel

Michael Jarvis

Field of Vision Books
Miami

The author wishes to thank Joslyn Pine and Justine Tal
Goldberg, independent editors whose work significantly
improved the manuscript.

For Beverly, with love

As a matter of fact, it would be easy to show that the more we are preoccupied with living, the less we are inclined to contemplate, and that the necessities of action tend to limit the field of vision.

—Henri Bergson, *The Creative Mind*

Gentlemen, I'm joking of course, and I myself know that I'm not joking very successfully, but you see you mustn't take it all for a joke. Maybe I'm joking through clenched teeth.

—Fyodor Dostoyevsky, *Notes from Underground*

• CONTENTS •

Part 1

I nearly step on a chicken, a crazed rooster running for its life. I drop the receiver and raise my arms, pressing myself against the wall, trying to move my feet out of the way as the trapped bird flaps up against the wood and turns back between my legs so that I'm dancing in place around a blur of white feathers and beak. He bangs into my legs, pecking and squawking and beating his big wings, his red comb and wattle flapping wildly as he looks for an exit in a hopeless cul-de-sac.

A small boy kneels over my bags at the open door of the booth and reaches in for the rooster with both arms as I attempt with one leg to guide it out without actually kicking it. The bird explodes upward and seems to fill the space entirely with its panic and noise, and in self-defense my arms push away and send it out over the head of the boy. It hits the floor running, turning left then right, legs working in long strides of airborne alarm, cartoonish in its movement, the people in line at the counter shifting back and forth as the chicken darts among them. The door to the Cable and Telegraph Office has been left open, I notice, as I turn around and pick up the dangling receiver. There are feathers on the floor of my booth and one stuck to my sweaty shirt, which I brush off as I put the phone to my ear and speak.

"You still there?"

"What the hell's going on?" Tom says.

The connection is okay but the delay makes everything seem shaky.

"A chicken's loose in here. It ran into my booth and pecked me."

"A what?"

"A rooster, a cock, a barnyard animal. Foghorn Leghorn."

"I say, I say, hold on boy—are you telling me—"

"It's back outside now. Some kid's chasing it."

Through the slot of the open door I see a vertical segment of island life, clouds riding over a peaked metal roof covered with rectangular patches of rust, the tops of coconut palms sprouting between buildings, the one across the street a battered shell of turquoise and black peeling away to reveal a layer of pink like an inner skin, the roof gone and banana leaves slowly unrolling out of windows like weeds. The irregular asphalt of the street is a dusty charcoal with a sandy rose patina across a surface worn with potholes, the hot light playing over everything so intensely that the colors vibrate together and the shadow of a light pole lies black as tar on the gray pavement, its shape as sharp and flat as an etching scratched into the road.

Crossing this narrow view, a sizeable woman passes with a round wicker basket on her head, laundry visible at the top, a solid weight with a circumference greater than the woman herself. In the shadow of the basket her head is featureless. She has one hand to her face and in the other she carries a white

2

plastic bucket by its handle, her heavy black arms reflecting russet highlights as if her skin has been rubbed with cinnamon oil. She wears a blue blouse and a white skirt that dazzles in the sun, its brightness an overexposure flashing through my sight.

Tom clears his throat. "Aside from being attacked right off the plane, how is Soufrière?"

"Hot and sticky, otherwise a far cry from Miami. Looked cool from the air. Small and rugged, really mountainous. Misty, green, visually intriguing."

There is a pause longer than the delay. "I hope it works out for you."

"I feel good possibilities here."

"What happened with the other places, Puerto Rico and—"

"The Virgins. They were okay. I just never quite broke out of the tourist thing."

"Hey man, this call's going to cost you a fortune."

From the next booth I can hear a woman's muffled voice. I look down at my bags, make sure they haven't moved. A man and a boy in line are watching me through my own open door. My shirt shows dark stripes of sweat from chest to waist. An old metal fan rattles on its stand near the counter, none of its air reaching me.

"Tom," I say, "this is something—"

"Yeah, I know. Sometimes you have to jump off a cliff."

"I can't do weddings and babies all my life."

"You don't even make money doing that."

"It's a couple of months."

"Jake, whatever you had will be dried up."

"Gwen Gilmore will give me a show."

"Maybe you'll get a coffee table book out of it."

"She has New York connections."

"I understand. The lease was up, the timing was right."

"Don't you have an artistic bone in your body?"

"Call me the voice of reason."

3

"That's what's wrong with the world."

"What, me, or reason?"

"Gotta go. That kid actually caught the chicken. Looks like it's dead. I need to get a shot of this."

"Why?"

"It's dripping blood in the street, man."

There is no answer on the other end. In the silence another thought occurs to me.

"Have you seen Marla around?"

"Once."

"Did you talk to her?"

"She was with some guy."

"Yeah, okay."

"Look, I'd help you any way I could, right? I'm barely making ends meet here."

"I wouldn't even ask. I'm totally fine."

"I have to get back to work. You take care."

"You too. Hey, look for a package soon."

"Okay, I will. Good luck, man," he says. "I mean that."

"Yeah, thanks." I hang up and slide my bags away from the door and get in line at the counter. By the time I pay my phone charges and get outside, I'm certain of two things: The kid with the chicken is gone, and I have made my last long distance call here.

Planning to stay in Granville, the capital, for a couple of days, gathering information on the country, getting some feeling from its nerve center, sampling its nightlife, I rent a plain room in a cheap, clean guesthouse in the heart of town. Then I go back out immediately with my camera to nose around in the late afternoon light. From the broken jetty I shoot the vibrant reflections of fishing boats waving in the sea, stews of color tossed and stirred in fluid collages. I wander along the water's edge to the mouth of the river, where in the current people seem to be collecting minnows in sacks weighted with stones. On the beach the skeleton of a car rusts in the sun. As my lens roams over it two young boys tumble out of a back window.

"He tryin steal you soul!" one of them yells. They plunge into the river and swim underwater to the other side. The minnow-catchers watch me shoot the car, but I doubt any good pictures will come from it. I can't seem to find any of its soul remaining.

Back among the buildings at the edge of town my eye is drawn to faded wood, peeling paint and cracked plaster surfaces—once-rich colors, time-textured and seasoned by salt air—of stores and houses emblazoned by a relentless sun. Outside a small house I stand looking through the lens, working on a composition that involves a streaked lavender wall, the black square of an open window, and a brown dog resting under the edge of the raised floor. Out of the darkness of the window a man's voice comes to me.

"Take me pitcher I break dat fuckin camera." The voice startles me out of the lens, but I can't see anyone inside. Behind me a few people pass on the street.

"I can't see you, the camera can't see you," I say. The dog looks up with a puzzled expression and I put my eye back into the lens. The window is a black hole.

"Doan take no fuckin pitcher here!"

I bend my knees slightly, lowering the frame. "I see the wall and the dog, okay?"

"De fuckin dog doan want it!"

"The dog is begging for it," I say, and shoot it.

The man appears in the window, filling the frame with dark rage; muscular arms press down on the sill, bloodshot eyes burn red in a black face; wild clumps of dreadlocks hang like ropes around a heavy black beard that opens as he shouts.

"White muthafuck!"

The motor drive provokes. At the same time, it's hard to

5

resist a photographic moment: hostile man framed above barking dog—prologue to a crime. My finger reacts involuntarily and the motor drive fires again. And as the hostile man climbs out of the window, it fires again. I get out of the lens, stepping backward into the street. Adrenalin shoots through my limbs; my brain blurs with possible actions. On the ground the man shouts again.

"Ass-fuck touriss!"

I stand there wrapping the camera strap around my hand. "I don't mind ass-fuck, but I have a problem with tourist."

He glares at me, his face a mixture of revulsion and amazement. In the street people are stopping to watch. He steps forward.

"Gimme dat fuckin ting."

I feel someone close behind me but I can't look away. "I keep the camera. You get some tranquilizers."

"Devilfuck!" He comes toward me spouting a stream of patois, of which I understand the tone, if not the exact meaning.

One of the onlookers speaks. "Leave de mahn be."

Bolstered by the indirect support I yell out words as they assemble in my head. "Get a therapist, man, or get some better weed." He stops an arm's length away but I keep it up, as if this verbal barrage is not more fuel to his flame. "Are you a real rastaman or just a racist with a religious hairstyle?"

More voices come out of the street. "Take it easy mahn."

"Pitchers nothin to fight about."

And from farther back, more urgently, "Rollo! Police come!"

Rollo freezes, holding himself like a coiled spring, and leans forward so I can better see the seriousness in his eyes. He points at me and speaks with trembling quiet— "Dead touriss, dead devil,"—before he turns around and moves off down the lane beside his house.

I offer a universal goodbye —"Fuck you!"—but he's gone.

Field of Vision

In a daze I wade through the black faces staring at me—hearing, "Okay mahn," "Free up now," "Take a motion"—and pass two policemen walking together in stiff, clean white jackets and hats, their dark faces smooth, saying nothing.

I turn the corner, letting the strap loosen around my hand while neurons are rapid-firing inside my head.

I don't believe in omens, good or bad. I don't believe one person can represent the character of a place. But I do believe travel plans can develop quickly and I realize rather acutely that I might benefit from seeing some other parts of the island as soon as possible.

In a state of high tension, I enter the guesthouse and go straight to the bar. I order a beer and drink alone to a rediscovered philosophy: Life is short—keep moving.

The next morning, seeking the mountains of the interior, I travel by bus—actually a truck with bench seats and local people in the back—up the twisting, tortuous road traversing the center of the island to Rocklee, a village nestled among cool, misty peaks. There are no accommodations in Rocklee itself, but I hear about a place a couple of miles farther up the mountain road and set off on foot. Sure enough, I find Sheila's Red Ginger Restaurant and Rooms. Right away it feels like home, but I'm near the end of my trip and Sheila's place is not cheap. Since it's off-season though—if there is a season—and the rustic cabins clustered behind the restaurant are empty, I convince Sheila to let me pitch my tent near the cabins and pay half the price of one, but be permitted to use the bathhouse showers and toilets. I point out that with the cabins empty no one will be inconvenienced, and argue that half a customer is better than none.

Although plainly skeptical, she gives in with the condition that I buy something from the bar each day. Reluctantly I agree, as long as there is some kind of snack provided to accompany the drink. She accepts this with a smile, probably

7

figuring that I'll frequent the restaurant as well. And she's right. An outstanding cook, she wields her talent like a weapon, and though I try to rely on my own food, it's no match for the promises held in the rich odors that waft back to me from her kitchen. On the first morning, my lump of oatmeal has to compete with cheese and mushroom omelets, potatoes with onions and spices, bowls of fresh fruit, pots of fresh coffee, loaves of bread fresh from Rocklee, butter and all the homemade mango jam one can stomach. That night, when my peanut butter sandwich comes up against steaming vegetable lasagna and garlic rolls, the battle is over.

Compared with the other islands on my list, Soufrière seemed to offer an untrammeled remoteness, but I didn't know what I'd find here. Now, after a few days, I realize I've stumbled upon an absolute jewel—a rough green rock of lush feral forest, as yet uncluttered, uncut, unfucked by foreign clowns—that's working a spell on me. Only here am I beginning to realize the obvious—that I've come to find images I've never seen.

For several days I'd been exploring the forest, gaining higher elevation with each successive outing. Now I've paused to examine a few wildflowers. In the bland light they are nothing special. Bending down, I squint. Why did I stop here? I don't see the reason now. The whole mountain is beautiful, but it's a question of selection. Hidden still lifes are everywhere. Nearly invisible compositions. Tiny tropical color arrangements. Blown up, they'll be like abstract paintings. Will the photos be lost in exquisite detail? Or vice versa? Won't the subject of the image be obscured by the overall abstraction?

In the cool green silence these questions plague me like a swarm of insects. In the profound solitude behind the camera they bore into me like parasites.

The sun is gone. I climb the trail to a clearing where I can see something of the weather on this side of the mountain. It's apt to change quickly up here. Through a hole in the trees, I see clouds move into view, swirling ominously, rolling downward toward the valley. Beyond the mountains a strip of blue sea shines in the light about five miles away. Beside a small stream I sit down to eat my lunch: a sardine sandwich, some avocado slices, tomato, pepper and lime, coconut chunks for dessert— the same as yesterday. I drain my canteen. The forest is full of water. I just need more light.

Every day I go a little farther, working my way up to the cloud forest. Every day I see less sun and spend more time hiking. But the forest is so sublime that I've begun to experience a disorientation I find pleasing, partly because I'm working in macro—finally, after a long process of scaling down, of reducing my vision to the elemental patterns at arm's length, to the abstractions underfoot—where composition is everything.

Searching the floor of the forest I examine ferns and fungus and fecundity, the arrangement of objects dropped from trees and the strange white shapes sprouting from dead wood into short-lived shafts of light; the sand designs in stream beds, where water deposits a macro-fortune in juxtaposed matter: floating petals and leaves, seeds, feathers and bark, whole crustaceans and claw segments, insect wings and legs, shells and stones, fragments of egg and bone. Down to areas of small detail, places where compositions emerge at the speed of decay, where color hides in a frog's back. Down to the drab world of slugs and termites, to a level where direct light is a surprise—where decomposition is everything.

No more scenes of island life. No more quaint streets, humble people or sailboats in the harbor. No more colorful fruit markets, idle taxi stands, dilapidated docks or dinghies at dusk. No more ragged children playing inventive street games or fishermen unloading their catches. No more humanity in all its rustic guises. What I seek now is beneath us, behind us, out of our sight. Things unseen, unnoticed, unknown. No more stunning blue bays, white sand beaches, coconut palm silhouettes. No more tourists with rumrunners and straw bags. No more sunburnt chumps in matching outfits.

I reload the camera and refill my canteen. The cool sound of the water takes over the forest. There is still no sunlight on the ground and I lean back against a tree and sit with the camera on my lap. My eyes are closed. High above me the trees whisper to the ground. Grainy patches of pale orange march across the olive surface of my eyelids.

I'm standing near the rim of a sunken lake, trying to photograph something on the ground. I can't tell what it is, but neither can I tear myself away even as I feel the earth beginning to crack under me. A wall of dirt and rock falls away. I keep my face pressed to the camera and I hear the motor drive firing into a massive splash. Then all sound is gone as I plummet into cold water and sink below the surface. I drop the camera but the strap hangs around my neck and I continue to sink as I try to swim, falling like a stone in the dark, afraid of passing out as I struggle with the strap, going down headfirst to get myself vertical. I wrestle the strap over my head and the camera disappears into the muck below. My lungs are bursting as I kick my legs and claw upward like a frantic cat.

I wake with a start, gasping for breath. The camera rolls off my lap to the ground. Tree ferns hang over me and heliconias grow by the stream. I rub my face and stare at the running water. It seems too simple, this drowning dream. But maybe I could use a little break. Tomorrow I'll leave the camera at home—separate myself from it. I need to break the tension and bring it back in a new form.

With her white legs up on the railing Sheila Faber sits on the front porch of her restaurant reading a paperback. She looks up as I approach the steps, her intelligent blue eyes appraising me, the corners of her mouth upturned in a slight smile that seems to signal amusement. Her brown hair falls to her shoulders and she is dressed casually in khaki shorts and a loose white cotton shirt that does little to hide the curves beneath it. She's an attractive woman in her mid-forties, long-legged and slim and quite buxom.

"You had a nice time?"

"Yes, thanks."

"You are having dinner tonight?"

"You have me figured out," I say.

She cuts through the small talk and gets right to economics. The question is merely a formality, and actually more of a statement. We both know the answer. I no longer even ask about the menu.

"Something from the bar?"

"Sure." Another daily standard.

She makes me a rum and fresh fruit juice—today's juice is passion fruit—and lights a cigarette as she returns to her chair. She will keep me company for as long as I spend money. And later, when the dinner guests have gone, she will sit behind the bar, smoking and talking, serving me drinks and matching me one for one as long as I want to stay. It's just business, and though she goes about it in a casual, easygoing manner, the bar tab is always precise. For my part, I do enjoy the conversation after being alone in the forest all day.

Sheila and her husband had opened the Red Ginger Restaurant ten years earlier after moving here from Frankfurt. She spoke of the industrialization of Germany and the cold gray sky there. They had made some money and been happy to leave, tailoring their business and culinary instincts to an isolated spot in the Caribbean. They succeeded for several years before a hurricane hit the island and destroyed their business. During the lengthy and frustrating period of reconstruction—at which time the cabins were added—they had separated and then divorced. Her ex-husband remained in

11

Germany.

Sheila lived above the restaurant. Her life, as she explained it to me, is simple—tending her garden of vegetables and fruits, cooking, playing hostess to her guests, driving to Granville for business errands and supplies, and taking an occasional trip to Europe. She has everything she needs here, she says, and she runs the place, if not single-handedly, then certainly to her exact specifications. She's a loner who's found her place in life and acts as though she doesn't care if anyone else shares it or not. And if she pretends she doesn't care whether potential customers stop for lunch or keep on driving, it's because she knows that enough of them will stop. No doubt she takes pride in the fine reputation her restaurant enjoys. She mentioned that on numerous occasions the Prime Minister himself has driven up from the capital and dropped in unannounced.

She and I had haggled the first day, but an odd coincidence cast me in a light that may have appealed to her eccentric nature. After I'd registered, putting my name in her guest book, she examined me as she smoked.

"Jake?"

"That's it. Jacob Mayfield."

"There was a hurricane with that name," she said. "In 1980. It broke the house and the bar." She gestured with her cigarette. "Trees came inside."

"I heard about that storm. And I'll try to be a little less destructive."

She studied me through the smoke. "Why are you here?"

It seemed like a serious question. "To penetrate other worlds. See what hasn't been seen, if that's still possible."

She smiled and went to the kitchen, effectively ending our first conversation.

Four local people, all residents of Rocklee, are employed by Sheila. The senior employee is Connie, an elderly cook who's been with the restaurant from its beginning. She stays in the kitchen and is rarely seen but I often hear her humming when the bar stereo isn't on. At first I mistook the sound for wind blowing through the trees and later began to think I recognized church hymns. Her daughter Josephine, or Josey, helps her mother in the kitchen when the place is busy, and otherwise washes dishes, cleans the cabins or the restaurant or whatever else needs cleaning. Some days she washes laundry in a large basin behind the restaurant and hangs it out on clotheslines that also support vines of pink bougainvillea. She seems a bit slow to me and though she is friendly she speaks so softly I usually can't understand what she says. A silent young man named Clifton performs the maintenance on the buildings and keeps the jungle at bay; he works the day shift only, carries a machete most of the time and rarely looks me in the eye. Rita works the bar and the dining room, setting up, taking orders and serving, clearing tables. She appeared a reticent, conscientious girl who seldom smiled, but in whose black, glancing eyes I detected traces of curiosity and spirit. The women are permitted the use of two small utility rooms behind the kitchen for resting between shifts or passing the night if they desire, and they have a bathroom back there. Connie has her own room; the younger women share the other.

I finish my drink and set the glass down on the floorboards beside my camera. In the west the sun drops below a band of clouds, suddenly infusing the treetop mist and creating a layer of floating gold light between us and the distant gleaming sea.

Sheila looks up from her book. "What a beautiful picture."

I lean down and press the button on the motor drive, opening the shutter, capturing a porch-level panorama with a wide angle lens.

"You waste your film," she says.

"You haven't seen the picture yet."

She puts the open book down on her lap. "Why do you make pictures?"

13

I think about this for a few seconds. "I take pictures for the surprises. Sometimes I remember an image I saw through the lens and I carry it in my head. But when I finally see the photo I'm often surprised at the translation. And when I don't remember the image the surprise can be much greater. There's a fantastic random quality about looking through a batch of new photos and finding a bull's-eye, a winner that lives on its own."

At my feet the empty glass has caught the passing light and recast it in an oval shape on the wood grain, leaving a design like a translucent barnacle. "Also, I like being inside the lens." I look up to see her watching me and I shrug. "I'm an abstract kind of guy. Composition is everything."

She lets out a little laugh. "You wish to make order from chaos."

"The other way around," I say. "I'm only human."

Rain begins to pelt the metal roof, plunking a forceful, tuneless song, as if from a child's toy xylophone. On the porch streaks of sunlight are still hitting our faces.

"Rita!" Sheila shouts.

The girl comes around the corner and looks up under the railing at her employer. Her wet arms shine in the warm light and droplets explode off the tightness of her hair, its rippled surface pulled back into two short braids that stand out behind her ears. With her high cheek bones and sharp nose she might possess some Carib Indian blood.

"Has Josey put the laundry in?"

"Yes ma'am."

"The dining room is set up?"

"Yes ma'am."

I reach down and press the shutter release, firing a shot in the girl's face. She twitches slightly, glances at me and then looks down to hide an almost imperceptible smile.

"Then find Clifton and ask him if he changed the bulb in

the drive." Sheila looks at me as the girl moves away. "I prefer you don't take her photo," she says. "She may think you are interested."

"I am. I'm interested in everything. It's a sickness. You just saw me shoot a sunset."

"I don't allow the staff to mix with the guest."

"Look, I'm sorry to break your rule. My rule is to shoot anything I react to. It's a hard principle to keep but it keeps me working, keeps me going, keeps me alive."

Her face becomes rigid and some redness creeps into her cheeks.

"It's also killing me," I say, smiling as if this last part is hardly worth mentioning.

Her blue eyes are as hard as quartz but her mouth softens a little. "The client is sometimes a problem," she says. "Would you like another drink?" She gives me a half-smile. "On the house."

I laugh. "Well, hell. I'll need one to toast this historic occasion."

As she stands I raise the camera as high as my knee and shoot her looking down at me. "General interest," I tell her. "Everyone's equal."

The rain falls harder, and makes a comforting racket overhead. Sheila sets my drink on the railing. "You want a cabin?" Every day she asks me this. Twice if it rains.

"My tent still doesn't leak," I say, and she turns to go inside. "What about the snack?"

"Chips on the bar," she says, passing through the doorway.

Darkness comes slowly as the mountains and jungle soak up the remaining light. Over the metallic drumming I hear the first whistles—like hesitant questions—of arboreal frogs, and the last excited twitterings—the hurried explanations—of roosting birds. Then the generator starts and the steady chug-chugging fades into background noise as the stereo comes on with Radio Antilles.

I stroll down the concrete path past the generator shed—Clifton is inside, bent over the machinery with a flashlight—to the other buildings, where I can barely discern the rain-battered bushes of red ginger and the loose circle of dark cabins. On the concrete around the bathhouse, black snails crunch like seeds under my shoes. I hit the light switch for the showers, find my damp towel and turn on the cold river water. The rain is warm by comparison. Under the splattering stream I cease to hear the river frogs, the steady pumping of the generator, or the pounding rain on the roof. As I bathe, moths flutter haplessly around the ceiling bulb while bats cut through the space, whisking the insects out of the cool night air. It's great to be alive; it's great to be clean.

I leave my wet poncho on the porch and pass through the bar on my way into the dining room, an open, comfortable space with tall windows on three sides. Paddle fans and brass lamps hang from the ceiling. The tables and chairs are local hardwood and the tablecloths are fine European lace. The front windows open toward the road and the slope of the tallest peak on the island, Morne Matin, so named because its cloud-shrouded top is usually seen in the early morning. A stone planter outside these windows is full of red ginger plants which flower profusely against the glass and summon hummingbirds who arrive each morning like brilliant sweet-seeking helicopters to find the white blossoms hidden in the crimson. On the east, French doors lead to an uncovered patio looking out toward lesser hills. The opposite side overlooks the orderly vegetation of Sheila's garden and the land's irregular descent to the sea.

A European foursome sits in a corner at the front and a young American couple with a video camera occupies a table by the French doors. I take a seat on the porch side, as far as possible from the video people. The man nods at me; I rearrange my silverware.

Sheila wears a long brown dress and a multicolored scarf, and when she brings the bread basket and water to my table she greets me cheerfully, like she would any hungry patron with a wallet. "Guten abend, Herr Mayfield."

"Good evening, Lady Faber."

"A beer?"

"Please."

I start with callaloo soup. The American couple take turns taping each other eating their appetizers, capturing precious moments of their incredible saga. She laughs with the camera as he makes his crayfish dance across the plate. When she gets caught with melted cheese hanging from her chin and he refuses to rewind, she protests and hides behind her napkin. I figure they might be with the State Department.

The man stands and says across the room, "Hey pal, would you mind shooting the both of us?" I say nothing, thinking: point-blank or from here? "All you do is press this button," he says, taking a step toward me.

"Je ne parle pas anglais," I say.

He stops and looks back at the woman.

"He's speaking French, honey," she says.

"Oh! Sorry," he says, raising his hand slightly. He turns around and sits. "Excuse me, Pierre," he says, grinning at me.

If she speaks French, I'm prepared to run out into the rain speaking in tongues. As it is, I sit looking at them with my head at a jaunty tilt.

She smiles at me. "He certainly looks American."

"You never know with these frogs," he says, "until they open their mouths."

Rita brings out their entrees. "Bon appetit," I say, raising my fork.

"Yeah, right," the man says, "same to you, Napoleon."

After the meal—curried lobster, dasheen and rice—I sip

coffee and nibble on a succulent rum-soaked fruit salad of pineapple, watermelon and grapefruit. Rita brings a cheese and fruit board around the room but I decline. Sheets of rain streak down the windows. Low strains of Bach flow from the bar speakers. A few more diners arrive, stamping their feet on the porch. I hear Sheila speaking German with them as they are seated.

I retire to the bar and sit under a corner lamp looking at a book on Caribbean wildflowers. The room has several rattan chairs, some small tables with ashtrays and coasters, a large woven grass rug that covers the middle of the floor. The bar itself—with five bamboo-legged stools lining it—is one long, irregular slab of mahogany about three inches thick. A wall shelf holds an array of paperback books—thrillers, romances, and Nietzsche—and a stuffed parrot. Mounted high on the wall behind the bar, a black boar's head looks out over the room; from one yellowed tusk hangs a blue ribbon cooking medal from Munich.

When the last tail lights turn out of the driveway and disappear around the mountain curve, Sheila comes into the bar, lights a cigarette and puts on a reggae tape. I want to believe she likes to unwind a little after the restaurant closes but with her it's hard to tell. If I didn't have the look of a man with a sizeable bar tab in his future maybe she would go to bed. Whatever the case, she pours us equal glasses of rum.

"Another classic feast," I say, clinking her glass with mine.

"Not so bad," she says.

We drink the first drink quietly, feeling the sweet burn, listening to the music, me watching her smoke and her watching me watch her smoke. By the middle of the next one we're discussing the loss of wilderness in Europe and America, the rampant squandering of tropical forests, overcrowded cities.

"The world's changing," I say. "The cities have become the norm now, the wild land more and more rare. It's out of control, like advertising."

"In the end we will sell all," she says.

I nod in agreement. "I spend most of my time in an urban jungle and I'm not even sure why anymore. I know it's a sellout too. So then I find myself standing there in the beautiful forest feeling wonderful one minute and pissed the next."

"Drunken?"

"No, pissed like angry. And I realize the fact that it's all going away keeps me from totally enjoying it."

"The problem is here," she says, tapping her head.

"I know, but it's also out there. It upsets me, maybe beyond reason. I just can't accept the way things are going."

"I was the same," she says, "so I make my great escape. And now my small life is normal, no?"

"Well yeah, you built a tropical holiday for yourself and people pay you to share it. That works, but what about all the tourists. Isn't it a conflict for you?"

"Business, my friend. Without me, without my nice place, where would you be drinking now?"

"There's no way out is there? Everyone wants everything." I tap my empty glass. "We all want it all. What's wrong with us, Sheila?"

She refills our glasses, lights another cigarette, and turns the tape over. "I have only what I need but I am happy," she says, but I can't believe her on either count.

"Are you really happy? Are you living the good life?"

"I live the life I choose."

"I suppose that makes it good. That and the wild land."

"It's not so easy as you say. There are problems here also, my friend. Serious problems."

She looks a little high now and I watch her over my glass, looking for the wildness that must have brought her here. "Tell me about Hurricane Jake," I say.

She gives me a curious look, her eyes glassy as she plays with a pack of French cigarettes. She pushes a loose strand of hair behind her ear and takes a swallow of her drink. "That was seven years ago," she says. "Since then nothing so exciting has happened."

"It devastated the island, but you make it sound like a positive experience."

"It changed my life completely."

"Because you survived?"

She studies my face as if she is calculating something, while her fingers mechanically turn the cigarette pack end over end. "Not only that," she says with the faintest hint of a smile at the corners of her mouth.

"So what, you had a party or something?"

"Not a party but a lot of excitement," she says. "I had never seen anything like this." Then she rushes on, trying to finish the story. "The wind and the noise, trees flying. It was terrible." She finishes her drink in a gulp.

"I'm not really getting the whole picture," I say.

The music stops. She reaches under the bar, fumbling for another tape. "What was it like?" I ask, taking her wrist in my hand. She looks up at me. I'm not squeezing her arm so much as I'm gripping it firmly. "Please go on," I say. "Pretend I'm not here if you like, but tell me a story." She stares at my face and I cross my arms on the bar. She looks down again. The cassette door clicks shut; a few seconds later some slow saxophone jazz eases through the speakers.

"Alright," she says, picking up the rum. "I will tell you a small story." She pours two more drinks and sets the bottle down between us.

"I hope you're not counting those."

"Don't worry."

She takes a sip, licks her lips and stubs out her cigarette.

She gives me another look and her eyes move to the open space through the door. "We knew the storm was coming. We heard about it for many days, coming across the sea, getting stronger. It was making a straight line to Soufrière." She pauses, still staring ahead, as if she's watching the weather. "I became a little bit excited but also frightened. We heard it was becoming a class five storm so we try to prepare—my husband, Connie and me. I didn't wish to evacuate because I was making my new home. My husband was a nervous man and he wanted to leave, so we had a great fight. I was hoping the mountains would protect us." A little laugh escapes her.

"The day before—when we are thinking the direction will not change—we close the restaurant. We bring everything inside. We put wood on the windows. We put stones on the generator house." She laughs again. "We didn't understand how strong the wind could be." She takes a swallow of rum and coughs softly.

Rain is still pelting the roof above us. The music is low. From the yard come the voices of the amphibian chorus, and on the other side of the wall I hear the sound of pots banging together in the kitchen.

"In the morning the sky was so dark and wind was crying in the house. It became difficult to walk outside because something could strike you. We had breakfast together in the kitchen. Connie was praying all the time. We made a box of food and water, flashlights, candles, some medicines—for after."

"We went under the house with our box and blankets—here"—she taps her foot on the floor, then adjusts her weight on the stool and looks outside again. "Then we waited. We could do nothing more. I became afraid when the storm came. The noise was so loud I felt stupid. We were like animals under the house. I wanted to go away but it was too late." She closes her eyes and continues.

21

"Rain came under so we crawled back in our blankets like snakes. The wind was like a great machine coming down. I could hear Connie praying and my husband cursing, but the noise became too much and I was alone in darkness. It was like the end of the world. The house began to make strange noises, like a sick dog. Then the roof came off, glass and metal was breaking, like a train smashing." She squirms on the stool and speaks so quietly that I have to lean forward to hear her.

"I felt the power of nature, like a god, but I didn't feel afraid anymore. I don't know why but I thought this great power would not hurt me. I was holding the earth like a friend. I had earth in my hands and my body was moving, pushing down to dirt and stones to get inside the earth, to hide there. I heard noises but they seemed far away. Then I felt dizzy and sleepy and everything was like dreaming. I believed the storm was raping the island. I felt the same pressure inside my body, raping me too, but I didn't care. I was pushing myself down into the earth. I felt my heart beating fast, my body was shaking but not cold. Inside, I became hot and wet. I was crying, laughing, a little bit crazy.

"I had orgasm. Class five. Then the storm was past and everything was quiet and peaceful like the time after lovemaking." She opens her eyes. Her cheeks are slightly red. She glances at me, then looks down at the bar and finds her cigarettes. She lights one and blows smoke at the ceiling. The music has stopped.

I'm speechless. For some reason I imagine her telling this story to a group of elderly tourists over lunch and I almost laugh out loud.

She gives me a sharp look. "You find it funny?"

"No, I love a happy ending."

"Since that time I have been an independent woman."

"Congratulations. Was it a direct hit?"

"No. At the last moment it moved to the north, away from

the mountains."

"To independence," I say, raising my glass.

"I knew I had finished a big test. I felt positive to stay here."

"To bad weather," I say, taking another swallow and dispensing with the toasts. I am feeling the rum too; I might tell a story about groping a continent and from there we could move on to screwing the planet.

"I thought it could not happen again so soon." I don't know if she means the storm or the orgasm. "But it didn't matter. I felt strong. I had no more fear."

"And you were in love with the land."

She blows smoke in my face. "I was very happy to be here, to be alive."

"It's great to be alive," I say. "You don't have to know why."

"We have nothing more," she says.

We are quiet for a few minutes. I can't help but wonder why she told me of her relationship with Hurricane Jake. She must be drunk. And when she is, she probably tells everyone the same story. No, that's nonsense. She just means to be amusing. She wanted to tell me because of my name.

The kitchen is quiet, the dining room dark. Falling among the calls of night, the rain beats flat botanical surfaces and plays haphazard metallic scales, keeping rhythm for the nocturnal notes of whistle-piping voices.

"What music do you like?" She is rattling through some tapes.

I didn't want to talk about music. Or art, or economics, or politics, or religion. I wanted to talk about the weather. "It may get stormy tonight," I say.

She looks up. "What do you mean?"

"I mean I feel some rough weather building up."

She stares straight into my eyes for a few seconds, but I

can't tell if she's smiling or not. "How do you feel it?"

"I don't know. It's a gift, I guess. I'm like a human barometer."

"You have a special instrument," she says.

"I'm sensitive. I know pressure when I feel it."

She fills our glasses again. "Perhaps you want to take a cabin." Her face is inscrutable.

I turn my head to look outside. "You can feel the electricity. If I was ever going to take a cabin, tonight would be the night."

"You would be more comfortable."

"No sense putting myself in danger."

The room is quiet. We sip our drinks listening to the rain. The only appropriate mood music would be a recording of howling winds and flying debris. Outside, the weather hasn't changed much but inside me a low pressure system is developing.

"Would you show me a cabin?"

"Of course." She smiles. "Anytime you want a cabin, you must first see it."

We finish our drinks and I wait on the porch while Sheila locks the doors. An umbrella hangs at the end of the railing and she opens it and turns her flashlight on the path. We walk down the narrow strip of concrete awkwardly, stumbling off the edge, bumping into each other, sharing the umbrella, our arms and legs brushing together as the rain encircles us. The generator pounds away in the wet air like a deep steel drum muted with fabric. The rain-flecked beam jerks from the path to the last cabin and we move up the wet steps carefully. Sheila unlocks the door and turns on the light. I step inside next to a desk with a lamp on it; beside it sits a low bureau. A double bed juts out from the back wall and takes up most of the floor space. A night table with a lamp stands in the far corner. A grass rug, a ceiling fan, and three colorful paintings complete the furnishings. The walls are dark wood and each has a window. We stand inside the open door with the umbrella dripping on the floorboards. The air is moist and musty. Rain pings on the roof.

I throw open one side window, then kneel on the bed and open the back window.

Sheila remains by the door. "Do you want it?"

I open the night table drawer; inside are candles, wooden matches, an ashtray. I melt the bottom of a candle, stand it in the ashtray and light it, then open the third window. A cool river breeze rolls through the cabin.

"You should take it," she says.

Leaning over the desk I fling open the last window; it bangs on the outside wall. When I turn off the lamp, the candle flame in the corner dances up the walls. I click on the fan switch. On its high setting, the fan whips the air violently. The flame jumps around and flickering light flashes across the ceiling. I pull the umbrella from Sheila's hand and drop it on the floor.

Sheets of rain slide off the slanted roof and splatter on the ground. The fan stirs a blustery funnel in the center of the room; the leaping light is dim and strange.

"You must take it." Her voice is nearly inaudible under the noise in the room.

The candle blows out and the room drops to pitch black. My hands find hers and pull her forward. She resists, pulling back toward the door, but I turn her to the bed and she sits on the edge without a word. She attempts to rise but I push her down, catching her scarf in my fingers. I loop it around her wrists and pull her arms over her head so that she lies on her back as I wrap the other end around the bedpost. We cannot see each other or hear anything besides the stirring wind but I feel my way around to her legs and kneel at her feet and place my hands on her knees. Her dress has risen and I push it higher, my hands spreading her thighs, my mouth following to kiss the soft flesh there.

She begins to shiver, or quiver, and I realize I'm blowing at her pubis like a fanatic. Suddenly I see an image of myself as a demented forecaster in a suit and tie, kneeling on the ground in a blinding rain, feeling my way to safety. Hyperventilated, I slump forward between her smooth thighs and the darkness is full of blinking points of light. Her heels dig at my back as she pushes me in farther. I gasp for air at the thin, musky fabric there, my face nuzzling her moist sex. She squirms on the bed, pushing her pelvis outward, her thighs clasping my head like she's trying to pop a balloon. I pry her legs apart and raise my head to catch my breath and check the weather. I don't want her to panic but this storm could be turning into a typhoon.

I manage to loosen several restrictive garments that might endanger us in the mounting turbulence. Wrapped in the close humidity of a warm blanket I find her open mouth, her heavy breasts, her wet crevice. I turn her onto her stomach, stuff a pillow under her hips for comfort during the melee, and enter her easily. Pinning her down, impaling her as she rises to join me, we ride it out together, and over the gale I hear husky cries in the darkness. I lose track of time and rain, and finally pitch forward, carried away in a drenching release, exhausted but safe in the coming calm.

I wake briefly when Sheila gets out of bed. A few minutes later, the fan's rapid spinning winds down to languid revolutions that turn to stillness and absolute sleep.

When I wake next I know it's later than usual but I don't care. I don't plan to take any photos today, so I can't be overly concerned with the brilliant light pouring through the open window with the whistles of songbirds and the frothy gurgle of the river.

I shower with the stall door open, standing in sunlight under the cold water, singing, "What a Wonderful Monsoon," a song I've never heard until this moment. I feel good; there may be a few cirrus clouds at the upper reaches of my skull, but the sky is clear and the future looks bright enough.

The restaurant is quiet. Sheila's car is gone and Rita sits in the dining room reading a magazine. Broad stripes of light cut through the windows and fall across the tables and the floor.

"Good morning," I say.

"Mornin," she says, standing up.

I walk out to the patio. Clear mountain light shimmers over the wet leaves of an arena of trees. Hummingbirds and bees sample the yellow allamandas gaping open around the edge of the patio. Rita brings out coffee and a basket of toast with butter and sea grape jelly. Her clothes—white shorts and a pink polo shirt—glow brightly in the light. Her arms and legs are the color of polished walnut.

"Where's Sheila?" I ask.

"Town."

She leaves and returns with a glass. I hold it up and watch the particles drifting in the brownish liquid. "The juice of the day." I say.

"Das tamarind drink."

A few minutes later she brings me the special—a freshwater crab omelet and grilled tomatoes—and I pick up an old newspaper from the bar and leaf through it while I eat. Rita comes out with the coffee pot as I'm finishing my toast.

"Please," I say.

She refills the cup and steps back from the table. "Somethin else?" she says.

I fold the paper and toss it on the table. "You can join me for a minute."

She stands quietly for a few seconds, looking at my cheerful face, then says, "Miss Sheila doan allow de staff to sit wit touriss."

"Yeah, so I hear, but can't you think of me as something

else?"

Rita lifts slightly on her toes and comes down again. "Such as?"

"A visitor, a passerby, a stranger, a provocateur. How about a photographer?"

"All de touriss take picture."

"This is true," I say, "but the pictures are not all the same." She shrugs.

"Have you ever taken a picture?"

"No."

"Do you want to?"

She shrugs again.

"I guess it's not a priority," I say.

She stands there a moment longer, then turns and leaves the patio.

I sit wondering how to tackle the day without a camera. No big deal—within minutes I have a growing list of interesting possibilities: follow the river; throw rocks into the ocean; go fishing; go cliff diving; hitchhike someplace; juggle coconuts; read *The Portable Nietzsche*.

When I walk back through the dining room, Rita is sitting again with the magazine she had before, looking at a picture of a wall of television screens. "What if I sat with you?" I say, pulling out a chair.

She closes the magazine. "Miss Sheila—"

"She's not here," I say.

Rita sits up straight, glancing at the driveway before looking at me again.

"Look," I say, "I'm not trying to get you in trouble. I'm the only one staying here. I just want to ask you a question. I don't see the crime in that." She looks as if I might ask her to help topple the government, but I sit down anyway. "I was trying to come up with something to do today and I thought you might have some ideas. Something unusual to see nearby.

Like, I don't know, a cave or some natural wonder. Or someone interesting, a craftsman, for instance, or a bush doctor."

She looks back and forth from my face to the magazine, continually smoothing its wrinkled cover. "To take picture?"

"No, just to see. Anything worth seeing."

"Dere's a cascade."

"A waterfall?"

She nods.

"Okay. Where is it?"

"Up de river."

"This one behind us?"

"Yes."

"Upstream from the cabins?"

"Yes."

"How far?"

"Not so."

"Thanks," I say. "Pleasure to meet someone who never took a photo."

I wash a couple of tee shirts and hang them on a line under the roof of the bathhouse. As I'm kneeling at the flap of my tent, stuffing some things into my daypack, I hear footsteps on the path and look up to see Rita going by, holding a plastic bag.

"Hi," I say.

She waves and keeps walking.

I zip the tent shut and catch up to her. "Where are you going?"

"To collect de wild spice."

We start down the ravine on a path to the river. "What if someone comes to the restaurant?"

"Miss Sheila is dere."

At the bottom, tall grasses and trees line the rock-laden river. Flowing smoothly over flat sand-pebble patches, rippling over irregular stone fields and rushing through boulder chutes, the water creeps and runs and flashes, pouring itself along in a voice chattering the language of mountains and rain.

"Are you going to the waterfall?" I say.

"Not so far," she says.

"You mind if I come along?"

"You are free to go wheer you choose."

The narrow river cuts a tunnel through thick forest; holes in the canopy allow spotlights of sun to hit the water. Behind smooth round rocks, leaves and brown debris swirl in the pockets of eddies. Ferns and flowers spill over the lush banks to brush the water. Huge green elephant ear leaves hang out over the shallows like wrinkled umbrellas, their thick pliant stalks home for lizards and snails, their shadows cover for skating beetles and tiny darting fish. Among muddy roots, orange crabs back into the darkness of their holes. Across patches of light sand, long gray crayfish shoot backward under rocks like retracted torpedoes. Giant philodendrons snake upward, clinging stiffly to their hosts, climbing into the weave of foliage over the winding river.

I carry my shoes, stepping from stone to stone or wading in the brisk, clear water. Soft brown finches chirp and flit among the reeds and stems fencing the banks. A bright green hummingbird—what Rita calls a frou-frou—follows us for a few moments, hovering in the open space over our heads, buzzing and flashing in a wild geometry of lines and angles before it vanishes upstream.

In a little meadow beside the river, Rita gathers the top sprigs of an olive-green shrub growing low to the ground. She brings a bushy clump of it to the river and sits on a rock, washing each piece and putting it in the bag. I sit across from her on another rock, my feet dangling in the water. The sun is hot now and as I watch her pull a sprig loose, dip it into the moving water, and slap it against the rock, over and over again, the task becomes a cycle of continuous motion. Performed and repeated in a perfectly peaceful setting, the simple action—wet hand swinging, plant striking stone, droplets showering—gives me a pleasurable sensation that lulls me into a state of repose. The rhythm of the task matches the rhythm of the day, and I stare unfocused at the stone, caught between the movement and the sound in the innocent workings of a natural clock, its ticking pendulum marking the slow passage of a time without implication. I feel I could stay this way until I'm forced to move, but these moments are as temporary as they are elusive.

"You like it here," she says, rustling the plastic bag. She looks relaxed, and I feel like I'm seeing her for the first time. Strands of her hair have escaped the braids and I wish she'd shake it all free. I watch her smooth round face, her black eyes shining at me, her small nose wrinkling under my scrutiny, her full lips forming a modest smile.

"I do, very much."

"I myself love de nature world."

I look around us, thinking of a future theme park, some bogus approximation of this. "What do you do in your free time?" I ask.

"Tonight we have a dance," she says, picking weeds off her shirt and dropping them deliberately into the same spot on the water.

"In Rocklee?"

"Sure, but people come from all over."

"Is there a band?"

"A DJ," she says. "A lot of people."

"Where is it?"

"Club Camou."

"You're going after work?"

"Sure." She stands and hops to another rock. "Now I muss go." She leaps downstream a few more rocks, then looks back to where I'm still sitting and points over my head. "Soon you will hear de cascade."

31

Field of Vision

It is the sound of power. The water falls forty feet, crashing in a broken column and flattening to a round pool, the middle plane between the dark, cavernous hollow below the surface and the green clearing above it—two halves of a spherical space carved by the dropping river. The top of the falls is a screen of fine spray onto which the sun projects the thin, illusory arcs of concentric spectrums. From the rim, pale vines dangle down the wall. Ferns sprout from cracks. Behind the raging chute the rock is slick black, green and gold; across its face endless rivulets run light and lacy like watery cobwebs. At the edge of the pool half-sunken boulders wear waving algae skirts and grow deep green mats of moss like heads of hair on top.

Inside the jungle enclave the falling water creates a natural static, a mock-deafness. Moisture collects on my skin and hair and eyelashes as I stand looking into the pool, seeing as deep as the spectral shafts of light penetrate. I dive in, piercing the light and sinking below it, my hands outstretched and groping. Cold-jolted in the darkness, my heart beats wildly. I hear the muffled churning of the water above. Deeper, there is nothing but colder darkness; my skin numbs and I feel only the pressure in my ears. Then my hands touch rock and I turn and kick off the bottom, reaching for the vague round light above, clutching at it as I break the surface.

Thrown spray lashes my head. Shafts of water tunnel into the pool. Underwater I take the roaring massage. The head-drumming force of the cascade turns me playfully with a loose, erratic pounding, and I roll in a swarm of bubbles, sinking and spinning in the turbulence, my tumbling brain filling with watery images. I wiggle through the water like an otter and come up in the pool's smooth middle, seeing sketches of shimmering, shallow water and flat, dark shapes in my head. Some of the images appear to float, but the shapes are solid— the crook of an arm, the curve of a shoulder, a hip, a fist. No face presents itself, but I know the model is Rita. Maybe it's not a vision, but I could call it a premonition. I think I see the next bit of land ahead, the place where I will live and work until there is nothing left to sustain me. Then I'll be back at sea, floating like today.

I climb out onto the rocks. The air is rich and still. In the space above the falls the sun is moving; in the spinning spray the rainbow illusions fade, evaporating into the sky. Peak-time at the pool is over. I put on my clothes and leave, whistling and weaving back along the river's solitary course, refreshed and reaffirmed.

I spend the rest of the afternoon reading Nietzsche and napping in my tent. Then I dress for the evening in wrinkled clothes and go to the bar, where Sheila is listening to the BBC news on the radio. Without a word she mixes a tamarind and rum and puts it on the bar for me. I'm quiet; when she listens to the world news it's with a religious intensity.

The Pope, on a twelve day tour of Africa, visits Our Lady of Lake Togo and welcomes another opportunity to remind millions that starvation has nothing to do with birth control; the Titanic is found but the passengers are still lost; a devastating Mexico City earthquake kills nearly five thousand but a dog has been rescued for a man who lost two children; there are riots in Brixton and West Germany, racially motivated in England, but simply hooliganism and destruction under a pretense of social reform on the continent.

When a local health program follows with a broadcast about fighting anorexia nervosa, Sheila lights a cigarette and starts our routine. "You would like dinner?"

I take a handful of nuts from the bowl on the bar. "Not tonight."

Her eyebrows rise. "You will eat nuts?"

"And berries," I say.

She smokes, watching me. "Maybe you have lost your

appetite. Maybe you have eaten too much."

"I don't want to become a creature of habit."

"We are all making our habits," she says.

"It's a constant battle, isn't it?"

"If we like something we do it again."

I crunch on some nuts and drink the tangy drink. "The food's great. I could possibly eat it every day. But if you expect me to, you'll be disappointed."

An announcement concerning the contagious nature of pinkeye comes on the radio. "Are you eating in your small tent?"

"In Rocklee," I say.

She lights a cigarette from the previous one and makes herself a drink. "Ah. You are going to the dance." It sounds like an accusation.

"I thought I'd take a look."

She draws smoke into her lungs and lets it out with a whistling hiss. "There won't be any tourists there."

"Sounds like heaven," I say, watching her eyes through the smoke. "Oh! I see what you mean." I rummage through the bowl, picking out the cashews. "You mean white people."

Her expression doesn't change; she isn't sure of the territory.

"You mean white people," I say again.

"I mean visitors," she says.

"But I'm a visiting white person and I'll be there."

She drinks. I eat nuts. Music plays on the radio and she makes me another drink. She's said all she wants to on the subject. In truth, I don't want to see her anywhere but here, and I'm pretty sure she feels the same about me.

She finally moves the conversation back to our narrow spit of common ground. "Do you want the cabin again?"

I smile at the nut bowl. "Depends on the weather."

"What is the forecast?"

"There's a storm warning but who knows? It might blow over or it might hit us. We'll have to wait and see." I finish my drink and stand up. "You might sleep right through it."

"It's the weekend," she says. "I'll be up quite late." She goes into the dining room, her cigarette still smoldering on the bar. I stub it out and head up the driveway—catching the citrus smell of Sheila's orchard—and out onto the road. Behind me the sun has dipped deeply into the cloudy horizon and a steady breeze blows in my face. It's great to be free.

Darkness falls on the winding road down to Rocklee and with it comes the sweet, unseen moisture of the mountains. The walk is wonderful. A few cars pass and one stops to offer me a ride but I turn it down.

The village center, with its stores and box-like houses, runs alongside the road for about half a mile, outlined at night by pale, yellowish streetlights; branching off the main artery are dark dirt side streets. I get directions from one of the shop owners, and set off on a steep curving road that leads down to Club Camou, a white warehouse-type building beside a field. Strings of bulbs hang between the front door and two trees on opposite sides of the road, making a luminous point to the entrance. Over the door the words CLUB CAMOU are painted in a black scrawl.

At the edge of the field is a booth with a group of people standing around it, and as I get closer I smell fried food. Under the glow of a single lantern, two sweating men sell fried chicken, fried banana and fried potato on paper plates, and bottles of Heineken from a barrel of ice. I get a plate and a beer. A dog follows me under a tree where I sit on a root, toss him a chunk of chicken and eat in peace. Music spills from the club. People are milling around the door and cars are being parked in the field.

After a while I walk over to the front of the club and wait in the line to get inside. People stand close together, funneling toward the door, laughing, smoking, arguing in their lilting patois or speaking matter-of-factly in English. A big man sits on a stool at the door, collecting the cover and rubber-stamping a CC on the wrists of the incoming.

Once inside, I stand in the barroom, separated from the rest of the building by a wall with another doorway. On the other side is a larger, darker room with a stage full of equipment at the rear and narrow benches running along the walls. The room is filling up. I see one more open door at the back, apparently an exit, with another man standing by. There are no windows and the room is hot already. Marley is playing through large speakers but the DJ hasn't taken the stage.

I squeeze up to the bar. There are about four stools and maybe forty people there, and a line filing into the big room. The bartender at my end points at me. "What will it be, mahn?"

"Heineken." There are only Heineken bottles and plastic cups on the bar. He pops one open for me and I put some money down. "What else you got?"

"Vodka, whiskey, rum and no-label."

"What's no-label?"

"Das a cane liquor." He moves away, putting beer bottles on the bar with both hands.

The DJ's voice booms out over the music and echoes off the walls. The people clap and yell. I can't understand what he's saying so I push my way into the big room. I still can't understand what he's saying. From the ceiling in the center of the room a wheel of colored lights flashes and turns, flinging blue, yellow, red and orange spots onto the dark walls and the dark mass of people. Standing behind his equipment, the DJ spins a record, the volume cranks up and dancing begins in earnest. I walk around the room passing the benches along the walls and looking at the dark figures sitting there smoking and drinking and chatting in each other's ears. It is true: I seem to be the only white person here, the only person who can't understand the DJ. Making my way along in the near-darkness I feel an acute sense of myself as a minority, even though the term has never held much meaning for me. I imagine someone standing up in front of me to ask, "Hey mahn, how is it to be so white?" And me saying, "Fine. It's great to be alive." But no one seems to notice me. In the dark I'm invisible, ignored, a stranger left alone. I return to the bar. I think if I try some no-label I might start to understand the DJ.

The liquor is a clear fluid with the odor of a mild fumigant, something like the groundwater that might be found near a chemical plant. It has a strange, almost bland flavor and a burning aftertaste that leaves a sinister vapor in the nasal passages. I'm surprised that a plastic cup can hold it and amazed at the quickness with which one attains recognition by ingesting it. After one shot I learn from the bartender of the local corollary that unites consumption with concern. To publicly drink more than a taste is to admit you are reckless, insane, deeply religious, inquisitive to a fault, hell-bent on destruction or seeking knowledge through the use of solvents.

Soon I begin to witness my own unification with the people around me. We buy each other drinks and laugh. Alienation goes out with the empty cups. We see the ways of the world and reach agreements; we marvel at common dilemmas and wheeze at stupid solutions. Two of my closest friends at the bar, John and Earl, convince me that I'm at least brown, and we all promise to visit each other every year.

"Goddamn it, Earl," I say, clapping him on the back, "it's great to travel."

Back in the big room I hear the DJ announce his intention to play selections from Martinique and Trinidad. I move between the dancing bodies, bending with the crowd just to get by, swaying and bumping my way into the thick of the event. Colored spots fly by, catching faces and arms, whipping over walls, grazing my eyes. Caught in the tide of movement, lifted by the heat and the beat, I dance without trying, like a rafter at the mercy of ocean waves.

The air is thick and warm like blood, pressing close to my skin, filling my nose and head with the odor of island, the meshed smells of earth and sea—the dripping sweat of coffee and rum, sugar and fish, oil and salt. The fragrance of roots and runoff rain, the sticky liquids of pineapple, papaya and coconut water, the soft, ripe sweetness of brown banana. The air turns over and over, heavy in the closed room, the reused breath of people moving, the stale exhaled currents of beer and smoke, the floating perfume of soaps and potions. People squeeze together, pressing and grinding their partners, strutting and sliding. It is a hothouse of cross-pollination, reeking of musk and mango, oozing the sap of spirits and seduction. All the same, the only fresh air is outside and that is the direction my dance takes.

I reel out the back door into the field, exchanging the smooth madness for moonlight and mountain oxygen. Wandering along a row of cars, I see couples and small groups dotting the field and the chicken shack crowd a far corner away. Stopping between cars I urinate on the grass. The two vehicles on either side seem to roll back and forth and I think I hear someone calling. I turn to look over my shoulder— inadvertently peeing on a light-colored Mazda—and see a girl walking toward me. I correct my aim as she nears.

"Sorry," I say, "I didn't know it was your car."

"I doan own a car," she says, stopping behind it.

"Rita!" I zip up and turn around. "It's great to see you." We walk over near the club's front door where two other people are waiting.

"Jake, das my brother Blandy," she says. A skinny kid wearing a tri-color knit cap reminiscent of the Ethiopian flag stands with his hands deep in his pockets.

"And my friend Janet."

Janet shakes my hand warmly, smiling as she looks me over. "Enjoyin yourself, Jake?"

"Very much so."

"Wanna dance?"

"Very much so."

In the light of the doorway, Blandy eyes me sullenly and looks around like he's expecting to meet someone. He's wiry, about six feet tall, has a small round face, a small nose like his sister's, and close-set hazel eyes, lighter and odder than usual around here. His forehead is pimpled and his mouth is down-turned in what looks like a perpetual frown.

The two girls chat amiably, occasionally asking me a question, politely keeping me involved. Janet is very pretty, short and curvy; her clothes barely contain her.

Inside, I buy the girls whiskey-Cokes and myself another no-label, and we enter the dark dance chamber. The music is too loud for much talking so I follow Janet into the labyrinth. Somewhere inside, at a place where there are several inches between us, she begins to dance, wedging herself into position and giving me the rhythm she wants back. I find it, bumping off her with the beat, rebounding as she spins, hitting any part that comes around to me. One song runs into another. Without hands we rub together, getting personal I think, her round rump sliding against my rubbery hardness. The beat throbs off the walls and never stops. All around us people are touching, knocking and brushing their neighbors, bumping their partners in unison. I feel myself slipping into a giddy sensuality and close my eyes to the colored lights.

Lost in one world, I feel its heart beating. The motion is natural, instinctive. There are no individuals, just a body around the warm, pulsing heart of the world. I feel its heat, smell its wild scent. The body dances the rites of nations and animals, held by the bonds of earth, blood and sex. The body is bliss; there is no blame or misery, only the beat and the dance of the world tribe.

The dance becomes personal again, an erotic ritual. I open my eyes and find that Rita has become my partner—the surprise is electrifying. We push harder, lingering perceptibly to grind on target, finding points of mutual consent and staying with them, running together like wheels on a track. The music is relentless. I can't stop. This is the greatest dance of my life. Orgasm is imminent, conception not out of the question.

Someone steps hard on my foot, tripping me up. Suddenly the song changes and the DJ talks over it. People crowd me. I am too far from Rita and our contact regions aren't meeting firmly. The smoke stings my eyes. I find it difficult to breathe properly. The darkness is bad air, choking me to the floor. The wet skin of strangers is slippery against me. The room has filled to its capacity, but at the door more and more people are somehow getting in. There is no stopping it; no one knows how much is too much. Claustrophobia rolls over me like an avalanche. We will all suffocate. The world in a room. Everyone alive has come to dance and getting out is like swimming through quicksand. Finally I stumble outside.

I suck down great lungfulls of moist, night air, my hands resting on the cool metal of a fender through which I can feel the bass notes escaping the building. Turning my head, I see the strung lights and the people waiting to get inside. I laugh and notice someone sitting on the hood of the next car, watching me as he smokes.

"Getting thick in there," I say, standing up straight.

"You like my sister?" It's Blandy, looking me over.

"Yeah, she's a nice girl."

He stares at me while he blows smoke into the night. "You fuck her?"

I almost laugh at this abrupt inquiry. "You know," I say, rubbing my forehead, "I'm not certain, but she may have been impregnated during that last dance."

He stares curiously at me for a minute, then hops down off the car and flicks his cigarette away. "Mahn," he says, shaking his head, "you muss be crazy." He pulls air through his front teeth in a squeaky sound of confirmed suspicion and walks past me toward the front of the building.

I stand there feeling flushed and disturbed, alone in a changing atmosphere, waiting for the cooling rain. Rita and Janet come out and stand near me talking, but I am not included this time. The dance is inside, not out here. A ritual in the fetid dark doesn't mean anything is owed to anyone. Mystery and curiosity become awkwardness and swift glances in the night. World tribe is only a concept, a line you might hear in a song.

Rain falls upon us and the girls run toward the chicken shack. The drops hit my upturned face and run down my sweaty neck. I walk slowly, loving the rain—the clean beautiful impartial rain. I catch it on my dry tongue.

We huddle together under the roof of the shack, pressed against the grease-spotted boards around the sputtering heat of the cookers, breathing chicken fat, sharing molten fries and ice-cold beer with enough people to justify a franchise.

The girls depart—away from the club—with a quick goodnight, leaving nothing to link the future with the splendid gyrations of the previous hour. Nothing to advance the one-world theory. I am less than cheerful, seeing that the disappointment I suffer is proportionate to the swell time I had, the trough following the peak of high enjoyment. Now I'm the lone freak in a crowd.

I slog to the front of the club and hail a taxi. As I get in the back seat the driver looks at me in the mirror. "Granville?" he says.

"Red Ginger."

The car takes off. "Touriss?"

"Prime Minister."

Field of Vision

I nurse my beer. Sheets of water roll down the road as the car crawls up the mountain. The headlights peer around each curve, short beams that frequently light nothing and seem to be, aside from the dim dashboard, the only lights in the world. I get out in the driveway and stand in the deluge, watching the car leave. The rain clouds are invisible, black against a black sky. My eyes settle on the pale lamp light at Sheila's window, the parted curtains, the hazy face behind streaked glass. She stands, a blurry-white figure on undressed display, and I watch from below, standing in heavy clothes and swelling beneath them, soaked to the bone of contention, expanding into the cool night. I trudge up the stairs, open the door and step inside, dripping puddles on the wooden floor.

She hands me a towel, shuts the door and whispers, "Want a room, mister?"

"Any port in a storm," I say.

Saturday—the day of many tourists. Tropical thrill-seekers sampling strange fruits, braving the bestial insects and savage sun of the patio. Holiday humans—their grating presence comes through the upstairs window, hornets in my slumber. Wearing a towel and carrying my pile of sodden garments, I escape to the ground, retreating to the sanctity of the cabins, the forgiving grace of the river, where the birds are too loud and the flowers too bright. I sink naked into a pool, soaking my fiery head, rousing my haggard cells, absorbing the even flow of cool water.

Having reaped the river's restorative powers, I put on shorts and a shirt, take aspirin and walk up to the restaurant, slinking into the kitchen like a lizard, begging and then blessing Connie for coffee to go. I sit on the steps of the last cabin, a hot cup at my face, warm steam fogging my sunglasses.

After a while I climb down the bank and wander upstream

in the river. When I get to the place where Rita washed her spices the previous day, I stop and sit again, lingering over the memory and trying to recreate the image of her hand in the shallow sunlit water. There seems to be something to explore in this. I lean back into the foliage sprouting from the bank. It's important to remember the line between subject and object. She can be a subject, part of the intended picture, not the object of it. That's what I tell myself. Traveling alone and oh so detached.

Don't get involved. You're in the perfect medium—stand back and observe. Look closely but don't touch. Keep the lens between you and everything else. Take nothing but reflected light. This is the challenge. But how can you stay detached and also dig in deep? How can you penetrate from a distance? How can you shoot detail from space? How can you touch without touching?

Pain flares across my shoulders and upper back. I jump up, slapping at myself, twisting in discomfort, splashing about, getting my shirt off. Tiny red fire ants—barely above microscopic—have attacked me as a unit, a battalion of bastards demanding to be seen. I fall forward into deeper water and submerge, rolling over in a hole, banging my arm, getting my torso down in the current. Even underwater the little devils hang on like staples. Bracing myself between rocks I rub my back down into sand and pebbles, come up brushing at my shoulders and neck. Even with the ants gone it feels like they're still attached, so I stay in the water a little longer, soaking and scratching, thinking—Wake up, Jake! You're drifting with your philosophical head up your ass, daydreaming your way to peril.

Out of the water my back is a network of stings. I head back toward home, slapping my wet shirt over my shoulder, smacking my hot skin for relief. Flogging and castigating myself. Pay attention, man! Watch your back! Look alive, ass-fuck tourist!

I crawl into my tent and unzip the back window. In a fabric-tinted blue light I lie down on my back breathing the warm humidity. The door flap rustles occasionally, stirred by a merciful breeze. I read and nap, off and on, for a long while. I rest for my health, justifying the slack time before the all-important next phase of my life and work, utilizing the space between events. It is less a waste than a renascence. Maybe the ants have tired me out.

In the dream I am on a riverbank. It's sunny and mist rises off the water. A figure swims away from me, slowly moving into the current. I see the figure is a woman but she doesn't look at me. She is dark in the water. In her wake, papers float away, moving into the current also. They look like photographs though I can't make out their images. I move into the cold water, desperately wanting to collect the papers as they float away from me but I cannot get to any of them. The misty air darkens around me and I can hear a factory somewhere, the sound of machines. The sun is gone. The papers are gone. The swimming woman is gone. In the dark I stand waiting, frustrated at the turn of events, sensing but not seeing or hearing the river anymore. I hear the machines, the sound of bulldozers maybe. I look for their headlights in the darkness but I see nothing.

I wake confused in the dark, hearing the generator, seeing the fireflies on the fabric as stars, not knowing if I am indoors or out. I run my hand across the nylon of the tent, regaining my senses but still feeling disoriented. I dress for dinner and crawl outside, visit the bathroom and wash my face, then walk up the path flashing my light beam here and there.

Two men sit at the bar engaged in conversation. In the next room the battle of forks and plates rages furiously. I take a table at a porch window and watch Sheila moving among the diners; she makes them feel at home and some of them eat like they are. Eventually she comes over to me and I realize I haven't eaten all day.

"Evening. Thanks for stopping by."

"Guten abend," she says, her voice chirpy. "Are you okay?"

"On the verge of losing consciousness."

"You must eat, you starving artiste."

"I'll start with the pumpkin soup."

"I think it's finished. Let me look."

Rita brings water, pouring a glass at the table.

"Evening," I say, watching her eyes.

"Evenin." She glances at me but the contact is brief.

"Many tourists," I say.

"Keepin busy," she says.

Sheila comes back as Rita moves away.

"No soup."

"Bastards," I say, looking over the room. "Okay. The ginger salad and barbecue fish."

"To drink?"

"Heineken."

In a few minutes Rita comes back with a basket of bread and the beer.

"I want to talk to you," I say.

She looks surprised. "What about?"

"An idea."

"Which idea?"

"I need some time to explain it."

She looks over her shoulder.

"I know we can't talk here," I say. "I want to meet you after work."

She looks at me for a moment. Across the room some people rise from their table and we both look over. "Wheer?" she says.

"Down at my tent."

"You doan stay dere," she says, stepping away.

She leaves me in a dizzy spell, feeling uncomfortable and unlucky. Watching her move through the room I butter a piece of bread and take a bite. It sticks in my throat. Beer pushes it down. By the time she brings the food I've developed the strange sensation that insects are crawling on my skin.

"Rita," I say, watching her nonchalant eyes and feeling like someone in need of a pharmacist, "we all have our secrets. What I have to tell you has nothing to do with Sheila."

She looks pensive for a minute and then suddenly smiles. "Eat your food," she says, and goes away again.

I eat my food. Relax, mahn! Relax and enjoy it, I tell myself. Everything fine, mahn. No problem. Enjoy the evening. Tomorrow come sometime. Enjoy the myth of island life.

Several people leave, others linger at their tables over coffee, pineapple cake, mango crisp. The bar is half full of drinkers; Sheila attends to their needs. Music plays, and through the open windows the soft night air caresses us all.

Rita takes my plate. "Dessert?"

"No thanks, just some coffee."

She comes right back with it.

"Stop by," I say.

"Maybe so."

"What the hell."

She turns away, then says, "For dis you need another secret."

"That's no problem, Rita."

A few minutes later Sheila leans over my table. "I am having a brandy," she says. "You would like one also?"

"Sure thing."

She returns with two snifters and sits down across from me. "Prost!" she says, lifting her glass.

"Prost!"

A couple is leaving by the front door; they wave when Sheila turns around. "Sehr gut! Fabelhaft! Wunderbar!" the woman says.

Over her head the man says, "Phantastisch!"

Sheila laughs. "Danke schön," she says, and turns back to me. "Nice to be appreciated." She lights a cigarette and blows smoke at the ceiling. "And what have you done today?"

I swirl the heavy liquid around the glass. "Thought a bit. Philosophized."

She smiles. "Ah so, you take it easy."

"Whatever it was tired me out."

She sips the brandy, licks her lips and inhales smoke deeply. "So you won't be dancing tonight?"

"No, I feel much too anti-social for that."

She leans into the table and whispers, "Like me?"

"I guess we have something in common. With me though, it's not a secret."

"You are so funny." She gets up and goes to the bar.

I watch a car—the people who just left—pull into the driveway; the red tail lights move between the hedges and swing out onto the road, gone from sight.

Sheila sits down again and smiles. "You wish to discuss the weather?"

Across the room Rita clears a table. I see her glance at us as I look out the front windows. "Looks like a pretty good camping night."

"On this mountain the only certainty is rain," she says.

"Rain is good for sleeping," I say.

"And I think you prefer to sleep always in a different place."

"Depends," I say. "The important thing is to have a feeling of freedom. I realized it again today."

She glares at me, finishes her brandy and sets the glass down. Then she stands and says rather venomously, "We don't want to make a habit."

"Indeed," I say as she leaves the table. I am aware that she may harbor some anger toward me but I don't mind. We are engaged in a curious relationship, somewhat antagonistic, certain to be short-lived, maybe the only one possible for us. Luckily, with the help of weather and alcohol, we've been able to channel our mistrust into bouts of physical exertion that prove mutually beneficial. Now she has left me alone and it seems possible that our sexual concordance has already ended. If so, that's fine. It's fine either way—I just hope the outcome doesn't jeopardize the quality of my meals or raise the prices.

I leave by the front door instead of going through the bar, and as I'm going out Rita looks over. I wave slightly—motioning a reminder really—and she nods casually, the way she would in response to a greeting or a farewell.

For a while I sit on the concrete under the bathhouse bulb trying to read Nietzsche in the dim light and brushing insects off the pages until so many are crawling on me that I retreat to the zippered safety of my nylon chamber and sit in the darkness imagining how I might explain myself if I get the chance. Loose sounds drift down to me. I hear a car start up over the chugging generator and then later, after what seems like hours, the machine stops and there are only the staccato drills of insects, the sweet shrill calls of tree frogs, the river's throaty murmurs.

I crawl outside and stand beside the tent. The night is as dark and soft as loam. Rita isn't coming. I walk closer to the cabins and look around in the darkness, seeing almost nothing and listening for her arrival as disappointment clenches at my chest. Then I hear a low hiss and she steps away from the wall of the nearest cabin.

"Why didn't you tell me you were here?"

"I din want to disturb you."

"But I asked you to come down."

"I thought you were sleepin."

I laugh softly. "Never mind. I'm glad you came." We stand there a moment looking at each other but I can't really see her. "Let's sit over here," I say, feeling my way onto the steps. She settles down beside me, the cabin at our backs, between us and the restaurant. "This feels like a secret," I say. She is quiet, waiting for me to explain while I stare out into the porous darkness over the river, feeling her patience beside me.

"I came here to take pictures. That's what I do." I'm not looking at her. "When I get home I'll try to display some of them in a gallery, hopefully sell a few." I hear deep croaks from the river and from farther away, far above it. Big frogs, I think. "That's one thing. There are also weddings and jobs for other people, you know, little advertisements and stuff. But now—" I touch the air in front of me. "Taking these new pictures, it's different. I don't think about anything except the pictures."

Is this making sense? Maybe she's gone already, disappeared. I look to my side; there is a dim outline like a statue in profile and I follow her gaze.

"Usually I shoot what I see but lately, since I've been here, I've been trying to shoot what I don't see. I guess that may sound crazy. I'm trying to make some new kinds of pictures. But it's like looking for an idea, a sort of blurry image that gets into my head. I try to find it but I don't know exactly what it looks like." I rub my head with both hands. "It's a mystery. It happened to me in the forest, on the mountain." I point over my shoulder. "And now it's happening again with the river. At least the idea came from the water." My eyes are shut behind my hands, looking inside at a blank screen.

"But you're in there with the water and the mist," I say. Now there is more silence. I'm a comedian dying on stage. "I want a human element in these next photos," I tell her. The audience isn't laughing. I wait for her to say something. The heavy croaks seem louder. From different places. Bass notes from the mountain.

She laughs. "You wanna take my picture in de forest?"

I laugh suddenly, too loudly. We laugh together. "Yes," I say, nodding my head in the dark. Close by, the tree frogs lend their laughter in whistles. Ha ha ha ha ha! The audience is loving it; they want more. "Not really your picture. I mean, it's not your portrait. You're in the picture but maybe I don't know it's you. You're some part of it."

She says nothing, presumably reflecting on what her exact role might be in pictures that cannot be described.

"Well?"

"Cahn't say."

"Why not?"

"No time."

"Your day off."

She is silent.

"Monday, right?"

"I go to my home."

"We'll leave early in the morning. You can go home later. This is work. I'll pay you. It's just one day. You understand? I need help with this." I'm leaning close to her. "This is very important to me." I slow down, put my hands on my knees and say softly, "I need to make these pictures."

She sighs, an audible shrug, then draws air sharply through her teeth. "You doan need me for dese pictures. You can use any person. Me, I am too shy. I doan look good enough for a model. My—" She motions at her chest. "Dey're not big enough."

"What?" I say, trying to see her better.

"Dese," she says, patting herself in front. "I am workin, tryin to grow dem." Her palms are together, pressing.

"What do you mean, isometrics?" I can see her nodding and now it's my turn to sigh. "Rita, I'm not talking about big breasts."

"Doan tell me you doan like Miss Sheila's."

"Let's not change the subject, okay? We're not talking about body parts. Besides, you can't change those things except artificially. And anyway, there's nothing wrong with yours in the first place and I never mentioned them either." I shift my weight forward. "It's like this—I saw you in the river, the sun was perfect, an idea came to me. That's it." I turn my head; she's watching me. "It's not about you being a model, it's about you and I going somewhere to work on this. Away from here. We can go up the mountain. Once we find a good place and start working, maybe we'll find some answers. We'll just be looking. It'll be fun, a hike in the forest. We'll have a picnic. Then we'll keep going." I pause, remembering my quest. "Up to the cloud forest." I tap her knee. "Have you been to the top of Morne Matin?"

"No."

"No?" I suck air through my teeth like an islander, like a desperate man sucking up to her. "And you were born here. How old are you?"

"Eighteen. What about you?"

"Twenty-seven. So what other reason do you need?"

"I doan need to climb de mountain."

"You should know your country."

"I know my country."

"Then you should know me."

"Why is dat?"

"Because I'm not from here."

She looks away from me. The air drawn through her teeth sounds like a leaking tire. Among locals this common mannerism expresses doubt, disbelief, or wonder, among other things, and I feel sure she views me with some skepticism.

I can make out the roof line of the next cabin. Above it I see the moon's glow in a cloud's penumbra. The air is heavy and an abrupt chill shakes me. A distant, solitary croak comes to us like an exclamation.

"How much you payin?"

"Whatever you get here for a day." In the silence I can feel her waiting. "Plus twenty dollars."

"Forty."

"Plus thirty dollars."

"American."

"American, for the whole day."

"Alright, de photographer got a person."

I know she's smiling. And I am too. The money makes it official, but the potential seems priceless to me. I squeeze her arm, happy with myself and with her. We have conspired—first, to meet here, and now to explore the unknown.

"You know that great big stone up the road?"

"Sure," she says.

"We'll meet there at seven."

"Okay."

"Don't be late and bring something to eat."

We sit still for a while, silently acknowledging our partnership. Another great croak sounds, momentarily halting the thin, vacillating throats of small tree frogs.

"De rain comin," she says.

I look up at the moon revealed, the sky of stars. "Why do you say that?"

"De crapaud say it."

"The crapo—"

"Dat one."

"Sounds like a bullfrog."

"Dat big one." She spreads her hands.

"He predicts the weather?"

"He predict de rain."

A few light drops tap us and tinkle the metal roofs around us. The stars are gone. The mountain air descends cold and damp, slowly rolling down on us. As we rise there is a sound—a soft pop, like a large seed pod being stepped on—and we freeze on the steps. In the rain we hear nothing else, see nothing in the darkness.

"That wouldn't be Sheila would it?" I whisper.

"Maybe Josey."

"Wait here." I walk slowly along the side wall, keeping the cabin between me and the other cabins, and stop at the back corner. The rain is getting louder, pouring down. The cabins are in a rough circle, the bathhouse on the opposite side, but I can't see them now. I wipe my eyes. It's like trying to see through running ink and my flashlight is in the tent. I crouch and sprint across the distance to the next cabin, barely see the steps. I feel the railing to the door and try the handle. Locked. I peer into the opaque space between the buildings. Rain splatters off the ground. I run to the next cabin, grope around it and step onto the concrete slab of the bathhouse. I lean against the wall under the ringing roof and listen hard, staring into the void toward the generator shed and beyond, toward the restaurant and the orchard—all lost in the darker background of Morne Matin. This is useless, the blind searching for the invisible. Whoever it was has gone. Or is hiding in a stall behind me. I wait a few minutes, hoping to get lucky. Hoping someone will sneeze or turn on a flashlight. Clang against porcelain or flush a toilet. But nothing happens.

I cross the common area to the steps I started from. Rita is gone. Nor is she in my tent. I find my light and flash it over the area. Everything looks normal. I can't get any wetter so I go back to the bathhouse and make the rounds, gently kicking each door open, checking the floors for wetness, anything suspicious. There isn't. I circle each cabin, find nothing, and return to the tent. I strip outside, leave the clothes in a heap, and crawl in shivering with cold. I dress in a heavy shirt and shorts, get into my sleeping bag and lie bundled in dampness, holding the flashlight and watching its pattern hover on the blue nylon over my head. Gradually the beam stills as my own heat warms me from the inside out, and I cut the light and lie still in my cocoon. The rain pounds away, thumping and rolling off the tent, drumming me drowsy, pouring onto the ground, running into the river, sweeping onward to the sea.

Parrots wake me. Lunatic squawkers—for whom every flight is an emergency—winging down from the mountain heights into the riverside forest. I roll over in the stuffy air, unzip the bag and both tent flaps. Breathing against the fine screening I remember that it's Sunday. Whatever that means. A day of rest? From what, swarming brunchers? I decide to leave right after coffee.

Outside, the ground is soft, the air cool and fresh. Mist hangs over the river, clings to the ground, sits in the hollows of the eastern hills. I bathe, wash some clothes, pack for the day, and walk up the path feeling lively and alert. The sun hovers in a young sky the color of a blue crab's shell. I hear Connie in the kitchen but the restaurant is locked and Sheila's car is gone. I sit on the porch with my feet on the rail, waiting and wondering. I haven't seen Clifton around; he probably has the day off. And where is Rita? Soon the mongrel hordes will arrive.

Sheila's car drives up crunching on the gravel. She gets out with a local girl and they walk around to the kitchen without a word. A few minutes later the doors are unlocked and I go inside. The girl is opening the windows and I hear Sheila's footsteps over my head. Out on the patio the light is dazzling, the boards still wet. The new girl brings me coffee, sweet cakes and yellow melon. Turns out she's Connie's grandniece, Darlene, who helps out whenever Sheila needs her.

"Where's Rita?" I ask.

"I believe she gone home."

A car pulls up and when a family of six enters the dining room Sheila is there to greet them. It's my exit cue. As they take a table outside I corner Sheila in the kitchen doorway.

"Is Rita sick?"

"She is gone," she says, glaring at me. Over her shoulder I see Connie look up from the stove, heat in her eyes.

"Why? What happened?"

Sheila puts up her hand. "This is not your business."

"It is if I ask."

"You are a tourist. This is my business."

"Gestapo headquarters!"

"Goodbye!" Her voice carries. She pushes past me, walks out to the patio and stands with her back to me, speaking to the family. The father and two of the children look at me through the windows.

Shouldering my bag I walk through the dining room and down the steps and up the drive to the road. It's a beautiful day, hotter than hell already.

The churches in Rocklee—one Methodist, one Catholic—are doing a brisk trade. People are out and there is an unhurried busyness beneath their movements. On the main road old men sit together under trees, noting with spare gestures the strolling women dressed for the day. Toyotas and small Peugeots roll along stuffed full of families on weekend outings. In the dirt under an old Bedford truck—a spectrum of mismatched fenders and multiple paint jobs—a gang of dogs sleeps, scratches and rolls in a synchronized show of canine idleness. From their doorstep a mother and daughter sell flavored ices frozen in the rounded corners of thin plastic bags which are bitten open and sucked by a cluster of children fanning out under a lofty monkeypod tree. In small open houses meals are cooking; radios are playing choir voices. At another front-room store down the road people stop to buy snacks in cellophane wrappers and sodas in clear bottles colored by flavor—banana yellow, ginger brown or lime green. Near the edge of town the blue and yellow West Indies gas station attracts drivers and pedestrians alike, those passing through and those wishing they were. I find Janet there, occupying a side wall with some friends on the lookout for the unusual. She greets me happily.

"What you been doin, Jake?"

"Looking for Rita," I say, glancing at her associates. A girl laughs. A fat guy in cut-off overalls and rubber sandals hops off the wall.

"Need a petroleum product?"

"Don't we all?"

Janet says, "Rita not workin?"

"She went home today."

She stands, arms overhead, stretching like a cat. "You know wheer it is?"

"No, I don't even know her last name."

"Das Blanford. Come den, I take you dere."

We take a path down into the lower part of town and follow the road past Club Camou and its adjacent field, where a soccer game is in progress. As we walk by, the play moves toward our end, chasing several chickens from the goal area. A shot misses, the ball rolls into the road and someone runs after it. A few boys call out to Janet.

"You come to play football?" Blandy says, standing at the road.

"Not now," I say, and keep walking.

As the game resumes he yells after me, "Why she lost her job, mahn?"

The house is the color of the melon I had for breakfast. Rita seems quite surprised to see me. I meet her mother, Angela, her two other younger brothers and her baby sister. They have just been to Mass. Now she and her mother are preparing some sweetly aromatic meal. Angela is a heavyset woman with a big growth on her neck. She invites us to lunch and returns to the kitchen. Rita, Janet and I sit in the yard drinking lime punch under an almond tree. Rita is talkative, telling us she needed a change—implying that she quit the Red Ginger—and plans to seek employment in Granville, but also intends to visit Barbados, where her father is working, to explore possibilities there.

A car drives up and a middle-aged man and woman step out. The man wears a brown suit and has white hair, though he looks fairly youthful. The two boys run to him and he picks them both up at once. The woman is tall, statuesque in a dark blue dress and pearls. She waves in our direction and Rita stands. "Das my aunt Doris," she says, and as the woman gets closer I can see that Rita resembles her much more than she does her mother. Rita introduces us and Doris shakes my hand rather firmly.

"Are you havin an enjoyable visit?"

"Yes I am. I like it better here than the other islands I've been to."

She smiles. "We are truly blessed wit a beautiful land." She looks at Janet and Rita. "We are fond of sayin we have as many rivers as days in de year."

"I don't doubt it. And the beauty is they're so clean."

The three of us follow her into the house. As we take our seats at the table I speak to Rita's uncle, Roger Mathews, and he expresses interest in my photos. "I like to witness what others see in dis country," he says. "What truly attract dem."

"I don't have any prints with me. I send my film back home for processing."

"I see," he says, passing me a platter of brown meat and gravy. "Try some mountain chicken."

I picture a free-ranging sort of bird, clucking and pecking around a meadow between peaks, but I see a long webbed foot flop onto my plate.

He laughs. "You have not yet tried our famous crapaud?"

"No, but I'm feeling a little jumpy myself."

"Dis a delicacy, a natural resource."

"I guess it is. People eat these things in the southern United States too. Unfortunately, they're not used there for weather predictions like they should be."

There is some laughter and Doris says, "Das folklore, Mistah Mayfeel."

"Well, whatever works. Maybe if weathermen thought they'd meet the same fate, they'd be more accurate."

We have rice, mango chutney with the frog, okra salad, fried bananas, and the ever-present dasheen, all in great quantities. The mountain chicken tastes as much like real chicken as anything else that carries the claim, and I have soon eaten enough to feel as though I might croak.

"Mrs. Blanford," I say, "this is terrific food. I believe I've eaten more than my share."

"Juss regular food," she says. "Not like de Red Ginger people talk about so much."

"That's good too, but pretty costly."

Her sister speaks. "And how do you find de accommodation up dere?"

"I like the location but I have a tent. I take my house with me, like a turtle."

"Is dat not somewhat rough on de photographic equipment?" Roger asks.

"Well, it's not perfect, but it's good to be outside and it costs a lot less."

"Dis de rainy season y'know."

"I like the rain. For me it's always a matter of light, and there's often a very fine light right after a rain. Who was it that said you find freedom within your limitations?"

"Is dat what someone say?"

"Someone did."

"Is dat your secret to happiness?" he asks.

"One of them."

"You muss not have children," Doris says.

"My pictures are my children."

She chuckles. "Oh my goodness, Mistah Mayfeel, dey are juss paper. Cahn dey bring you such comfort and joy?"

"I see them as offspring, Doris, that might live on without me."

"You are too young now. You have not met de right girl juss yet. Later you will make a different decision."

"I've already made my decision. Call it a sacrifice if you want, but everyone shouldn't have kids. Too many people just do it, without thinking. Our numbers are overwhelming us. We have no natural enemies, except ourselves."

"Such a cynical opinion for one so young. Settin yourself against de strongest forces, de natural order of men and women and de laws of God too, Mistah Mayfeel."

"I'll just have to start abstaining, won't I?"

I notice Janet whispering in Rita's ear, both of them looking at me. Angela glances at them, and then looks at me as she works on a bone with her hands and teeth.

"Oh, you look much too healthy for all dat, young man," Doris says.

"It'll be easy enough. No one seems to want me anyway."

"Well, I expect you will find yourself getting married one fine day."

"Right. I don't mean to be disrespectful, Doris, but I'm only trying to lift myself above public opinion, to think for myself."

"Young man, dere's a reason opinions become public. Ask de outcast, ask de criminal."

"I'm trying to go my own way, ma'am, call it what you like."

"Now, now, young man, we woan be fallin to name-callin. You juss remember me later on when you sittin dere bouncin dat baby boy on your knee."

Rita brings coffee to the table. And some kind of lemon custard in a cinnamon crust. Then Doris has another question.

"What about de proprietor up dere?"

"Sheila?"

"De very one." She smiles without any hostility that I can detect. "Is she hospitable?"

"She runs a tight ship. She knows her business."

Janet speaks up suddenly. "She doan care for black people."

Everyone looks at me and I say, "She's not fond of any people that I can see. She has her own world up there and she's the boss."

"Sound like juss de girl for you," Roger says.

We have our coffee and dessert. The boys run outside. The baby sits on the floor. The conversation gets no closer to the topic of Rita's dismissal. I ask Roger where they live.

"Pagan Bay," he says. "Over de middle past de Red Ginger and down de coast."

"I should have a look."

Doris puts her cup down. "Does de name attract you?"

"I was just thinking ahead toward a change of scenery."

"De name is quite old, " she says. "Has no meanin for people today."

"Curious though. It must have come from the French or the English referring to the Indians."

"Our Soufrière is a pastiche, mahn," she says. "Like all dese Carib isle."

"To me it looks like a sort of paradise."

She laughs. "Mistah Mayfeel, you have not been lookin so closely."

"In some respects I would call this heaven."

"Oh my, hardly de next world."

"I don't think it could be much better."

60

"You flatter us poor people."

"I don't mean to, but there is something special about this place. I don't know what it is yet, but I've seen quite a few other places."

"You are fortunate."

"Sometimes I am, sometimes I'm not."

"We all got our problems, Mistah Mayfeel."

Janet leaves, and Rita and I go outside and talk under the watchful eyes of those inside. She tells me she got scared the previous night but did not see anyone as she returned to her room. She was dismissed early this morning, accused of collaboration with a tourist. She cleared out her room while Sheila waited, then was driven to Rocklee and coldly deposited on the main road. When I apologize for my part, she shrugs it off. And to my nervous inquiry about our scheduled meeting the following morning, she replies, "Of course mahn, I need a job." Which makes me laugh with relief.

I invite her to accompany me to Pagan Bay for the remainder of the afternoon, but she declines. So I say my goodbyes and leave, taking a shortcut she shows me up to the main road.

It takes me forty-five minutes to hitchhike over to the western coast. From the rear of a pickup truck descending to sea level, I see acres and acres of coconut palms and the flat locality of Pagan Bay, a narrow strip of town wedged between sea and swamp and abruptly elevated land. Like the stitches in a sewn wound, its dirt streets cross the long shoreline road and dead-end at the bay around the edge of which the town has grown. In the dead of afternoon, the truck crosses a rusted bridge over a stagnant, mangrove-lined lagoon. I step out into the humid, breezeless center of town. A hand-lettered sign nailed to a palm tree reads: GET CONSCIOUS, ERADICATE MOSQUITOES. The place is practically deserted; apparently all those able to have fled. Aside from an occasional car or the diminishing shriek of a moped whining around the long curve, the streets are as quiet as settling dust. Fishing boats bob on the bay, colorless silhouettes, matchsticks on the burning surface.

I walk north on the shoreline road past the buildings of town, glimpsing sandy beach between small bayside houses that dwindle in number as the pavement ends and the jungle begins. I reach a fenced property—surely the last house— which the tangled bush threatens to choke from sight. Seeking access to the beach, I notice a small sign attached to the front gate—BEWARE OF HOG. I knock and whistle, hear no snorts or grunts, and tentatively push on the gate; it opens into the yard on a spring, and shuts tightly behind me. The yard is mostly dirt pitted with shallow holes; a few flowering shrubs struggle to adorn the dark property, mushrooming into bloom at eye level, their bottom parts stripped bare of leaf and limb. Above the faded front door hangs another small sign that reads: AMBROSE INN PARADISE.

Jungle sweeps over the fence. Edging around the house I push through strands of vines and heavy hanging gourds, approaching the rear with caution. The house is staple-shaped, its center space a concrete slab of patio facing the bay, strewn with a motley collection of tables and chairs; the prongs of the staple are single rooms, one on each side, their doors leading onto the patio. Most of the middle wall, including the back door, is covered with a large, striking mural. As I get closer I see that it's actually a mosaic of sorts; the vividly painted surface includes broken glass, bits of tile, stone, shell and sea fan. The glass sparkles; jagged edges threaten the viewer. I step back to better see the pattern, and the picture develops into an intricate mix of elements and images: broad leaves and vines, yellow snails, tropical fish, birds, snakes, fruits and faces—or masks, it appears. Like a dense dream designed to sharpen the eyes.

At the end of one room an extension has been started—a

foundation laid and a wall of cinder blocks built two blocks high—the beginnings of another room now filled with leaves, berries, blossoms, twigs, bird droppings and colonies of insects. Stacked against the fence are more blocks and planks of lumber covered by a sheet of plastic. Most of the backyard is sand, well-shaded by a colossal sea grape tree. Ten yards from the back gate tiny waves break noiselessly. I step out to the beach, eager to feel the wicked waters of Pagan Bay.

A man is running toward me, followed closely by a lean black pig, both splashing through the low surf. The man suddenly dives into the water and disappears. The pig jumps up and down, squealing wildly. When the man comes up on all fours, the animal runs headlong into him. He rolls over in the water, pulling the pig off its feet, flipping it over with a wrestling move, then pushes it away from him with a slap on its wet flank. The pig scampers around in a circle, ears flapping, and faces him again, ready for another attack. On his knees now, the man looks over at me.

"Look dere, Smith," he says, "a curious touriss fellow."

"I must've been followed," I say, and glance over my shoulder.

"No more games, Smith." The man stands and walks over to me. The pig follows, its wet snout quivering.

"Lookin for someone?" He stands with his feet apart, as if a passerby might need his permission to pass, still breathing heavily from the exertion, his bare torso carrying a mat of coarse hair but no extra fat, his long dark face calm, inquisitive, and unshaven for a couple of days, his black eyes set wide, his hair standing out in unruly tufts, like maybe he sticks his head in the sea and gives it a good shake for his morning grooming.

"No," I say, as the pig smells my knees. "This your place?"

"I am Ambrose Jones, proprietor of dis paradise." He is half-covered in sand, wearing threadbare cutoffs, a solid-looking man making an assessment. "Who is askin?"

"Jake Mayfield, ordinary traveling fellow."

"Uh huh, like de hurricane."

"Occasionally leaving a path of destruction."

"Even so—" He shakes his head and a clump of sand falls out of his hair. "You doan appear too dangerous."

"Not today, I'm just looking around." The pig moves behind me, nosing my ankles and the backs of my knees.

"Need a room?" Ambrose asks.

"I will soon. Today I just came for a swim."

"Of course, dere's a bigger place up de coast road." He points toward town. "Wit a pool, y'know. Fancier."

"I don't stay anyplace without wildlife."

"Hah! At least, mahn." The pig grunts, its nose bristles tickling my legs. "Smith!" The pig looks up. "Leave de mahn be." The animal sits back in the sand, scratching an ear with a hind foot. "De pig doan come wit de room. Dat boy is strictly security."

"That's worth three stars. You must be affiliated with the Ministry of Tourism."

"Loosely." He grins.

"I met someone in Granville—a Mr. Rollo it was—who seemed to be affiliated also, part of the welcoming committee. He invited me to die here."

"Das a new campaign."

I laugh. "How many rooms you got?"

"Two."

"And another on the way?"

"A creepin expansion."

"Any vacancy?"

"One."

"Who's in the other one?"

"A Dutchman. White. Looks like you."

"We all look alike."

"More or less," he says.

I leave my daypack hanging on the fence and swim straight out, glad for the exercise. I consider pig wrestling but have to forego this contact sport after the black shoat runs up the beach and vanishes in the jungle. Sunlight flashes on the waveless bay. From farther out I'm afforded a broader view of the waterfront town, the gentle sweep of the coast, the thick hills beyond, the lush mountains lost in afternoon clouds. Rain up at the Red Ginger.

On the beach Ambrose stands before a green wall of trees, drying himself in the sun, eyes closed to the light. Hermit crabs crawl around his feet, stopping to become ordinary shells as I approach them. "You play chess," he says.

"Not lately."

"Wanna game?"

"Why not?"

We sit on patio chairs with a low table between us. The board is old and scarred, the opposing colors not much in contrast, the pieces simple, smooth, hand-carved from local wood. I take dark, he takes light; the actual game has less irony. In the first few minutes I lose a bishop and a rook and face the sacrifice of my other bishop to save the queen.

"Want some beer?" he says.

"Just enough to pass out of this game."

"We woan have a stalemate."

"No? How about a natural disaster?"

He steps into the house and returns with two cold beers. I notice paint stains under his nails and in the lines of his knuckles. Then my bishop meets his fate. I begin to play recklessly, trying to snare his queen without looking ahead. Ambrose is playing a methodical game, picking off pawns and harassing my queen in some long-range plot that I can feel but not see. Suddenly though, I trap his queen with the more stealthy of my knights.

"Check."

He moves his king without hesitation, apparently uncaring. I take the queen. Then become the victim. His rook moves across the board. "Check."

I run. A bishop moves in. "Check," I hear again, thinking: you can run but you can't hide. It's a bad feeling. Two more moves and the game is over.

"You played a good game," I say. "My people were lost."

"You had no plan."

"I play like a desperado. No patience."

"No concentration."

I point at the mural. "I was distracted."

"Das why I made it."

"You can get lost in there," I say.

"An escape for de curious," he says.

I study the painting again. "Nice work. I'd have to say it's more than a hobby."

"Doin a wall in town." He shrugs. "Den another I hope, and so on." He drinks some beer and wipes his mouth with the back of his hand. "Better to have two jobs here. At least."

"Where're you working?"

"Chez Lambi."

"House of Conch," I say.

"Das de one," he says, pouring the rest of his beer in a bowl as Smith pushes the gate open and walks in. The pig sucks it up in seconds, grunting continuously. When he finishes, he looks up at me.

"You're a fine beast," I say, "but my bottle is empty."

"Doan make him angry."

"I wouldn't. Why?"

"His father was a Chinese boar."

"What's that?"

"Das a wild bush pig. A solitary boar, mahn. A mean muthafuck."

Field of Vision

I put my hand down. "Come here Smith, you wild animal." He noses my fingers. I scratch between his ears—rough bristle fur, tough skin—and he closes his eyes. I thump his side, he snorts once and plops down, head under my chair. I stand, lifting my pack. "I'll be back for a rematch."

"Anytime."

"Thanks for the beer."

"For sure."

"So long, Smith." He lifts his head and watches me leave.

The return trip is an hour, two rides to the driveway, where rain is falling gently on the parked cars in the thin gloom of dusk. I put away my laundry, still hanging under the bathhouse roof where I left it, and take a shower, then have a meager feast of sardines on stale crackers, one overripe and misshapen orange, and water. Afterward, with the rain still falling lightly, I sit at the mouth of the tent taking a few hits from a pint of rum I have saved for days like this. I have no complaints, not for the moment. The great dark shape of the mountain looms above me, up there with the sky. I raise the bottle once more, screw the top back on and toss it inside as I get up. I walk a little closer to the ravine and listen to the river. It's great to pee outside. In the cool rich air of real heaven.

The alarm goes off and some strange dream is suddenly lost in the receding night. Dawn is arriving. I wash my face awake, brush my teeth, pack my gear and set out with a brisk stride. I get to the rock early and sit by the roadside cleaning my camera lenses, dreaming up pictures in the clear brightening sky. I've gone three days without shooting.

She arrives at seven-fifteen in a black tee shirt, black jeans and sneakers, a small red bag slung over her shoulder. We embark on a rough road of stones—a four-wheel-drive track to nowhere it seems—that becomes a foot trail, climbing gradually in a northeasterly direction through dew-bent grass under dripping tree ferns. We pass perfect cacao trees, their

67

dark-reddish seed pods hiding the essence of chocolate, and eat wild berries—like raspberries but smaller and redder—that grow along the way. Our fingertips become stained. Our clothes grow damp from the exertion of climbing.

The sun has not reached us, though the air is already steamy. We move among trees and vines, between pole-like saplings, thin palms and thorny shrubs, our legs parting clumps of ground ferns, our path edging around kapok, wild tamarind, blue mahoe and the peeling red bark of the gumbo limbo—also called the tourist tree for its thin flaking skin. And the sinister sandbox—its tall trunk densely studded with sharp thorns—whose rain-borne sap can cause blindness in the wide gaping eyes of stumbling strangers.

Walking is work, footing precarious on rocks and logs; shoes slip on rotten wood and slick leaves, trip on roots jutting from soft earth. We labor on a faint, circuitous trail, left to fade by earlier explorers, or barely made by cautious native woodsmen. We cross a trickling stream—a river to Rita—meandering downward as we ascend in roundabout ways, sometimes going down to go up. But always climbing. I set the pace, enjoying the pure endeavor of the hike but wanting elevation, knowing the light will fail in the afternoon. Occasionally I stop, winded and sweating profusely, to drink water, check my compass, or tie a tiny strip of red bandanna at eye level. In her damp clothes and muddy shoes, skin shining wet, Rita looks comfortable, naturally familiar with terrain she hasn't seen, unafraid and yet unmoved, like she's doing it for me. For the money.

We move on, absorbing the smell and feel of the forest floor, looking for the sun and the sky, breaking through thick underbrush and suddenly emerging on an open ridge to the sight of neighboring peaks, green-chiseled slopes cut with light, blotted with cloud shadows.

We stand under towering thickets of bamboo, hearing their

clacking and scraping in the breeze. Rita goes ahead and when the light intervenes, laying bright patches across our ridge, I take quick wide shots, loosening up, letting her hear the motor drive, setting the wheels in motion. Simple landscapes with a human reference, lush territory inhabited by one, a witness to the overwhelming bounty at hand.

Behind us boisterous grackles storm the bamboo, chaos aflutter, while our progression unnerves a black-whiskered vireo in the bushes just beyond our reach. Out in the drafts between peaks, hawks soar over sharp ravines, their harsh cries reaching us at times. They watch us from lofty lookout positions, from high twisted limbs, stark gray against an azure sky.

Under cover of the tall forest we continue upward on a broad slope, surrounded by giant gum trees, mahogany, teak, white cedar and pine. Vines and leaves interlock over our heads. Walking and climbing. Always climbing. Looking ahead to endless trees. And tiring. Sometimes it seems as if we have no actual destination. As I walk, I watch sweat drip off my head onto leaves on the ground. We aren't talking much.

I hear a woodpecker drilling in bursts overhead. A few moments later pine bark flutters down. We stop for water and I watch Rita's supple neck as she drinks, head turned way back. "Feels cooler now," I say.

She hands me the canteen. "Not many pictures."

"Not yet," I say.

From faraway—somewhere ahead, or maybe across a green chasm—comes the clear, piercing call of the mountain whistler, a two-note proclamation of altitude. The next time, though we have hardly gone any farther, the bird sounds much closer, almost with us. It makes a sound of unwavering clarity and optimism, hinting at secret knowledge of places still unseen but waiting behind the trees. Or over a knoll. Or in front of our eyes.

Field of Vision

It is difficult to know how far we've traveled. In a sense the entire island is one mountain peak rising out of a warm sea, like so many other islands, thrown up into view during a volcanic birth. The land itself is made of ridges, valleys and adjoining peaks. On a map of the island I know roughly where we are, but to be on these slopes under this layer of tropical foliage is to be inside an oceanic rain forest—out of sight in a disappearing world. A world enchanting in a way that has nothing to do with magic, but with something ordinary and fascinating—like rain perhaps—not secret or hidden at all.

I'm breathing rarefied air, nowhere near altitude sick, but catching an ill wind all the same. My feet are moving up but my thoughts take their own journey. I catch a scent of despair and follow it because it's familiar, my own human smell. It's the scent of self-serving parasites overrunning their succulent host. Ticks on the back of a planetary dog, a once-healthy animal whose fur is falling off, whose skin has become diseased, whose eyes have become oily, whose life—beset by still multiplying pests—is turning to sand and calcified cells. What a destiny! A legacy of waste and overkill determined by the short-sighted and the incompetent. Blessed are the moronic, for they shall inherit the Earth.

But don't worry. Things work out. They always do. It's just a phase, a bad mood, a cold sore. At the very least, God will fix it. Probably at the eleventh hour. We're just children shitting in our pants, but we'll be taken care of. It's okay, trash the place. A better one awaits. Ride the beast until it dies, then fly away. Take the soul train. Have a nice day!

Jesus Crisis! Must I have these sad thoughts while I'm walking through the gardens of heaven? What is it, the inverse law of perception? That for every wonderful realization there lurks some mournful hell of negation? For every golden meadow a rancid dung heap? For every clear eye a festering boil? Is this the balance of life?

We are alone near the top of the tropical world. Traces of mist appear among the trees. Large epiphytes grow at eye level with mosses and strange little flowers. Thick bunches of ferns sprout along soft, wet branches, dripping like saturated sponges. Now the canopy is lower, the air cooler. Gusts of wind whistle faintly through bent treetops. Light filters in, mystified. Small birds chirp, bobbing out of sight as we duck under fallen limbs, holding on for balance, breaking away loose bark. Various flies keep us company as we cross a black mud pit, keeping to the edge, the ground sucking at our heavy shoes.

There are no more paths. We ascend, traversing the spine of a narrow ridge, seeking the way to the sky. At the crest of the ridge we come into the open again. Below us is a shining lake, flat under the overhead sun, shielded by higher ground. Across the water the peak of Morne Matin rises steeply to its veiled summit, by my estimate an hour more of rigorous hiking. Above it white puffs scud across an open blue field.

The lake is idyllic, rimmed with long green grasses and small trees. It's almost round, a crater. I can see great boulders below its crystal surface. In the midst of green-surfaced planes of angular mountain it is startling to see this flat piece of water, clear as glass, like a porthole window to the center of the Earth.

We make our way down and sit on round lakeside rocks. Rita takes off her shoes and steps in, then turns toward me, grimacing a smile. "It's cold."

"You'll get used to it." I take off my boots and then my shirt, laying it over a rock to dry. The sun is warm on my shoulders. We walk along the shoreline, wobbling on loose rocks for a few minutes. My feet are sore but the water is brisk and invigorating.

"I'm hungry," she says.

"Me too," I say, looking at the sky, "but let's wait a little. I don't want to waste the sun."

71

I begin by shooting her feet in the shallow water, mingling with gray and brown mottled stones, strands of algae, blue and green surface reflections. Then her hands, fists and fingers, her snaky arms underwater. She thinks it's quite funny, getting wetter all the time as I search for abstractions.

"You should go swimming," I say.

"And you?"

"I should too."

Under her clothes is a white one-piece suit that stands out in marked contrast to her skin. She crosses her arms, watching me. Her brown body is lithe and fit. I stand on the rocks in running shorts and spread my mud-caked jeans in the sun.

We wade out together, stepping gingerly on the slippery rocks, making extreme expressions at each other. When the water is at my thighs I say, "Let's go!"

She laughs. "Let's go!"

I dive forward, submerging in the shock of the clear water, swimming through distilled liquid light, moving my arms out to the sides. Bubbles rise like translucent pearls. The bottom fades away in a blur of water vision and increasing depth. I come to the surface standing, the water at my chin. Rita comes up beside me, her face bearing a look of surprise, her hair shining like wire. She takes fast breaths, kicking in the water, and ripples start away from her and disappear in the flat glass of the surface. Her eyes are almost fearful. Words rush out with her breath. "Dis a special place."

"It's brilliant," I say, trying to stand perfectly still, watching her kick. "You swim much?"

"Not very," she says.

"You can rest on me."

She puts a hand on my shoulder. I move my opposite arm through the water, regaining a subtle balance. We are quiet for a few moments, looking around at the encircling slopes, hearing nothing but a few invisible birds and our own astonished breaths. My face is warm, drying in the sun; below the surface my skin is cool, contracting in minuscule spasms.

At the top of Morne Matin trees bend slightly in a wind we can neither feel nor hear. The lake is still. Distant clouds float in a washed blue sky. Nothing changes for a long time. Nothing moves but the air in our lungs, the blood in our veins. Ordinary seconds and minutes cease to pass as time slows to nothing. In this elevated arena our lives move at the speed of glaciers. The water holds us like gelatin. There is nothing to explain, no way to explain it. This is the spectacle we share.

At my shoulder—where her warm hand grips—I feel movement. She is shivering, I realize. We both are. Cold as sleeping fish.

She whispers through quaking lips, "No people been here before us."

"They could find our fossil bones in a million years."

"What would dey say?"

"They would say we forgot to swim and stay warm."

"Let's go!" she says.

We swim hard to shore, thrashing our limbs, coasting into the shallows with breast strokes, hand-walking over stones until they touch our bellies and thighs. We get to our feet and climb up onto large shore rocks, where we lie fully stretched out to steal the warmth collected here.

After a short time in the sun we return to the water. I am rejuvenated, energized for work, and I feel Rita is like-minded. I am fascinated too. In this open spring-fed hollow, high above the surrounding sea, there is a superb clarity of air and light. Over the lake the atmosphere is pure, ethereal. I squint at the surface, watching for evaporation. Bright condensation fills my eyes. Molecules leave for the sky.

I am fascinated by Rita also. By her color. By her wet form in the sparkling water. By her attitude. I want to translate these things into movement and shape. Into mystery or intoxication. I look into the camera, through the glass of alteration.

She swims underwater. I stand thigh-deep, seeing parts of her pass through the frame, flashes of sable darker than anything else I see, darker than flat gray stones or soft brown mud stirred from the bottom. I move farther from her, working the light that enters the water, gaining more refraction with distance and angle. The white of the suit is bright, an albino seal passing. She comes up for air and I motion her down. She glides by, a black and white form with scant color, a watery sketch.

At the edge of the lake she kneels on the stones, the water covering her hands and wrists, and her legs from knees to feet. I move around her, exploring angles, looking at the arch her body makes and the shadow below it. I stand over her, shooting down, seeing the back of her head and the round stones underwater. I squat beside her, roving slowly over her shoulders and neck with my capsulized eye. Her neck is straight, her face smooth, lips together, eyes closed, her profile outlined by fluctuating water. The motor drive fires but she does not move. I have asked her to speak as little as possible. I hold the camera in my right hand and whisper things about the warmth of the sun, the freshness of the water. I see my left hand enter the frame dripping droplets onto her neck, the sensuous curve where it meets her shoulder. The white strap annoys me and I hear myself ask, "Do you mind?" as my fingers tug it over the shoulder.

"It's okay," she says, and I put more water there. Droplets race down the arm, leaving darker lines on the baked skin. Close up they are like dewdrops or sap trails on a brown stalk. The shutter opens and closes. I stand to change film. She shifts her hands and knees a little but keeps her position.

I lie almost under her, in her shadow, shooting up at the line of her stomach, her breast, the white-suited contour rolling

74

upside down through sky or intersecting the blurred diagonal of mountain slope. Afterward I crouch quietly behind her, watching tiny silver fish at her toes, shooting her underwater calves through ripples I create. I wet the backs of her thighs, shoot them and the space between, seeing a sliver of white suit in the middle as I move up. I look again, working to keep the compositions abstract, keeping my eye inside the glass. I wet the thighs again. I wet the white suit stretching across the buttocks, pouring handfuls of water, watching trickles run down the recess and drip from the white patch where black curls sprout at the edges. The motor drive is quiet. "How are your knees?"

"Okay." She stretches her legs. The sun is still with us, hotter even. The water feels good. The stones are hard but very smooth. My stomach growls but I feel quite well. I love it here. I put my hand on her back and she looks around at me.

"You can lie down," I say.

She flattens out. A pool forms in the small of her back and spills out the sides. I stand looking down at it. At her. At the island her butt makes. Her legs are long dark shapes, streaks of poured coffee. I am wondering what photographs to take next.

"Turn over," my voice says. I'm thinking that composition is everything. She rolls over, gets herself into some sort of comfortable position, reclining on a rock pillow, looking up at me. Her face is impassive but I believe she looks happy. The white suit is completely wet, molded to every rise and turn. It is so bright I am nearly blinded. I take a few more photos but I think they might be overexposed. I change to macro and study her terrain in detail, seeing only small sections at a time. I hear the motor drive fire but I am losing touch with the images. I want to work but I'm losing sight of the subject. In every composition I see only the woman.

I stand over her. The camera hangs from my neck. I bend over and pull both straps off her shoulders, down her arms and over her hands. The white suit rolls down the muscles of her stomach. Her breasts, firm and pointed, aim straight up at the sky. They are the color of her arms, only the sharp nipples are darker. I look at her face. The expression is the same. The camera dangles above her. Maybe she thinks I'm still working. I'm not sure if I am anymore.

I take both sides of the suit and pull it down. It's tight at the hips, then springs loose, rolling a stone over beneath her, sliding down the long legs and over the feet, out of the water. I throw it onto the grass and look at her dark body. The uniformity is pleasing to my eye. Her feet are together, her legs as close as they can be. At her pubis the tight black hair grows untrimmed, beyond the boundaries of American bikinis, onto the insides of the legs, up to the lower belly. Watching me look at her she says softly, "Das a wild bush," as if I am in need of information. Maybe my actions tell her I am. She looks at the camera and I can sense that she doesn't want to be a naked subject. I take two steps and put the camera on the nearest dry rock.

I lie on my stomach next to her, my face near hers. We watch each other as I position myself on the rocks. Finally I say, "How do you feel?"

"Hungry."

"I know," I say. "We'll eat after this."

"After what?"

There is silence while I search for words. During the long pause I feel the sun on my back, a stillness in the air. I picture the lake from somewhere in the sky. Suddenly I feel a light touch of mist, light as a sparrow's breath, on my cheek, on my back. An infinitesimal wetness falling. I look up. There are no clouds over the lake, yet fine moist particles descend on us, noticeable in the sun's rays, twinkling in the bright air, unnoticeable on the water. It is so sudden and so slight that it seems imaginary, even though I watch it settle on her breasts, her lips, her eyelashes. "After the rain," I say.

"Das dew."

"From the sky," I say.

"From de mountain," she says. "It's good luck, y'know."

I lean up on my forearms and kiss her. The hardness at my loins wedges between the stones, becoming one of them, so hard that a mollusk couldn't tell the difference. We lie motionless in the water, only our mouths touching.

"I am not a virgin, y'know."

"You're just fine to me." My hand slides down her stomach onto the coarse growth of the wild bush. She is quiet, watching my hand; it moves underwater, rubbing its way down the middle. Her dark thighs spread slightly, my white hand wedged between them. My fingertips touch her swollen lips, the wet inflated cushions expanding to open the warm crevice. Cool lake water flows around my fingers, inside so easily, feeling the smooth warm wetness, warmer than the sun on my skin, smoother than ripe papaya. She moves, pushing up off the bottom.

"Let's get off the rocks," I say.

We push out easily into deeper water. I throw my shorts to shore and they smack on a rock. She touches my neck. We stand facing each other, lightly feeling each other's skin. She looks into the clear water where my erection noses at the wild bush.

"You muss be careful."

"What?"

She bites her lip, knowing I can guess.

"No birth control," I say.

"Doan discharge inside."

"I'll be careful," I say, holding her shoulders. She has stiffened and I tell her, "I won't. I don't take it lightly."

Pressed together fervently, we kiss, her arms over my shoulders, mine around her back. I hug her tightly, kiss her neck and whisper, "I didn't plan this."

"It's okay."

"These things happen."

"It's okay."

My arms slide down her back. My hands lift her buttocks, pulling from both sides, opening the way as her legs come up buoyant around my waist. Lowering her I guide myself, slide up inside, pull back and enter again, completely—a blind whitefish slipping into a narrow cave, backing out and going in again, testing the size of the chamber, rubbing back and forth on the close walls, enjoying itself. She's so wet. Breathing over my shoulder, holding on to my neck so tightly. I churn the water inside. Easy, easy. So wet and so tight. My foot slips off a stone. I stumble and focus on equilibrium, even in the still water. I shut my eyes and settle into a rhythm.

She whispers in my ear, "Doan discharge."

"Okay," I say. Think of something else—a car rolling into a carwash, suds flying. No, not that. Think baseball. High fly to left, backing up toward the fence. Think of the mist falling again, the sweet dew, like the kisses of angels. "It's okay," I tell her again.

She whispers my name, gripping my neck.

"It's okay, Rita," I say, thinking: one more stroke. Two. That's all. Three. I lift her, sliding out like a drawn dagger, bending over in spasms of transcendence, shooting my fluid into the crystal lake, introducing stringy globules that fall slowly, fish food sinking to the bottom. She giggles. We are both watching.

We eat lunch on the rocks—peanut butter and jelly sandwiches, dasheen slices, oranges—watching clouds come and go over the peak of Morne Matin, seeing the light withheld and released over the lake. The sun is into its western slide when we push on, rimming the lake and climbing once more, going for the summit.

Field of Vision

Fingers of mist stretch down to meet us. The trees are low and dense, sculpted into twisted tangles over our heads. Wiry strands of moss, olive-green and black, hang in long bunches like nests of spiders. We stoop low, walking with bent backs through a condensed world of tightly-sprung air plants, small unfurling ferns and miniature blossoms in primary colors. Hummingbirds arrive in flashes of electric green or shiny violet and disappear before the drone of their wings is gone. We have reached the elfin woodland, home to the small and the unseen, to undiscovered insects and rare parrots. In the near distance milky sunlight appears and fades with uncommon frequency. Fields of vapor suddenly vanish, and spindly, leafless trees spring into view. White air descends again moments later, cloaking the long furry arms of tree ferns reaching out over us. Here and there long stiff palm spikes stick up like the spears of prehistoric people hidden in the mist. Cool winds swirl as we continue upward, engulfed in a euphony of singing zephyrs.

The trees thin out and the spongy ground becomes firmer. At our feet, orange lichen and pale green moss cover the surface of rocks like rough skin. A shallow canyon opens before us, a nearly barren field of boulders riven down the middle by a vaporous stream. We descend a slippery escarpment, catching pungent whiffs of hydrogen sulfide. In and around the stream huge colored rocks—bluish-gray and reddish-orange—sit like natural icons. Yellow-rimmed vents in the banks hiss sulfur fumes into the cold breeze. Along the canyon walls bordering the water, steam clouds rise from a line of hidden pockets like geologic smoke signals marking a volcanic continuum.

I lag behind, watching the low cloud ceiling for a glimpse of the peak. Shielded from the sun, I shiver in the wind and put on a sweatshirt. I come to a place where twin fissures feed steaming water down slick, orange-faced rocks into a shallow pool that spills over and joins the meandering stream. I bend down and dip my hand in the water; the pool is a hot bath, a spa at the ephemeral world.

Picking a way out of the steep canyon we begin the final ascent, climbing from rock to rock over the cracked ground, reaching a scalp of short grass and exposed roots, thorny shrubs and brambles. We crawl over white boulders and under the intertwined branches of stiff, wind-bent trees. Finally there is nowhere else to go. We have arrived. There are no more inclines, only gusts of wind and the rapid movement of clouds all around us. White space.

We sit on top of a boulder drinking water, snacking on broken crackers, looking at names scratched in the rock. The clouds open on one side, revealing the ocean to the west and a quick view of a coastal village—minuscule white squares in a cluster—before the hole closes. A shower moves in from the north. We huddle under my poncho, sitting on the back edge while the front corners flap in our hands. The rain falls for less than five minutes and the clouds leave. In the northeast we see other peaks and green slopes with shadows racing across them. Then we're alone again, enveloped by opaque tentacles of cool white air.

I stand up on the rock looking out over the flat-topped trees nearby. When the mist clears I can see jungle spreading away on all sides, green and uniform, held in place by the encircling sea. I see the capital but it's nothing from up here, a distant arrangement of shiny spots. I gaze at stretches of irregular coastline, get a sense of the shape and size of the island. I see a miniature ship way out at sea. I am elevated in a sense, feeling substantial and lucky but not exalted, not special. Certainly no closer to God. I feel temporary and tired and not surprised by what I see, though I take a couple of quick shots for the record. I look down at Rita lying on her back, wearing my sweatshirt, looking up at me. I'd like to stretch out beside her and fall asleep. But it was a long way up here and it will be a long way back. We've peaked. It's all downhill from here. Isn't the journey always worth more than the destination?

We return the way we came, down the steep grade into the canyon of barrenness. A chill wind blows down the corridor. There is no sun, just the heat from the earth. At the hot pool I stop for a moment of consultation with my sore muscles. It's a quick discussion. I undress and slip into the steaming water, soothing myself in a private bliss for several silent minutes, sinking into such a deep state of relaxation that I briefly sleep. When I open my eyes, Rita sits waiting for me. After some coaxing she joins me in the water.

The heat is stimulating, the mineral springs no doubt healthful. Its recipients become pliant and passionate. We make love with only our sweating heads above water. She is quiet and more relaxed this time, trusting the promise of my timely withdrawal. And when the time comes and part of me melts away, I let out a guttural cry that echoes off the canyon walls.

"You say somethin?" she says.

"Yeah." My voice is a laughing whisper. "I said I love the Earth."

Backtracking through the elfin woodland, we climb down freshly wet slopes, going over and under the same slippery limbs in the same dense thickets, collecting mud and flies again in an arduous descent, no easier going down than it was going up. In either direction one must clamber. Down below, on the roomier slopes of the lower forest, we'll make faster time. I look at my watch; we'll be hard-pressed to get down before dark. Each landmark is a sign of progress, another step on the return.

Through wispy tree ferns we see the lake, a silver pie plate wedged into place under an overcast sky. Minutes later, cutting through the long grasses around the perimeter, we pass it. There is no evidence of our previous merrymaking and not a ripple disturbs the surface.

Once we find it I become absorbed in keeping to the trail. Everything is backward now but I feel comfortable with the landscape, with my memory, and with my sense of direction. Rita generally follows me but sometimes we ponder the way together, standing at places where the trail seems to end or split into options. Occasionally we make a mistake but always correct the error before we've gone very far. For the most part I feel mentally sure-footed, and though my legs are tired, I begin to move faster, running, leaping and sliding for the fun of it, to make better time in an exhilarating fashion. It's something like skiing late in the day on rubbery legs, moving downhill too fast, slipping, cutting around trees, barely avoiding collisions, racing oneself, feeling a little closer to danger. In the windless humidity I strip down to tee shirt and shorts. Running sweat-soaked, I fall and roll, collecting samples of the forest floor on my skin. Rita catches up laughing. I laugh too, and toss her the canteen.

Rain falls, sounding heavy above but reaching us in shattered drops that gradually slicken the ground. Still, we make good time. When it becomes clear to me where we are, how far we have to go and how much light we have left, I begin to search for one last stopping place. I don't want the day to end too soon.

We sit on the dry end of a log under a giant tree fern and split a soft chocolate bar. I set the camera farther down the log, set the auto-timer and come back to sit behind her. We freeze, staring at the lens. The shutter snaps—our formal forest portrait is taken—and an animal scampers between the trees thirty feet away, leaving only the residual sound of overturned leaves and the impression of an overgrown black guinea pig with longer legs.

"What was that?" I say.

"Agouti." She points overhead at the tree fern. "We call dis one parasol agouti."

"We call that a rodent umbrella," I say.

She pulls air between her teeth—playful resignation on this occasion—and picks up her bag. I retrieve the camera and sit wiping off the moisture. Drops patter around us, rolling off the feathery edges of the green parasol. When I look up she is opening a prickly pod from a lipstick tree we must have passed along the way. She crushes the soft red seeds into a wet paste and draws marks on my cheeks, my chin and down the sides of my windpipe. She makes two more dabs above each of my eyebrows and holds the pod out to me. I rub the substance between my fingers, watching them turn bright red, then make similar stripes on her. Wiping my hand I leave streaks on the log and smudges on my pants. Holding the camera away from us as still as I can, I take another jungle portrait—black and white faces in tribal color.

"Look through here, turn this until the image looks clear, then push this button." I give her the camera. She holds it to her eye and aims at me, turning the focusing ring back and forth. The shutter opens and closes as the motor drive fires to the next frame. She jerks but keeps her eye against the camera, leans closer to me and takes another. She roams over the log, out into the trees and up into the canopy, and slowly down the trunk of the parasol agouti to me again.

"I would like a picture of you," she says.

"You'll get one."

"When?"

"I don't know. When I get back I'll send you some."

"You will forget."

"No I won't."

I tell her I'm going to town tomorrow to send some film home and she says she's planning to look for work so we decide to go together in the morning. I tell her I want to see her again even if there is no photography involved.

"You leavin soon?"

"I don't know when."

She is quiet for a moment. Then she says, "Why do you hate de other touriss?"

Momentarily taken aback, I stare at her serious face. "I don't hate them," I say. "I hate the way they travel, like swarms of locusts. I hate the places built for them, the ones that are too big, take too much land, and that reduce everything to money. They need too much. And now there are too many of them. They make different places look the same."

After a moment she says, "I haven't been to any other place."

"You haven't been off this island?"

"Not yet."

"Well, at least you live in a great place. At least you can come to a spot like this and not see hundreds of tourists."

"I see only one."

"Yeah, only one. Not bad."

I've already seen several fireflies by the time we get to the stone road. The trees open over us. The sky is a cloudy violet but the drizzling has stopped. The air is cool and fragrant. Insects fly across the trail and birds squawk overhead, heading for higher ground. Walking on stones we observe the last western rays grazing the sky.

We come out to the main road not having spoken for a while. There is a kind of awkward tenderness between us, something half-sheltered in the unusual quality of the day we've spent together, and I suspect she's wondering, as I am, where to go from here. We've exchanged more than fluids and face paint, and now, walking down the quiet road, I feel the mixed bliss of fatigue and discovery.

Not far from the Red Ginger driveway I suddenly remember our financial arrangement and open my wallet, embarrassed. I have some cash, some traveler's checks. "Tomorrow I'm going to the bank—" I say, the words dying in my throat as I hand her some money, about half of what she's owed. She takes it, saying nothing.

"The gas station at eight," I say.

"Okay."

She walks down the hill. I cross the road.

"Goodnight, Rita."

"G'night, Jake."

The morning is wet and clean. The river trades pleasantries with me as I empty my bladder down the bank. Out on the road the stiffness in my legs feels good, like something needed and earned. I have no camera with me but carry enough exposed film to feel the weight of solid work. Under the circumstances I'm not sure things can get much better.

Rocklee is active, the people on the street friendly. The smell of just-baked bread floats on a flower-fragrant breeze. The faces of dogs wear reluctant smiles. Rita sits on the low side wall at the station reading a supermarket novel. As I sit down a look of wily speculation crosses her face. Not speaking, we might appear to be happy strangers.

The bus fills—women with empty shopping bags, young children, a silent teenage boy next to an old man—and we embark on our trip to the capital, leaning with the turns, wedged together in the open air under tree-framed slices of blue morning sky. Against the warmth of Rita's body I doze behind dark glasses, swaying and waking to the same peaceful monotony of the faces around me. The radio plays road music in tune with the wheels, upbeat melodies that drug the sluggish passengers. Sometimes I hear the driver yell to friends as we roll by, their brief responses fading into our sleepy wake.

A white sailboat leaves Granville harbor between cargo ships at anchor. A small tanker rests against the government docks. We rumble on, passing a pumice quarry and a bottling plant, taking Longbay Road into town. We slow for construction—the installation of underground, hurricane-proof cables—and then cross the bridge over the Granville river. Below us two women wash clothes in the rushing water, draping shirts and dresses over gray boulders along the shore. On the other side the bus stops at a bakery-restaurant that overlooks the river and everyone gets off.

The sun blasts off the roofs and walls and cars. Rita and I walk a few blocks to the Windward Inn for breakfast and eat in a courtyard shaded by palms and sea grape trees. She inquires about a job but is told no positions are available. Afterward we walk down the street to a Barclays Bank and she goes into a boutique next door while I cash my remaining traveler's checks. Fifteen minutes later I rejoin her and we continue down the street, walking along the edge of Goodwill Park. I pay her the balance of her fee and she walks me to the post office. We split up there, agreeing to meet at the park at two, or failing that, to catch the three-thirty bus together.

I send a package of film to my friend Tom, mail a few postcards and meander through the center of town among one and two-story buildings painted in tropical hues. The National Workers Union Headquarters bakes vacant in the sun, aloe green and deep-sea blue. A TV & Radio Service shop has faded lemon walls and a tangerine door. Second floor porches are trimmed top and bottom with gingerbread wood or crisscrossed white slats; the railings, posts and shutters match in accent colors. Ironwork grills and gates, lengthened by their sharp shadows, make spiderweb patterns or opposing zigzag diagonals like tire tread. Grass sprouts in the gutters and doors hang open three or four feet off the hot pavement of patchwork streets. Dormer windows jut out of high-peaked, rusted roofs, open-shuttered for any wind. Under the scathing sun, streets are off balance; people weight the shady sides, crossing the light to enter the shadows of listing balconies.

Next to a derelict building I find Island Dispensary and

step inside to a dark, high-ceilinged room which is reasonably cool, cave-like after the sunlight. My eyes adjust as I wander between rows of glass-fronted cabinets. The room smells of antiseptics and musty cardboard. Built into the walls are shelves lined with bottles, boxes, tins, tubes and jars. In the back of the shop a girl behind a cash register cracks her gum loudly. Fluorescent fixtures hang on long chains from the ceiling over the pharmacist's platform, where the man sits at his desk writing. Two elderly women who look like sisters occupy a bench in front of the pharmacy partition. One wears a straw hat. The pharmacist looks up over the railing of his domain. He is nearly bald with a salt and pepper fringe over his ears that grows down into bushy sideburns, and he wears a white smock with several pens in the front pocket. He looks at me over his glasses.

"May I help you?"

"I'd like to buy some condoms, please."

He pushes his chair back, walks across the creaking boards of his platform to a glass case, selects a silver box and hands it to me over the partition. The box has a layer of dust on it and the expiration date was two months ago. I look at the case and see that all the shelves and boxes have dust on them.

"Not a big seller," I say.

At the register the girl totals my sale and I pay and put the box in my pack.

As I turn to leave the lady in the straw hat says, "Shoulda brought his own."

I open the door—the gum cracks behind me—and step out squinting into the dazzling chaos of the street.

At the supermarket I restock my portable pantry—tinned fish, dried fruit, crackers and cheese—and wait in line watching the people around me, especially the foreigners. A French couple, certainly sailboaters, push two shopping carts, one filled only with bottled water. A band of Americans buys lunch meats, bread, sandwich spreads, sodas, beer and potato chips. A motley group of men—Asian, Middle Eastern, European—come in full of laughter and camaraderie, crew members of a cargo ship no doubt.

Outside the door I take a few steps and stop cold in the shadow of the overhang. Across the street I see Blandy on the stoop of a leather shop, turned almost toward me, his colorful knit cap a trademark, a cigarette in his hand, talking to someone in the doorway. I back inside and stand watching through the store window. I can see an arm and leg of the other person, a man. Blandy stops talking and smokes his cigarette, listening. The hands of the other person emerge into view, gesturing. One hand drops a piece of leather and the person bends to pick it up. Dreadlocks swing into the sunlight. The man straightens up and looks in my direction before his bearded face moves back into darkness. I recognise his large head, his unpleasant craggy face. It's Rollo.

I cross the front of the store and exit through the other door, moving among the people on the street, away from conflict. I stop next to a vendor's cart and look back. They're still there talking. Maybe they've just met. Or they know each other. So what? It's a small town, a small island. Probably a coincidence. Or maybe not. I wonder now if Rollo knows Rita too. I never mentioned that first day's incident to her. Now the vendor is trying to sell me ballpoint pens or incense or pocket combs, so I leave, entering the stream of humanity again, moving where my feet take me, wandering in thought and trying to separate suspicion from reality. But that's the difficulty—they're bonded like Siamese twins.

I stop in a little place near the park and have a coconut punch, sitting on a stool at the door, watching people and cars go by, watching for Rita.

At two I go into the park and walk among the benches and shade trees where we intended to meet. Way down at the other end schoolboys in white shirts play soccer. I can see a few people in the bleachers as I sit down to wait. The humidity is like an extra skin. At two-thirty I start walking to the other end on a dirt path along the perimeter wall. A cyclist passes me. A goat munches grass in the narrow shade of the wall. I sit down on the bottom row of the bleachers. Rita is nowhere in sight. I eat some dried pineapple, watching the game, dripping with sweat. I think she must have landed a job that started immediately.

I leave the park at three, walk past the boys' school next door, past the Government Printery, and follow the river to the bus stop. In the bakery I buy a bag of breadfruit puffs and stand outside eating them even though I'm not very hungry. I imagine that she is already hard at work somewhere nearby, or that she's run into an old friend and forgotten the time. Or that she's had an accident. I think of checking the hospital and the clinics. At three-fifteen the bus arrives and unloads. New passengers begin to take their seats. At the restaurant counter I ask about the next bus. Five-thirty. I stand at the window watching the driver finish his drink, hand the bottle to a boy, start the engine and light a cigarette. The last-minute people climb on and find places to sit or stand. Rita is a no-show. The driver blows the horn and starts a slow U-turn. As I watch the vehicle rumble away over the bridge my suspicions grow and I wonder if someone is watching me now, seeing that I'm still here. It's a fucking conspiracy, I think. She's setting me up.

I walk across town toward the hill overlooking it. I don't know what else to do but walk. Pausing a moment outside the somber cathedral, I round the corner onto High Street, climbing on cobblestones between the convent high school and the Catholic cemetery. The road gets steeper, each sharp turn angling back over the previous section, and there is little traffic. Near the top, beside a squat block building, a white radio antenna sticks into the air like an aberrant thorn. Across from the station is the library, an open, one-room house, the front porch of which overlooks the town, the river, the fort and the sea. The rest of the hilltop is given over to a police building and the prime minister's residence, a huge high-walled compound which has the appearance of a fortified botanical garden. Beyond the compound, hills become mountains—the island rising abruptly to shroud itself in a baleful sky.

The walk brings me an appetite. I meander back into town, taking another route from the bottom of the hill, and stop at a clinic I happen to pass. Rita hasn't been here; nor—I inquire by telephone—has she been admitted to the hospital. Minutes later I stand in front of the Victoria Cinema looking at the Now Showing poster for *The Kick of Death*, a martial arts movie. On the other side of the door the Coming Soon poster promises a horror film titled *Gone to Hell*. On the wall beside it another poster has been affixed, perhaps a quarter of the size of the larger, more colorful, action-packed ads. It's a simple two-color illustration showing a young girl's head thinking of several images: students at desks, an airplane, a girl in cap and gown, a theater. Over her head are the words, *What will you have to give up if you have a baby now?* And opposite the images are the corresponding answers: *School, Going Abroad, Career, Movies.* Across the bottom the poster reads: *Take Control of Life . . . Before Life Controls You! For sound advice talk to The Family Planning People. The C.F.P.A. Caribbean Family Planning Affiliation.*

I'd hoped to find Rita at the bus stop, but I don't. So I get a plate of dasheen tortillas and a Red Stripe beer and sit down at a formica-topped table with a salt shaker and a red pepper sauce bottle in the center. Outside, sunlight reflects off the windshields of cars coming over the bridge. The bus is late. I stay at the table reading until it pulls up. We leave at ten to six, and after that I hold no illusions and expect no more warning than I've already gotten. The breeze relaxes me as we climb slowly into the twisting roadway, riding on continuous curves away from the thick coastal heat and into the cool vines and the drowsy dew.

"You home, mahn!"

I open my eyes, wipe moisture off my face. The bus is pulling into the Rocklee gas station. Across from me a boy has spoken. I yawn, climb out the back and ask a man who works there if he's seen Rita.

"No, mahn," he says, wiping his hands, "not dis afternoon."

"What about Janet?"

"She neither."

A fine mist coats the surface of the road; the sky is grainy, a rear-screen projection of failing light. The tires of the few passing cars make spinning hisses as they overtake me, sounds that transform—once I've cleared the high side of Rocklee—into discomfiting whispers of ambush. At the first sound of a vehicle, slow on the uphill grade, I move to the side of the road—anticipating hostile wheel direction or incendiary actions from within—and wait, watching the approach with a demeanor of casual alertness and gripping a good-size throwing stone against my thigh with rattlesnake tension. The walk to Sheila's has never been so long. Nor have I ever been so pleased to turn into a driveway filled with the sights and sounds of rental cars and holiday gaiety.

Taking food and especially drink, I spend the evening among the vacationers, in the midst of their protective good time, filling the cavity of my paranoia with a fodder of touristic insipidity, letting them provide the bulk, the soft foam of banality against the fomentation of foreboding in my gut. And while I only want to cultivate a suitable distraction, I can't help but feel I'm making an unhealthy decision—like one who consumes his own skin to stay alive.

Curried crayfish, steamed cristophene, baked yams,

creamy pumpkin soup, avocado salad, passion fruit pastry in vanilla sauce, coffee, rum, Sambuca, Pernod. Keep the drinks coming. A toast to the Lesser Antilles! To the lesser evils of Antilles tourism. A toast to the Red Ginger Rooms and Restaurant. Or is it Restaurant and Rooms? To our hostess, Sheila Faber, a beacon of civility in the bush. Let bygones be under the bridge. Goddamn, she stimulates the economy. To her generosity. To her generous breasts. A toast to her cumulonimbus chest. Great thunderheads for a drunken weatherman. Drink up, Shriners! Then get the hell out. I want this busty nimbomaniac all to myself.

We close the place. It's a late night but the take is good. While Josey cleans up, Sheila is jubilant, smoking behind the bar with the music louder than usual. She raises a glass to her last paying customer. "Welcome back."

"To the Faber of the day," I say, and down whatever I'm drinking.

She pours us both a rum. "You were so friendly tonight."

"Do me a Faber. Why don't you sit on this side?"

She lights a cigarette. "I'm playing the music. Why don't you come here?"

I bring a stool around and sit beside her. "Let's not talk," I say, putting my hand under her dress.

She rests her elbows on the bar and shuts her eyes. Wild, incongruous jazz plays into the night. Her cigarette ash grows long and the smoke rises in a thin plume. The music makes me crazy. Everything does. Moths crashing on the bar. "We go upstairs," she whispers.

"Here," I say. "Let's stay here."

"Not here." She stands, holding her cigarette. "Upstairs." She finishes her drink in a gulp and fumbles under the bar for a flashlight. "I must stop the generator," she says, moving toward the door.

I take refuge in the music, staying in the moment, nodding

with the tempo. Insanity that makes sense. The lights go out. Everything stops. Bright moonlight creeps across the yard, then darkens and withers. Without music the night becomes unfriendly. In the great blank space I occupy, resurgent concerns about misunderstandings and unseen surveillants begin to intrude. The silence bothers me until I hear the reassuring sounds of nocturnal life. The frogs are cool. Everything's fine. I wait in the dark, whistling in imitation. The flashlight beam appears at the door and shines on the porch boards.

"Come out." Keys jingle and fall to the floor.

"We need music," I say.

"I have a portable machine."

My hands find the lighter on the bar and the flame lights the room. I pop the cassette out. "We need continuity."

"You are drunken. Bring the cigarettes too."

Upstairs she lights a candle, I start the tape and the jazz continues. Anarchy is the order of the night. But I'm wondering about Rita as Sheila unbuttons the top of her dress. I reach in and pull her breasts to freedom, hold the soft white flesh in my hands and announce my need for refuge and the place I intend to seek it. "I have to fuck these."

"But not only," she says.

We have it both ways, and while I'm inside her and we are romping loudly across her bed, images of Rita flash in my head—lake pictures. I see her white-suited butt, an island of ass waiting to be explored, and the thoughts of her push me over the edge.

In the aftershock of orgasm I feel good but nothing feels right. Ripples of guilt begin to roll out, and with them a muddle of sobering, half-baked thoughts on secrecy, trust, desire and delusion. I don't know what the fuck is happening. The music stops. I roll off Sheila and lie watching the light flickering on the ceiling.

She sits up against a pile of pillows and lights one of her French cigarettes. After a few inhalations she coughs and clears her throat. "Have you lost your little Negress so soon?"

"That's funny. I was just thinking of her."

The world is quiet for a moment, a feather of smoke curling at the ceiling.

"Do you pay her much?"

"A lot less than I pay you."

"You know, you are disgusting. Sleeping with anyone you meet, like a dog."

"Thanks. I fuck anyone I want, as long as they don't mind. Don't you?"

"Typical American."

"Sure. We have an expression, 'They're all pink on the inside.' Don't you say that in Europe?"

"You're a pig. You care nothing for others."

"Which is it, a dog or a pig? Maybe a pig-dog. And what are you, Sheila, with your money and your superior attitude? Queen of the jungle, charming cheeseheads on vacation. This is not your personal New World, Fräulein."

Her voice rises. "I have made a place for civilized people. You don't belong here. It was a mistake for you to come. You should stay with the blacks."

"I'll take the bill with my coffee and I'll be gone, like it never happened."

She stares out the window, smoking, while I get dressed.

"Can I borrow a flashlight?"

"You can fall down."

I leave, shutting the door on the only light, and move carefully on the stairs. Darkness is complete. I stop halfway down to listen. And think. Sobering thoughts are arriving more fully baked now. Maybe I acted too hastily, leaving the security of her room. I walk down the stairs unable to see anything. The moon is a ghost hidden by clouds. I move by memory, staying on the path, staying quiet. It's a still night, only tree frogs and crapauds and a few billion insects are doing anything much. I pass the crouching generator shed and decide to avoid the bathhouse, place of many leaping doorways. Cutting across the grass I'm invisible; anyone would expect a light beam ahead of me. Beside the looming cabins I find my tent, with the loudest zipper in the world, and grope for my flashlight—leave it off— and pocket knife and canteen and toothbrush and toothpaste. Everything is fine. I take a leak right here. Quiet piss, beautiful night. Night of the Living Dread! All I have to do is go to sleep, wake up and clear out. Sweet dreams, Jake. We all got our problems, Mistah Mayfeel.

It seems to me I've forgotten how to sleep. I can only remember how to listen—to hear little sounds that add up to nothing and long spaces between them—and then at some point I forget that too. But my eyes aren't shut long enough for dreams. I sit up in absolute darkness. My heartbeat feels erratic. What noise woke me? An animal? A bat squeaking? Something on the ground? Agouti? Chinese boar? I hear nothing unusual and lie back down, fidgeting, getting strange ideas, like putting crunchy snails in a circle around the tent, a perimeter alarm system that slowly crawls away. I sleep badly—being awake is being alive—and wake minutes later. Maybe an hour. The tent is lighter and I think it's dawn, but when I look outside, a full moon is exposing me completely to the dread of night. Deep breaths come next. A long, uncounted succession of slow breaths, and when I awake again, the tent is blue, the real blue of the sky behind it.

I visit the mellifluous stream for the last time. Things are changing. I don't seek trouble but it's always nearby, like a crab in a hole, coming out sideways with strange eyes and dangerous claws. All I want is to take some photos and get laid once in a while. But other people get involved. There are repercussions, energy rebounding but not lost. I can certainly appreciate that, lying naked and cool in my preferred pool. Alcohol and sleep-deprivation notwithstanding, I feel okay, even somewhat stimulated, and I laugh hysterically for several minutes. The hummingbirds don't hang around for too long; any absurdity greater than their own tends to make them nervous.

I pack my loose items, then fold and roll the damp tent and stuff it in my backpack with the poles. Leaving only a flat spot in the grass I go to the restaurant for coffee and the bad news. Sheila is waiting and wordlessly brings me the bill for my entire stay. My financial troubles are starting today. Darlene brings coffee, which is already on the bill, and I drink it slowly, squinting at the columns of neatly printed numerals. I put the money on the table and signal for more coffee. Sheila picks up the money, walks into the bar, and returns with the change and a tidy receipt that has the name and address of the establishment printed below a color illustration of a red ginger flower.

I finish the coffee, leave some coins for the waitress, pick up my pack and walk out. Sheila is sitting on the porch smoking like the first time I saw her. As I walk down the steps she says, "Good luck, mister. Don't come back."

"Thanks for the pussy," I say, waving from the driveway.

She is smiling.

Part 2

No breeze worms its way between folds of heat stacking up on the coast. There are no interludes on the long walk through open sun and thick shade alongside mangroves and brackish water. There is the smell of warm stillness and ripe organic fusion as the day advances to sweltering dullness and mosquitoes come in noisy clouds from the shadows. I am their laden prey, driven from lassitude to running through the heat, offending barking, ramshackle dogs standing in the husk and dirt of small coconut properties near the bridge into town. Welcome to Pagan Bay.

On the main street heat waves wiggle up like the clear trails of schooling fish. In dormer windows lace curtains hang as still as the brown silent fronds drooping from palms in the yards of sidestreet homes. Cars rattle over ruts, churning dust into clouds that rise into open doorways and settle on the shaded porches of stores where dusky old men sit in spindly chairs watching the day unravel.

I find Chez Lambi and step inside. The room smells of paint and fried seafood. At the back of the room people line the bar but there's no one behind it. Empty tables and chairs fill most of the floor space except for an open area in front of one long side wall. On the wall is a mural about three-quarters done, an undersea depiction of fish and other creatures that features a congregation of conchs in stunning colors. Affixed to the wall, giving it dimension and contrast, are real conch shells; the protruding spines and ridges seem to provide some rough protection for the painted surface where their artificial brethren lie rendered in flat brilliance, scattered like pearls over an opulent ocean floor.

The wall behind the bar is decorated with product posters: FANTA, 7UP, 555 CIGARETTES, GUINNESS IS GOOD FOR YOU. I ask for the painter and a man shouts, "Ambrose!"

His voice comes out of the back room, "Alright," and when he appears his face breaks into a smile. "Hurricane Jake!" He comes around the bar and grasps my hand. "Leavin a path of destruction." He holds a brush and a rag.

"The wall looks fantastic," I say. "How's it going?"

"Movin at a sea snail pace."

I hear the back door close and a few seconds later a woman in a yellow dress walks out from the kitchen. Someone calls for service and all the customers watch her open a beer and set it down. She moves down to our end and leans on the bar. Ambrose nods. "Jake . . . Sweet Sharon, de queen of Pagan Bay."

"Your highness," I say, extending my hand.

She shakes my hand once and releases me. "Stayin at his place?"

"I guess so."

"Of course, mahn," he says, "if you claim de room." He tosses the rag on the bar and sticks the brush into Sharon's hand. "We may even get some lunch dere," he says, heading for the door. "Some fresh breeze and a view of de sea."

I nod to Sharon. "See you."

"Probably so."

We walk down the street toward the sea, turn away from town and walk past the end of the pavement into the narrowing curve of sandy road between the bay and the trees. As we approach the house I hear Smith grunting loudly, standing up against the inside of the gate. Once we're in, he nudges our shins and prances around in a circle. He seems to remember me.

My room has two beds, two windows, a bureau, a round metal chair with no cushion, a standing floor fan and a green-tiled bathroom. I take off my shoes, wash my face and stand in front of the fan clicked to its highest setting.

We sit on the patio having a lunch of crab cakes, fried okra and beer, and I tell Ambrose about Rita and her curious disappearance the day before. I also mention her brother and Rollo and the unknown implications of their meeting.

"You scared?"

"I'd just like to find out what happened."

He rubs his chin thoughtfully. "Someone may have spoken to her. You woan know unless you see her yourself."

"I'll have to find her," I say, suddenly feeling very tired. "It's a little strange."

"At least." He brushes the air with his hand, putting the subject aside. "Care for a game?"

"Later. I'm a zombie right now. I'm going to take a siesta and go into Rocklee." I drop half a crab cake on the concrete for Smith and take the dishes into the kitchen.

Under the drone and wind of the fan I lie on the bed feeling weird about Rita's absence. I get up, string a line from a window to the bathroom door, unpack the wet tent and hang it up, lie back down again. At least I have two new friends, even if one of them is a pig.

I wake up groggy, confused about time. It's after three. Ambrose is gone and Smith is sleeping against the fence. Out on the road I feel listless, lacking imagination and drive, like a half-formed somebody at the edge of a dream.

I get a ride to Rocklee with a Canadian engineer who is overseeing the installation of a plastic floating dock at a fishing village on the southern coast. He asks if I'm a journalist and I tell him I don't have any assignment at all. After that he's less talkative.

In Rocklee I become nervous, but take the steep shortcut down to Rita's house. Several geese honk and scuttle away as I cross the front yard. I hear hammering from the back. Then I knock and Angela answers the door.

"Hello, Mrs. Blanford. Is Rita home?"

She looks at me sadly. "She is not here."

"When do you expect her?"

"I doan know."

There is a moment of silence. "Is anything wrong?"

The woman watches me closely for a few seconds and there is nothing light-hearted in her stare. "She is not herself for de moment."

"What do you mean?"

"Feelin poorly."

"I don't understand," I say. "Is she alright?"

"She is not here."

I pause for something more, any kind of explanation, but none comes. "Will you tell her I came by?"

She shuts the door partway. "Good day, Mistah Mayfeel." Then she closes it.

I walk into the yard and look around stupidly, waiting for a missing ingredient, a motion at a window, a voice behind a tree. But there is no sign of Rita and I start up the path to the main road.

Behind me I hear the sound of running feet and look back

to see Blandy coming up the path with a piece of wood in his hand. He stops beside me, on equal footing, breathing hard, holding the wood at his side.

"What de hell you doin here?" he says, his gold-green eyes blazing and strange.

My leg muscles have tensed and my left arm is rising between us on its own. "Looking for your sister."

He shakes his head. "Why you treat her like a whore?"

"Blandy—"

His mouth is twisted. "Why you wanna beat a little black girl?"

"You need to get your story straight because I don't know what the fuck you're talking about."

"She all bruised up, mahn," he says, and lunges at me. The wood catches my left elbow, glancing off as I duck, pain shooting through my entire arm as I dive into him, ramming my head into his stomach, reaching around behind him as he falls backward. The wood comes down on my back as we hit the ground hard, scraping into dirt and rock. I lift up, pulling my arms free, blocking the stick with my left hand, punching his face twice with my right. He arches off the ground, throwing a leg up. Both of us are holding the wood as I fall off him down the incline and he comes over me. We roll down a few turns into an amorphous thorn bush and I scramble free, pulling strands of brittle vine, tearing loose with rips at my neck and shoulder, my right hand. He lies under the bush catching his breath, his mouth open wide, his nose bleeding, the wood at his side. I sit in the dirt holding my aching arm, breathing sharply.

For a few minutes pain and light combine in a dizzying heat, like I'm sitting in a bright circle under a great magnifying glass. Then my breathing normalizes. My hearing seems acute. Blandy drags himself away from the bush and sits up, touching his face. I look at the blood on the back of my hand and my mind begins to operate more quickly, taking an inventory of my injuries. I haven't felt so clearheaded all day.

"I saw you with Rollo."

He just glares at me.

"Did Rita meet him too?"

He wipes blood from his swollen upper lip. "Got nothin to do wit you, white bwoy."

"If it was me who beat her, do you think I'd come over here like this?"

He doesn't say anything, trying to blow the blood out of his nose without using much force. He picks up the piece of wood, begins tapping it on the ground.

"Were you talking to Rollo about Rita?"

He keeps tapping, his face a grimace. "He will get you."

"Yeah, he already got me. And you set her up, man, her own fucking brother!"

"You doan know shit! He got job for her, muthafuck!"

"Really? A friendly interview? Whatever happened is your fault."

"No, white bwoy, das your fault. Playin wit her."

"You fuckhead, you don't tell your big sister who to play with." I get to my feet. "She's not like you." I brush dirt off my pants. "Nothing like you."

He stands too, without the wood, and runs his tongue over his front teeth.

"I'll find out what happened. And I'll see her again."

"Go away."

I laugh a little, shaking my head, then take a few steps and look back. "Not until I see her."

"Go—away," he says, emphasizing each word as if his patience is at an end.

"Rollo's poison, man. Think for yourself." I walk up the path. Near the road I look back again. He is still standing there, watching me go away.

The wearing of blood and dirt gives one a certain veneer of temerity. A stain of desperation, perhaps. An appearance too unsettling to the drivers of passing cars. A truck comes by, slows down for a closer look, and moves on.

"C'mon, man!" I cry out.

Brake lights come on. A man's head sticks out the window. "Wheer you goin?"

"Pagan Bay."

"Jump in de back."

I sit on a roll of fencing wire and we take off. I hold the side of the truck with one hand and cradle my left arm in my lap. Once in a while the man looks back through the rear window of the cab. Rushing air fills my lungs and lifts me as we fly back and forth, sailing downward to the sea. Near the coast, rain begins to fall and the man looks back at me and points at the front seat. I shake my head. It's a warm rain, a blessing. The sun shines favorably and the rain smells like almond water.

Back at Ambrose's place I'm greeted by Smith, who expresses some interest in my suggestion of a swim. When I let him out he comes in for a dip, then trots off down the beach. The good bay water stings my wounds. My swollen elbow wants to float like driftwood. I lie back in the sand and let small waves rake me fresh and clean.

After a shower I pour hydrogen peroxide on a few spots, dress in loose clothes and sit outside watching the sun drop, absentmindedly rubbing my skin, obliterating sandflies. Ambrose comes through the house, throwing open the back door.

"Cane-Jake!"

"Brose!"

He stands beside me. "What happen, mahn?"

I tell him about my fact-finding mission.

"Okay, mahn, some pain for progress. You gotta plan?"

"How about a drink?"

"Excellent plan."

He brings out a bottle of rum and two glasses, no ice, and pours. "To de object of your affection."

"To Smith," I say, and we drink.

"So wheer de girl now? At home actually?"

"I don't think so. Maybe right here."

"In Pagan Bay?"

"She has an aunt and uncle here. I should try them. Doris and Roger Mathews."

"Look in de phonebook."

"You have one?"

"No phone either."

"Tomorrow I'll find out where they live."

"At least, mahn."

We set up the chessboard. The late slanting sun spreads a mango stain on the bay. Sandflies are joined by mosquitoes. Ambrose shuts the door to the house, lights a green mosquito coil under our table. The game resumes, smoke curling up around the edges of the board, our drinks in hand. I try to stay involved in the course of my chess game but as I become rum-relaxed and sedated, separated from the pain in my arm, I see myself more and more as a player in another game. Staring at my pieces but dwelling on Rita and the opening moves of Rollo's revenge, I play two games, neither very well. The contest at my fingertips hardly seems to matter. The other game, missing pieces and lacking rules, revolves around a strategy of despair involving violence and rapid flight from the island. High-risk bridge-burning.

Even with divided loyalties the board game goes better than the previous time; it takes me twice as long to lose. But if I am to act in life as have my errant knights on the field, I should expect a fate worse than checkmate.

"You are distracted," Ambrose tells me, displaying his gift

for insight.

"My bishops are bunglers."

"You muss focus on de game."

"My queen is dizzy."

"A dizzy queen kills her subjects."

"I'm thinking about getting even. It's not right, man."

"Go slow, mahn, go slow."

The light is almost gone. I can barely see the motions of shore waves lapping at the sand. Smith comes in the gate, a black shape snorting. In the jungle next door the insects begin in earnest. Ambrose gets up and puts the outside lights on. "You wanna get some lambi?"

I scratch the pig's roaming head; he smells of rotten fruit.

"Wake up, mahn. Experience de nightlife."

"Okay." I stand up and we walk through the house. The pig meets us at the front gate and I look down at the animal. "Sorry, Smith, someone has to hold down the fort." He looks up at me, waiting to be left behind. "Take no prisoners," I tell him as we go out. Everyone appreciates a little humor when they're feeling lonely.

The road is dark at our end. We pass small houses that barely show their interior lights, then brighter places with people on doorsteps, then streetlights into town. An ice cream shop with people on stools, a television blaring on the counter, a dog outside. A movie house and a muffled soundtrack escaping into the street, sounding like arguments in foreign languages. A store selling cigarettes, candy and shirts. A bar with music and a revolving light collecting a ring of unmoved patrons. We turn up a quiet street. Over low roofs I see the lights of hillside homes outside of town.

Chez Lambi is full of people. Music is playing loudly and red glass candle holders flicker on the tables. We sit at the bar, where Sweet Sharon is sitting as a customer, and promptly order two beers and two house specials. Ambrose spends a lot of time talking to Sharon, who is nice to look at and probably worth talking to as well. I'm left to my own devices, which aren't functioning real smoothly. The conch is excellent— fresh, tender and batter-fried spicy—and I eat in silence, hearing the music and the voices around me, sitting like an island in the midst of a calm sea, accessible but remote.

Whenever the door opens I turn around thinking it might be Rita but I'm not that lucky. I feel responsible for her troubles, indirectly or not. Also, I miss my new muse; she's departed with her image. But worst of all, I miss the woman. So I just keep drinking with myself even though I can scarcely afford to. I will soon be broke and forced to leave. Therein lies the answer and the problem, an impossible solution for me at the moment. I buy drinks for the three of us, drink up, pay up and leave. Stars shine brightly over the dark road to Paradise. The guard-pig is home alone, no intruders. The day is over and it's been memorable too. One little puzzle, one little fight, no deaths of any size.

There are public phones and phone books at the Cable and Wire Office. The address of Roger Mathews is simply listed as Smallhill Road. Ambrose gives me directions as we walk in the street. I think about taking a taxi and driving by first, but I don't like the idea of spending money. I don't like the idea of knocking on the door either, assuming I find the place. "I guess I'll stake it out," I say.

"Take some food."

"Good idea."

He goes to Chez Lambi. I continue down the street, pick up some crackers and two oranges at a store. Then I'm walking along again, wrapped up in my own thoughts, barely taking in the scenery.

Rita's mother was obviously protecting her, and she seemed far more suspicious of me than before. Which leads me to Blandy's role in this. He asked me why I beat a little black girl. He said Rollo had a job for her. So she went to see him. But why would he offer her a job? Unless it was just a ruse. And what's the point of beating her except to send a message. Meaning Blandy had to have mentioned me to Rollo. In what respect? That I'm a white photographer hanging around with his sister? I feel like a detective on the warm trail of a tropical mystery.

Standing at the bottom of Smallhill Road I can only see a few houses before the road curves away. I start up, fearful of passing the house without knowing it, or being seen too soon by the wrong person. Just before the curve I spot a kneeling woman—too heavy to be Doris—placing tin cans with flowers in them around a tree in her front yard. As I step into her driveway a car comes down the hill. I turn away and it passes without me seeing who's inside, though I don't believe it's the car I saw at Rita's house on Sunday. When I look up again the woman is staring at me from her hands and knees.

"Good day, ma'am. Can you tell me where the Mathews' house is?"

"Who you lookin for?"

"Doris."

She sits back on her legs and wipes her brow. Her palm is red with dirt. "Two more up." She flings her arm out. "On de opposite side."

"Thanks."

"Good day, sir."

The house is a small, well-kept place with a trim lawn, flowering bushes below the windows, two coconut palms of equal height. No car is there, no visible activity. Across the road is an open shelter, a bus stop maybe, and I walk toward it, edging into the weeds. Behind the shelter the ground drops off dramatically. I move to one side, hidden by vegetation, and lean against a tree sloping out over the hillside. If I move my head around, I can see most of the yard as well as the front door.

Nothing happens. I spend as much time watching for ants on the tree as I do watching the house. The sun is higher now. I watch the light on the ground slowly change position. I eat the crackers and the oranges more out of boredom than hunger. An hour passes. It's barely midmorning. Four cars pass. No one walks by or uses the shelter. I count the pieces of orange peel on the ground. I squat by the tree, tying grass blades into knots. I watch a red-legged thrush hopping in the branches, cocking its head at me from different angles. I curse myself for not bringing a book. I wait. Another hour passes, a man on a bike passes. The heat is putting me to sleep. I think of rain, the beautiful sudden rain, and a chain of pleasant thoughts follows.

I hear a door shut and open my eyes. Two figures on the steps become two women in the driveway. Doris and Rita, aunt and niece. I smile to myself: go with your instincts, Jake. They walk toward the shelter. My exuberance sinks as I imagine them either seeing me in hiding, or worse, being driven away, leaving me to wait in the roadside shrubbery until they return. But they stop at the road and speak briefly, then turn in opposite directions, Doris heading toward town and Rita going uphill. I wait a minute, then move behind the shelter and look into the road. Neither of them is in sight. I glance at the house again and step into the open.

Running lightly up the road I hear the cellophane cracker wrapper bending noisily in my pocket. At my approach, Rita turns around and stops, startled for a second. So am I. Her left eye is swollen to a red slit; the other is round, strained, making her face look out of balance. Her nose and lips are puffy, and there is a bandage over a lump on her cheek. The longer I look at her, the more she looks like someone else.

"Hi Rita," I say, trying to sound natural. "What are you doing?" She's holding a folded sack and a long knife.

"Walkin to de garden."

"I'd like to go with you."

"Alright," she says, and we start walking along the quiet roadside.

"Are you okay?" I ask.

"Yes, fine."

"Didn't you think I'd be wondering what happened to you?"

"I had a problem."

"Yeah, me too. I went to your house and your brother attacked me. Your family thinks I beat you."

She shakes her head. "No."

"Your brother accused me."

"I told dem."

"Told them what?"

She won't look at me.

"You told Blandy who hit you?"

"It was a stranger."

I keep looking over at her but she watches the ground as we walk. "I told him who did it. It's not that hard to figure out." I kick a stone across the road. "Goddamn it, you took a beating. Look at yourself."

"It was a mahn who tried to rob me."

"Come on, Rita. It was Rollo."

"Were you dere?"

"Why are you lying to me? We're both involved in this."

"Whas de problem, Jake? Are you hurt so bad?"

"Not as badly as you."

"I am not hurt bad."

"Why are you hiding here?"

"I am not hidin."

"What are you doing then?"

"I juss wanna be alone a few days. Okay? Okay wit you?"

I'm on the verge of yelling, so I shut up and try to stay calm, walking silently, thinking, fuming at the truth.

We turn off the road onto a path. The tangled hillside becomes more level as we walk down to an acre or more of cultivated land. There are fruit trees—banana, guava, papaya, lime—and rows of ornamental palms. At the lower end, along a border of shade trees, a low wooden framework supports a draping black screen. Underneath it grow bunches of ferns. Sprouting from this greenery are stiff red anthuriums the color of wax candy lips, each with a pale pink organ drooping from its center. They look like strange sensors, or the flattened cartoon hearts of animated lovers.

We walk between rows of engorged, soft-spiked aloe plants into the center of the eclectic garden, into the edible heart where the vegetables grow. She points them out to me: the infamous dasheen, its great leaves unfurling into wrinkled green elephant ears; pumpkin squash, heavy on the ground like brown leather medicine balls; pods of pigeon peas; bushes of shiny red peppers; the disheveled wiry vines of groundnuts and the yellow-flowered shrubs of fuzzy green okra.

I wander among the plants as Rita selects vegetables and sets them on the spread sack. I have a stomachache. I want to kick holes in ripe squash and make a scene. I walk back to where Rita squats on the ground.

I squat beside her and touch her arm. "Rita, I want you to tell me the story."

She is digging up some dasheen, scraping her knife in the dirt. She looks at me, sighs and returns to the task, pulling up a brown tuber, brushing the soil off.

"Tell me the story."

She sticks the knife in the ground, stands up, tosses the big tuber at the sack; it tumbles and jumps, knocking peppers in the grass, and rolls to rest thirty feet away. I stand up beside her and she begins to speak.

"I was leavin de Creole Castle. Blandy found me in de street. He was tryin to help me wit a job. Okay? He told me to

110

see a friend of his knows a lot of people workin in town. So I went to a wheerhouse to see de mahn—das de time de bus leavin."

"That was Rollo?"

"Yes." She looks at her hands, rubs off dirt between her fingers. "I was havin no luck wit restaurants. Blandy told me about an export company wit some position open. I was goin dere, passin between de wheerhouses. A mahn caught me and grabbed my arm. He tried to get my money but I kicked him and he started to hit me." She looks at me, her face lopsided.

"That's it?"

"Das it."

"One man?"

"He was drunk."

"Could you recognize him?"

"I doan know."

"So you went to the police?"

"No."

"You went to a clinic?"

"No."

"Why not?"

"I was not hurt so bad."

"What'd you do?"

"I went to de sea to clean my face."

I turn away for a moment, watching a pair of grassquits chase each other in the weeds around the aloe. "I suppose that's a possible story. But it doesn't add up because of Rollo's involvement." I turn to confront her. "I say this because I've met Rollo and he didn't seem so friendly and helpful. Quite the opposite. He expressed a strong desire to see me dead." She makes no attempt to hide her surprise.

"Your brother's not the brightest guy in the world. Like most people he only believes what he wants to believe, doesn't bother with reality. But he's only fooling himself, he's not trying to fool everyone else." I pause but she isn't willing to comment. "I don't think he knew you'd be hurt, and he didn't know Rollo would see it as an opportunity. Rollo must have said something that made Blandy believe I could do this to you." She's looking at my elbow, the scratches on my arms. "I'd really appreciate it if you'd tell me the story again, but this time tell me what really happened after you met Rollo. It doesn't matter how bad it was. I won't desert you. I'll help you any way I can."

We stand there together with the birds playing near the ground, the clouds moving slowly over the center of the island. Rita stares out over the garden toward the hills. Several minutes pass, time enough to drag the truth out of storage and hold it in the light, to forget the personal listener and begin a monologue to the impassive land. She speaks flatly, as if she is remembering something that happened in a dream long ago.

"De wheerhouse was hot, many boxes stacked in de room and packing materials on de floor. Rollo close de door behind me and I notice de quiet. Dere are two others sittin on boxes across de room. Dey look at me but doan speak. Rollo says he can help me, he needs to take my information in de back office.

"Back dere is a room wit a desk and nothin else. No chairs. He close de door and ask me if I want a job fuckin touriss. I say no. He says I already have experience. I cahn barely get my breath but I tell him I wish to leave now. He slaps me hard across de face, tells me I am a disgrace, fuckin de white devil wit de camera. He says he will kill dat devil and I woan have anyone to fuck.

"My face is burnin and I try to leave before I cry. He hits me again and pushes me against de wall, calls me an ignorant bitch who muss learn her lesson. He punches me and now I doan even know wheer I am but I hear him speakin about me. Unclean, he says. Contaminated. Full of white filth. You muss be turnin white, he says. He wants to see my black body.

"But I cahn't move and he punches me again and de sound is so loud in dis small room. I take off my clothes and stand lookin at nothin, shakin wit fear, cryin wit shame. You look black, he says, but what about de inside. Dat white stain muss be covered. You muss be filled wit black seed.

"I see him open his pants and I close my dizzy eyes. He pushes me down to de floor and I am lyin dere like a corpse, my head split, my face on fire. He lies on me and pushes himself inside me. Black woman, black seed, he says. Crushin me. Black woman, black seed. Again and again, slammin himself inside me.

"Den I remember at time at Carnival when I was a young girl knocked to de street by accident. I was frightened but not hurt. Black seed, I hear. Noise and bodies passin, so much energy coverin me. Black seed, he says. Den someone liftin me up. Rollo groanin, pushin hard. Den he is still for a time. Everything is quiet. He rises and speaks.

"If you see de white mahn again I will kill you next time. If you speak about dis I will kill you. De door opens and slams. I open my eyes and start dressin on de floor. When I stand I fall on de desk. Feel drippin between my legs. Taste blood in my mouth."

Suddenly she turns away, begins walking swiftly, brushing past dasheen leaves, looking down, and her voice is as loud as I've ever heard it. "Happy to hear dat? Happy for de truth? You gonna say you want me now?" I catch up to her, taking her arm. I feel as if something is stuck in my throat. The air is dry and white, like sand. Her crying is soft under her hand. I hear little squeaks and swallowing sounds. Tears roll down to her elbow and escape to the hot ground.

I hold her loosely, rubbing the space between her shoulders, saying softly, "I'm sorry. It's okay," over and over. I can't think of anything else to say. Nothing poignant or cheerful or inspiring. All I can see is her lying like a corpse on some dirty floor. The sun blazes over us. The heat comes not in waves but in a continuous beam, as if we stand in a tube, a clear cylinder of pouring sun. From the weeds all around us the sound of unseen grasshoppers makes a tremendous hissing, like skillets of bacon frying too fast.

We walk on. The information is between us like a yoke, holding us together and keeping us apart. She has confessed— though I am neither priest nor avenging angel. And there are no rules for the wounded.

As we near the house I tell her that the worst is over, and then wonder what the hell that means. That she's lucky? That it's good to get it over with? "He did it to get to me," I tell her. "It's something bizarre between him and me. Something that makes no sense. I'm sorry it happened, really sorry, but I'm not sorry I came here. And I'm not sorry we met. Some people are full of hate. We can't let that stop us."

She turns on me. "Nothin to do wit me. Is dat right? Juss between de men. You want sex. Any woman is a chance. Doan worry about it. Okay? Now you had a black one too!" She runs across the road and up the driveway.

"Rita!" I call out.

She looks back from the top of the steps.

"I'm at the Ambrose Inn."

She goes inside and slams the door.

Well, that's it. I've reached the end here. Things have progressed to a point where I can see the journey's conclusion. Sometimes you finish the trip, sometimes the trip finishes you.

I walk home in a state of detachment, talking to myself in my salesman's voice, neatly wrapping up the loose ends of a deal. When I mention the unfinished business, the violence certainly necessary to even the score, to balance the game, the salesman shakes his head sadly. Why do you expect a balance? Because you see it in the natural world? Do you see it in the human world? I protest, trying another approach: But what about the emotional attachment, the woman? He scoffs. Are you stuck so soon? Consider the octopus, one tentacle severed in a rockslide. Regeneration occurs, life goes on, fluid as water. It's inevitable.

The arguments are sound, but they're too clean. He wants to close the deal, that's all. It's not that simple, I tell him. I need a few more days. That's my answer: I need more time.

When I tell Ambrose what's happened and press him for a response, he gives his usual advice: "Play chess." So we have a quick game. My forces are scattered. I get killed in minutes. Smith could have made a better opponent.

"I have no moves," I say. "I have no woman. No money. No work. No ideas. Nothing. I don't feel stable."

"De perfect startin place."

"The beginning of a long period of suffering."

He leaves to work on his mural. I begin the long period of suffering. Waiting, essentially. For what? An idea? A tidy conclusion?

I make suggestions to myself: Don't think about home. Occupy yourself. Take photos. Work at something strenuous. Get tired. Sleep all you want. Eat cheaply. Drink rum. Get plenty of rest. Don't worry. And suddenly I arrive at the idea that I'm not living my life actively anymore, that passivity is equal to suffering.

I run barefoot along the cusp of the bay, away from town, with Smith as my partner. He's fast but takes time for other pursuits, frequently slipping into the bush only to pop out elsewhere and rejoin me. The beach ends in sharp pock-marked rock. The coastline resumes its rough and abrupt character. I run the return trip harder, in long strides, the balls of my feet crunching into wet sand. Sweating like a pig, I think, realizing the injustice. While the sun bears down on us like a diligent posse.

We cool off. I swim vigorously while Smith sleeps in the

sand under palm fronds, each of us immersed in occupational therapy. A little later I creep close with my camera and take a few wide-angle shots, lying in the sand at the animal's snout, creating a ground-level perspective of a porcine mountain. It's not work. I take the shots but in my mind I see a frame devoid of images. A vision that's been shut down.

I nap in my hot room, the world obliterated behind the humming air of the bedside fan. Sleep is shallow, difficult, strange. Rita is trying to tell me something across a road. I can't hear her even though there is no noise around us. I check for traffic and cross the road. There are no cars or people in sight. She points behind me and as I turn I sense that I've just missed something; leaves flutter with its recent passage. The situation doesn't make sense to me but I'm too groggy to understand what she's saying. I tell her I'm dreaming, that we're not really together. Then I'm awake and staring at the ceiling.

Outside, Smith is sleeping in the shade against the fence. I take another photo, comforted by the feel of the solid apparatus in my hands and by the rectilinear control I wield through the eye of the lens. I stand looking through it, reassured by simple compositions I have no intention of recording, taking particular notice of the cinder blocks, the wood under the plastic tarp, the groundwork. The unfinished business, the disturbing incompleteness.

I carry the camera in my hands like a favorite pet, then sling the strap over my neck and shoulder so the weight hangs at the middle of my back, familiar equipment along for the ride, a third eye watching the rear. I clean my sunglasses as I walk, squinting hard into the burning glare of the road. Behind the dark lenses my eyes relax and water. I look out from a cool cloudy haze that coats everything.

At Chez Lambi, using a chair for a tripod, I photograph Ambrose at work on his mural. Work lights burn at the last unfinished corner, but the colorful wall of sea life is destined to live by what little natural light the front windows afford. Most of the sunlight in the room seems to come from the painting itself, from the long silvery rays striking the ocean floor like knives in a glass.

The photos are mere documentation, gifts for Ambrose and a record for me when these days have become memories. I sit forming what I hope will be a lasting mental picture of Sweet Sharon standing on the other side of my chicken sandwich. Her hair is pulled away from her face in smooth lines converging at the back of her head. Her dark brown eyes absorb the room without comment. Her skin is a perfect unblemished finish over her forehead, across her wide cheeks. Her mouth is broad. Full lips form a softly pursed pout, suggesting a kiss considered but not delivered.

I watch her as I eat, thinking about taking her portrait. Instead of asking, I say, "Maybe I've taken all the shots I'm going to take here."

She watches me a moment. "Maybe time to go."

"I don't know if it is or not."

She leaves a respectable silence for the thought. "Need another beer?"

"I guess I do."

She moves unhurriedly, walking to the cooler as if she is attending a coronation. She is regal, the princess of Pagan Bay. Moving very well, I think, and let it go at that.

Ambrose stops working to have dinner with Sweet Sharon. After she leaves he brings a chessboard out of the back room, sets it up under a work light hooded with a red bar towel. More people come in and the music is turned up. The noise is soothing, a barrier of sound that divides me from the world outside the game. My play improves. Ambrose is pleased. He wants a struggle and he gets a small one. I'm beginning to remember the game. Or relearn it.

117

We start another one. Gladiators in the arena. The board is a grid, the grating of a cage, as my mind wanders unfairly. The pawns, all the pieces, are absurd little objects, useless weapons, playthings from another age. I think of Rita, healing without me. I think of Rollo, plotting and waiting. I rub the knot on my elbow and realize I'm losing the game.

"You are not seein de whole board," Ambrose informs me.

A man slides a chair up to our table and sits. Ambrose glances at him. I move my queen, putting Ambrose in a bit of trouble. The man beside us sits quietly, holding a bottle and three stacked glasses. He wears an unbuttoned vest and has a big scar on his neck, lighter than his skin, like a gray flatworm crawling under his ragged beard. He stares at the board, his eyes black as bullet holes.

Ambrose begins an assault. I counter, appointing troops for suicide missions, assuming the posture of a field general outnumbered and desperate, waffling between haggard intensity one minute and dispassionate observation the next. My horse is saddled, I seek an exit. The greasy smell of fried fish is the odor of death on the battlefield.

The man with the scar says, "Ruthless in retreat," as he sets the glasses alongside the board. I take a pawn but my king is on the run. The man sings as he pours, "Check one, check two." He looks at me as he pours the third. "And goodbye to you." The bottle has no label.

"It's not over," I say.

"Check, mahn."

"Is that your favorite word?"

"It's never over," Ambrose says. "De players change. Dey switch color."

My once-white pieces take on the gray pallor of cadavers. We drink the clear fluid, one swift shot to the liquidation of my assets, rocket fuel to fire the games—brought by this man Glenroy: jack-of-all-trades, as Ambrose puts it, local master of one, who drinks to ignite the rivalry. To heat the competition and burn the opponent. His hair is close-cut and neat, in contrast to his patchy beard. His forehead is high, his nose and mouth wide, as if warring forces composed him. His eyes are so keen I get a feeling that he sees things around him without looking. His black arms are thick, his shoulders broad, and he's darker than Ambrose. Dark as a moonless night.

I leave them to it and step outside into the soft salty air where I'm alone but for my own irresolute deliberations. I'm thinking about this particular trip—life condensed between departure and homecoming—a geographical trip, physical and communal and abstract and solitary, a sensory exploration of landscape and color, a personal search for light and composition. For private value. Meanwhile, there's this other trip added on. It has to do with external responsibility. With justice. Am I not free to go? To forget loose ends? But if this is a game, what's my plan? I see Rita's cut face and try to remember if Rollo wore a ring. There's no question, is there? I have to see him again. I go back inside. I'm not yet ready to stand under a weak streetlight thinking the unthinkable.

The game ends, Glenroy the winner. We all have another shot. Ambrose laughs, positioning the pieces in their rightful order.

"When do you plan to finish the third room?" I ask him.

"What?" he says, and the question registers. "Soon."

"Let's start tomorrow."

He looks up from the board. "You doan mean dat."

"I do. We can work like hell, finish the big stuff in a couple of days."

"Why? You enjoy dat work?"

"No, but I'm broke. For pay I'd get my room free and a few meals here and there. That's the deal."

He points at the wall painting. "I gotta finish dat."

"You'll finish in the morning. After lunch we can start

laying block."

He hesitates, fingering his queen.

I push on. "When you finish a project the best thing to do is start another. Right away. That's a known fact."

"De room already started," he says, smugly exploiting a loophole. He looks at Glenroy for assistance.

Glenroy has a hand splayed across his mouth. The hand slowly slides down over his beard, down his neck, over the scar to his collarbones, and rests there as he returns the look. "Check, mahn."

I don't know if he's helping or not, but I keep at it. "Practically free labor, man."

"Take a little push, mahn," Glenroy says.

"When is another chance going to come along?" I ask.

"Check," Glenroy says, and I believe he's affirming my argument.

"You'll have three rooms."

"Check."

"More money."

"Check."

Ambrose lays a hand on the board. "Alright, mahn, ease up."

"Great," I say. "Well spoken, Glenroy. I appreciate your support."

The series continues until after midnight—the third man watching and pushing the players through laggard periods, each game crowned with shots of no-label. People wander past our table, pause to watch a few moves. Smoke hangs around our light. The place thins out. At the bar a man sings drunkenly; someone shouts for silence. Alongside us stands the clear water wall of conch: seashells in shades of sand, coral and pearl, yellow tube sponges, purple sea fans, wavy green grasses and sharp blue fish. Brilliant to see, one vast window at Chez Lambi. I start swimming with delight, beating Ambrose in a drawn-out, topsy-turvy game during which I suppose he momentarily forgot his color, and suddenly I am wonderfully purposeful, one-worldly, capable of staying.

Sometime later my dream is one of fire and murder. I am crouching in the utmost silence. The sudden rasp of the lighter's wheel is harsh. In the small flash of flame I see a metal can against the wall as I touch the flame to the corner of a wooden house. Fire shoots under the house, races to other corners in a rush of sound that yells in my ears, 'Too late now!' The ground is bright as daylight. The heat is frightening. I run across the street to hide in the darkness of an alley, safe from the jumping light. The house is engulfed in a roar. There are strange, faraway cries and a few people appear, moving in shimmers through the crackling orange light. I feel terribly excited, compelled to watch, but there are louder yells and I crouch lower. The alley is too bright now and I'm afraid, looking over my shoulder for escape. I stand to run as a figure stumbles from the doorway of flames. Against the wall of fire the person is indistinct—waves of heat and burning hair—but I see an arm rise pointing toward the alley and the sight horrifies me.

I am running away from the buildings, I think, even though I can't see anything. There are no cars, no lights. The town is behind me. I am running hard, nervous and hot, but not tired. The road turns uphill. I know there are trees on both sides but I don't know where I'm going. The road goes on and on, but I see nothing. Desperation is on me like a animal as I keep running, hoping for a light, a place; I want to stop but I can't. Going higher and farther on the dark road I feel more and more anxious. There is nothing ahead, it seems, but I can't get far enough away. I don't know how long I can keep running.

My mouth is so dry it wakes me. I stumble into the bathroom, groping along the wall, and drink endless handfuls of water, splash it in my face and over my head. I stand in the other room, water dripping to the floor, my head reeling. I see dawn at the edges of the curtain. I sit on the bed and turn the fan off. I am nauseous.

I nap off and on for another hour, then submerge myself in the sea and lie like a mass of seaweed in the shallow water, gently pushed and tugged in the low rolling surf. I keep my eyes closed, aware of the salty taste and the sweeping sound of the water drawn back over the sand, repeating itself in variations too subtle to be heard.

Back in bed, eyes under a wet towel, I hear Ambrose on the patio—a rattling cup, a scraping chair—and drift off again. Waking in stillness and sweat, I lie unmoved in silence. When I stand in the diffused light of the bathroom, the image in the mirror seems an achromatic photo of me. For a terrible moment I feel like I'm starting to fade away.

On a patio table I find a pot of lukewarm coffee, a cup, a spoon, sugar cubes, three hard-boiled eggs, and toast. I brush the flies away and sit down. My mind holds a memory of liquor and my hand holds a spoon, stirring, clinking the inside of the cup. The black coffee spins in a spiral, a dark hole through the table and into the world. My mind travels down uneven streets to blue sea, bright sun on rippled roofs, sharp turns in the breeze, laughing ladies, river baths, roaring falls, bamboo thickets, mountain views, frogs splashing and hummingbirds flashing, flying motors and radio voices, whistling winds, smooth wet flesh, running blood, dead chessmen, mango pigs, sea fans and sea grapes, rustling leaves and hanging vines, scraping plates, music, bottles, honking horns, slamming doors, cries in the street, sex in the water.

I begin by cleaning the foundation, sweeping out debris, dislodging the crawling population at home there, swinging my arms like a coal shoveler. I move furniture, sweep the concrete clean and carry blocks from the fence to the patio two at a time, stacking them carefully and brushing them off, sweating but

not whistling.

After the long walk to Chez Lambi I drink a lot of water, admiring the mural while Ambrose cleans up. With the doors open and the floor just cleaned, the place is as bright as it gets. Outside the back door we borrow the cook's pickup and drive into the street. At the first stop I stay in the truck and Ambrose comes back with a wheelbarrow and shovels. At the second stop we carry bags of cement together and sling them into the truck bed.

The yard has never been hotter. In the shade we mix cement with sand and water. The radio plays music from the back door. A jar of cold water sits sweating on a table. Bent over trowel and board we spread mortar and follow the foundation, turning the corners, pressing blocks into place one after another. Fingertips rub raw. The walls rise, the house grows; a new room is joining mine. Even in the wet heat dust forms, and our arms turn gray. When it's time to eat we rinse our hands with a hose. Water splashes in the sand as I douse my head and neck. The rest of the world seems far away. Right here it's easy to see how much work is done and how much remains. We sit down to eat between the radio sounds and the glossy bay. The sun comes filtered through sea grape leaves. Thus begins the pattern of passing days.

I have no passion for the work but perform it eagerly and quietly, taking any advice from Ambrose, trying to envision the finished room. We don't talk much; when we do, it's of about the work at hand. We stop when the blocks are all us Tomorrow we will need a ladder and more blocks. We begin to think about the roof.

The sun hangs over the bay like a burning eye. In the w my hands burn, my arms and back loosen; soreness flows to sea. Clouds hang over the interior, clinging to the spir the island. Rain is not far away; it may even come dow Pagan Bay. Everything seems possible.

We drink beer on the patio, more secluded now by the extended wall, our eyes channeled toward the bay and the sight of the dying sun. I tell Ambrose about my fire dream. We're just relaxing; the chessboard is on the table but there are no pieces on it. He makes a sound like bubbles escaping a can of carbonated soda. "Be serious, mahn."

I'm watching the sun without looking at it. "There has to be some kind of confrontation."

"You cahn bet de mahn never leave Granville. Okay? Half de people in de country live dere. What you wanna do? Attack him in de daylight? Go to his home in de night? You wanna shoot him? You wanna talk wit him beforehand? You wanna cut out his heart? You wanna see his blood? What do you want? Das de question."

"Something more subtle, perhaps."

"What? Like de dream of fire? Burn him in de night? Lot of people round dere. Some of dem already seen you two wit a problem. One witness to a white face and you will be found. You wanna spend time in a prison shithole wit people like Rollo for neighbors? Hah! Dat woan be a disco club, mahn. In dere you will cease to be."

"Fuck, I don't know. I feel bad about Rita."

"Rita cahn take care of herself, mahn. She come around."

"He threatened to kill her. I'll feel pretty good, won't I, if I wait until he does."

"He talkin about police, mahn, if she talk dere."

"Maybe if I tell Blandy his sister was raped, he'll take out some family revenge."

"Hah! You feel so lucky de boy gonna believe you and forget his angry doctrine? You gonna ask her help on dat? So she cahn help de boy get himself fucked up and in de process tell everyone de story. Consider de woman, mahn."

"Brose. He's got to pay, man."

"He is payin, mahn. He fuck de poor girl outa hate, not

love. Das a miserable life. You cahn pity de muthafuck if you like, but doan waste too much time."

"You call that justice? Leading a better life?"

"Dat may actually be your best chance, de only way certain."

"Give me a fucking break!" I stare at his face, black eyes reflecting fire spots, the sun at the water level, full of surrender. What are my options? Airmail insults? Racist graffiti? Slander? A voodoo spell? A street fight? And if I should win, what then? A court case. A claim of self-defense. The court hears the case of Mr. Mayfield, trouble-making tourist, versus Mr. Rollo, citizen of the Commonwealth. And then? My incarceration in a foreign cell.

I hold my bottle like a grenade. "You're telling me everything will take care of itself, that I should be on my merry fucking way!"

"Ease up, mahn. Dis not a fairy tale."

He goes inside a moment, comes out with a small box and sits down again, dumps some grass on the empty chessboard. I watch him roll a joint. "Are you the doctor now?"

"Reduce fertility."

"Oh. Let me guess. You have a date tonight."

"Uh huh." He licks the paper.

"Sharon."

"Das de one."

"Lucky you."

"Life got some sweet spots."

"She's got several, I'm pretty sure."

He lights the joint, inhales short puffs and smiles at me. Smoke trickles out of his nose. "You cahn be sure of dat. Un ensemble par excellence."

We pass it back and forth a few times, then he stands, leaves it with me. "No chess?" I ask.

"Play wit yourself."

"Real funny."

He laughs. "De game cahn wait."

"Because it's never over," I add.

"Hah!" he says, and goes inside.

I lean back with my feet on the chessboard, my neck pressing numbly on the bamboo at the top of the chair, listening to mosquitoes and crickets, the shower splashing inside. Arms loose, body relaxed, brain hanging off the back of the chair, induced with passivity. Peace on Earth, man. Let the good times roll. Be cool, brother.

Ambrose comes out and stands over my upturned face. "Dere's food in de house. Drink. If you go out, lock it." He smells of talcum powder.

"I'm not going anywhere."

"Alright." His head moves away, opening my view of the sky.

Alone under faint new stars I think of possible resolutions, snapshot endings vivid in the mind.

Rollo's dead—face down over a spreading stain, leaking fluid like a rusty radiator. Tight moonlit sailing, smooth passage to the next island, and the next. Home free. Almost anyone can believe in capital punishment if it's personal enough.

Or, island life: living with the injustice—me and Rita splayed across a red raft on an emerald sea. Dancing on forest leaves. Fucking on mountaintops.

Or, back in the States: Rita with me—at home on the couch we watch an old black and white film and eat popcorn. I explain things; she sees them fresh. The neighbors talk, but then they always do.

Or, we don't realign; it's over between Rita and me, as it seems, and I am home again, sorting through photos. Light hits the hardwood floor. A cat sleeps in the window. The phone rings. There will be a gathering here later. Marla comes over in the afternoon. She is attractive without makeup, braless under a frayed tee shirt. She adds nice touches to the place and still makes me laugh more than anyone.

I have a working life. I travel alone. There are new photos in Indonesia. I lie on my belly in Borneo, inside the lens. The forest is different here—more dangerous—but then also the same. Un ensemble par excellence.

But what place is safe? Not here. Will the pig warn me?

I take responsibility. I'll sit down to write my own ending, but this is like something out of Kafka or a Dada joke. What was it that Duchamp said? *There is no solution because there is no problem.* But I don't understand the question. Must we simply accept our various hatreds? They say this: the woman allows, the man causes. Generalities put me to sleep. Mental pictures change without warning. Life is so short. Composition is every . . .

In the morning I run with Smith to the rocks and back. When I return Ambrose and Glenroy are having coffee and making a list, measuring. Lizards move along the edges of the highest blocks. We take a trip in Glenroy's truck, borrow a ladder, pick up more blocks, more cement, corrugated tin, rebar, roofing nails and a new saw; the truck rides low and slow.

By one we've finished the walls; we have a roofless room with two small interior walls outlining the corner bathroom. After lunch we level sand and build a frame for the patio extension, adding rocks and rebar for strength. Cement is mixed with sand and pebbles in a cut-off barrel, then poured, spread and smoothed into a slab. Load after load of gray sludge, only just thicker than the heavy air. It is back-wrenching work—stirring, pushing, reaching on all fours to finish. While it sets the pig stays outside; we don't need his footprints to complete it.

At sunset we take a cleansing swim—there is no rain near

Pagan Bay—and afterward stand on the beach drinking beer. The pig digs for a crab, flipping sand with his snout, leaving loose, light-colored trails away from the hole like a crude drawing of the sun.

As darkness settles we're sitting on the old section of the patio discussing the work. Smith pushes open the gate and comes in limping. Glenroy scoops him up, takes him to the back door, turns on the light and sits down on the concrete. I stand to watch while he's holding the pig in his lap, examining a front hoof. When I bend closer the pig's eyes roll over to look at me. Glenroy is taking out a knife.

"What is it?" I ask. "A thorn?"

"A shadow."

"A what?"

"Sea needle." He holds a black spine up for me.

"An urchin," I say.

"Urchin," he says.

I take the spine over to show Ambrose and hold the point up between us. "That'll slow you down," I tell him. "The man's got a way with pigs."

"He raise it from a baby."

I drink some beer, watching the man holding the pig. "Where'd he get it?"

"In de forest." He lowers his voice to a whisper. "He was stayin in dere, avoidin some troubles. He trap de mother for food and den find dis one baby." He laughs softly. "He became de daddy."

"And gave you the gift of a piglet?"

"After he came out he went to Granville for a time and juss leave de pig here."

"Is that how he got that scar, hunting Smith's mother?"

"No, mahn."

The pig hobbles over to the sand and lies down. Glenroy gets up and sits in a chair near us. He sees me looking at him.

"A bit wayward, don't you think," I say to Ambrose.

"At least, mahn."

They play a game of chess in the time it takes me to shower, then Glenroy leaves. Ambrose rolls a joint and we smoke, setting up the board. I am so tired and hungry my pieces might have moved faster without me. Part of the pattern of passing nights.

The next morning is Sunday and we begin the construction of the roof, using the long boards under the tarp to make triangular supports, crossties, braces and ceiling beams. Creole radio songs dance in the air. Hammers jar the sunny stillness. The smell of a trash fire drifts along the shore, scraps of smoke against a pale sky. Thick leaves and branches are right above us, a green screen against the sun.

At lunch I swim first, and then sit dripping for a while in the shade with a chopped chicken sandwich and a cold beer. Afterward Ambrose and I work on the roof—anchoring wood to block, connecting beams—while Glenroy works below, running plastic pipe to the new bathroom. In the haze of labor my sweat pours, my mind loosens and travels, returning sharply to hammer blows and splinters. Out of the work comes a mindless meditation that accepts any thought—like a receiver left on at some remote outpost, picking up signals, sentences and static—about plans, plots, passing days, pieces of work, pictures and people. I see Ambrose next to me but I'm not thinking of him. I'm remembering Rollo and considering the woman.

We start adding the metal to the framework, one of us holding a tin sheet down while the other nails it in place. The noise is horrendous. The pig goes to the front yard. The metal gets warm. Knees and hands scrape on the rough surface. My ears ring from the pounding; the vibrations spread into my arms and legs, my brain. Stopping for the replenishment of lost liquid, we check on Glenroy and the white PVC plumbing running outside along the foundation and branching off inside with segments for a sink, a shower head, a drain, a toilet. I notice other things: shadows on the sand, a dog snooping at the fence, ripe fruit in the air, vine blossoms full of bees. On the roof I smell rain coming. The hammer is an erratic metronome banging off increments of time. We are making progress. Sometimes I consider staying in the new room; other times I consider my own death, my body machete-cut to pieces in the dark of night.

The rain blasts down, bending leaves, hammering tin, rinsing hard concrete. We stand inside laughing at our good fortune, at the timing of providence. There are no leaks. We adjourn to the house where rum is poured and the work is toasted.

I go to my room for a shower and when I return, Sweet Sharon is helping Ambrose prepare dinner. I play chess with Glenroy. The music is loud, the rum is kicking ass. Ambrose brings me a burning joint. The game absorbs me. I don't care what day it is or how much money I don't have. Between songs I hear the rain on the roof. Whether my luck is good or bad I can't say.

Later, on the patio, I watch a delicate mist spinning around the outside light like fine morning webs in the breeze of a field. In the new room Smith lies sprawled on the cool floor, the first occupant; he lifts his head with a grunt, like he's surprised. We're both squatters, I tell him, but I'm not sure how much more I can take.

In the morning I run with the pig as usual. The sky is clear, the air fresh. We have a tussle in the surf but I never feel like he'll bite me.

After coffee and toast, Ambrose and I drive to town in Glenroy's truck and pick up plywood, plaster, electrical wire, light fixtures, switches and two wall outlets. We buy some gas, drive home and unload the materials. We run wire from the house under the edge of the roof and into the new room, hanging leads for lights in the middle of the ceiling and in the bathroom, dropping lengths into the wall, breaking in to retrieve them at the positions where switches and outlets will be attached later.

During the afternoon we work on the installation of two old aluminum louver windows scavenged by Ambrose some months earlier. He has most of their panes and the mechanisms work, even if they are a little stiff. We build wooden frames into the window spaces and fit the metal into those. For the bathroom he has a smaller louver window that needs panes of glass and a handle.

In the evening Ambrose goes out. Sharon picks him up for a drive to visit some friends on the north coast. I stay home, temporarily opposed to travel, but thinking of leaving. Smoking weed and drinking, reading Nietzsche—*But the worst enemy you can encounter will always be you, yourself; you lie in wait for yourself in caves and woods.* Staring blankly into sustained waking dreams of copulation with Rita. Feeling the pull of departure while keeping to the pattern of passing paralysis. Falling asleep with the light on and the rain playing on the new roof like unwritten music.

The next day we hang two scarred red doors taken from the scavenged goods in the storage room of the Ambrose Inn, shimming and planing to make them fit.

Inside, we nail plywood to the crossbeams to make the ceiling. With that done and the door closed, we have the rough solid box of a real room. Wires hang from holes in the ceiling and the walls like loose threads.

The rest of the day we plaster, mixing batches to the right consistency, applying layers to the interior walls, working until the light is gone. Outside the sky turns a golden rose, the bay goes flat, mosquitoes leave the fragrant trees. We light coils, set up the game, add our own smoke to the other. Reaching over the board with our dry dusty arms we share the last beer, finish the rum and sit opposite each other flecked with plaster, unified in labor and disposition. The game ends in a stalemate—my second non-loss in a week but no victory at all—and it's disappointing. Our moves are becoming habits of thought, predictable as morning coffee. I begin to feel I'm overstaying my welcome.

In the morning Ambrose goes for supplies while I start plastering the outside walls. He brings paint, bathroom tiles, window screens and rum, then returns the truck to Glenroy. We plaster all morning. My arms hurt from the motions of the day before and I silently resolve never to do any plastering after this for the rest of my life. Still, the place is looking okay. The walls have a rustic texture that doesn't appear especially accidental. Ambrose has already said he'll do a mural on the wall facing the patio, and he shows me a sketch of his idea. Forest insects. I laugh. On the wall, they'll be huge. Traveling entomologists might like it. Tourists might have nightmares.

Ambrose wires the lights and switches. In the bathroom I construct a short wall which will be the lip of the shower, and begin to lay tile. The radio plays songs outside. We are working in a sweatbox at the end of the Earth, inhaling moisture and heat like plants in a greenhouse. Once in a while a newscast interrupts with dire accounts of misfortune from places out beyond the sprawling sea. Then the music comes back washing over us, closing the holes in our fragile isolation. In the late afternoon, as I'm wondering what's become of Rita, Glenroy shows up with a toilet and a sink—white porcelain sculptures for a plain and basic room. They are bolted in place and fitted to pipes. Crowded together in the small room, we finish the job under the bare new light of the overhead bulb.

Flipping the lights, flushing the toilet, proclaiming the room a modern success, we drink in celebration of electricity and plumbing as Smith inspects the results of our work.

"Progress," Glenroy says, "does not mean exactly dat."

"Even if it does," I say, "the population is overrunning itself, stepping on its own toes, using everything up."

"Neither one of dem cahn stop or even slow down," Ambrose says. "Das de way we do it. We muss adapt to anything dat happen."

"We can only play games and watch the scenery change."

"De clock always tick. We juss record de time."

"Check."

We don't play chess; there is an unspoken accord this night that the game will not suffice as a legitimate pastime. A phase is ending. Something else is coming along. Waiting for it is depressing and dangerous but there are times when no other course presents itself. They leave and I stay, though I doubt Rita will come by so late. I wait anyway, but with none of those three around my only allies are the pig Smith and the dead philosopher Nietzsche—*What? Is man merely a mistake of God's? Or God merely a mistake of man's?* My best weapon is a crowbar and I sit on the dark patio without music, watching a quarter moon climb into the sky, so hungry and tired I sleep.

Thursday is for painting—the ceiling, the walls, the whole place. Also for tiling and for odds and ends. It's midday when I hear a whistle and step out to the patio.

Rita's at the back gate. I walk over and stand across from her. She puts her hands on the gate and says, "You are still here," but I don't know if she's really surprised.

I nod. "Building a luxury hotel."

She smiles. "First class."

"Wanna take a motion?" I ask.

She laughs. "Sure."

"Hey, Brose!" He appears in the doorway. "This is Rita." And to her I say, "That's Ambrose."

"Alright," he says.

"Okay," she says.

"Going for a walk," I say.

"Of course." He goes back inside and we head down the beach.

Her face is no longer swollen but her left eye is still red, and there's a small line on her cheek where the cut has healed."You look better," I say.

She shrugs. "Everything is normal."

"Have you been to a doctor?"

"I goin to de Granville clinic tomorrow."

We walk around to the rocks. Looking back we can hardly see the new room under its shady seagrape. The bay spreads out before us, a languid blue sheet. The thin pale beach draws a curve to town, where walls and roofs glow in the sun. Above the buildings the sharp rising land holds its own weather, defines itself as a collector of clouds and a rain-maker. An overgrown garden at sea. A covered rock, steaming inside.

The water is warm and Rita seems relaxed as we swim. There is a trust between us and we smile, enjoying the realization that after all, we are here together. Standing on the sandy bottom she moves close to me, getting over the past even as she reaches back for certain moments. I admire her strength. I admire the white suit I'm touching under the water.

"Always in de water," she says, laughing softly. Her head lies against my face.

A layer of warmth joins the front of our bodies. "There's a lot of it around," I say.

We kiss deeply and the warm layer spreads into our faces and through our encircling arms. The soft sea envelopes us and our liquid tongues run together. We move toward the rocks. Small waves push into them, racing ahead to find hollows and pools. It's low tide. Moist sand lies farther up between the rough rocks, untouched by moving water. We lie down at once, kissing and touching anyplace our hands want. She squeezes at my crotch. I work my hand under her suit, pressing the source of her heat, feeling her liquid center. She squirms, biting at my neck, friskier than I've ever seen her. We rock on the sand, my hand stretching her suit, her hand stroking me through mine. I groan with pleasure, and also with deep regret at my failure to carry my condoms on every outing. The thought that her aggression might yield to caution hastens my actions, and I pull her suit aside as I struggle to free myself with my other hand.

"One more time," I say, my face at her ear. "Like before, okay. I'll pull out, withdraw." Then I'm free, my suit down, my cock scraping sand. She isn't helping anymore but I'm aligning myself, my eager fingers prying.

"Wait!" she says.

"What?"

"Next time."

"What's the matter?" I'm ready to find a crab hole and fuck that, if necessary.

"Not dis way. After de clinic, okay?"

The thought of examinations and instruments has a negative effect on me. I stop and roll off her onto my back.

Her lips press at my ear. "Another way." Her tongue goes in after the words and a hand runs down my stomach; fingertips brush my foundering fish. She kisses my cheek and neck, getting a grip on me as she gets to her knees. She kisses my stomach, moving her tongue down to meet her hand pulling the other direction. She licks the head timidly, looking at the thing as she might an eel—judging the size, estimating the danger—then puts it in her mouth and holds it there, tasting it, breathing through her nose, moving her lips a little. I swell against her teeth. My hands dig into sand. I stop watching her and see edges of jagged rock, flat blue sky. Close to us the waves make sucking noises at rock crevices. I lift a little off the sand, pushing at her mouth. It tightens around me and slides down. I feel her short, sucking strokes, her hand grasping at the shaft. Then she moves with me, in slow opposition, going down as I rise, pulling up as I sink. Grinding sand in my fists, my stomach tight as a dry sponge, I arch upward and let go in jerking spurts. I sense her face moving away, feel her hand pumping me as the moments pass like ripples in oil and my hearing seems unreliable. She falls back on the sand and I lift my head and squint at the burning bay, the trenches my heels have dug, my beached eel dying in the sun, her bright white suit, her glossy lips and sleepy eyes. I lie beside her. Among the rocks hot air lifts the smell of drying seaweed but keeps us from moving. Marine salt tightens on our skin in a thin crystal layer that protects us from nothing as we nap unceremoniously in the sun, holding hands.

The water revives us and we head back. Walking along the beach she grins at me. "You like it?"

"That's a fair approximation."

"I wanted to practice."

"You're a natural. But that doesn't mean you shouldn't practice constantly." I hook an arm around her neck and pull her close. "What are you doing tonight?"

"I gotta watch de little ones."

"Tomorrow?"

"In de mornin, Granville."

"Yeah, I forgot."

"After dat, lookin for you."

"I'll be easy to find."

"I will be stayin de weekend at my aunt's. One evenin you cahn come for dinner."

"Sure."

At the gate she hugs me tightly. I kiss her goodbye and go inside to the patio where Ambrose is at the paint tray pouring a creamy saffron. He glances up. "A good time, I hope."

"There's a time for work and a time for love."

He draws air between his teeth. "Are you possibly one of dose people dat start fast and den fall down someplace?"

"Without question this room is the center of my life."

I'm in a fine humor, happy to get back to work. Painting puts me in a loose delirium, brushing stroke after stroke, breathing paint fumes in the indoor heat. I am the perfect laborer, smiling to myself, content with repetition, loving every song on the radio. The hours roll by. Eventually the paint gives me a dull headache. Flies annoy me. A few nagging questions come to the surface: What am I waiting for? Why don't I just leave? Where is my desire for composition?

As evening comes around Ambrose and I walk to a bar called Pinder's Place, a dark, narrow establishment with fewer people and greater tension than our usual choice. At the front are empty domino tables, pounded and worn to smooth cornerless surfaces. At the other end a thin shaft of spotlight strikes a dart board's round face. Low wattage red bulbs in wicker shades hang in a line over the long bar and a row of unlit red booths lines the opposite wall. From one booth, two young men watch us as we take stools across from them, their voices low mutters. A cigarette glows in an ashtray, its faint orange spot reflected in three glasses. Another young man comes out of the restroom and pauses to look at me before sliding into the booth across from the other two. We get beers from the bartender, who holds up four fingers to indicate how much we owe.

"Who are these guys behind us?" I say.

Ambrose shrugs without looking. "Maybe Dreads come to practice deir political animosity."

"Sort of an Opposition Party?"

"De seeds of revolution always bein sown, mahn. Somethin to talk about."

A young woman walks out of the restroom and joins the young men in the booth. The front door opens and an elderly man enters and sits near us at the bar. At the other end two fellows are talking to the bartender but there are no other women here. I glance back at her again. She seems to be looking at me but I can't see her well or the faces of her companions at all. They are hunched over their table in a private discussion.

"What are we doing here?" I ask Ambrose.

He fixes me with a straight look. "Havin a drink, mahn. Whas de problem? You feel better goin to de same place all de time?"

"No sir, that place isn't nearly dangerous enough. I like this one. I don't need to be liked to have a good time."

He finishes his beer. "I know you gotta maintain yourself, de well-rounded travelin mahn."

I can't tell if he's irritable or merely sarcastic. "I feel safe just being in your presence, Mister Enigmatic."

The young woman appears next to me. She has long braids with yellow beads at the ends that rattle when she moves her head. "Desmon, some rum," she says, leaning on the bar. She gives me a long look while she's waiting. He puts a bottle down, she takes it back to the table and we use the opportunity of Desmond's visit to order more beers. A sign on the wall reads: PAY AS YOU DRINK, so I dump my pathetic wad of crumpled Caribbean dollars on the bar. He selects what he needs without a word, puts the money in a metal box, moves to the other end and slumps forward facing the door. I glance back at the booth again, at the girl watching me.

"You restless?" Ambrose asks.

"That's all my money right there. Except for a twenty stashed with my plane ticket. Almost the end of the road, pal."

"You finish takin pictures?"

"I sure as hell hope not. But whenever I stop, I'm afraid I won't start again."

He looks at me quizzically a few moments, maybe thinking this over. "Not havin seen any, I naturally cahn't say what dey might be about. I assume you know what you lookin for."

"I'm not looking for anything. I just take pictures."

"Be true, mahn. You hope to find somethin in dere."

"Of course. I want to find more than I thought was there. You know the process. When you hold a brush, what comes out?"

"Nothin mystical, mahn," he says with a wry smile, "juss de wild and colorful and beautiful mélange of life."

"Yeah, your forest wall reminds me of Rousseau, but even dreamier."

"Doan know de mahn."

"Really? What about Duchamp?" He shakes his head. "He changed the course of modern art and then gave up painting to play chess all the time. A brilliant joker. He said a painting that doesn't shock isn't worth painting."

He chuckles. "I doan think about any of dat, about makin history or who did what. I juss paint, mahn."

"Maybe you're better off that way. Once you know something you can't escape it. It's harder to be original."

"Originality," he says. "Is dat de big problem, bwoy? You gettin it yet? You got a brand new destination?"

"Not that I know of. I look for the abstract because it's more interesting to me. I try not to practice self-delusion, but unfortunately I have a really bad memory."

"You doan need it, you got all your pictures."

"Don't make me sound like a tourist."

"Hah. Dey pay for my paints."

"One day you'll be painting the forest and they'll be overrunning it. What'll become of this clean little jewel then? People will want those trees, that good wood."

"What becomes of any place?" he says.

"It gets fucked up. Every clean little world—"

"Only samples of de bigger one."

"That's right, man. This is the saddest time in history."

"Dey all are, at de time dey occur."

"No, Brose. Now we *know* we're losers. No doubt remains."

"Too early to say. We go on, das all."

"I'm not a visionary, man. I feel the loss right now. I'd rather die in the jungle with some privacy, some tall trees around and beetles for pallbearers."

"Hah! Doan wait too long."

"If I stick around here I might not have to. Hey, where the fuck is Mr. Friendly? Is there any chance of more beer?" The bead-headed girl returns to stare at me, smiling a little now, like maybe she's falling in love all of a sudden, and Desmond graces us with enough attention for Ambrose to get us two more cold ones.

"Haven't seen you round here," she says.

"Change of pace, darlin. Lovely, homey sort of place, ain't it."

She smiles, a little coy this time. "Whas your name?"

"Fred. Fred Nietzsche. What's yours?"

"Jaydee."

"Jaydee? Like a name or initials?"

"A name."

"Like deejay in reverse."

She chuckles, beads rattling. "I could play a song," she says, motioning toward the silent jukebox. "Any request?"

I sing her a few words. "You ain't nothin but a hound dog."

"Which?"

"Cryin all the time."

She laughs. "We doan have dat one."

"Anything you like is fine with me."

She sashays over to the jukebox, knowing I'm watching her walk, and puts in the coins and punches the buttons and turns around as the song starts playing, some kind of island ballad, romance with a beat, and she's barely dancing her way back to me, taking her sweet time and watching me watch her move. "You like it, Fred?"

"It's only my favorite song."

"Really?" she says. "I knew you like it cause I like it." She shrugs, coy again, and shakes her head like a little shiver is running through her whole body. "You wanna buy me a drink, Fred?" she asks with an impish grin.

"I thought you were drinking with your friends."

"Who?"

"Those boys back there," I say, tilting a wicker lamp up so that it casts its pale red glow on the booth of three. Two squint up at me like it's a floodlight, while the kid in the corner, wearing a big tri-colored knitted hat, glowers at me in a familiar way, and grumbles 'Put de fuckin lamp down'. He hunkers lower, drawing on his cigarette and scowling severely. I drop the light back to its normal position.

"Dose bwoys not drinkin wit me," she says.

To Ambrose I say, "The kid in the corner looks a lot like Rita's brother."

"Whas de matter, Fred?" the girl says, touching my arm. "You doan wanna have no company? You doan like Jaydee?"

I look at her earnestly. "You look totally fuckable," I say, "and I mean that as a sincere compliment. But I bet your friend from Rocklee wants you back."

She stares at me while Ambrose is laughing so hard that Desmond is actually drawn to us, and she says finally, "What you sayin to me, mahn?"

"My last verse. You ain't never caught a rabbit and you ain't no friend of mine."

Desmond puts two more beers in front of us, Jaydee looks over at the booth and then back to the bartender and then straight at me and says, "You gettin drunk so soon, Fred, sayin all dat after I dedicate a song to you."

"I'm sorry darlin but this is a bad time to start with rabbits, today's world being what it is. Say no more. Let's hold on to what we might have had."

She looks like she wants to laugh but can't. "I gonna have to excuse myself," she says, "and I hope you doan get yourself in trouble talkin rude like dat."

"Me too, Jaydee. Nothing personal, you understand. It's just not easy being me."

She gives me a long and doubtful frown before she leaves, and though I soon hear the muttering of derision behind me, I look only at Ambrose drinking peaceably in this atmosphere of dim hostility.

"Careful she doan stab you in de back, mahn," he says.

This sparks the remembrance of an earlier question. "You never told me how Glenroy got that scar of his."

"De neck?"

"Yeah, that one. On the outside."

"Hah!" He takes a slow drink, then examines his bottle at eye level. "He was fuckin a Swedish woman."

I burst out laughing. "Jeez, she was rough, to say the least."

"No, mahn. His girlfriend was rough." He's laughing now too. "Stuck him wit a vegetable peeler."

"No shit! What'd he do?"

"He bled, mahn."

We laugh some more, having too good a time for this dour place, and then Ambrose gets quiet and wipes his eyes.

"He went a little crazy."

I lower my voice. "He killed her?"

"No, mahn."

"What happened to her?"

"She move to London."

"What about him?"

"He took up de game of chess."

"Okay. He became thoughtful."

"He doan fuck like he did."

We switch to rum and it's late when we leave, no one but the booth boys still there. They leave right behind us though, and follow us a few paces back. After about a block I say, "Let's just stop here."

Ambrose says, "If das de way you want it."

"If they're going someplace else they can pass us."

But when we stop, they stop too, and we all stand there looking at each other in the street-lit night. Blandy lights a cigarette but no one says a thing, all of us silently testing the situation for weaknesses. I'm wondering if any one of them over there is as drunk as me, or we, but there isn't much time for sociological considerations.

They come walking at us and I brace myself for a fistfight. Two of them are strangers to me and they are all young, seventeen or so, mean-looking, bored and angry and unemployed, I imagine, dropouts wanting to release their rage and frustration at things they don't understand, wanting action instead of talk, fast deeds to feel some kind of power, any kind at all, right now, because the future is totally fucking obsolete. They must have come from Rocklee and I'm wondering where they parked their car. The biggest of them breaks into a rush, as if to what? Split us up, overpower us with speed, make us run in fear? But he stops in front of Ambrose and waits for the others to join him. They surround us as best they can. The other one unknown to me steps up and throws a kick but I slap his foot away. Blandy pulls a pistol from his waistband and points it at me, my chest, as the boy kicks again and catches me in my sudden stillness, lands his foot on my hip. Ambrose is fending off the bigger boy who is scrambling madly to smack his face until the click of the cocked hammer intercedes and everything slows to a standstill, all of us focused on the gun now, waiting for the shocking report, the sound to send us spinning into another dimension.

History is meaningless now. All I've ever done or seen or thought or known or expected to happen is completely useless at this moment, absolutely without value on the cusp of this absurd change. I know I'm drunk, but why am I not dead yet? I'm looking at the barrel. Is it a .22 or a .25? It looks so small it might be a fake. He holds it in one hand—bad procedure, too casual—and he's still smoking, the cigarette in his mouth, the barrel shaking a little, but his eyes look normal, not crazy, just intense and unsure and pissed off like millions of other people. I can't believe how long this is taking. I want to speak or look around but I am definitely paralyzed. The world is a blackout. We're on a tiny stage and no one can remember their lines. There are no lines. There is only the standing threat: If I wish you dead, then you are dead. Gone, nonexistent, not here.

"Shoot him," Ambrose says, "den shoot me and shoot dese two bwoys, and go back and shoot Desmon and find Deejay and shoot her, and den shoot yourself."

"Hey," I say, "why'd you save him for last?"

Blandy steps a bit closer, the pistol extended, roaming up to my neck, my face, making his point and I see it too, the cigarette in his lips and some small enjoyment on his face. He doesn't have to say a word, I get the idea. He's in control.

"I'm sorry," I say, "I didn't know you were a gangster."

Ambrose snorts like he's about to laugh.

A quick pop occurs in my ear, so close, an explosion amplified by its range, and I jerk down and away, my hand covering my ear, my head shot through with noise, not lead. I'm reeling in a crouch watching the boys backing up, turning to run into a side street, Blandy walking slowly backwards with the pistol still up and pointed, no cigarette now and his lips moving, my other ear working to hear.

"Go away, bwoy. Bye bye."

It's like a hangover too soon, only this ringing will surely

144

go away too, won't it? Tomorrow, at least. No permanent damage, a night on the town. I have a finger in my ear to keep sounds out, but they are already in there, a minuscule crew of power tool operators trying to fuck up my equanimity.

We get home in something other than a straight line but no further ills befall us. Of course we wake the pig, who snorts sleepily, both disgruntled and comforted by our untimely arrival.

The morning comes sluggishly, waffling in vague degrees of brightness and heat and unbalanced sound. The ringing is down but not gone, an alarm still going off. I face the world in profile, left side listening. Instead of running on the beach I stagger into the bay, Smith looking on in apparent disgust. Even in my lousy condition I feel his disappointment.

Ambrose brings the coffee outside and we sit in the shade in relative coolness, each lamenting his personal excesses. In front of us are the paint cans, the waiting walls, the end of the job, my imminent departure, all very clear. In silence I breathe the organic air, my physical condition stolid yet kinetic inside, my queasy stomach a cavern of foaming liquids. Though locked in a bellicose relationship with this volatile island, I am not a captive. On the contrary, I have consumed the place and it's moving now, a sulfurous, churning pressure pushing to get out. I have to digest or regurgitate. Restless, gaseous, in a state of burning flux, I'm waiting for release, for a fissure to crack open, an explosion to propel me to the sea. In a moment I will surely vomit lava or charcoal trees.

"I'm thirsty," I say to the world at large.

Ambrose doesn't answer. I walk inside, bring out a jar of cold water and tip it up, pouring splashes down my throat into the fire. Ambrose takes the jar and drinks long swallows, glances at me with bloodshot eyes.

In the heat behind our whisking brushes there is no conversation, no radio noise. The bay rolls up and back, the sound of endless tedium. In the trees above us insects tick like fast clocks—there are moments when I want to run off down the road to the airport—but I can't work any faster than slowly and I can't leave until it's done. I tie a bandanna over my nose and mouth but it barely cuts the tainted air. I paint with the uniform strokes of self-hypnosis. A white coat spreads out across the plaster wall. I am a working man, a vessel of liquid. My hands move back and forth, oozing paint wherever I touch.

We eat sandwiches in the kitchen. I make a pitcher of iced tea and cut up a lime. We sit at the table drinking it, cooling down. After that I feel better. Ambrose lies on the couch and falls asleep. Outside, the paint is drying. The sun is high in the west; its rays strike parts of the mosaic wall. I stand close to it looking at sparkling glass bits, leaf shards and green eyes, bright forest eyes shining in broad daylight. A work of art at the end of the road. Across the patio the new room is a blank canvas. I imagine the future sight of glass insects. Dappled daylight will hide the creatures until the sun streaming under the tree catches their hard glazes and fires their sharp wings for dusk. I go into my room to rest. We think it's the work that's important but it's the outlet. The release is what really counts. We end up with byproducts of our energy to look at. Everything we do leaves our residue.

I sit on the bed, back against the wall, thinking about release and residue. Across from me the camera sits on the bureau, an inert mechanical eye, the lens cap its black eye patch, still loaded with the few shots I've taken in Pagan Bay, half a roll unexposed. All the rest—pictures to be, the art of the trip—are in transit or waiting at home. The journey is virtually over, yet nothing is conclusive. I am unable to see, lost in my own life, blinded by residue. My investigation investigates itself, like a salamander chewing its own tail. All travel leads to the traveler.

I slump into the strange land of afternoon sleep. Soon I am

standing in line at a ticket counter watching a clock on the wall. My flight leaves in minutes but the line barely moves. I shift my weight from foot to foot, craning to see what kind of moron the ticket agent might be. I push my bag ahead with my foot and kick at cigarette butts on the floor. At the counter the man takes my ticket and looks at it for too long. In my restless state I point at the clock, telling him my flight is leaving. He tells me the ticket may have expired and turns away to consult with another agent. I have an overwhelming desire to get on the plane and I yell at the man, telling him I have an open ticket. He hands it back, saying calmly that the plane is leaving and that if I run I may make it. I take off running to customs and shove my passport at the agent. My heart races and I'm sweating through my shirt. The man flips slowly through the pages looking at every stamp. I mention the time of the flight's departure. He doesn't look up but finally stops turning pages and hands me back the open passport. He says the visa has expired. I stare at the stamp, frantically adding up the days, ending with today's date. Tomorrow it does, I tell him. Today, he says. Outside the door, engines start up. I can see the plane through the door's glass window. Today's not over yet, I tell the man. He shrugs and says nothing more. I struggle to control myself, asking him about an extension. He points to a desk where no one sits. The engines are roaring outside, calling me. I bend down, open my bag, set the camera on the floor, then straighten up, lifting the bag and holding out the passport again. I have no money, I say. He looks down at the floor, then up at me. The stamp is the sound of a single slap in a domino game. I burst through the door. The plane is moving slowly in the brightness as I run toward it. From the side I see the pilot looking ahead. I drop my bag, waving and jumping. The plane is turning away, the cockpit moving out of my view. I watch the plane taxi and lift off quickly. The engine sound gets fainter and fainter. I lie down on my back and close my eyes against the hurtful glare, waiting for the next plane. The runway is warm through my damp shirt. Soon I hear light taps on the surface around me. They become louder. Drops smack my face but I don't get up. I listen to the pinging rain on the roof of the terminal behind me and dream of sleep.

The tapping becomes more insistent, waking me. I open my eyes. My face is pressed into bunched sheet. Rain is falling but there is another knocking sound. "Come in," I say thickly, sitting up. The room seems drained of color.

The door opens and Rita steps in, water dripping from her face and hair, rain rolling off the roof in thin streams behind her, her dress clinging to her flat stomach, making a dark circle, her bra straps raised tracks under the wet cloth. Her eyes move around the room and land on me, and I get up and bring her a towel. She holds it against her chest, moves past me and sits in the metal chair, her eyes downcast. I shut the door, go back to the bed and sit across from her. We stay quiet, the rain drumming, the light murky, and I watch drops rolling down her legs into the wet canvas of her shoes.

"What is it?" I say. "Did you go to the clinic?"

She sits hunched over the towel, knees pressed together, staring at the floor. Behind her the curtain moves infinitesimally, catching the edge of a breeze that never penetrates the room. She straightens up and looks at me, puts her hand under the towel, holds herself. Her voice is feeble. "I'm spotting."

I stare blankly at her dark eyes, her pained face. She drops the towel to her lap; her hand is splayed wide open across her wet belly, held there tenderly, as if she feels something inside. "I'm spotting," she says. "Dey took a blood test."

I stand up, groping for some response, moving about the room. After a moment I pick up the camera, drop the lens cap on the bureau and sit down across from her again.

"Maybe it's your period."

"Too early for dat. And de spots are brown."

"What's your personal feeling?"

She looks at me with some assurance, her dark eyes steady.

"Have you ever been pregnant before?"

She shakes her head and says softly, "I feel it now."

I lean forward, looking through the lens, moving closer to her face, reading low light, reducing the shutter speed, composing with half the curtained window, confronting the issue, the hidden dilemma in her repose.

"You wanna remember me dis way?"

She is absolutely still, watching the camera, defined by a pale rim of light over her hair that traces one side of her face. Her eyes are barely visible but I see in them a look of guarded amazement. "What are you seein?" she asks.

The mechanism fires—loud motor, slow shutter—and cracks the layer of apprehension I feel. "Your beautiful face," I say, steadying the instrument on my knee. At the end of a measured breath, I fire again, liking the solid noise, and again, releasing more tension each time.

"Wanna see it cry?"

"If you feel like it." I get closer, knees on the floor, one elbow on the metal chair, seeing her face full in the frame, a woman alone and vulnerable, emotion spilling.

"When are you leavin?" she asks.

"When the room is finished."

"It looks finished."

"There are still things to do," I say, and shoot again, striking at my frail uncertainty, keeping the camera—the tool and the barrier—pressed tightly to my eye.

I lean against her legs, getting closer to her, farther from indifference. She stares straight into the lens, hiding nothing anymore. There are tears, yes, but no breakage, no shattered life. I fire again and again, shocking myself, breaking down the disbelief with every shot. I smell the rain in her hair, feel the quiver in her heart.

"You got it now?"

I take the camera away from my eye. "Rita, you're shivering."

"You see love?"

My pupils feel disparate, my vision divided between two hazy planes of weak light, readjusting to one. But I can see there isn't much distance between us. "Get your clothes off."

"You feel it?"

The towel falls as she stands and grasps the bottom of her dress, arms crossed, and wiggles it up, her slip too, water squeezing out on me watching on my knees as the garments rise to hide her face, elbows struggling with a wet wrapping, her arms covered overhead, two pieces of underwear pasted to a sleek body squirming. I put the camera on the bed and begin to dry her legs, holding the towel in both hands and rubbing her calves, behind her knees and inside her thighs. I unlace her shoes and pull them off as she lifts each foot. She drops her dress over the chair, removes her bra and waits for my help in tugging the last piece down, then she steps free.

"Cahn you take *us*?" she asks, sitting on the bed, pulling the sheet up around her shoulders.

I look at the frame counter as I stand; one shot left. I move to the bureau, set the camera on the edge, look through the lens, focusing on her, composing the shot, setting the aperture, the speed, the auto-timer. "It'll be slow, so don't move." My finger hovers over the exposure button. "Okay? Ten seconds."

I push the button and begin the countdown, sliding behind her and becoming still, aligning my face with hers, holding her tight in the sheet. At the last second she turns, kissing my cheek as the shutter blinks and our images are transferred to film. One single picture of passion and possibility—sudden love, somewhat blurry. She leans against me and we fall back together.

I hold her, listening to the slow ringing of roof rain. She lies docile, a solid mass beating her heart into me, her back against my chest, her skin hot where it touches mine. Our breaths are the modulations of alternating current.

I think of her brother's latest stunt but I can't add that to her burden, I can't mention any more hardships. She's staring overhead, listening to her own thoughts or the rain or my breathing, her ear inches from my mouth, her eyes shining at the ceiling. On the outside our bodies remain still, free of voluntary motion, but inside there is movement in lungs and veins. Blood is running; I feel it everywhere. Without moving, she's writhing against me and I'm reaching out to her, stretching to join her, to bridge the spare gap between us. I lean closer, breathing at her neck, pushing my shorts down and kicking them loose, reaching in front to press and squeeze as we kiss over her shoulder, my hand kneading her breasts while behind I am cocked, spring-loaded against her round bottom, running to and fro along the line of division. She lifts her leg and I nudge into the space. Her hand joins mine between her legs as my fingertips feel the fine silky channel. Her fingers curl under, guiding me as I prod forward, sliding in like an oiled bolt, splitting the wet crevice as it takes hold of me. She pushes back against me and we buck sideways across the sheets. I roll her over, her stomach flat on the bed as I cling to her backside, my hands gripping her tight bottom. Her face under mine, her mouth blowing air noisily, her arm cast out to the side, hand grasping the edge of the bed. To stop crushing her, I lift up on my hands. She is splayed across the sheet, her perfect butt raised, the small of her back concave. We begin again, gathering speed as I pound into her, watching her flesh shake with the impact. She pushes with more vigor as I dig deeper. But even as I'm shooting into her I know that my ejaculatory ecstasies are not enough, that more work is required. In the time remaining we will need to create more residue.

We nap for some time, tangled in twisted sheets and strands of semen. When we wake, the windows are pale squares barely distinguishable from the walls. The rain seems to have passed. She gets up and sits on the toilet, shutting the door as she looks at me. Over the top of the wall I hear the sound of her peeing. When she flushes, I get up. In the small shower we bathe in ashen light. She washes my hair, then my back. We stand kissing under the weak spray. I turn the water off and lather her body from neck to knees. She spreads suds on me by the handful. I lift her—a great slippery fish—against the slick tiles and slide her down onto my soapy erection. She hangs onto my neck and rides me, and I stay inside her until the end. Standing under the falling water she tells me she feels tickling bits dripping out of her. The stuff washes away in the dark, a byproduct of our stalled goodbyes. We are only adding to our brief history, lubricating the space between us, accidently gluing our lives together with things we can't see or even keep track of.

The air is gentle and cool after the rain and a number of people are out on the streets as we come into town. Houses are open for the air. As we walk, music follows us, one source fading out as another grows more prominent. People sit on stoops murmuring among themselves. Rita's wearing a pair of my shorts and a shirt of mine with rolled up sleeves. Once in a while someone greets her, casually including me with a nod or a word. I have walked to Chez Lambi enough times now that I'm beginning to feel like a local, no doubt experiencing a common delusion associated with arrested travel.

Still, I feel at home in the restaurant. We sit on stools at the bar. Sweet Sharon smiles at me, and when I introduce her and Rita, seems pleased to see us together.

"What's new?" I ask.

"We got a band comin." A drum set and a couple of small amplifiers sit on the floor in front of the mural wall, and the closest tables have been pulled back to leave a space for dancing. Already people occupy the nearest tables. I notice two white guys with beers watching me from across the room.

"Look at that wall," I say. "The man's good."

"People love it," she says, her hand on the bar between us. "What are you havin?"

"How about rum and Coke? Rita?"

"Juss Coke."

Neither of us has any money to speak of but we split an order of conch and fries while the band—three local boys who call themselves Radication—take their places and warm up. We move to a table after they start in earnest. Since there is no stage, people dance right beside the band members. Rita and I watch, sipping our drinks. The bass player wears a bowler hat and sings lead vocals with his eyes closed. They play original versions of island standards, reggae, and ska tunes with fast and scratchy guitar licks. After a long first set the bassist comes around the tables with his hat in his hand. The clinking of coins is the simplest music, weaving its way back to us.

I get another drink, running up a tab I can't pay. The band comes back with a slow number that crowds the dance floor. I hold Rita close, turning in a tight spiral of music and heat. Her skin is flushed, her breath hot on my neck. Her pelvis pushes against me. We stay this way well into the next song, then break apart and dance with more energy, bumping each other as we did at Club Camou.

It's a beautiful night for a stroll but once we're on the unlit unpaved road we walk swiftly. We rush through the gate past the wary pig, burst into my room and lock the door, feel our way out of our clothes and into bed without lights. I put her legs over my shoulders and enter her, leaning forward on the strength of her thighs, sinking closer to her face as she lowers me.

"I want you to come," I say.

"To de States?"

"I'm talking about right now, coming right now."

"Oh, climax."

"You have to relax."

"I'm troubled."

"Everyone's troubled. You can still come."

I coax her, speaking softly of the excitement she causes me. I tell her how well we fit together. As we move I touch her sweet spot and she reaches a state of vocal passion. I consider her obvious arousal a partial success and erupt, tingling like a tuning fork, without her.

I get up for water and by the bathroom light set the clock for pre-dawn, intent on pursuing the last landscapes of the journey, preparing to practice the art of the intimate trip one more time.

We sleep peacefully, touching in long common lines, meeting at surface junctures across the slack terrain of our bodies. I wake in quiet darkness, wrapped in an amorous bear hug. Swamped in the thick fog of interrupted dreams we kiss, gently sleep-fucking through the lapse of night. Her earnest rhythm carries me, her melodic trills encircle me. We spin a viscous cocoon in the hollow night—my rigid convulsions tear us open, spewing more juice on the unexpected fire.

I lie quietly, my brain idling, fixed in the present, listening to her breathing and measuring time with the only sound outside my own heartbeat. Then I hear the ticking clock, swing myself out of bed and stand swaying like an addled cat. I click off the alarm, squint at the luminous clock face, and find myself twenty minutes ahead of schedule. Leaning over the sink, I trickle water and rub it into my eyes. I dress by flashlight, pack camera and film, water, knife and hat, and creep toward the door. Her sleepy voice follows me.

"What are you shootin?"

"I won't know until I see it."

"You woan see anything now."

"I'll see first light. Go back to sleep. I'll see you in a couple of hours."

Outside I shine the light in the pig's face, then redirect it to the sand by his snout. "Ready, Smitty?" He lifts his head, squinting unhappily at my rudeness. "Come on boy, let's go." Sandflies sting my ankles and I walk toward the gate. The pig gets to his feet and shakes himself, ears flapping like banners in the wind. I hold the gate open, he trots out beside me and we walk down the beach. In the darkness I hear the gentle surf, my shoes biting the sand, and the pig's faint incessant grunts.

Somewhere behind us a rooster crows. The sky lightens over the barrier of trees beside us. The rocks at the end of the bay gain texture. Dark crabs scuttle over the sharp surfaces. It's high tide, and the bay waves scour the myriad pores and hollows in the rock, sucking and slurping like a thousand nursing puppies. We leave the beach, moving through shore brush and marsh grass, trading sandflies for mosquitoes, dawn for day. Under the high migration of pink clouds we skirt white mangroves, their breathing roots sticking out of the soft soil like new hairs growing from the face of the Earth. We wade through swamp ferns, knocking off snails, leaving spiders dangling, alarming herons spike-poised in the midst of the wetlands. In the distance, fresh sunlight rakes across a wet hillside. On the mud flats, white crabs withdraw to their burrows in loose unison. Smith digs for them, thrashing about, ripping the ground open, tunneling with his snout. Pulling one up, he quickly flips, stomps, cracks and gobbles it as I shoot the action. In his wake he leaves savage irregularities across a field of holes.

On higher ground the sun reaches us, spilling onto reeds, trees and aerial roots. I shoot planes of gold light, textures of peeling bark, millipedes and moss. Wild ducks scatter the morning mist. A mangrove cuckoo spies on us from shadowy branches. Smith finds fallen green fruit—some wild variety of annona—and momentarily loses interest in the world around him. I drink some water and move on, looking for simple complexities.

I come to a pond. Black-faced grassquits hang in the reeds around it, their high-pitched chirps mere accents on an air of solitude. At the water's edge I become still as stone, shooting down at a mat of white heron feathers—a delicate drawing of cross-hatched lines—while my other eye sees freshwater prawns moving in the shallows, translucent shapes drifting back and forth like minuscule ghosts. In the water I find aquatic plants, pond scaters, and light-filled bubbles. I shoot into reeds, seeing parallel lines, backlit beetles, egg sacs and broken patterns. Webs hang in gossamer etchings over the water. My sweat drops explode below them like bombs rippling the background. When Smith finds me I'm wet and muddy, wearing sticks and seeds, the same as him. I hang the camera from a low limb and take our tilted portrait.

Heading back the way we came I find things unlit or unseen earlier. I shoot places where the sun hits the ground, convergent lines in drying mud, animal tracks, shells, twisted white sticks, a bird skull, a dragonfly—rattling wing-stuck— upside down. The compositions are not obvious. It's a matter of seeing the stately tension of natural objects, feeling the clash and pull of shapes in a frame, following the chase of line and space. The terrain is a stage, the camera a conduit between the drama and the viewer.

At times the work seems mysterious or senseless to me. I look at fragments and see arrangements in their details. And in the next moment I can see that by connecting these things I am somehow connected to them. I am an integral part of the arrangement I create. I feel the tremor of my own life being lived. In one sense I can settle into the mud, content with the elements around me, and live a kind of observant solitary life for a time, an earth-life with my friend Smith. In another sense I am not welcome here at all. I am a disturbing presence, leaving soon to look for more humans, going onward in discomfort and uncertainty to gather with the others. It seems to me a universal puzzlement—being lost but thinking you are found. Have we somehow become, or have we always been, strangers in our own world?

Down the beach I see Ambrose in the water. As we get closer and he swims in, Smith becomes aware of him too and charges along the water's edge, zigzagging in the wet sand. Ambrose flips him into the surf and their game begins. I go inside to rouse Rita.

She rolls over as I shut the door. The room is warm and soft. Blinking sleepily and stirring under the thin sheet, she watches me undressing beside the bed, my clothes dropping in a rank heap. Pig squeals come through the window.

We take a leisurely bath in the bay—she swims in my tee shirt and shorts—and join Ambrose on the patio for coffee and toast. He is leaving soon for a cricket match in Granville, and I confess to the further debt I incurred in his name the previous evening at Chez Lambi. To compensate I swear that I'll finish the bathroom tiles this very day.

"And den we are even?"

"Then we're even." There is a tone of finality in the appraisal of our contract which brings up the subject of my departure, something we never discuss using specific dates. Rita leans forward and there is a pause at the table.

Ambrose makes light of the topic, gesturing in mock pain at Smith, sitting quietly at our feet. "If I turn my back de mahn may leave wit my beast."

I smile, dropping a corner of toast for the patient pig. "He likes me better anyway. Give him a choice."

Rita and I wash the dishes without much talking. After Ambrose leaves we sit outside with the radio playing. It's hot and the pig is napping. The work is waiting. Rita is waiting. I feel the tension in her look, an unspoken acknowledgment of the changes that must come. "Let's get started," I say.

"Who?"

"Us. Partners in work and play."

"You want me to help so you cahn leave sooner?"

"You can work slowly if you like. What else is on the schedule?"

"My aunt will be cookin."

"Is this the night?"

"If you have time enough."

"What time should I come?"

"Six."

"Fine." I take her hand. "Are you still hungry?"

In the room she lets me strip off her wet clothes without a word. How can I ask her to relax? Rollo said he'd kill her and yet we lie naked on the bed. She is so willing, so sensual despite the disorder in her eyes. Time is flying whether we have fun or not. I turn away from her face and move down. We eat in bed, dining on each other with upside-down appetites. I taste seawater and find grains of sand in her shell; she nibbles at my brittle coral. I can't get enough. I have her in my mouth and Rollo is gone, left behind, out of contention. I am the ravenous winner, a bear at a seaside salt lick. But I only get hungrier. I want another portion and I kiss her grave face to get it, taking her tongue as I churn the pot below, turning solid to liquid, cooking the consequences until we come without an outcome. And lie stirring in silent disarrangement.

Rita works outside painting window trim, the missed ends of roof beams, neglected details. I work in the tight confines of the shower, laying the rest of the tile. Divided by walls and radio songs we work in separate parallel worlds, making personal decisions, wrestling with private concerns, knowing the other's whereabouts and feelings even as we know our plans together go no further than the evening meal.

She finishes first. I hear her dragging a chair into the empty room but she doesn't come into the bathroom or make another sound. I continue to place tiles, tap them down. When I stand up and look around the door, I see her sitting in the chair, staring at me as if she has long expected my voice to issue from the bathroom with the weight of authority and address questions about the composition of our lives. I go back to work; I don't know where to begin with such a vast subject. Haven't I already said that composition is everything?

When I come out, we put towels on the concrete floor and make love fast and hard, noiselessly until the end when her surprising cries summon Smith into the room for a few vicarious sniffs before he's invited to leave. Then we're quiet again, flat out on the floor like make-believe characters on the hard surface of reality.

Rita leaves, saying she'll see me up the hill and expects me to come hungry. I laugh to myself, famished and weak, sitting in a patio chair and gazing out at a lone fisherman—a traveling image burned into the hot light on the sea—who appears not to move as he passes the mouth of the bay.

I gather my clothes and pack, leaving out a shirt and pants for dinner and for traveling. I shower and shave and dress, then sit down and write a note to Ambrose.

Brose,
All you need now is a shower curtain. The job is done. The trip is over. I'd like to get the 7:00 flight tomorrow morning if I can get a ride. That means leaving Pagan Bay more or less by 5:30 as you know. I just decided. A bitch for a Sunday but it might be worth it to see me go. I've gone to the Mathews' for dinner. See you later.

Cane Jake

P.S.   For your information Smith has indicated that he might enjoy a change of scenery at this time in his life.

I tack the note on the front door and leave, taking the camera with me. I have nothing in mind but it's my policy for the last day anywhere. And it's an old friend—I always like the feel of it, the weight, though I hardly notice it this time; it's lighter than the air in my lungs. Or the pang in my heart, for that matter.

Up on the hill the late light is striking the front of the house as I arrive. Rita meets me at the door in a green dress with yellow flowers on it. In the kitchen she gets us something to drink while I speak to Doris. Roger is not home yet so Rita and I move into the backyard and walk around together holding glasses of sweet, frothy seamoss drink. There are hibiscus and bougainvillea near the house, fruit trees here and there. On a grapefruit limb two large brown leaf-shaped butterflies draw sap face to face and I put them on film; to me they look like a natural Rorschach test. At the back of the yard a great yellow poui tree towers in bloom, its top half ablaze in the low wash of the setting sun. The blossoms are like those on Rita's dress and I ask if she'd mind posing among the fallen flowers. My inclination is to shoot, somehow delay the talk.

"Would dat make a pretty picture of a girl you know?"

"I wasn't thinking of it like that."

"Would it show how intimate we have become?"

I look back at the house where Doris is watching us from the kitchen window. "Rita, I'm a visitor, I didn't move here. When we started this we always knew I'd be leaving sometime."

"How convenient, now I got dis baby."

"Don't call it that."

"What should I call it den?"

160

"Anything else. A seed, a larva, a groundnut."

"You doan care, Jake. Now you think it's funny."

"No, but maybe it's not true. You have to get the results."

"Alone, it seems." She turns toward the house and I hear a car driving up, see a few fireflies flashing above the weeds at the edge of the yard like bits of light fallen from the sky. "My uncle is here," she says.

I put my arm around her shoulders as we walk. "Look, I would've gone already if it wasn't for you." We are behind the grapefruit tree when I stop and turn her toward me. "This doesn't have to end, but I don't even know what you want. Maybe there's a way for you to come with me. We don't have to end it if we don't want to. But I have to go back now and finish the work I'm doing."

She looks puzzled. "When?"

"Tomorrow."

"Tomorrow?" She takes a step back.

"I know it's sudden, but I'm totally broke."

"How cahn I go tomorrow?"

"I don't know. You have a passport, don't you?"

"I doan have enough money."

I nod toward the house. "Maybe you can get a loan. If not, I could send you a ticket when I get home. If it has to be later, then it has to be later."

She puts a hand to her forehead. "You make it sound easy."

The back door opens and Doris calls us to dinner.

Rita shouts to the house, "Okay!" and looks back at me. "You want me to come?"

"Yes, I want you to come all over me; I want you to come your guts out; I want you to come like there's no tomorrow. And I want you to come on the plane with me. Take a vacation."

"What, be a touriss?"

I laugh. "We'll see how you like it." I kiss her then, find her lips hot, her face hot. She's trembling a little. "Are you alright?"

"I doan feel so fine."

"Let's go eat."

Inside the house, Roger shakes my hand and offers me a drink; I think he's had a couple already and hopes I'll accept, making it easier for him to continue. Doris interjects. "Maybe Mistah Mayfeel does not drink." It sounds to me like wishful thinking.

Roger gives me a quizzical look. "Oh, he drinks."

"I drink," I say, and to her, "on occasion."

He straightens up from a cabinet near the dining room table holding a bottle of rum to show me the label. "Wit soda or Coke?"

"Any juice from those trees out back?"

"Grapefruit."

"Perfect."

He takes the bottle to the kitchen, saying, "Dere's a healthy mahn, takin de natural juice of de land."

In the dining area a heavy wooden table occupies most of the space. Set against one wall is a cupboard which prevents the chairs on that side from being pulled out very far. A collection of straw baskets sits on top of the cupboard and mounted on the walls are flat straw weavings with market scenes painted on them. In the adjoining living room are two long couches with thin legs and thin plaid cushions indented with permanent impressions in the favorite spots of their users. At the end of the room is an old television set with a plastic enlarging screen mounted to the front. On the mantle behind it a blue-robed statue of the Virgin Mary stands among candles and plastic flowers. Against the front wall a bookcase holds several bridge trophies presented to Doris Mathews, and family pictures showing the couple with a boy and girl at various ages, now grown. Hanging on the opposite wall is a heavy-looking metal crucifix of the bent knee variety; its outward leaning position makes me wonder whether gravity will pull the figure from the cross or the whole thing from the wall.

My drink arrives. The women bring the food to the table and we take our seats on the four sides with Doris near the kitchen, Roger at the other end and Rita up against the cupboard, across from me. Doris blesses the meal and the passing of platters begins. There is a pile of whole baked goatfish—their eyes stare through the cataract glaze of a delicate sweet sauce that possesses a hint of anise—along with dasheen, cristophene, rice, bread, and green tomato salad. The small bones in the fish invite careful consumption or choking, but it's delicious and I remark on the fact.

"Seems like you been here long enough to taste most everything," Roger says.

"It's only made me hungrier."

He looks at my camera on the cabinet. "Took many pictures—true?—documents of your experience."

"Quite a few."

"And nothin to show at de moment." He shakes his head. "Will dey tell your story of de place?"

"I don't know about a story. There may be a couple of good images. From the forest, mainly."

"Which is de first image dat struck you?"

I take a bowl from Doris. "A green jewel, I guess."

"From de air?"

"Yeah. It looked beautiful, mysterious."

"Heh. Nothin mysterious down here. People livin in an overgrown garden."

"Probably all the clouds, the shadows and the mist, gave me that feeling."

We eat in silence for a minute. Rita hardly touches her food. Out on the road a car with a poor exhaust system drives by. She keeps looking at me like I'm guilty or she's unwilling to be the victim. The situation begins to feel more immediate.

"You have quite a garden yourself," I say.

He nods. "We are eatin some results."

"Have you always worked the land?"

"More or less. In de past I did some loggin, most recently after de hurricane—" He smiles. "—Jake it was, knock down so many big trees. But lumber, das a real slow business here. Land too rough, y'know."

"So far, until it's wanted badly enough."

"De government has now made parks to protect de mountains, de water supply."

"Well, I hope your luck holds for a long time."

He finishes his drink. "Like another?"

"Yes sir, thanks."

He gets up and goes to the kitchen.

"When do you expect to return home?" Doris asks.

"Tomorrow," I say, scraping my plate.

"Tomorrow," Rita says, staring at me as if it hasn't sunk in yet while Doris catches the looks between us.

Roger returns. "For a number of years I worked indoors at de Coconut Products factory." He sits down with our drinks. "You seen it?"

"Outside Granville."

"Makin soap."

"Now there's a clean living."

"Heh, heh. For de management, not de labor."

He seems such a balanced fellow that I feel sure he's seen both sides, but he doesn't elaborate and I don't pursue the topic. I put down my fork and work on my drink.

Rita leans forward and grimaces, her hands at her waist.

Doris holds her with a long hard look. "Whas de matter, child?"

Rita gives her a sickly smile. "Juss some cramps."

164

There is a pause as I set my glass down. Doris is looking at me as if I'm a beacon of impropriety, a good guest gone bad.

She stands and leans to touch Rita's forehead, then looks at all of us in turn. "Girl, you are flushed hot. Is dere some special news you wanna share?"

"We gonna speak straight here?" Roger asks.

I look at Rita. "Everything out in the open?"

"You know about dis?" Roger asks.

"She had a blood test. It's not confirmed yet."

Her aunt's face is grave. "Child, what have you done?"

Rita looks stunned. "I am not a child," she says, "I am a woman."

Roger stands. "You ready for more?"

"Please," I say, handing him my glass.

"Congratulations," he says, maybe sarcastically.

Doris leans on the table with both hands. "Not a child, she says, but carryin one already. And you." She picks up her plate, staring at me. "Leavin your quick work behind. I imagine dat airport will look like salvation hall tomorrow."

"You're making an assumption," I say, looking at Rita.

Rita pushes her plate away. "He may not even be de father."

Doris puts her plate down. "Good Lord! What are you sayin, girl?"

As he enters from the kitchen Roger sets my drink down, barely within my reach. "She sayin loud and plain she cahn't keep score."

"Lord have mercy, Rita," Doris says. "How many possibles in dat bunch?"

I want to stand too, and feel less like a defendant, but I stay seated in commiseration with Rita, and because Roger stands behind me with his hand on my shoulder.

"We are not havin a tribunal here, but maybe someone could share wit us who else de father might be," he says.

Rita is touching her fork lightly. She shrugs. "Juss a mahn in Granville."

"Who?" her aunt demands. "A black mahn?"

Roger grips my shoulder. "De mahn got a name?"

Rita raises her eyes to me, then to him. "I prefer not to say."

Roger's hand lifts. The ice in his drink rattles. "Wait now, hold still, dis dat drunk mahn you say hit you?"

I take a bite of fish, cold now, and watch Rita as I lean over to reach my drink.

"He was not even drunk," she says, "juss a riffraff huckster."

Doris reaches for Rita's plate and sets it on top of hers. "I see," she says, and looks around at all of us. "Not a drunk, not a thief. We heard some fabrications de first time around. You were ashamed. De mahn was forceful. Is dat not so? De mahn was rough. Dere was no consent at all. You were disgraced and you told a story."

Roger takes his seat, sits rubbing one temple, looking at Rita and then at me.

I take one more bite of fish as Doris leans toward me, and I think she might hit me. "I suppose you feel yourself off de hook now," she says. "De good mahn by comparison."

"Not exactly," I say. She reaches for my plate and I flinch, swallowing a bone.

"You had enough?"

I drink some water and clear my throat forcefully, then drink some rum. "Yes ma'am, thank you. Very good."

She picks up the plate and stacks it with the others. "Well den, you got any good advice for your sweet friend?"

"I've said she can come with me."

"Okay, fair enough," Roger says. "Let me mix you another." His chair scrapes backward.

"Doan be gettin de mahn drunk," Doris says.

"De mahn sittin in de hot seat," he says, heading into the kitchen.

Doris looks at her niece. "Soufrière is your home."

"America cahn be a new home," Roger says from the other room.

"It's her choice," I say.

"She will need help," Doris says.

Rita looks like she could laugh or cry, but says nothing.

"Stand yourself up," Doris says. "Make de coffee." She turns to me. "Dessert for you, Mistah Mayfeel?"

"How could I say no?"

She speaks to Rita. "Get up. Bring dose dishes. Make de coffee. You are not lyin in bed yet."

Rita gathers the platters and bowls in the method of a professional food handler and strides into the kitchen indignantly.

Roger puts down my glass. I clear my throat and we sit waiting for the next course or the next surprise.

Doris comes in with a pie and a knife, talking as if she is thinking aloud. "Who is gonna help wit de baby way over dere?"

In the kitchen doorway Rita shoots back, her voice a low flame, "Which baby? De dark one from a street pirate? Or de light one from a fly-by touriss daddy? Which good baby you like?"

"One and de same in God's eyes."

Tears well in Rita's eyes. "Maybe dere woan *be* a baby!"

The older woman whirls around. "Hush dat talk!" She shakes her head. "You doan wanna make a bigger mistake. You doan wanna cut yourself from de Church," she says, slicing air with the knife.

"Could be a blessing in disguise," I say.

"Not for a Catholic, Mistah Mayfeel. We doan forfeit salvation so fast."

"Anyone can change. Just because you're born a Catholic doesn't mean you have to stay that way."

"You speak from outside de Church. You doan know."

"I know one thing, though. This idea of forbidding birth control is the most ridiculous policy in existence. Bar none!"

A hush falls over the room as if the air has been sucked out and I realize my voice has risen to the leading edge of anger. As I watch Doris, her eyes lock on me with such intensity that I wonder if she's noticed an insect on my forehead. Without moving my eyes I see her knife hand steady over the pie and I see Rita standing in the kitchen. Doris cuts the pie, saying evenly, "Das a matter we choose to leave in de capable hands of God." She sets a piece in front of me. "You heard of a higher power, true?"

"I think it's political. The Church is an outdated organization and the policy is a way of keeping membership up, of staying in power."

"As you say, anyone cahn quit, but de Church been existin for hundreds of years, growin all de time."

"So has the population, by leaps and bounds, so that's no great claim."

"De claim is de duration, like a rock, givin strength and shelter to de flock down through de ages."

The pie is creamy and tart, not too sweet, perfectly cool for a heated discussion. "What's this called?"

"Sour lime pie."

"It's really good, not too heavy."

The smell of fresh coffee creeps into the dining room to appease us and push the meal along to its civil conclusion. Rita brings in the pot, pours all four cups, and sits. "The Church," I say, "reminds me of the Dark Ages, makes me think of plagues and famine and superstition and torture. It was right at home there and that's where it should've stayed."

"Except dese present times are not so different," Roger

says.

"Good point, but there's no reason to think that humans will die out anymore, not by lack of breeding, anyway. Now it's the opposite, too many rats on a sinking ship. Someday soon we'll be running over each other in the scramble for a bag of rice, killing each other for a cup of clean water."

Doris scoffs. "You are a pessimist, Mistah Mayfeel. Look at de fish and bread you consume. Turn round and look out at de garden. We are not so lost. And dis one a poor country, not de wealthy one you come from."

I savor the rich coffee. "That's your good fortune, living here. Every place doesn't have such good land and water. Imagine if a hundred times as many people lived here, or a thousand. There'd be no trees left and the water would be gray, not fit to drink. Then you'd really be poor."

Rita is watching me, sipping her coffee and listening, seemingly relaxed for the first time this night. She looks so young and pensive, relieved probably, her problem in the open now and classified as a tiny fraction of the much larger issue.

Her aunt speaks. "It's a great and complex world. Wit de Lord's help we cahn surely right our problems. And be ready for His terrible intervention as it is ordained."

"Looks to me like this Lord's help is widespread suffering. I'll tell you how I see it: here on Earth we're like fleas on a dog, sucking the blood out of our host. The dog can handle quite a few and goes on living its life as the fleas live theirs. But they keep multiplying until the dog becomes visibly disturbed, then unhealthy, unable to care for itself, finally diseased and dying. But as long as there's blood the parasites won't stop. When the animal dies they just jump off and find another dog. The obvious problem for us is we have nowhere else to jump."

"If you doan worship, you cahn't see de next place."

"What I worship is trees and streams, the rain and the sun,

plankton and squid, all of it, the whole system."

"God's handiwork. You worship dose things you worship de Lord."

"Even if this Lord loves people, and that seems very doubtful, he doesn't love the Earth. It's only a waiting room. Why should you care about it? Heaven waits, isn't that right? If you look around you see that all religions are really the same: bad explanations. But instead of unifying us, they drive us apart, make us kill each other, keep us looking backward, make us irresponsible toward our real world."

"Dey give us hope and relieve us from sufferin."

"They increase suffering, dwelling on it for political reasons. Their leaders are like maggots under rotten bandages, forever festering in guilt and shame. Original sin is the worst concept ever devised. It's devious and destructive. People should leave it alone and keep their reverence for the Earth and for other species. The acceptance of heaven is fatal to this world."

"People will always put God above everything else."

"I know they will, but it's like believing in a trick to make yourself feel better."

Doris shakes her head in disbelief, glances at her husband, who sits with his arms folded across his chest like a watchful mediator. Suddenly he laughs the laugh of the practical man. "De mahn's a free thinker, Doris. Das okay too."

She gets nothing but an amused grin from Rita, but she goes on, protecting them both from irreverence and hostile declarations. "May de Lord have mercy on you, Mistah Mayfeel, for de things you doan mean."

"Oh, but I do mean them, Mrs. Mathews. I'm a one-world heathen, believer in birth control, advocate of swamps, jungles, plains and deserts. Lover of pigs and lizards."

"And what about people?" She leans on the table, her elbows out like wings. "What about *people?*"

170

"They need condoms and abortions, as well as advocates."

"Abortion is killin."

"It's a form of birth control. The worst form, for sure, but we seem to need it for survival. Education is too slow. And those Roman boneheads sitting around in robes telling you how to live your life are not helping at all. Just the opposite."

"Evil is not de solution to any problem." She smiles obliquely and pulls a small silver crucifix from the front of her dress, kisses it and holds it out in plain view.

"I doan think de mahn appreciate de symbol," Roger says, "but he seem to me a sorta spiritual fella all de same." He smiles. "But not a preacher for de pulpit, oh no."

"Everywhere you look someone's preaching—to the young, the old, and the gullible—the same mythical stories over and over again," I say, unable to stop myself.

"Den dey muss appeal to many, many people," Doris says.

"Faith can be mass-produced a lot easier than it can be argued."

"Faith is personal, Mistah Mayfeel."

"And so is choice. So no matter what anyone else says, Rita makes her own choice. It's her life, she lives with her decision."

"And you want nothin to do wit dat."

"Maybe my plane goes down. Maybe I go crazy or go to jail."

"Mistah Mayfeel. So dramatic!"

"Okay, I'm exaggerating to make a point."

"Whas de point?"

"That every tub has to sit on its own bottom."

"You tryin to pass dat as wisdom?"

"I've heard worse."

She looks at Rita for a few moments and her niece returns the look. They resemble each other and though Doris surely sees something of herself in the younger woman, she sees no decision. To me she says, "If your mother had chosen abortion instead of you—"

"Then I wouldn't know the difference."

She looks at me sadly, her great dark eyes telling me I still don't know. The conversation is over. I haven't seen the light and I never will. Not the blinding light of faith. Instead, I see the faint pinhole light, the light of stars maybe, whereby I can navigate with nothing else in sight. I see what light comes to me, the light that shines sidelong to illuminate infinite compositional possibilities. There is no need for artifice. Discovery is inherent in the process of selection.

"I am glad you could join us," she says.

"Thanks for having me."

She gets up and goes to the kitchen wearing her faith like an old robe, it seems to me, musty and weak-threaded, worn not so much for its appearance but because she has nothing else, because maybe it was a gift handed down.

"You sleepin over dere?" Roger says.

"Gatherin my strength," Rita says.

"Gather it up to help dat woman who loves you like her own child."

He and I move to the living room and he turns on the television. A cricket match is being shown and we stand in front of the black and white picture talking about sports. I have never understood cricket so he explains its basic rules and objectives to me, using examples from the match in progress and comparing it to baseball. He tells me the name comes from an Old English word for stick. Then he wants to know something about American football, as much a mystery to him as cricket was to me. Even as I reveal how the game is played I realize how complicated the rules have become. His mouth smiles under serious eyes.

Then he clamps a strong hand above my elbow. "You know dis other fella?"

Caught by surprise I look at him for several seconds, considering how much to divulge. "I know who he is," I say.

He maintains his grip. "How you gonna handle it?"

He knows I'm leaving so I assume he's referring to my emotional state. "Nobody likes it," I say, "but none of us can change what's already happened."

He looks into his glass as if he might be watching the ice melt. His breathing is audible. "Our actions influence de future," he says, "not de past."

I drain the last of my drink and tilting my head back feel for a second like I could pitch backward onto the couch were it not for his hold on my arm. My feet shuffle for balance and he releases me and I stand somewhat wobbly, his implication pushing against me like an inescapable weight.

"You know de mahn's name?" he says as our eyes meet again.

"I know who he is," I say again.

"Den we leave it up to you," he says.

A little later Rita and I are sitting on the front steps. A patch of yellowish light from the living room window falls on the grass. It's a cool, moonless night. We can smell the moisture in the air. From our position on the hill we can see some town lights below, the edge of the black bay. Beyond that, nothing, the future. From inside come the low garbled sounds of television, the voice of the present.

"They're good people," I say.

She's been looking out at the black sky, maintaining a kind of silent vigil.

"Tomorrow you go back to modern time."

"That's a funny way to put it. Over there we walk faster, talk faster, drive faster, make love faster. You want that?"

"Sure."

"Everyone's in therapy. We all need analysts because we're driving each other crazy. You want that too?"

173

"I might like it."

"People go shopping every day and buy things they don't need. They always want bigger houses just to hold the things they don't need. Stores are open all night. Nothing ever closes. You can wake up at three in the morning and buy a bigger house or a television for your dog. Every house has a phone and a TV in every room, even the bathroom. How's that sound?"

"Funny. Scary."

"There's nothing to be scared of. Lights and roads and buildings are everywhere. There are no more dark places, no rough spots. You can drive anywhere and never have to step on dirt or grass. Are you ready to go?"

"Of course."

"You'll be sorry. You won't be able to come back."

"You de one wants to go back. Das why you came here."

I sit quietly for several minutes, cradling my camera, floating in the moment. Her breaths are like Pagan Bay waves. I think of us back in Paradise and want to make love, but it seems too late for that now.

"I doan know what to do," she says. "Dere's no time. Everything is in Rocklee." She shakes her head. "I cahn't go so fast."

We're leaning forward at the edge of the step, our faces close, staring at each other. She reaches over and touches my hand. "You hold dat thing juss like a baby."

I look down at the camera for a minute, considering her observation. I take a deep breath. "That's all the father I care to be," I say. Thunder is starting to roll above us like colossal ball bearings.

"A dark baby doan sound so good?"

"You know that's not what I mean. I've already said I don't want kids, any color. I don't think this one's mine, anyway."

174

"Woan know till you see."

"Are you listening? I don't want to see it."

"If you get angry wit me, it's easier to go, true?"

Rain is falling out of the invisible black sky. We huddle under the eaves of the roof with our backs against the house. Thunder crashes behind us and tumbles down the mountains like breaking wood. "You heard me at dinner. That's how I am, I wasn't pretending. It's completely up to you; it's your body. I can only give you my opinion; I think abortion would be the smart thing to do. If you disagree, that's fine, you have to make your own decision. I just think it would be tough, for us I mean, if you had it. Practically impossible. I didn't mean to influence you, but you have to know the truth."

I don't know when she started crying, weeping silently, not shaking or sniffing, but tears rolling down. Rain lashes at the house, spattering us. We stand pressing back against the wall, our arms touching, our fingers intertwined while the wind whips the trees across the road.

"I'm sorry," I say. "I should've given you more time. I haven't been able to see very far ahead lately. I don't know what's wrong with me."

"De sky weeps angry tears tonight, sad tears for us," she says, her voice choking.

I squeeze her hand. "Everything will be alright."

She looks up at me. "You truly think so?"

The camera dangles at my side, slung over a shoulder. Her dark eyes appear warm and wise to mine, the smooth surface of a resilient spirit. And I stand at the edge of a clean new rain, reborn in the winged, exhilarating wash of imminent travel. "Sometimes," I say. "Sometimes I do."

She takes my other hand. "You doan mind bein alone?"

I kiss her forehead. "No, it's essential not to mind it. These days it's a privilege even, a rare state." I hold her close for a few minutes, feeling my melancholy erection between us, contemplating my chances for one more definite, sure-fire, solid grounding with her, weighing these uncertain, slipping moments together against a near tomorrow and the pale encroaching future. "I should go," I say.

After a few seconds she asks, "You want an umbrella?"

"Yeah, for the camera. And these are my only half-clean clothes."

We step inside. From their living room places, Doris and Roger regard us. I thank them both and they wish me a safe flight. Roger offers me a ride but I tell him I want to walk. Rita picks up an umbrella, closes the door behind us and walks me down the driveway. The rain is steady but no longer a deluge. I hold the umbrella and she holds me, and we hug and kiss pressed together at our loins and stomachs and faces, squeezing each other tight, our faces slippery with kisses, holding on to a hard parting.

I start to pull away, keeping the umbrella between us, rain hitting my back. Tears are running down her face. She presses a note into my hand. "Das for de plane, okay?"

"It's not the end," I say, backing away into the dark.

She stands blurred in the rain, then runs to the house, a fading vision in the night.

I turn down the hill walking on sheets of running road, descending in darkness under a drumbeat fabric dome, all other sound seized by the rain, only its obliterating static allowed.

Slogging down the winding stream, I follow the dull shine gathered from feeble house lights glowing mysteriously behind wild botanical shapes reaching for the road. I pass through Pagan Bay with tempered sadness, alone on mud-washed streets flowing to the sea. The town looks empty but for its lights flickering like candles in a pre-industrial rain. I look back. The drowsy mountains of this wild, lightless land follow me easily between weather-beaten buildings, touching everything with their resident rains. Their hidden rivers pour downhill, bountiful water courses plunging to the surrounding sea from places deep within their landscape, connecting in all directions to the circular world of passing ships and fragile passengers on similar trips.

I walk on, hearing the voice of Nietzsche: *I beseech you, my brothers, remain faithful to the earth, and do not believe those who speak to you of otherworldly hopes! Poison-mixers are they, whether they know it or not. Despisers of life are they, decaying and poisoned themselves, of whom the earth is weary: so let them go.*

I push open the creaking gate, whistling for Smith. The yard and the house are wrapped in darkness like a vast blanket. I knock at the front door, feel for the note I left. It's still there, wet paper. I knock again, try the door—locked. "Brose!" I call out. No sound, only stillness. "Brose!" No one home, the pig gone too.

I walk around back, the umbrella pushing leaves away, a scratching on the fabric and rain falling through trees and dripping off the eaves, spattering the patio, a blackness like deep purple dye beyond the yard, over the bay. I crouch against the house, staring into an impenetrable soup, waiting and listening suspiciously, hearing the taps and plinks and splats of drops drumming sand and plants and metal and wood and concrete all around. What I'll do is cross the patio, open my door and flip on a light. I straighten to get the key from my pocket, then close the umbrella and turn the corner with the point weaving in front of me like the cane of a blind man.

With one hand following the wall I tap the patio and step onto concrete, shoe scraping sand grit, reaching forward with my cane and tapping a chair, going around it, another step and I stumble over a bundle—stifle a cry—and poke the soft form, bump it with my foot, and then jab toward the door like a swordsman, one foot slipping a bit, my other hand finding the knob as I drop the umbrella and rattle the key into the lock.

Field of Vision

The door is pushed open, my hand comes up on the switch inside, brightness fills the room, floods my light-deprived eyes, and I flatten myself against the doorjamb, ready to lever my body inside or out, squinting into the rain for any threat revealed—the light cutting a hazy lane across the concrete to the fence and up into the branches, reflecting off wall and ground into the yard in a wide wash of paltry illumination.

Scattered furniture. Smith lies on his side right before me. I squat in the doorway, searching the yard, the sea grape, the fence, the gate, for a shape or a motion. "Smith," I call, my throat constricting. He doesn't move. I pull the strap over my head and leave the camera on the floor inside, crawl through rain running off the roof and kneel beside the animal. A short length of rebar protrudes from his underside like a stiff extra leg. Blood seeps from multiple wounds, flowing away unpooled in a thin spreading stain, diluted and washed over the concrete, growing amorphous in the dark, absorbent sand. Bent over his face I see nothing unusual: the eyes are closed as in sleep; the restless rubber nose twitches under falling drops; the mouth remains slightly open, upturned in its porcine grin. Rain shifts his fur, the only movement. I wait for an eye to open, an ear to twitch. Streams of water run out of my hair, off my nose and chin onto the pig's sleeping face. I put my hand on his bristly head and feel beneath the fur the knots of blows that landed there. "Smith," I say in his ear, "Smith." I put my fingers in his mouth, feel his teeth and soft tongue. "Bite me, I won't care. Bite me hard."

Matted stomach fur like the fringe of a dark red rug holds blood where the weight of the body meets the concrete. Rain and blood, rank fur, a smell like edible garbage, odor of a clever scavenger. Pink draining wounds, irreparable damage, a trace of excrement, the last rites of a lost life. Between the front legs, metal pierces the heart. I lift one leg gently, grasp the cold rod and pull it straight out. There is a sliding sound like cut fruit and the body drags a little. New blood runs after the crimson point. Steel taps concrete and the sound reminds me to look around, holding the weapon like a knife.

I drag him by a hind leg through the gate. Rain falls with salty tears and will not stop. All is fresh now. In rancid color. Purple stinking surf. I splash his face, wash his dead eyes, talk him toward revival in a saltwater healing. "C'mon Smitty, c'mon boy." Dark bloody sky pissing red rain. I stand in putrid yellow light holding the rebar weapon, wrought with sickness and loathing. I walk on sand before the black jungle, talking to myself, or thinking out loud: *Motherfucker.* Before rotting trees. *Motherfucker.* In a blurry rain. *Bloody pigfucker. Smitty boy, where's your motherfucker?"*

Light cutting through the trees, a car coughing, backing up. I stand listening. A floodlight fires over the fence and I whirl toward shadows in the yard, sprinting to the gate with the metal in my hand.

"Whas wrong, mahn?" Ambrose at the back door.

"Look at him," I say, pointing with the bar, holding the gate open so he can see the lump in the surf, the black remains at the edge of the bay. We stand over the bristled body being jostled like refuse in the waves. Like some child's stuffed animal gone overboard in the night. The man's face, under its usual serene veneer, bears a look of surprise and agitation, as if he's just heard that a marina will be built on his property. I look around, see rain falling through the outside light in brittle streaks like optical fibers.

He squats beside the animal, lays a hand on its soggy side, looks at his palm afterward, looks up at me. "What de fuck?"

I stab the bar into the sand beside him. "This was stuck in him." I turn away squeezing my head.

He stands with the spike. "Wheer—"

"The patio, right outside my door."

He looks back at the house, closes his eyes tightly, then

looks down at Smith again. "You plannin a burial at sea?" He looks at me and slings the rebar down into the sand, sinking it deep in a standing position.

The surf is starting to pull the pig's body so I grab his leg and drag him back across the sand in his dirty track, back on the patio, into what's left of his blood and stains, return him sandy and salty to the scene of the crime.

"Goddamn it, I'm sorry, Ambrose."

He walks over to me."My little black pig, mahn!"

The sight of his face makes my throat tight. "He was a friendly little guy."

"Crazy fuckin touriss! Dat could be you lyin dere."

"What are we going to do about it? It was Rollo or Blandy, one or the other."

Ambrose just stares at me, his dark eyes filled with disgust or anguish, or both.

"Okay," I tell him. "I'll hunt this motherfucker down myself."

"When? Before de plane leave?"

"I'm not going now."

"Hah! You gonna change your plan for my dead pig?"

"Enough is enough."

"You gonna make everything smooth here?"

"Not everything."

"Sure, sure. Let's get out de rain, mahn."

He turns to go; I grab his arm. "You have to do something about this."

He jerks his arm away from me. "Come inside and take a drink."

I stop at the door, look back at the lifeless animal who appears now on this drizzly night like some bush beast taken to sea, swallowed in a storm and belched back up in the surge. Or maybe just ordinary livestock, market fare, a farm creature we mean to gut and skin and soak. A jamboree feast still whole.

I take a shot of rum before I wring out and hang up my traveling clothes. After that I sit in a chair beside the couch where Ambrose sits leaning forward, elbows on knees, looking at the note I left for him on the door where anyone could see it, a message of rain-bled words that seems stupid now. A bottle sits on the table and the doors are open. Rain is drumming on the roof, a fan oscillating in the kitchen. The room is hot to me and I hold my glass like a rock.

"Should we bury him?"

He doesn't look up. "Tomorrow."

I watch a gecko on the wall over a lamp across the room. I could probably hit it with my glass. I could probably put my fist through the wall. The chessboard is set up on the table below the lamp, armies in stalemate. I could kick it through the ceiling, kill them all.

"Can you get Sharon's car?" I ask.

He nods.

I pour another drink. With each one the twitching in my guts grows more diffused. Warm burning rum, falling rain, shelter in the night, nothing makes any sense.

"Ambrose, I don't know what to say. I mean, the fucking note says I'm leaving. There was no need for this shit."

"A last goodbye for you, mahn, das all. Or de muthafuck never saw it."

He rubs his eyes, squeezes the bridge of his nose. I drink, looking at a map of the island on the wall by the door. A big place when it's the only one on the map. When you consider mountainsides where nearly no one walks.

We are quiet. He sits back for a while sipping his rum, then leans forward to examine the note as if he might have missed something. The gecko runs down flies, sluggish lamp-thudding creatures unable to sleep with a light on. I feel my drinks sinking in pretty well.

"I can't understand this," I say, "but it's fucking me up.

It's like a curse."

He rubs his neck with both hands, looking tired, then lies his head back on the top of the cushion and closes his eyes. "Anyone cahn get de blame."

I sit listening to the rain, thinking of Rita in the crater lake, thinking of the pig running on the beach. I drink, looking out the open door. The drumming on the roof fills the warm room with soothing tones while moths beat on screens and indoor crickets and rain-tuned frogs play chirp-and-whistle duets for a yawning insomniac.

Ambrose slides down to the side and stretches out. I stand and take the glasses to the kitchen. A column of ants is marching in the sink. I walk over to the lamp. The gecko runs up to the corner, a cartoon animal. "Brose?" He doesn't answer. "You feel free?" I wait by the lamp, watching his immobile form. When I look up the lizard is watching me with great staring eyes.

"More or less."

I turn off the lamp and leave him alone, locking the doors behind me. An animal dashes from the fence into the trees. I imagine I can smell Smith's body as I cross to my room but the smell is the same inside. I set the clock and collapse on the bed. Despite the rain and the proximity of my dead friend, I have neither wet dreams nor nightmares in the brief dark interlude. But my heart jumps at the buzzing alarm, a rude sound from some future world arriving too suddenly. My traveling clothes are still damp but I wear them anyway. Outside, the world is exactly as I last saw it but without the rain. I bang on the back door. "Let's go!"

In a moment it opens. While Ambrose fumbles around in the bathroom I bring my pack and the borrowed umbrella inside by the front door and go back out to the patio. I kneel beside Smith, smelling his blood and fur, feeling his stiffness in my own body, hearing the buzz of imaginary flies, saying a silent goodbye, asking forgiveness. Welcoming the maggots.

We walk in darkness while roosters crow. A hidden dog barks at us, raspy and uncertain. Inside the glow of a streetlight a grizzled old man peeks over a fence as we pass. A gentle breeze comes off the bay. My clothes dry and become damp with sweat. At Sharon's I wait in the street. Ambrose taps on a window, comes back with the keys. We drive through town and up the coastal rise. In the headlight beams mist floats across the road, rolling down the hillside.

I look at my watch and then at Ambrose. "I need to see Glenroy a second."

He doesn't hide his disapproval at all. "What for?"

"To say goodbye."

"No, mahn."

"Why not?"

"He is sleepin and we got no time."

"I'll wake him. It won't take long."

"You wanna deliver bad news."

"He should know."

"Doan be sure of dat."

"The man should see the pig."

"De mahn is not completely stable. Okay?"

I can see he isn't going to stop so I grab the wheel and yank it. He hits the brakes, we fishtail off the side of the road and stop. I hop out and start walking back into town. I don't even know where Glenroy lives but I walk fast and don't look back. The car pulls alongside me, backing up as I walk. "Sit in de fuckin car, mahn!"

We spin around in a stone-throwing U-turn and drive too fast, sliding to a stop with the lights shining on the blue door of a blue shack. I bang on it and hear a rustling inside. The door opens and Glenroy stands there in shorts, deranged with sleep, looking into the lights behind me.

"I'm on my way to the airport," I say. "Last night Smith

was murdered. Someone mistook him for me in the dark."

There's a long pause while he evaluates me, but if I'm a practical joker I don't have a next trick. "How is he dead?"

"A piece of rebar stuck in his heart."

"Who did it?"

"A guy named Rollo, from Granville."

"How is he your enemy?"

"I took his picture my first day here and he said he'd kill me but he beat up my girlfriend instead. Now this."

He squints into the headlights and they go off. "You can check it with him," I say.

He looks at Ambrose sitting behind the wheel. "Check."

"I have to go. Put your address down and I'll send you a picture of this guy."

He looks at me, at the pen and notebook I hold, then takes them and writes against the door.

When I get back in the car he walks over and asks, "Wheer is de pig now?"

"On the patio." We start backing up. "I'm very sorry, man."

As we drive away, I look back. Glenroy is in the road, walking under a streetlight, barefoot in his shorts. He hasn't even shut his door. Ambrose is looking in the rearview mirror and I have never seen such sadness on his face.

We speed through the outskirts and climb the coastal road. Light is seeping into the sky. Our raking beams swing through curve after curve of blurred road outlined by glimpses of missing guardrail on one side and cut rock walls on the other. I have one hand on the dashboard. The driver watches the road.

"Leavin a path of destruction," I hear him say over the wind whistling through the windows.

"I can't help it, man."

"You doan even know what happen behind you."

"It's more important to look ahead."

"You cahn't have a fuckin picture of everything, mahn."

We come upon the tail lights of a slower car. Ambrose accelerates, hits the horn and whips around it on a curve. "Not if you kill us both, I can't."

"You wanna walk, mahn?"

"No."

"Den shut de fuck up."

I watch the road intently, my arm pressed flat on the outside of the door. After a while he glances over at me and says, "I know dis road like de corners of my bedroom."

I settle back and close my eyes, surrender to hypnotic turns, cool morning breezes and erotic visions of Rita, lulled half asleep for brief periods. The sky turns blue. I peer out at stirring villagers as we slow for them. Strutting roosters, scratching dogs, trickles of smoke, a man on a bicycle, a woman sweeping a doorstep between metal cans of bright flowers.

At the airport, taxis disguised as ordinary cars deliver their fares to the small yard around the terminal building. On-lookers, well-dressed passengers and uniformed officials gather in unhurried participation. On the skirt of the runway a yellow and white twin otter sits waiting, a small plane in the presence of so many people.

We park and get out. Ambrose waits in a short line at the snack bar window while I carry my bag to the ticket counter. After a few moments there I walk over with just my daypack to the customs area where the captain stands smoking a cigarette and I ask him a few questions about the British West Indies Airways schedule. Then I return to Ambrose, who hands me a coffee.

"Thanks," I say. "Thanks for everything."

"Dey got a seat for you?"

"They have a couple left."

We stand there sipping coffee for another minute. "I'm all

set," I say. "You don't need to wait."

"Okay, mahn, okay."

"You don't want to see me weeping."

We step outside by the parking lot. Far out at sea, sunlight is starting to catch the water. The sky is clear; it's a good day to fly. Through the fence we see the pilot and copilot walk out with their papers and flight bags. Passengers are congregating around the doorway.

"All the best, Brose. I appreciate the hospitality. And the chess lessons."

"Have a good trip, Jake." We shake hands. "See you next time," he says.

I watch him walk to the car and get behind the wheel and back up and turn and pull out on the road north. Then I walk back inside with my coffee and retrieve my bag and take it to a chair in one of the bolted rows and sit down. I listen to the rotary warm-up of the otter's twin engines, the pitch slowly rising to a choppy but sustained whine, the sound turning in another direction and I can hear it finally moving away, taxiing to its takeoff position, the sound diminishing momentarily. And this seems like a long wait, as if an error has been discovered and some rethinking is needed, as if maybe someone is not aboard and there is still time for a quick dash across the tarmac.

When the sound returns, accelerating, I'm standing at the door watching the plane running desperately, bouncing and shimmying over the field, watching its yellow rising in the blue morning sky, a successful lift-off for all concerned, watching it fly out of sight, its whine receding and then gone, all of us down here in relative silence, staying.

I want to laugh at myself, at this world, at everything and everyone around me, but I can't right now, not out loud anyway. I could more easily cry but I might start feeling pity then, and I don't want that. That would disgust me more than anything. Better to fail at laughter.

Field of Vision

I remember Rita's letter and take it out of my pocket.

Dear Jake,

Now you must be flying over my home. I know you are looking down for the clearwater lake from up in the sky. I have never been up there but I know everything must look very different, very beautiful. Maybe you are taking pictures.

As for me I miss you already so much. I don't understand love even if I feel it. I am still troubled. Sometimes I think I will go to Barbados and see my father. There I would get the abortion. After that I would try to find a job and then go to see you when I had enough money or when you send a ticket. If I have this baby I think I will never leave and never see you again unless you come back again.

The times with you were different than my life before you came. Now I feel sad. Life is hard for me now. I don't know if it is hard for you too. I don't know if you love me but I know we had a special time together. I would like to go in the forest with you again. I didn't know that was a place where love waits.

Soon I will give you this letter and maybe see you for the last time. I hope not. I would like to go with you but at this moment I can't. Please write me soon or call me. Please send me a picture of us.

I hope your photos are what you want. I know they will be different. Not like a tourist. Remember the island of forests. Remember me here.

Love, Rita
P.S. My aunt says you are an infidel.

I have twenty dollars and a return ticket. I don't have any plans of substance. I don't know exactly why I'm sitting here while my plane is heading west in the direction of my home, my former life. Maybe I'm taking a later flight. It's a perfectly beautiful day to travel. Also a good day to read. And since I'm free as a bum, I'll remain where I sit. Maybe I'll become a bum. I don't have any idea what I'm doing. My allies get raped or killed. I guess I'm curious as much as anything. I open my book and stretch out my legs. Between flights this place is like a reading room. I plan to keep to myself, just me and Nietzsche.

For that man be delivered from revenge, that is for me the bridge to the highest hope, and a rainbow after long storms.

I read random passages for what they're worth to me.

Alas, this black sorrowful sea below me! Alas, this pregnant nocturnal dismay! Alas, destiny and sea! To you I must now go down! Before my highest mountain I stand and before my longest wandering; to that end I must first go down deeper than ever I descended—deeper into pain than ever I descended, down into its blackest flood. Thus my destiny wants it. Well, I am ready.

I wish I could say the same. But he was only human, like the rest of us, and destiny is a thing of the mind.

Part 3

So I'm gone now. I've spent my time, taken my shots, had my run-ins and my fun, had my ups and downs, and now people think I'm gone. Limbo, so to speak, unless someone sees me and calls my name or taps me on the shoulder. I'm just sitting in the Granville airport terminal. Middle of October.

I'll need to get down to basics. I'll need to get resourceful. Not run-of-the-mill, but exceedingly, deviously, maybe even fiendishly resourceful. Everything is juggled now. The borders have shifted, realigned to a new order, tighter or looser, depending on your view. First, I'm thinking two things: food and shelter. I have enough cash for one night in a guesthouse and a few portions of cheap, portable food—sardines, raisins, nuts. Alright. Forget beer, forget rum, forget ice. Then I'll need a camp, a base camp, someplace either here in town—unlikely, unsafe, but close to where I'll need to spend some time—or elsewhere, farther from here but safer, in the forest, let's say, with fresh water nearby and maybe free fruit, but involving more travel time and inconvenience. Otherwise it's just time spent, period.

I have to think about a weapon of some sort. I don't mean my Swiss Army knife. I mean something a bit more task-worthy, to be on the safe side. Something to make a man, alone on the streets, or in the woods even, feel more comfortable in the event of a problem, a hassle, a robbery attempt, for instance, or a racial incident, that will keep him self-reliant, just in case—and I'm thinking hypothetically now—he is forced, in his own defense, to commit some kind of crime, legal or moral, it will not matter at the time.

I'm already hungry. Food will be a problem; it's always needed. So it's time to move into action, not swiftly, but just to start rolling, make an immediate plan at least. Get rid of this big pack, carry the small one. Get a bite. Find a place to sleep. Roam around. Check out Rollo. Look him up, take a little peek, see what he's up to, how he spends his time. Maybe see where he goes, who he sees, things like that. Go slow, be patient. I look at my watch—almost eleven—and look around. No one seems to notice me just yet. I stand and stretch, yawn like a tired traveler. I feel peculiar but try not to show it.

I take up my pack and vacate the premises. It's hot outside, a fairly long walk into town. A man asks me about a taxi. No thanks, I like to walk. And that's what I'm doing.

When you travel alone, time is more elastic than your regular time at home. You may feel you've been gone for weeks when it's only been days, or months when it's only been weeks, and so on. You're occupied in being leisurely, to some extent, getting away from your day-to-day routines and job problems. Time is more carefree, lazy, sliding into the next day, the next place. And right now it's really stretching.

I cross the river and return to Petit Paulette's, the guesthouse I stayed at one night previously, my first on the island. Once I have an adequate room on the third floor and

190

half my money is gone, I shower in cold water down the hall and lie naked on the bed under a wobbling fan. Now I have my room, I'm respectable, I come and go as I please, no questions asked. Another visitor enjoying the hospitality of the capital town.

I need to get better acquainted with these streets. I need to walk around in this sea level heat and be a part of it, feel inconspicuous and easy-going but purposeful. I need to find the next place to sleep and it won't be here. How strange! Suddenly I'm so fond of my little room—#11—the lumpy bed and the clean sheets, the fan, the light under which I'll be reading later tonight, the chair, the curtains fluttering faintly before the two louvered windows, the door and the view from the landing, the red roofs and rain barrels, gutters, pipes and porches, people passing on the street, moving in and out of sight along narrow lanes, wires and walls and backyard chickens, laundry in the sun, a visual puzzle locked and moving at once, its pieces shifting with light and shadow and the motions of its inhabitants, the town and buildings arranged in some order of stone and wood and steel and smoke, a live mosaic below misty mountains so green and close, their white clouds grand and still as a painting hanging in place like a backdrop of perfect weather.

In ball cap and shades I take nothing for this outing but what's in my pockets. I don't feel like working. I'm in the wrong frame of mind at the moment. I nod to the young barman on my way out—no beer this time, my friend. Who knows when? I imagine not knowing simple things like this tend to shake you up at first, but the not-knowing part is where the pleasure will be found. Maybe pleasure is the wrong word. Maybe it should be excitement or aggravation or breakdown. Ah, the fun has begun. Such as it is. I'm smiling about as much as a sparrow smiles to itself.

Around the corner is the pharmacy and across from that

the grocery store, Continental Super Centre. Closed on Sunday. It's the heat of the day and partly cloudy. I stand on the corner thinking. Down the block is the leather shop where I saw Blandy and Rollo, closed also, like most businesses. A few people out but not much traffic. At the end of the street the market, the mouth of the river, the sea. Over to the left, the dilapidated warehouse district with some houses mixed in, Rollo's included. Then the jetty, then Fort Rodney, English-built in the eighteenth century. A couple of quality hotels along the coast. Back to the right, the bridge, the Riverside Bakery, where I waited for Rita that day, and upriver to Goodwill Park, behind it the land rising; then around to the Roman Catholic cathedral, the cemetery, and up the hill to the library, the Prime Minister's place; and then down in front, in the central area, the post office, the cinema, banks, offices and so on, ten or twelve square blocks of varying length and regularity. I have a map, I realize, from my prosperous days. For a moment I think back fondly to the old me, the traveler staying anyplace, eating and drinking anything he desired. But this turns out to be a bad idea if you're hungry. Even thinking you're hungry is bad.

Walking toward the park, the cricket grounds adjacent, I'm a man about town looking for a game plan. Walking along with my hands in my pockets, strolling really, no hurries, no trouble. Looking at the people, young men on bikes, women in doorways and windows, young girls laughing together in self-absorbed and sassy cliques. Then I'm daydreaming, remembering the meal, the many fine dishes made by Doris and Rita, seeing that table and that food, the plates and platters and bowls, Roger making those drinks—Christ, was that only yesterday?—and seeing the pitiful pig. I shudder at the memory, the brutal death. And then I'm wondering again: Which one actually killed him? Came in that gate and let him have it so hard. Both? Unless there was a third party, a favor owed, a bad deed needed, a payment, a mercenary act, or some kind of initiation undertaken. No, it's the kind of thing you do personally.

I can hear it two blocks away, a big event at the cricket grounds. So this is where everyone is. A crowd of young boys is gathered around the gate, apparently unable to pay the entrance fee, but trying to catch a sliver of action anyway, at least near the noise and near the door, some of them no doubt hoping for a friendly benefactor or maybe at some later stage to be let in free of charge. As I turn away I hear the crack of a bat and the roar of the enthusiasts.

I wander over to the cemetery, walk along the street wall considering my Granville lodging options. In one far corner of the graveyard, where the hill begins to rise behind, a mass of vines has grown over the wall to the ground. Peering at this green drapery I imagine the space inside against the wall, some shelter but not rainproof, my tent hidden from view but certainly not its occupant as he comes and goes. I imagine some sharp-eyed priest coming over to ask me what I'm doing. And what about a bathroom? I wouldn't foul my own nest. But there's the church itself. Are the bathrooms open just as the sanctuary is? Would I be struck dead on a holy toilet? If I asked for mercy, a small spot on the floor at night, would I pretend to be a believer, a convert, an apostate coming home? No. I keep walking, knowing I can neither accommodate such blatant hypocrisy nor place enough trust in the priesthood to get any proper rest. I'm not nearly that desperate; I have not yet descended to the appropriate level. Maybe later.

There are derelict buildings here and there, monuments to natural disaster, the unpredictability of island weather, the unreliability of economic recovery. Some structures are vacant and boarded, merely awaiting eventual repair, others too severely damaged, stripped of roof or wall, standing decrepit and unwholesome, undeniable legacies of Hurricane Jake.

The problems with these structures are trespassing, high

visibility, being too close to too many people, attracting attention with unusual or antisocial behavior. I would have to find one on the outskirts, somewhat hidden or unremarkably located; but then, if it was that ideal, it would already be occupied. There are plenty of people here poorer than I am, and who have been so for a much longer time. I won't actually be poor until tomorrow.

Climbing the hill to the library it occurs to me that I must wash my clothes while I still have a room. There goes the afternoon. The library is closed too, sitting shuttered and solitary on the hillside. Part of its foundation is supported by posts that allowed level construction and created an open space under the front porch, open on three sides to anything that wants to crawl under it, the ground unlevel of course, but a roomy and roofed enclave existing there nonetheless. I sit on the porch resting, stomach hollow, looking down on the town and thinking this might work in an emergency. Cooler up here, quiet at night, out of the mainstream, nearly the same view as the Prime Minister.

Without food one becomes tired, listless, lonely and unenthusiastic. Weak and muddle-headed, sleepy, headed down the road to crazy. I brought it on myself but it's just a situation I'm in right now, it's not permanent. A challenge, I'm calling it. When I'm satisfied, I'll move on.

I pass a corner store that's open, turn around and go inside. An old man sits on a stool, having a drink and a smoke, passing time with the man behind the counter. From the sundry items on the food shelf I select two small cans of sardines, a package of saltines, and take a cold bottle of soda from the cooler. The man writes and adds the prices on a paper bag, then puts the items inside as I add them in my head too, handing him a bill and thinking that I'm paying a little more than I would at the supermarket, counting the change carefully, bidding the men good afternoon.

Field of Vision

I walk down to the waterfront, over to the jetty. No boys diving, no fishermen, the sun out over the sea ahead, high in the west and angling its glare at the land below the clouds, a couple of small boats way out, working men with no time for stadium games. As I'm walking onto the jetty a man rises from a squat at the water's edge, his pants down and paper in his hands, casting a wary glance at me as I turn away, not meaning to intrude on his privacy and doing him the courtesy of looking out to sea as I pass. I walk out to the end and sit with my legs dangling over the edge, holding my food and gazing into the greenish depths below, watching the fish weaving back and forth while I wait.

After a few minutes I glance back, see the man moving away scrawny and shoeless along the rocky shore, clothes hanging disheveled, hair wild and stiff, some sort of wharf rat leaving this public toilet behind. A vision of the future, I'm thinking, digging the food out of my sack.

Crackers with sardines in tomato sauce. I wipe the sides of the cans with a finger to get it all and burp Orange Fanta happily. I put the empty cans and the bottle in my pack—they might prove useful—and observing the pieces of fishing line, the dried and hardened bits of bait stuck to the surface around me, I'm wondering if I shouldn't get a hook and line myself, maybe catch a few little keepers. I lie back in the sun rubbing my belly, closing my eyes to imagine Sheila cooking them for me, dishing up some special recipe out of the goodness of her heart. Soon she's mixing the juice of the day, making drinks for us, and then we're fucking like rabbits when she turns into Rita and I'm behind her on the bed, dozing delusional on the warm jetty.

Walking along the shoreline toward the river I look for the right rocks to keep on my person, picking up and sorting through potential weapons, finally selecting three in keeping with my needs, smooth and rather flat palm-size throwers that fit my hand and feel like they'll go where I aim them.

Up ahead I see several figures sprawled around the market tables, either sleeping or just hanging around near the water. I turn up the street I'm adjacent to, a block before the market, and at the next cross street head back the way I came, passing the waterfront buildings and thinking I'll just take a look up Rollo's street on my way home, make sure I know exactly where his place is located.

I believe I've got the street, strangely desolate today, except for a man getting into a car two blocks ahead. There's a depot, shuttered, a few pieces of crate on its loading dock; next door, the office of a shipping agent. The car ahead drives on, turns off the street. Homes across from these freight houses, some smoke from a side yard, a baby's head sticks through the slats of a balcony railing, watching me; behind the child a woman in a chair doing the same, eyes craning over the rail, her hands busy in her lap. I hear a radio somewhere as I move to the other side of the street. In the next block I see Rollo's house, pale lavender, quiet, catching the sun pretty well right now, just about the same time I took my pictures there. I remember the small brown barking dog. Was it his, or did it just happen to be under his house? But I don't need to see the man now. I don't want to be surprised; I want to do the surprising.

The house is on the corner of this street and the lane that cuts through it. Across the lane are several stucco buildings that appear old, unused. I don't see the dog or any activity in the lavender house. On its other side sits a factory-type place, a three-story structure with long windows on the top floors, none on the ground. A truck is parked in front of this one. Behind Rollo's house is another nearly abutting it. In front, across the street, more old houses, a newer air freight office, a small packing house. I turn up the lane on this side and head toward Paulette's. I'll come back here after dark.

Twine strung in three sections around the room and my clothes washed down the hall handfuls at a time, a long and tedious task. I'm hungry and tired by the end but I'll eat no more this day. Instead I lie down for a nap, getting whatever I can from my room, my bed, safe and restful and hidden inside the hanging triangle of my own wet wardrobe.

I wake to shapes and sounds—gek, gek, gek go—in a gloom of pale beauty, the fan stirring ghost shirts, sock spirits, friendly underwear. An evening coolness drawing in the windows, mountain dew descending, street heat rising to form night clouds, a cloak before the Granville sky. The fan waving moisture from my damp clothing like primitive cooling to ease me through the night if I choose. But night lizards are calling: Gek go. Gek go. Get going.

Downstairs half a dozen patrons occupy the bar. I smell the kitchen warming up as I pass the screen door. With each step I find myself reviving, blooming to nocturnal capability. I could've been home by now, seeing my friends, having drinks and dinner, telling tales of these past two months. Instead, I am still here, walking up to speed, anxious and furtive and glad too, somehow excited by the unpredictable predicament, the danger and craziness of everything in the world and in my mind. I could almost laugh. A man with three rocks and a pocket knife out to have some fun. Looking to make some kind of opening move, start a new game, sacrifice a pawn perhaps.

By a circuitous route—just walking, passing among those out at this Sunday dinner time—I arrive on the lane from the other side. What if I meet him, if we pass in the dark? Will we feel it in the air? Auras of ill-feeling and then flashpoint violence? I think of Rita and then summon the beaten image of Smith, the carrion on which I now feed. Behind a sludge of pain and anger is a fury held back, kept locked, rare and exquisite, a cache of rage whose value is not known, unredeemable in emotional currency, precious as diamonds.

197

Oh, I prefer detached, indifferent, anything but this—investing in the lives of those I would rather only read about, or know nothing of at all. Be a cynic, be a clown, but don't be involved like this. Where's the value in justice and revenge? It's a sport, a game, an inning in a life. This is an intuitive move but intuition cannot be sustained, it's only a spark. What follows is the fire, the actuality. Am I not getting there by these very actions? Am I not becoming a marginal man?

Coming up the lane I am alone. On my left the old stucco buildings are dark, neglected, three very close together, quiet and peeling in the weak light cast from Rollo's rear neighbor. I am moving so slowly I can only look suspicious if I'm seen, but I must proceed with caution. This is not the time for abandon, my heart racing, blood running hot and cold. The house behind contains movement. Smells of onion and meat seep out the side window. A chicken clucks, strutting away in the dirt, startling me still. I cross to the shadow between the stuccos, slip into a slot of darkness, watch the back door open and bang shut, a woman standing on the stoop scraping the contents of a bowl onto the ground. A middle-aged woman in a dress and a headscarf, no one I mean to bother. As she goes back inside, a form moves out from under Rollo's house to investigate, the small dog I've seen before. Doesn't it smell me? It moves to the food and eats whatever it is. I recede deeper into the slot, check the other side and step into the open here, move quickly along the wall and vanish into the next space between these dark bunkers.

I come forward, opposite Rollo's place now, see light in the front room, hear music and voices on my smooth shadowy approach, flat against the wall beside a window now, light fuzzing out like toxic rays above me. Men talking, but I can't tell what's being said. My face eases like a snail to the window's corner and I see the interior—two men across from each other, beers on the table, radio on the floor, posters on the wall—and smell something like curry crawling out. One man leaning back, hands behind his head, about my size but younger, hair in short tufts, baby locks, while the other talks, the one with the full mane of cascading dread-clumps, a man bigger than me in a sleeveless tee shirt, jeans and sandals. He's the one. I move before I'm caught, slip across the lane as the dog appears with a growl and a clipped bark like a question mark, and then Rollo's in the window leaning out. Glancing up and down the lane, the full-bearded face, the hair swinging, a different window frame now but much the same image as our last encounter. He doesn't see me but I have him in my sights.

No camera, no gun. He withdraws from view and I am gone, slipping out the other side and moving down the street, his head behind me like a balloon on a string tied to my wrist. A face made huge by its surrounding mass, like moss grown thick and spongy around volcanic rock. He looks dangerous, looks also like a guy at home having a beer with a buddy. But I know things about him. I know him better than he knows me.

I walk along Bay Street toward the market and come to the snack bar just across from it. I tell the girl at the window that I've found a dog in bad shape and I'm wondering if they have any scraps they can spare, anything at all that a dog would fancy. She turns around to the cook and relates my request. He looks over her shoulder at me and steps back and bends over a can and plucks at it with a fork for a few moments and brings me a greasy box and tells me I should look in the trash barrel out here as well. "Thanks a lot," I say, "and the dog thanks you too."

A young couple sitting on stools and sipping sodas watches me rummaging through the barrel, turning over papers and cups with my hand, holding the box and picking out chicken skin and bones and gristle and a couple of fish heads. Trying to tune them out of this task but feeling their eyes on me and hearing the girl giggling, I imagine my explanation even as I'm throwing off my self-consciousness, choking down my petty embarrassment like a bitter drink, reeling over the mixture of odors uncovered and the thought that I'm already seen as a bum, smirking at the misconception and telling myself: I don't care, I don't care, I don't care. So what! Stick to your own maniacal program, bwoy.

Back at Paulette's I transfer the scraps to a plastic bag outside my door and then wash my stinking hands in the washroom. I change into darker clothes, a long-sleeve shirt, running shoes, load my pack with twine and flashlight. No camera tonight. I drink about a liter of water and leave, taking the scraps on the way out, prepared for an evening's adventure.

Half past nine. The nearest streetlight to Rollo's is at the corner where the Super Centre's located, about four blocks away. I approach as I did before, from the far side of the lane. All is quiet, the neighbor's lights on, Rollo's too, but no sound that I can hear. I slip into the first of the stucco slots to wait and watch. No sign of the dog. I move around back and into the other slot, routine position. I feel like a spy. Well, I am a spy, and a stalker too. A man with a new hobby, letting the minutes go by. I'm just watching his house. I assume he's there but I'm not sure. At the edge of my dark lane I listen hard, hearing no voice or music, seeing no movement. I walk to the other end, patrolling my narrow territory, staying alert, checking my exit. There is no way up the sides, no windows or pipes or means to the roof. There's front and back, a channel about forty feet long. From this end there is a dark office to be seen, the dark street, the house down the way where the upstairs baby and woman were. I believe I hear ambient domestic sounds, dull and sporadic, a sneeze, a window shut, a laugh, but these sounds might be nerves and silence mixing in my own mind. I hear a clattering, a car coming, a rattling roar that passes clunking up the street. The stillness returns. I go back to the other end. I wear my pack at all times. I can smell the scraps in the bag on my back. Fishy and fried. Can't the dog smell it? Does it ever go inside? Maybe it belongs to the neighbors. Doubtful. It's probably under one of these houses sleeping right now. I have to be careful though, not let myself fade into numbness, the blandness of waiting. Because something will eventually happen and if I miss it, there may not be another chance.

I see a shadow cross a window at the back. Must be the kitchen. The front room I've seen, there's probably a bedroom across from the kitchen, and a bathroom. The back door is opening and Rollo comes out alone carrying a bicycle. Takes it into the lane, climbs on and pedals past me into the street and turns right, passes the parked truck as I'm walking toward it, the truck between us as the bike rolls on. Alongside the truck I move, hugging the cab, watching Rollo ride away slowly, looking too big for his bike, and I feel someone watching me as I turn to see the dog standing between the house and the truck, appraising me silently, and soundless still as I move ahead beside the looming factory and on up the street, seeing the man turn, and then breaking into a run to follow.

When I make the turn, he's about two blocks ahead, not riding too fast. I can keep up by running, my pack bumping up and down. I stay at the curb, along the gutters, ready to leap next to a wall if he looks back, glancing down often to watch my footing. There are very few people out now, almost no one, but someone running like this looks strange. A man running at night with nothing to be late for. Fuck it, stay back a safe distance, hope he's not going too far. Heading straight for the river. I pass the Super Centre, cutting through the pool of streetlight, returning to semi-darkness. Jogging on my toes to avoid scraping my heels. No loud scuffs of a running man, but a smelly shake-up of the nasty scraps in the bag on my back.

He turns again and I make my next turn. At the next block he comes into view, resuming his prior direction, wheeling for the bridge over the Granville river. I slow to a brisk walk, coming up on a man who gives me a long look in passing. Rollo riding over the river now and I start running again, breathing hard, a car coming alongside me, its lights showing the bike up ahead, the driver checking me out, head sticking out his window to look back and see me still running. Crazy fuckin touriss is all it is, mahn.

I'm past the bakery and over the water myself, the rushing river near its mouth here, churning over stones and shallow patches below, Rollo turning left past the gas station and another car behind me, my shadow stretching far forward, elongated like a paper giant already reaching the other side.

I slow down, gasping for air, make the turn before the station and jog to the next block, this area north of the river, more dark homes, the small shabby district of Hopetown, its streets sandy and potholed. I bend over huffing, barely able to make out the movement of the bike in the grainy darkness ahead. I start walking, hear a car passing up on the main road, leaving town. Then suddenly I see a man walking toward me. We pass in the night, no words spoken. I hear a radio talking singsong. Some people on a porch.

"Goodnight," someone says, and I answer the same.

I smell a cigarette burning, sense shadows of a family quiet. A few lights ahead, homes alive and pallid. The bike has stopped, pulled off the road. I'm hardly walking, my eyes straining into the murky distance. I stop too, squat beside a car and watch him taking the bike up onto a porch, light spilling from a front window. He coughs, taps at the door, it opens almost instantly. When he steps in, I move forward, the successful surveillant.

At the railing I stand listening, hear the floor groaning in the front room, the muffle of voices, maybe a woman. I spend a few minutes where I am, smelling the garbage I carry on my back, glancing down the side of the house, up and down the silent street, seeking discernable motion and wondering if those porch people are still out, if they can see me looking at the situation and regaining my breath, settling down for the next move. The town seems shut down. The front room seems vacant.

I mount the steps without hesitation. A board creaks like a rusty nail extracted. I take the bike by its crossbar, lift it to my shoulder, turn and carry it down to the street. One glance at the house, the door, the pale curtained window, and I'm off, standing on one pedal and pushing the ground with my other foot, rolling away on an old and heavy and clanking cruiser, swinging my leg over and taking a seat as I look behind. No running, no shouting, no pursuit. I make my first right laughing. Right again on the main road. Picking up speed and watching the cross street for a man running to cut me off. And when he's not there I'm home free, heading to the bridge.

Wind in my face, a thief in the night, I'm the last man out in Granville. Over the river, I turn off the main road, clanging over bumps and weaving back toward Rollo's, giddy with adrenalin and speed and this first new stage of the war. My criminal career just beginning. Aware suddenly of hunger and thirst—the wind-hollowed dryness of my mouth—and the sweat running under my arms, the sap of fear, gush of victory. I left my water bottle in my room but there's no stopping now. Tonight's mission is not over yet.

I ease into Rollo's street, stealthy as I can be on this bike, coasting up between the truck and the factory. I get off and lean it against the truck's rear fender, walk toward the house like Rollo returning home, removing my pack, withdrawing the smelly bag of food scraps. I squat at the corner of the house and whistle softly. In a moment the dog appears at the edge of the house's undervoid. I open the bag and wait, the dog inching closer, materializing into some sallow representation of itself, neck stretching forward and nose working at this unexpected treat.

I toss over some chicken skin for starters. "There you go, Muttly," I say soothingly, a friendly food service making my rounds. "You hungry, Muttly?" I toss a chunk between us and the dog comes to it, crunching eagerly as it watches me. I'm in my pack, rustling around nonchalantly, muttering to the dog, letting it salivate and get a nasal reading on the reeking contents of the open bag.

I take out my twine, pull it through a loop to make a slipknot, a hand-snare for Muttly. I hold out a bone. The dog creeps forward, pulls it from my hand. With the next piece I coax it closer. Then closer. I lay the loop around the bag and give the animal some room, holding the length of twine wrapped around my fist. The dog puts its nose in the bag and I yank upward. It darts to the side, a fish head in its jaws and the noose pulling tight behind its ears as I stand. The animal growls and shakes its head, dropping the prize, pawing at the twine stretched taut between us, the noose threatening to slip over the head. I lift the front paws off the ground, choking the dog. It yelps and I let it down and scoop up the plastic bag, stuff it into my pack, sling the pack over a shoulder and change hands on the twine, get my other arm into the other strap.

The dog is making a sort of gargling noise in its throat, not too loud though, as I'm half-dragging it, convincing it to come with me to the bike. I'm looking around nervously, anxious to vacate the premises. I half expect Rollo to come raging out of the night at any second. The dog is not getting the idea whole-heartedly but we have to leave. I decide to drag it away from here and somehow hogtie it if I have to, then carry the hairy bundle by hand.

I straddle the bike and move it into the street, the dog trying to back up against its restraint. The harder it pulls, the tighter the tether becomes, and then I'm riding slowly, one arm stretched behind me, the dog gagging and retching beside the back wheel as we head precariously for the waterfront.

Some kind of circus act in the dark, me trying to keep the bike balanced while the dog, performing its act of recalcitrance, tries to upset it. I might be better off walking but I'm enjoying the absurdity of this small town rodeo, the animal thrashing and whining while I'm looking around for witnesses unseen, turning left on Bay Street, riding along parallel to the waterfront, peering into the spaces between buildings, catching sight of the sea rolling black and sleepy to the shore, turning right to reach the seawall at the end of the street.

Another block back to the right on my roundabout route and I dismount, holding the bike upright, the tether in my other hand, looking out at the jetty. Still no witnesses for the late show. Down the cracked concrete road we go, a walkway to the ocean, the dog reluctant, dragging its feet, scraping its nails like someone facing a gangplank. No moon, but the concrete showing whiter, and up above the eternal movement of the heavens, the clouds cracking open to reveal the evidence of stars, bright and abundant swimmers in a vast pool without fathom or shore. Down here a smell of sea floating on a sea breeze, an island asleep beneath the swirl, Muttly choking on stubbornness.

I wrap the twine around a cleat, pull it snug, continue on with the bike. The dog sits pawing at its throat, both of us revealed somewhat in this scanty starlight. I look back at the shoreline, searching for friend or foe or neutral parties, anyone in the open nearby. Looks like there's only me and Muttly though, so I start running with the bike, bringing it up to speed, wheeling it straight for a launching, braking myself and shoving the back of the seat, sending this old creaking conveyance flying off the end, diving to a reckless splash—a huge shattering of quiet rippling out into the night—and sinking like an anchor to the dark depths. You won't see it in daylight green either; must be at least thirty feet deep here.

As I walk back I see the dog standing on all fours like it's seriously considering the noise, looking past me, curious or maybe relieved that the thing went down alone."Okay, Muttly," I say, sitting down beside the confused animal, "this is the new deal. Relax and you won't choke." The dog stands looking at me, breathing raspily, while I remove my pack and plop the food bag down. The dog takes notice.

Muttly is scraggy. The dog is even leaner in this thin moonlight, ribs and some skin visible beneath light brown curly fur, a skittish demeanor and faithless expression, no hellhound but a spooky canine who doesn't know how to behave toward me, the man with the food and the tight leash. Even in this minimal light shining on the calm sea I can see a row of nipples. Muttly is a female. I push the bag to her and she stands smelling it a moment, watching me, her head low, her eyes rolled high, before she puts her face to the food.

Soon she's swallowing skin and cracking bones, her head sideways on the concrete. I feel immensely tired all of a sudden, longing for my last prepaid bed. We're both thirsty but I forgot my water. "I know this is crazy," I tell her.

I yawn, lean back on my arms while she finishes, coughing and gagging on split bone, getting the marrow, leaving nothing edible. I'm almost envious.

I stand with my pack, pick up the bag as it starts to blow away. We have to get some sleep. I'm wondering if Rollo has missed his bike, if he'll even bother looking for it. Been stolen, has it? I laugh. He doesn't know what hit him yet.

We walk back up to the street, cautiously make a turn. The dog is more cooperative now, generally walking beside me, accepting this strange situation somehow, occasionally pulling where her nose leads her. We follow the seawall a few blocks to the old dark fort, then turn toward the cathedral, toward High Street, with nary a soul around. A somnambulant tourist out walking his dog past midnight. Exhausted, I talk to the dog as I walk. The feeble sheen of light from the sky comes and goes, clouds moving all the time. Way up the hill a dog barks and moans, a far sound drifting away. We come to a streetlight and start to climb. Looking down behind, I see a loose grid of weak orangish lights spreading into sections as I rise. No cars in motion. A small town, looking smaller now. "We'll have to get out of here," I say. She looks up at me. Maybe she's glad to move on, who knows?

I crouch under the library porch but she's not eager to enter. I don't know where else to put her. Maybe she smells things, doesn't care for the unfamiliarity. "I'll be back early," I tell her, tying the twine to a post. "Don't let anyone take you." She smells my hand and I pat her head. "I'll bring some water in the morning," I say. As I'm walking away I remember one more thing. "Be careful. Don't hang yourself."

Time has a way of slowing down when you're alone. It stretches out into personal details that make you feel you can't get away from yourself, the idea of yourself, make you think you're missing the big picture. I start thinking this as I'm slinking back home so late like someone up to no good. "Sorry," I tell the watchman at Petit Paulette's, "I got lost." He doesn't say a word, shutting the door behind me and locking it.

I trudge up the stairs, overcome with fatigue and hunger, unwilling and unable to read or even think much. There's only sleep now, survival. I unlock the door and drop my stuff. The smell of the greasy bag is making me sick to my shrinking stomach. I don't want it in my trash basket so I take it to the bathroom and leave it there, wash my hands and arms and face and brush my teeth, drinking the tap water until I feel full. Stumble back to the room, strip, and collapse on the beautiful bed, every lump in place. A reasonably safe haven, full of clean laundry and the sharp stuttering calls of night lizards out prowling the walls. It's been a day, hasn't it? As I'm sinking away I see Rita standing in a pine forest. Guess what? I tell her.

I'm still here. I have stolen a dog.

Seven A.M. Horns and trucks already active. Curtains bright as rice paper. I lie rested and drowsy, desirous of another hour but experiencing a mild panic concerning the dog. I feel hollow and odd. There are gears grinding on the street. I step out on the landing, shielding my eyes. People everywhere, the day bustling along. Down the hall, someone using the shower.

Downstairs I get a cup of coffee, sip it like it's my last. It does a good job, gets my mood up a notch. I want another cup but I can't afford it. The other three people in the room are each having a proper breakfast.

I take off with my water bottle full, dodging cars and hopping gutters, walking briskly, climbing the hill in the early rugged shadow of the island itself. The dog sees me coming, as if she remembered my promise. I whistle and her tail twitches, almost a wag. "Hey, Muttly," I say, and she yelps once. I squat at the post and pour water in my hand, and she laps it out. She takes about half a liter before she stops. Needs a good bath, probably a deworming too, and breath mints. I untie her, she shakes herself and we start across the grass to the road. She stops and squats to pee and then we head down the hill.

We walk along the cemetery and around the edge of the town's center rather than through it. I don't believe she's well known, but I don't know that for sure. I have the feeling she stayed pretty much around her neighborhood, under the houses, though she was free to roam. Maybe she roamed some, had a bad experience and then stayed home.

I take her into Goodwill Park, tie her to a tree near the wall, a place that will stay shaded for an hour or two. Across the field I see another dog trotting along nose to the ground. There are a few people walking through. An elderly lady sits on a bench watching me. I give the dog more water and she takes it readily. I have the feeling she could be harrassed here, but all the young boys are in school now. Later, school kids will take recess in the park, mostly at the other end, I believe, and we'll be gone by then anyway. "See you later," I say, and walk off to conclude my short stay in the capital.

This will not involve much: a quick trip to the Super Centre to spend the last of my money, a shower and packing. That's it. I'm temporarily out of ideas. All this congestion and traffic is making it hard for me to think. I can't figure out what I mean to accomplish here. I need to back off, take stock, listen to the wind in the trees. Maybe I need love. How long's it been? Two days. Pretty soon I might not have the strength required.

Combing all the aisles in the grocery section, I'm looking at prices and figuring exactly which purchases to make, inexpensive and nutritious being the major criteria, this translating to sardines again, plus a mix of peanuts and raisins, entree and dessert all in one. I'm walking around with my few items, looking at choices, adding up small numbers. I look at the fruit longingly, planning a trip back to town on market day, Wednesday, then Saturday, eons in the future. I pick up an orange, put it back down, walk around some more. A few minutes later I have a small can of tuna and two small cans of peas deep in my pockets, standing at the register with the food I'm paying for, smiling at the girl who takes the payment, walking out with a small plastic bag and a few cents, no buying power, another crime behind me.

I walk down past the leather shop, glance over at the open door, a shadow entrance, and keep walking. I don't have my rocks, just these hard little sardine cans, food weapons. Not doing too well in this department. Maybe it won't be hand-to-hand combat. Maybe it'll remain guerilla warfare, the unseen enemy. Who the fuck knows?

There is the market area, empty, the river and its mouth emptying into the brilliant sea. As I get to the seawall I can see the jetty sticking out, a couple of boys fishing off it. Some boats beached right here: blue and white, blue and burgundy, red and lime green; fishing nets piled up in some like bundles of translucent wire. Good color, good light, but not shocking. Not new.

From the shadow of the single market building a man is watching me. He's an old man, gray-bearded, waving me over. As I get closer I can see the fellow muttering, wearing cardboard clothes, his suit dirt-colored, pieces tied together or sewn to allow movement. A sort of shingle tunic hanging from shoulders to knees, rags underneath. On broad calloused feet he shuffles back and forth in a cardboard hat, a round brimless affair that reminds me of those Russian bearskin hats, without the fur. The outfit shifts and flaps a little as he moves, his skin dark and dusty, wrinkled like an elephant's. He's working his mouth, glancing at my bag from time to time. His odor is strong and it's not a cardboard smell.

"Fah goo dollah dat bike go penty," he says.

"What's that?"

"Fishy doan rye down dere bwoy." He grins toothless.

"Try it again, Pops."

He points a hand toward the boats. "Catch he up, sell dem wheel." He makes a motion, fingers to the mouth, points again.

It's the jetty he means. "You're talking about a bike?"

He grins nodding, tunic scratching like rustling leaves.

"Had to drown that thing," I tell him. "Too late now, too deep. A bad businessman, Daddy-O, same as you."

He's looking like he may or may not see the similarity, tongue running over his gums, lips puckering into doubt or a kind of skepticism that seems to mean he lost out on the deal nonetheless, missed another opportunity, somehow got screwed. He keeps looking at me and glancing down at my bag, making it seem like he's owed something just for witnessing my wasteful act.

I move over beside the building, digging the cans out of

my pockets. He looks impressed by this, even more so by the knife following. I sit against the wall and he squats in front of me, arms across his wrinkled knees, watching intently as I lever the opener around the rim of a can, set it down and work on the next one, then the next. Three cans, two eaters. I hand him his peas and lift the other in a toast. "Cheers, Daddy."

He holds the can, looks inside, and gestures at the tuna.

"Eat your peas first," I say.

He's immobile as a resting cat, more interested in the tuna.

"You'll get your half, Gramps. Just eat the peas first." I bend back the lid and drink the liquid, eat the soft peas in small mouthfuls, chewing elaborately while he begins the same procedure, until I'm tapping the bottom of the can and he's gumming a green mush like it's hard to swallow or I need to see it, the first course in this breakfast of champions.

I divide the tuna, push half of it into my pea can and give the rest to my fellow diner. He stares at me eating with my knife blade.

"What, you gotta have silverware?"

"Whey de brid?" he says. "Whey de samich?"

"There's no bread, no mayo either. This is the meal."

He eats with his fingers, then runs his tongue around the bottom of the can, pushing it into his beard. I wipe my knife clean and stand. He arranges the empty cans in a triangle and shifts in his squat, twists off the circle of a lid and places it too, absorbed it seems in some crude geometrical figuring as I prepare to leave. "So long, Pops," I say, and he looks up, an ancient knight in cardboard armor; no lance, no steed, no windmills in his wanderings. No enemies but life itself, an urban ascetic walking through island days. "If you see Godot," I say, "tell him I couldn't wait any longer."

A saturnine and fastidious packing, a shit, a long and thorough shower, a shave, and then I'm on the road, pack on my back, the weight of Granville lifting as I walk. Hot now and

I intend to walk some distance, out of town and beyond the construction and big business sites, past the airport and harbor activities, before I start hitchhiking. Hitching with a dog, no less. Like it's too easy without an animal to dissuade most of the drivers.

She's there, right where I left her, and this time she's wagging her tail. I'm the guy with the water, remember? We take the path along the wall to the other end, behind the bleachers, and exit to the street, walking along the south bank of the river. Until the sweet and yeasty aroma of the Riverside Bakery stops me in my tracks. Breads, cookies, cakes, pastries. I stand outside breathing deeply, letting these warm and rich fumes overpower me and work on my mind. I tie Muttly to a signpost and step inside, drop my pack by the door. The owner is in the back, baking. He's busy mixing dough but listens as I ask about old bread, anything he'd like to toss out, telling him I got robbed and I'm waiting for some money to arrive from home. But he says no, he was closed on Sunday, he just started the fresh goods this morning. He says come back tomorrow. I thank him and turn to leave. I'm hefting my pack, cinching it up, when he comes out with a little loaf and slips it into a paper sack and hands it to me.

The sun rippling off the rolling river, me and Muttly crossing the bridge among the throngs of pedestrians, people taking notice of a dog on a leash and a foreigner with all his possessions. Everyone's helping me lose my pride. That's okay for a while. Now I'm a beggar, a liar and a thief, succeeding on some level, I tell myself. Now I can make a samich. I try to see who's looking at us without looking concerned. We're walking at a pretty good clip, the dog on the inside away from motorized traffic but smelling too many people, as if she's looking for someone she knows, for the way home. We're exposed out here. I'm glad to be leaving town but this area is like a funnel that handles everyone on the island, the point through which all residents must pass. It sounds strange to say it but I'm not terribly displeased. I just don't want to be seen. I don't want to show my hand or drag anyone down with me.

But look at this day. Hot and clear, the sea so fine and easily seen from this coastal road. I've got some bread and all my clothes are clean. I'm going camping now, up into the forest again. I know my way around. Here's the road to the technical college, and to the hospital, if one were to need such a place. Plenty of traffic on this work day. Anyone might give us a ride, toss the dog in the back of a truck. Once we get through this industrial sector we'll be clear, take a turn to the interior, start climbing. If I could only walk without thinking. If I could only meditate, and not talk to myself.

Passing the road to the quarry, to the prison. Another mile or two and things will change. I see landmarks—cement silos, petrol storage tanks, the airport tower, banana sheds, boxing plant, fruit juice factory—points along the human stream, while off to my right the land is always rising, heaving up in rifts and tangled hills to the untamed peaks, the lonely and indifferent forests of rain and silence. Bear with me, Muttly.

Finches roadside, coast and capital gone behind green curves, the folding, twisting switchbacks, the beginning of elevation. A few turn-offs to houses seen standing in their chopped-out plots, a sort of suburb, this Mount Pleasant settlement, with much less traffic and most of it presumably local. The road running jagged up through the middle portion of the country, some fifteen miles or so angling in a southwest to northeast direction between the major peaks, an alternative to the more traveled coastal highway, this is the way to Rocklee. We stop to rest and try for a ride.

People are looking at the dog tied to my pack. I wave as they pass. Hitchhiking is mostly luck. Auto-stop they call it in Europe, which sounds like a demand, but you have to have luck. If you're walking, drivers are less likely to stop. They reckon you're getting somewhere, closer to wherever you're going, which is true. You don't seem serious. You're not paying attention to the act of begging. You're nonchalant, like you don't really need much help. On the other hand, if you find a good spot—a place where the traffic slows, where you're clearly seen as a non-threatening gentleman bum, or just some regular someone who momentarily needs a hand, where there are no other ride-beggars nearby and where it's convenient for the car to stop—you just stand there facing each possibility with an honest, amiable face like you mean business, like you need to get somewhere, same as the people looking you over. After an hour with no luck you start thinking about changing your spot, like fishing, about moving up the road just to feel a sense of progress, about what you'll do if no one ever stops.

My hand is out to gently flag a Land Rover on the slow upgrade. Grinding and spitting smoke and going so slow I could reach out and smack the driver who's staring straight ahead and pretending he doesn't notice me. A red Toyota traveling the opposite way comes flying downhill, squeals and brakes to a skid across from me, a white woman at the wheel.

"Hello, Mister," she says, her accent music to my ears.

"Sheila! Well, hello there. Good morning!"

The car idling, brake lights on, she watches me wave, noting the pack and the dog, about to move on it appears, but staying instead. Her arm reaches between the seats, the emergency brake ratchets a burp. I cross the road and stand beside the car staring at her, neither of us knowing quite what to say. Her brown hair's hanging loose, windblown about her shoulders, her eyes blue and clear, no sunglasses worn, and she has on a touch of blood-colored lipstick. As I lean forward looking inside I see she wears a white dress shirt not completely buttoned and blue jeans. With my hands on the door I feel as if I'm bending to her level, that I'm about to whisper something important or kiss her. "How are you?" I ask.

She shakes her head a bit. "This is amazing to see you," she says. "How long is it you are here now?"

"I don't know," I say. "I can't leave."

"Why not?" She's looking at me curiously, then she looks across the road. "Mein Gott, now you have a dog too."

"You're going to town," I say, close to the window. "You look well." I feel I'm being drawn into the car almost, some sort of vortex powered by the engine vibrating into the palms of my hands and pulling me, and I'm suddenly feeling genuinely excited to see her, this proximity working on me, making her a long lost love, someone I never expected to see again.

"You look different," she says, pulling back, focusing her gaze. She seems to be trying to recall something.

"I'm glad to see you," I say. "I don't know why. I just am. It's a shock to the system."

Her mouth turns down at the corners and she looks away, glancing at the passenger seat, at the shaking gearshift, at the gauges in the dashboard. She reaches up and turns the key, the car shudders to stillness and quiet, and she clicks on the hazard signals and their regular blinks sound like a timer on the conversation, time allotted for an unexpected meeting. And in that brief period my eyes drop to her shirt front and past the two open buttons and into a cleavage so deep it looks to be the softest and most wonderful place on Earth, a place one could revisit easily and therein make a home for the night.

"Where are you going?" She reaches to the floor for her purse, finding her cigarettes and lighter.

"Up near you someplace, in the forest for more camping."

"What?" she says, a kind of funny frown on her mouth. "You have to be so near me?" She glances at me, cigarette in her lips, thumb on the lighter wheel.

"I didn't think I'd see you. It's a pleasant surprise." A

tobacco cloud rises into my face. "You know, Sheila, what a marvelous time I had at the Red Ginger. Naturally, I thought about another visit, thinking if I was in the neighborhood I might stop in, but I thought since you threw me out—"

"I did not throw you out," she says, smoke leaving her nose, lipstick on the filter between her fingers. "You ask for the check, Mister Weatherman."

"Maybe so. I got mad, you got mad. It just happened. It was nothing serious, was it? I don't remember. I remember the good parts. I'm not mad anymore. Are you still mad?"

She shrugs, flicks her ash between my arms. "Das macht nichts," she says. "It is nothing to keep inside."

"That's good to hear. I'm glad to hear it. I feel better about the whole thing."

"I should be angry with you," she says, "because you have stolen my book."

"What? Oh, you mean Nietzsche. I didn't steal it, I only borrowed it. He's been a great friend to me. You don't know. But I'll return him when I'm finished. I promise."

"I don't think your promises are so strong."

"It's right over there. I can give it to you now or give it to you later."

"Give it to me now."

"Sheila! I might be stranded out here for hours. All I have is Nietzsche and that mangy dog."

She smirks, smoking, looking at my hands. "You're a bad boy," she says, and starts the car.

"It was nice to see you," I say.

"Are you alone again?"

"Just that bitch over there."

She shakes her head, lips pouting. "How can you auto-stop with a dog?"

"Not too well so far."

She puts the car in first, it jerks and I step back. She sits there giving me another look. "Bring the book," she says, and pulls forward.

"Wait! How long will you be in town?"

"Three hours, no more."

"What if I can't get a ride? You'd pick me up, wouldn't you?"

She smiles and shrugs, hand on the wheel, two fingers holding her cigarette, and looks back to check her clearance. "We will see." The car lurches into the road and rolls on around the curve.

I pet the dog. We take some water, settle into the shade, rounded clouds roving high overhead, popcorn clusters floating in off a hot sea. Cars pass. Butterflies and grasshoppers enter my vision but my eyes stay mainly on the page, stomach grumbling to interrupt. Chickens cluck and scratch at the edge of my hearing. A girl with a stick leads three black and white goats past us. A red truck clatters uphill, crates of soda bottles rattling and clinking.

You flow for me almost too violently, fountain of pleasure. And often you empty the cup again by wanting to fill it. And I must still learn to approach you more modestly: all-too-violently my heart still flows toward you—my heart, upon which my summer burns, short, hot, melancholy, overblissful: how my summer-heart craves your coolness!

Sheila drives past me and then stops up the road and lets us catch up. I guess she thinks this is funny. I put the dog in the backseat with my pack and I get in the front. She tells me she knew I would be here, and I say I'm grateful for the lift, but then I get the feeling she wants me to be a bit more obsequious, more like Muttly, so I don't say anything else, just let her drive while I look out at the dense, unmanaged world we are entering, the thickets and the steep drop-offs into feather branches and vine netting, the road we are on a thin and perilous track barely allowed to hold its place across this craggy eruption of landscape.

"Have you found the photos you want?"

"I don't know," I say. "I doubt it."

"Are you working still?"

"I'm between ideas at the moment."

"Is the dog helping you?"

"The dog is just with me."

She gets herself a cigarette and lights it. "Are you having some troubles?"

"I don't know. I might be."

"The more you stay, the less you know."

"It's all work, Sheila, and the spaces in between."

"Like a bee, from one flower to the next."

"Something like that."

"So where is the honey?"

"You're the honey."

We drive on in silence until she clicks on the radio, punches up some island music, the car dancing into turns she knows so well. She brakes for geese, honks, and they honk in return, scuttling along the road in single file. Soon the engine is working harder, the altitude is less gradual and I feel light-headed, lost or kidnapped in a swaying motion, the terrain too abrupt and prevalent, all views a diorama of green profusion, a rain of leaf and vine, my stomach hanging apart like one piece of a mobile, separate, flat and hard, turning on mild currents of breeze, a smell like garden herbs blowing through the car, stirring the dusty fur and bad breath of the dog staggering to and fro across the backseat.

"What troubles you are in?"

"Financial."

"Oh, that. But you still keep your freedom, no?"

"It's enlarging even as it shrinks."

"I don't understand."

"Vast possibilities I'm not sure I can choose."

"Are you playing a game with me?"

"I've temporarily lost my descriptive powers."

"You are making no sense, Jacob."

For a second I feel like she's mothering me. "What's on your menu today?"

She looks over at me, I know, but my eyes have closed and I slouch as we pass the gas station, ducking any citizens of Rocklee. I pull my cap lower, just some sleepy white man being brought to the Red Ginger, a disinterested tourist passing through.

"For lunch we have swordfish omelet with carrots and peppers. Tonight I make eggplant linguine with shrimps and olives." She pauses and I feel her eyes caressing my face. "I will bake pastry with kiwi fruit and papaya inside." For some reason she's speaking with a heavier accent. "Does that sound good, mein Liebling?"

"My stomach is drooling but I can't afford it."

"You are masochist, to hear, to dream, but not to eat."

"I can take the pain as long as it feels good." I conjure up a vision of sardines. "I feel tired but I like the way you drive. I feel weak but I like the way you're helping me."

"You sleep outside but you like the bad weather."

"That's it. You're so astute, so bold. No one can touch you. No one can hurt you. So solid and yet so soft." I turn to see her. I see the dog gagging to vomit but spilling nothing.

"What is the matter with your dog?" she asks.

"Carsick. Don't worry, it's nothing but air."

She glances back at the animal's head-dipping. "I don't want sickness in this auto," she says. "I will put it out."

"She's fine. We're almost there."

"She is empty. Do you not feed her?"

"She likes leftovers." I say. "Table scraps."

Sheila looks from Muttly to me, to the road, to me again. "My food is too rich for animals."

219

"Too rich for people too."

Her eyes shift between the road and me. "You hurt me already," she says. "You know that."

"I didn't think it would be so easy. I thought you were the boss. I thought you wrote the menu."

"That is true. And now there is no more pussy on it."

"I have to say at this moment I'd prefer linguine."

"Ah," she says. "In this game everyone must tell lies—why?—hide what they feel, what they want."

"You don't want to hurt me, do you?"

"Perhaps, but I am too busy today." We pull into the driveway between hedgerow flowers waving like heaven's marionettes. "I can offer you a cup of tea."

"I'd love you dearly for it, I swear to God."

She stops the car and stares at me. "Don't look so sad."

The restaurant is empty. I sit at the bar waiting, gazing out over the railing and the dog tied there, over Sheila's orchard and into the western valley's slopes, my view stuck in clouds piling up like dumplings rising to cling to the mountain spine, rain slaves assembling before Morne Matin, in whose rough embrace I'll make my camp.

Sheila brings out a pot of hot tea and a cup and saucer and places them on the bar as a van pulls up outside the open door. I can smell the strong black tea as I slide it closer. The cup rattles against the saucer as I take my first sip. There is no sugar but I can't release the cup or bother to look for any. A local man in a knit cap gets out of the van and walks over to the base of the steps. Sheila steps out onto the porch and lifts her hand in greeting. "Hello, Jonathan," she says.

"Good afternoon, Miss Sheila."

"What do you have for me?"

"I got fresh fish and fuel, ma'am."

I'm looking at the dog looking at me drinking my tea when I feel someone else watching me too. I look over my shoulder and see the boar's head on the wall staring down at me and in my head I hear a voice. *Smith get fucked up bad and dead too, bwoy!*

"Yeah, where does that leave me? In a loop of repetition. Here I am again, right?"

Beat dat sweetheart, slaughter dat hog!

"I know all about it, but I didn't see it happen."

Woan be no reincarnation nor resurrection reward.

"I'm with you on that."

"With me?" Sheila says. "Who are you talking to?" She stops beside the bar with a bag of fish in her hands.

"Nobody," I say. "Do you have plenty of ice? I don't hear the generator." Suddenly I'm interested in the preservation of food which I am no longer entitled to eat.

"Of course," she says, frowning at me. "The ice maker is running every day." She looks either concerned or displeased, or both.

I leave the saucer, take my cup, and walk outside. I stroll into the orchard and stand among the trees, in the citrus air, looking up through the leaves, but not seeing much of anything, sipping my tea and thinking about foraging for food, thinking about pictures of food. Every still life I can remember blends together in a wooden table painted full of food. Pheasants and rabbits, harvest vegetables and plump fruits, all of it fresh and beautiful and abundant. Warm game and cold fish, grapes and melons, huge walnuts and meaty pecans. Leeks and kale and squash. Texture and taste for every palate. Every hunger. Every tongue and every eye. Entrails and organs, tripe and sausage and kidney pie. Cider and ale and black bread and corn. Squirrel and dove and deer and hog. And somewhere you can bet there's a still life with dog.

Bunches of hard green bananas, fruitless mango trees. I move down the rows, shopping for ripeness and photogenic quality. I stoop to rescue two grapefruits from the ground. They are dull to the eye but smell worthy of consumption. I find a rotting papaya and poke it with a stick until it breaks open and I can see its rosy flesh, the color so sensual and pleasing to my hungry eye. But I don't know what to do with it. I feel loopy, like I can't depend on anyone, least of all myself. My surroundings seem confidential. Sheila has become obscure. I see Clifton at the end of the row dragging a tangle of brown vines. I follow him past a trellis to the barrel in the open yard where debris is stuffed for burning. He glances at me, the teacup and grapefruit I hold, and returns to his work.

I stand by the barrel imagining the subsequent fire and my resultant photos, sensing the abstract value in a man burning trash at dusk, the cinders rising in waving demise, the flames and smoke against a purple sky, the man working in hazy action behind the waves, his race and common standing perhaps known though his identity is not, the work itself of interest, the ordinary made original, the bizarre allure of fire, its elusive nature, its light and heat shaping the man behind it, disparate images of flux and loss revealed.

To turn it around, what would this man think of himself recorded? Of his mundane task imbued with meaning beyond its due? Looked at for explanation and drama where none exists? By us, by the viewers, by me, capturing such an event with solemn presence and manner detached, just as likely to invest my time and see equal worth in a pile of plump figs nestled in a sun-crossed bowl. I can't weigh the value of a photo against any effect triggered by gaining it. I stand aside and shoot. This is my fabric and my bane, my work and the source of my worry. With the click of a shutter I commit acts of pathos and harm.

Does this make me abstruse? I'm trying to become involved, maybe change my doctrine, but it's hard to be both detached and immersed; one seems to occlude the other. We think without acting and act without thinking. And right now I need to get my esoteric ass up in the woods and camp, keep myself going.

Muttly doesn't know what to make of the forest. Has she always been an urban waterfront dog? By her haunted glances she appears surprised and curious, but I can't say whether she feels more of a feral freedom or a foreboding. The sun is high but heavily strained through torn clouds and the land's green covering. We take our time. Along the trail I find again the sweet red berries and remember that spectacular day with Rita two weeks ago. I eat the berries as soon as I find them, pebbles of juice that tingle with flavor and vitality. The dog tries a few from my hand, biting slowy with her gums showing, looking unsold on tart flavors.

The trail narrows. We walk on leaves and sticks now, the trees huge around us, the dog looking around suspiciously, unlike me, who feels grateful to be here again—the place remarkably quiet, relatively dry at the moment, a few birds here and there, lizards shifting position as we near. Muttly stops to sniff a centipede and jerks back at her discovery. The air feels good. I stop to breathe, to listen, to feel the substance, absorb the wonder as much as I can. I don't know what to call the feeling I have here. Beauty doesn't begin to describe it. The clean ripeness of the air, the tree ferns unrolled, the colors of bark and moss, the encircling pillars of jungle, protective yet open to the unhurried. The absence of sound—no cars heard down on the mountain highway, no machines or engines of any kind—save the wind, that steady presence of air in the trees above, a faint whistling that blows and fades around small skitterings and buzzwing passings, the chirps and wingbeats woven into their element like threads of tone. It's like I'm standing amid a treasure that cannot be held, and I feel blissful shivers that seem to penetrate to the cells of my blood. Doris would say this is simply the touch of God but I don't have a name for it. I don't have a picture of it either.

223

We come to a stream, the dog gorging here on a liquid diet. I tie her to a tree, drop my pack and leave the trail, treading crackling steps along the watercourse, scanning the slope for any semblance of a flat spot to harbor the tent. I'd like to be near water and only as high as I have to go. I don't need to be up with the mountain whistler, the hawk or the bamboo view. I need a compromise. I'll be a commuter using the highway for my trips to Granville but I'll need to be hidden when I'm here. I mustn't discount hikers or hunters or criminals on the prowl.

The incline steepens. It's clear that the flattest spots are part of the trail itself. I pause to consider direction and weather. What I can see of the sky is opaque. Soon it will rain. I want to maintain privacy and freedom, safety without walls. And surely as much comfort as possible. But there are no meadows here, no beds of grass, no fields of clover.

Returning to the trail, I come across a tamarind tree and pluck several hard pods. I crack one open on the trunk, pull out the brown sticky center with my teeth, scrape its tart acidic meat from the seed while I walk. Muttly looks somewhat befuddled, standing in the water as if she's cooling her heels. She is certainly hungry. I fill my bottles upstream and we continue our search. I'll have to clear an area to make camp. What I need is a machete, but what I find instead is a heavy stick, forked at one end, to use as a rake. Maybe I could find a hefty stone in the stream, use it to beat down roots and shrubs and young growth, use it to force a flat spot, but I don't do this. I keep climbing, dragging myself and the dog ever upward.

At the first stand of bamboo I drop my pack. Muttly is breathing poorly, looking out of shape. "At least you're not going to the elfin woodland," I say. "Up there you'd be crying for a doggie sweater." Much farther up I know there is an area of pines, an accumulation of needles on the ground, but I'm not exploring anymore, I just want a base camp. What I do now is locate an acceptable spot above the trail—one place is nearly as good as another—a space among trees clear of serious undergrowth. I rake it with my stick, pushing leaves, snagging roots and erupting shoots. The place is sloped, of course, so I move the leaves and matting to the lower area. I tramp around in my boots trying to flatten what I can, create a surface that will accept the tent. Muttly is watching and listening to the cracking of sticks, the breaking of limbs, the scratching of my jungle rake. My shirt is soaked, my arms already tired. I look camouflaged by debris. I tremble with weakness and hunger, but the tent must go up before we eat. We must have shelter beneath the canopy. This is not an easy place to live, though we are alone. I'm trying to make the best of this stubborn beauty, letting my mind wander, letting all creatures know we are here, a man and a dog from town. I rake bamboo matting onto my ground sheet, carry loads back to my spot, build up a mattress of sorts, spread a layer of leveling cover, sucking a clean tamarind seed, drinking my own saliva, thinking about Rita and Blandy with his little pistol, picturing people I've known— those at home and those more recently met—a phalanx of family and associates and lovers and friends and enemies, and none of them here. They are out there, down there, over there, in towns and across the sea. I'm on my knees spreading forest mulch, shuffling leaves and rearranging the lives of earwigs and spiders, millipedes and beetles. The dog scratches her resident fleas, probably collecting fresh parasites. And I'm making a home, wondering about human lives. How we regard each other. What value we have. Examining the old precept that people have the most value, that everything else is secondary. Other species get pushed to the far reaches while we crowd the expanding middle with our banter and orchestrations, our moral wars and take-over moves. Our sheer numbers. The enemy is all around.

The blue tent stands again, leaning but stable, the edge of

the ground cloth a front stoop where I sit arms on knees facing downhill and feeling completely dizzy and worn-out, like I've just landed here and don't know where I am, resting on the slope of a heavily wooded ridge spiked along its valley side by bamboo thickets, beyond which opens an airy ravine sunken among a family of rugged peaks. Still no rain and it's after four.

I wash my hands and spread out our meager supply. Cut open the bread and make a sardine sandwich, soak up all the liquid so the dog eats what I give her, pieces doled out so she doesn't wolf it all down too fast, so she appreciates the situation. The leash allows her to sit near my feet and her snapping bites almost take my fingers. It's a game, eating slowly so we might almost feel satisfied. The bread and the sauce and the salty fish are not too bad. We drink our thirst away—we have water in abundance—and now there are only nuts and raisins left, plus the grapefruit. And the tamarind seeds.

I walk down to the trail toward the bamboo. Looking back up the ridge I can't see the tent. On the other side of the thicket I glimpse clouds settling deep in the mountains. I can smell the rain, the air moving cooler, and shiver pleasantly while the bamboo rattles and scrapes in hollow wind chime sounds. I hear no birds and see no lizards. The trees are sighing, exhaling around me. The wind and thickening clouds push me toward sleep. This is what is meant by being alone.

When I lengthen the tether, Muttly is able to crawl under the edge of the rain fly and into the unzipped doorflap of the tent. I lay out my sleeping bag and stretch out in my clothes listening to the first drops falling, the pits and pats like light-footed animals forming a circle around us. But there is nothing out there except rain falling through trees, forest music, a sleeping drug, and all is forgiven in rest.

I wake in total darkness, fumble for my light, startle the

dog, who lifts her head at my feet. The rain has stopped but I zip us mostly shut, Muttly inside, and lie back down. If a pig or a possum comes nosing around, the smell of the dog will turn them away. You stink, Muttly, but please sleep well.

Fatigue is our king but I toss and turn while the night creeps close. The dog stirs and growls. I dream of confusion and wake on the slope as if I'm about to stand, the bumps under my body poking at my bones, dampness seeping into slumber, the dog turning in circles and curls of repose.

There is the comfort of trees. There are twigs and leaves falling and a green dawn dripping. We emerge like mushrooms peering timidly from the earth to the sky.

I take the dog down to the stream to stretch our legs, to drink. The walking, the cool air and the wood-songs enliven me, her too I imagine. She smells where we have been before and does not look frightened. She lowers her head and laps at the water trickling down this good morning mountain. My back's a little stiff but I feel pretty strong, pretty wild. When I piss on wet leaves the rising steam smells like cereal, like corn flakes soggy in the bowl.

With the dog secured out of reach of the tent I put a few items in my daypack— water, food, book, clean tee shirt, rain jacket, toiletries, camera and my last three rolls of unshot film—and sit down and eat a grapefruit. Then brush my teeth and head down the trail whistling quasi-carefree.

No customers. No cars except Sheila's but no sign of her as I walk past the dining room and down to the cabins. I can hear the river rolling over its rocks in the trough below. I could bathe up the mountain but this bathhouse is so convenient, so unused, it seems like the place to be. It's all the same water, isn't it? Or nearly.

Tree frogs waiting for night on the wall behind the door, dormantly adhering, bodily functions cool and slow, brown skin permeable and moist, their white throats beating infinitesimal pulses like soundless diaphragms worked in swallows. A cricket escaping the spray crosses the floor. I rub my bare itching feet on the rubber mat, cold water running over my face, down the pale topography of my body. Turn off the water and lather my head, soap myself joyously. Quietly. I hear someone coming down the path, walking around to the door behind which I stand chilled and suds-covered.

"Do you believe you are a guest here?" It's Sheila. Of course.

"Hi there. You don't miss a trick, do you?"

"Are you trying to irritate me?"

"I'm just trying to get some special treatment."

"You must ask me before."

"Excuse me. Do you mind if I shower?"

"Next week I have reservations for two cabins."

"Okay, I won't come next week. In the meantime I'll try to stay clean."

I hear the rasp of a lighter, her deliberate inhalation. "Did you get too dirty in the forest?" she asks.

"Yes. Could you come in here and wash this thing for me?"

I can smell the smoke while I'm waiting. "You think you are so shocking to me?"

"No, I'm only pushing my limits a little further. It's a crazy feeling."

She pushes the door open and stands holding it with one hand, cigarette at her side, looking at my nakedness, my skin cold as a frog's, but some warmth percolating in the loins as her eyes draw heat to the region. "Now you need more soap," she says. "Your thing is growing."

I hold out the bar in my hand but she shakes her head.

"You do it," she says, and takes a deep drag of smoke.

"Sheila, don't disappoint me like this," I say, rubbing the soap along my springing appendage, this slippery, mindless animal trying to live its separate existence. I drop the bar, continue the motion with a ring of fingers, hoping the sight will pull her in and draw her fitting hand to mine.

But she just stands watching, cigarette smoldering. "You don't disappoint *me*," she says. "If it goes you get a coffee."

"You know it goes," I say, thinking back, knowing she is remembering too, these mutual thoughts driving my hand like a milking machine, letting her play me for anything she wants, this handjob hers in my mind, while her devious eyes roam all over me and I tighten upon images floating by, her heavy breasts hanging over my face, her hips riding me as I take a swollen nipple into my mouth, my eyes closed as I lean back alone, a logical conclusion being reached, the outcome dripping in soapy foam to the mat.

There is a hiss as she drops her cigarette at the doorway. "You see, you don't need me for this," she says, turning on her heel, letting the door shut. "When you are finished you can come to the front."

I'm famished. I'm always hungry after sex but now I feel weak in the feet, not just the knees. I know she's jerking me around some but I don't care. I'll play her game and maybe she'll play mine. No big deal. I need things; otherwise I'm fine. I'll have some coffee and probably use her toilet too.

She's sitting in the dining room, a coffee pot, sugar bowl, milk pitcher and two cups on the table along with cigarettes and ashtray, and a notebook into which she's writing. Her cup is empty so I pour coffee for two and take a seat.

She speaks without looking up. "Did you bring the book?"

"I did, yes, but I'd prefer to hang onto it a bit longer. As I said, my only friend at the moment and all that."

"Ah so. You do not think of me as a friend."

"Sort of hard to say. Look what just happened down there. I can more easily trust a dead guy."

She seems about to laugh. "You know, you are going more

strange." She rolls her finger over and over in a loop beside her head.

"Do you object?" I slurp my coffee, both hands trembling.

"No, no. This is not my problem. It is only interesting to see. Like a film.

"I'm just trying to survive."

"What do you mean? With no money, just an ugly, smelling dog. Living in the forest. I don't understand your motivation. Why do you not go home? You are like someone who cannot find his life again. Is it a game? Do you find it funny?"

"Yeah, it's funny but I don't laugh as much as I used to."

"So it is not very funny."

"Not too funny, but funny in a new way. At a lower level."

"You should go up, not down."

"When you're up you can fall. Likewise, when you're down you can rise."

"You bore me with this talk. I am a practical woman." She lights a cigarette, looks at her watch. "Do you have some other business to speak about?"

"Yes, in fact I do." I finish my coffee and refill the cup, add sugar and milk. "I plan to be around here a few days and as you know I don't have any money." She is blowing smoke in a fine stream over the table as I look at her. "So I'd like to sell one of my cameras."

"I have camera."

"Maybe some customer—"

"You see any tourist without camera?"

"No, but maybe a local, who knows?" She looks at her watch again like I'm wasting her time. "The other idea is a very good deal for a businesswoman such as yourself. Say I take some beautiful photos of the Red Ginger for a brand new brochure, or even postcards. I give you the film undeveloped and you use it whenever you want. You don't see the pictures right away, but then I don't charge you a normal rate, either. I don't charge you anything, really, but you help me with a few things I need."

"I have brochures."

"Those pictures are bad. The place looks like a dump."

"I took them myself."

"I can't tell what I'm looking at, a brothel, a factory, who the hell knows? You need something fresh."

She pushes her cup away. "What things do you need?"

"Not much. I need a kitchen knife. For camping. And some scraps for the dog, stuff off the plates that you're going to throw out anyway. Little things I might think of, maybe a beer some evening."

While I'm waiting for her answer the phone rings. Sheila stubs out her cigarette, stands and goes to the bar. When she returns she collects the dishes silently while I sit light-headed and hungry, wondering if we have a deal. She turns away. "Sheila, what about a sandwich?"

She stands looking down at me with some degree of pity. "Come back later," she says, "I'm thinking about it."

"What's with the accent? It seems heavier."

She frowns. "I am speaking the same like always."

I start with the bathhouse, reckoning I'll document the entire place for her, sort of a bonus. The sun's out so I snap a couple of shots, then go inside and take a seat. Sitting on the toilet rethinking our shower encounter I experience another stiffening, and when I'm finished with my main business, I stand in the doorway light pointing myself to the sun and the next picture is of the thing itself.

Another bonus. There, stick *that* in your brochure!

Muttly is wrapped around her tree, head to the trunk, watching me approach. "You idiot," I say, reaching for the twine. I start to lead her around and she snaps my hand with a bite like wire cutters and I leap back falling to the earth, holding up my left hand to see blood running freely from the flesh of my thumb down my wrist. "What the fuck, Muttly!" The dog sits watching me like I'm the crazy one. I stand and fling my hand down, spotting the leaves in carmine-dotted lines. "You don't bite the hand that feeds"— I stop myself. "Oh, I see. Goddamn you, is that it?" The dog is displeased with my care, or diseased in some way not visible to the naked eye. She cowers against the tree at my return. "Yeah, you expect the usual treatment, don't you, you schizophrenic ingrate." I untie and unwind the twine from the trunk and drop the loose tether on the ground. "Go ahead and take off you miserable bitch!"

I sit down and unzip my pack, get the peroxide out of my bath kit. The dog comes forward, seemingly remorseful. I offer her a look and she smells the blood, gets a lick before I can snatch my hand away. She sits and watches me treat the wound foaming and burning under the antiseptic poured. I dry the area with my shirttail, stick a few band-aids over the cut. "Bad dog," I say, and she waits to see what else I've got.

She likes the peanuts, spends a long time chewing each one. She eats a few raisins too, but when I cut open the last grapefruit she draws the line. "If you ever bite me again," I say, eye to eye with her, my hand throbbing like a toad's throat, "I'll throw you off this mountain."

I scavenge the vicinity for dry wood, dead bamboo, make a pile near the tent, cover it with my poncho. The dog follows unleashed, seemingly content with my company now that it's not forced. I'm sucking a tamarind seed like it's hard candy, no other food in sight, wandering the woods, examining the shapes of leaves and the assorted spores underneath, thinking of digging for roots and snails and cooking them over fire. I lie down in the open tent to nap the midday heat away, wondering if the dog will kill me in my sleep.

When I wake, the dog is nowhere in sight. I shut the tent and shoulder my bag, embark again on the steep and lengthy walk down to the Red Ginger, looking for work in Sheila's world, badly wanting her now and desiring any dose of decadence she might provide.

I am amazed at how quickly I've succumbed to a day-to-day rummaging. What a narrow rail I walk to be free.

I shoot the cabins, make them look lovely this afternoon, and red ginger blooms born into soft crimson cones, signature images good for the cover page. The sun comes and goes, clouds thick but frayed formed over a warm companion, this fervent jutting earth of tree and stream a perfect mate for atmospheric intercourse.

I wait in the dining room for light to strike, for sharp western rays to cut between the clouds and under the roof and through the room to the patio, where a party of four sits finishing a late lunch. I position Sheila and the new girl, Darlene, at the edge of the foreground—as elegant profiles only, I say over their protestations—and focus on cutlery and crystal at a table the viewer is invited to take, as the sun peers teasingly and then bursts radiant upon objects of silver and glass that catch the light as it ricochets from surface to surface, the patio people seen as background clients.

Sheila brings me a cup of conch salad with hearts of palm and purple cabbage. The clients push back their chairs to leave.

"Did you ask them if they'd like to buy a camera?"

"That would be strange," she says. "I told them you were a professional working on a new promotion for me."

"I'll ask them."

"You must behave yourself. I sell food and drink here."

"What about their scraps?"

"They have eaten all."

"Sheila, I need food for the dog."

She turns to see them out. One man salutes me so I salute

him back, and after they've piled into their car Sheila brings me a beer, and sits. "What happened to your hand?"

"Nothing." I put it in my lap and guzzle a mouthful of good cold beer and glance over at Darlene clearing the patio table. "How's the new help working out?"

Sheila is tucking strands of hair behind her ear, rolling my lens cap back and forth on its rim over the tablecloth like a wheel going nowhere. "She is not so good yet but she is learning." She smiles. "You wish to have her also?"

"Only if she begged me."

"You are the beggar, not she. You are the vulgar one."

"You're right. I'm hoping to appeal to you again."

"You want me to feed you, don't you?"

"I want you to be the platter, the bowl, the fountain."

She looks over her shoulder as if to make certain we have not been overheard, and turning back says, "I don't know if you are hungry enough yet."

"I need the key to cabin five," I say. "I might find some light still lingering in there."

She gets up and goes to the cabinet behind the bar, comes back smoking, and hands me the key. "I invite you for dining later," she says.

"What have you got?"

"Calamari with basil and mango-apricot sauce."

"Sexy, but I don't know if the dog likes it. What else?"

"Chicken breast with cilantro and tomato."

"Save some for the dog or I'll feel too bad to eat."

The light in the cabin is unsatisfactory to me. I sit listening to the river through the open windows, then remove my boots, lie back on the bed and slip into a deep nap. In a dream I'm being pursued by a rabid pack of dogs running up the trail behind me. I scramble up a tree just in time and hold the trunk in a panic as the animals leap and snap and snarl below me. I'm gasping and sweating, wondering if Muttly is among them.

It's night when I awaken. I have no idea where I am until the generator sound—a vessel in the harbor of an island civilization—ships my mind back to cabin number five. Around the room my flashlight beam roams like a flickering ghost, finds my feet in a pale spot that flutters and vanishes with the spirit of dead batteries. But I'm alive, lying here in the whispering dark.

Sheila enters and locks the door, lights a candle on the bureau, carries a wooden tray covered in foil and linen napkins to the bedside table, the contents betrayed by the aromas they give off, hints of chicken and seafood and basil-tang and cheese emanating in claims of epicurean marvel from a private bill of fare. The queen chef herself sits on the bed to remove her shoes, surveys her subject, not some complementary king but a kind of cabin boy in waiting, hungry but not starved to ineffectuality, simply unfilled, somehow sustained by insufficient decisions.

The subject lies fully clothed, inactive but amply attentive to this silent supper, his stomach leading all other organs in anticipatory homage to the courses to come. The river's evening breath blows through the room like a cool accomplice and the woman pulls her dark dress over her head and lets it fall, stands over her laden tray of bait and her craving prey like some Saxon priestess, her skin in the wan light sallow as uncooked dough, the black undergarments just thin packaging strips across edible flesh.

Her fingers pry and stir into a bowl and move across the pillow to my ready mouth. Sweet and minty mango sauce drips from a squid curl I suck from her hand, and she traces the sticky remainder in a line downward from the base of her throat. She the server becoming the served by illustration, this motion telling me all I need to know, that she is the surface of this healthy repast. The rules I'm able to intuit: a meal taken slowly and thoroughly, all of it eaten if dessert be desired.

She lies beside me, breaks baked brie over her breasts, flakes of crust litter her skin like confetti and warm cheese drools like blond mud over the mounds, drops of apricot almond glaze trickle on the tips and soak nutty-sweet to the skin inside the cloth, quantity far surpassed by flavor, a buttery blob of cheese in my throat and stains of glaze licked from the ends, the sheer lace encasement a barrier now but not to be removed by me the feeder, for I understand my only task. I don't speak. I don't touch except by mouth. I don't do anything but eat these gourmet morsels. I don't hear anything from her except breaths caught and released, and single vowels escaping with air. I am the happy cabin boy.

Each taste enriches the next. Cheese and fruit and tender chicken. I understand the game, but I have never seen her so sloppy or wanton. She lies on her back and brings stewed juices—tomato, cilantro, bits of meat in broth—across to her belly and down to the silk panties left wet and savory as her ladle passes. My mouth follows her tasty trails, gets whatever sustenance I can raise while on my knees, hands at my sides, tongue grazing and working as a supple pick, lifting an almond sliver from the pit of her navel, these minuscule servings meant only to advance salivation. She doles out the ladle's contents in small measure. I search high and low for meat, bloodhound maw rippling over soft, slippery terrain, sucking the cloth at her crotch for flavors held, lips running down ribcage curves—she squirms at the tickling—and up the slope into the hollow of her arm, brie-streaked but free of perfume or powder, nothing but a culinary fragrance until I delve deeper, up into the musk of heated regions.

I have not kissed her; there is no food in her mouth. I pull hard at the scalloped lace of the bra, teeth clamped to reveal hidden skin, hungry as an infant. I don't want cloth here. She reads my wishes, loosens the material and pulls it away, her hand returning to drizzle mango sauce, basil leaf draped over a nipple and sucked away. She offers another and it too is taken, then more. Every ingredient is sucked off these summits that suckle me like wineskins—sucked in hunger to get drunk, sucked hard. She whimpers and cries sharply. I am biting too, a cannibal in the making, carnivorous and so dangerous she is slapping my head, knocking me away with the heels of her hands until I fall back, my own hands uninvolved but my vision twitching, my head resting on her belly, my eyes blinking after sharp blows, while she trembles and shudders under my face. Her hands come down to her hips, plucking the waistband and pushing down as she wriggles, tossing me off the surface as her knees come up, no cloth needed for the last course at this table. She spoons up liquid and leftovers, spills it over her pubis and I become a dog at the bowl, a pig at the trough, a pig-dog rooting out bits of flesh in her flesh, lapping at broth, spreading her thighs to deepen my feeding.

A squid tentacle caught by tongue and brought across the succulent slit, everything edible for the omnivorous glutton, an apricot devoured so personally and every last nutrient masticated until nothing is left but sopping sexmeat and one little standing giblet still in need of nibbling. Sheila cries out, muffling herself in a pillow, scratching the sheets, releasing more broth.

With the candle flickering I lie in troubled pain, restless tongue still moving, cleaning my teeth and savoring the meal, playing a good game but needing to be eaten too. I have an idea. I'd like to feel some squid rings pushed on, worked down this swollen shaft, forced on if need be, stretched and slid, as many as will fit, one above the other from base to head, squeezing bands of elastic meat applied and then eaten one by one, her diligent teeth pulling the top one off, chewing it there with her lips brushing the squid pole, crawling down for the next, then the next, sliding each tight piece up the shaft and over the head, reaching lower for the next, deep-throating for the last band held fast at the sack, lubricating the squid with her mouth's fluid, working it up in a long pull as if it's troublesome to remove, dragging it up slowly and finally popping it off as my captive ink is expelled for empathy and consumption and deliverance.

But the imagined second half of the meal—the banquet on me—does not occur. Sheila has no appetite—too much tasting in the preparation perhaps—or no interest in reciprocating, or the food is gone, for she sits up, slips off the bed and stands to pull her dress back on, then collects her underthings and lifts the tray. I'm thinking in horror and consternation that I'm to be left behind—sex slave and cabin boy, fed just well enough to clean the bedclothes—when she leans over and whispers, "Come wash me," and I dutifully rise and follow.

She flashes her beam on a bag hanging from the porch railing, says, "For the dog," and we start up the stairs. She unlocks the door and we go through the dark living area with its couch and chairs and TV to the galley kitchen where she deposits the tray. She lights a lantern on the counter, moves into the short hallway and enters the bathroom and shuts the door. I wander past the adjacent office room into her bedroom, find a thick white candle on its own pedestal and light this too, and pass through the connecting door back to the living room and remove my boots by the entrance. I spot a bottle of rum on the coffee table, partake of a few sips while I'm standing at the window watching a car pass out front on the mountain highway, the shower running now and Sheila calling me. On the bookshelves I see pictures and light a match. Sheila, and her husband, I assume, smiling at the camera during the construction of the Red Ginger; Sheila on a Caribbean beach; a very young Sheila in a bikini on the deck of a boat on the river Rhine, I guess. Then I get undressed and make my way back to her poster bed of white pillows, see myself in her wardrobe mirror, swilling rum and standing naked as a newt.

"Where are you, mein Leibling?"

I draw back the shower curtain, step in beside her in the warm spray, the smell of herbal shampoo in her hair, candlelight fluttering at the curtain. She is soaping a washcloth for me, breasts jiggling between her arms. Such a lure, these fine assets! Naked and wet and driven by senses and thoughts seeking further stimulation, we are powerless against the well-felt urge, the internal forces of provocation. Our parts like magnets muscled by potent codes. How are we to combat or resist or withstand this primal pull? Only immediate survival takes precedence. For now, let no one and nothing disturb us here at the easy edge of a smooth union. We live in endless cycles of attraction and consummation. As soon as we recover we want more, like food. No wonder there are so many births. The deck is stacked against us.

I wash her back and front, holding a hand on one side and pushing the cloth across the other, rubbing the front's upper contours over and over until her big breasts are swimming in suds, and she stands with eyes closed while I work down the flanks and into the middle pass, my hand slipping down between the cheeks to reach the soapy cloth and tug it under, working it up and sliding it back and forth in a froth of cleaning, the cloth then dropped and hands continuing over the territory, running up and down to meet below, slipping into any crevice, probing with soap every entrance opened.

Sheila leans into me sleepy-looking and says, "Clean me well."

My fingers find further purchase—two in front, one in the rear—while hers hang useless at her sides and her body goes limp as a dishrag until I kiss her. She shuts off the water and opens her mouth to mine and we stand close and slick together, her arms around my neck and me holding her low, fingers inserted in the places found, my bobbing cock lathered and lonely out on its own.

"I am ovulating," she says, squirming on my hands.

"What?" I say, not quite getting her meaning. "Right this second?"

She's ovulating! No longer on the pill she means. All out of conventional weapons. Okay, you can always work another angle, but you like to feel that thing get inside. I'm working her with my hands but she has not taken me in hers, my poor fellow nosing sadly against her thigh and needing only a destination. Anyplace tropical. South of the border.

"Not in front," she says, her eyes dewy, the corners of her mouth turning up in a naughty grin. And when I wiggle the posterior finger she nods, lips brushing my face.

She turns away and bends over and places her hands at the corners of the tub. I'm yearning to take this place, one hand free but the other still in possession, holding a reservation in the auxiliary canal, savoring the offer of her posture, this view of hips wide at the bend and the cleft before me, middle finger digging into the target path, free hand roaming for soap, its edge like a squeegee blade pushing suds to her ass, reaching under to pinch slippery nipples, returning to stroke the rigid probe.

She moans upon its throttled entry, a forbidden journey into the tight fist of God. An uncanny evolution this joining of parts. Who can argue with it? Sing the praises of whatever fucking you like but if the shoe fits, wear it. Who can be faulted? Who can toss the first stone of condemnation? Who can deny this gripping pressure, the suck of the savage anus—no fear of ovulation here. Jesus, how the mind wanders! Holding her hips, milking all I can from this lesser slow-hole. How do we keep from repeating ourselves when we love our own patterns? I can no longer name my old mistakes. I can say anything, do anything, think even more than that. Standing easy-headed with my hands groping at the physical world, striving to be wild and honest and concerned with a comely partner I don't even love.

I'm aware of her one-handed stance, the other touching herself, so I'm careful not to knock her over or bang her head on the wall. I don't need to move much in this exquisite grip but I can't focus solely on her, even stuck deep as I am in her barren socket. She's mumbling in German it sounds like, and I've got my own problems just below the surface. I'm so glad to share this time with her, to make love anyway she wants, but I wish she were Rita. And it's Rita I'm thinking of again—my apologies to Sheila, Germany, and all of Europe—as muscles are tightening and noises are rising, the squishing of soap squeezed out of our meeting, the mutual moanings of love-making in general, Sheila sounding like she's muzzled, and I think of dogs and feel my hand bleeding, the bandage hanging like loose skin, and in the downy furor of my spermatic firing I swear to God I hear the ringing of bells.

"Ah, the phone," she says, "so late." Sighing and coming uncorked, I stagger back under the showerhead, propping myself against the wall and turning the water back on. "Something is wrong," she says, stepping out.

"Wrong number," I say under the fine spray, a vermilion trickle flowing between my feet to the drain, thumb burning, prick dripping in hot tingles.

There are only two or three more rings. She comes back from the office and steps under the shower. "Something is strange," she says. "No one spoke."

I step out, my bloody hand wrapped in the washcloth. "Is the door locked?"

"Of course," she says, but I wrap a towel around my waist and walk through the bedroom to the front door, find that it is in fact locked. I pick up the rum on the way back, pour a splash over my thumb at the sink, groan quietly.

She towels herself and tousles her hair, puts on a robe taken from a hook behind the door, stands looking at my hand, then watches me drinking at the sink. There is already a secretive impersonal air in the room, separate tracks of thought leading off into the night.

"Can you dress this for me?" I ask, and she steps into the kitchen for the lantern.

She opens the cabinet, takes out scissors, tape, gauze and antiseptic cream and has a good look at the wound. "Maybe you want to get—" She makes a motion like sewing stitches.

"No, no, just make a good bandage."

"You don't want infection," she says, fussing with the materials nervously, like she expects another call. "I forgot," she says without looking up, "there was a call for you."

"When? You don't mean just now."

"This morning." She's trimming the wound's ragged edges.

"Who was it?"

"I don't know. A man."

"What did he say?"

"He only asked for you, and I said you were not here."

"What, like I'm not here right now, or like I haven't been here in a long time?"

"I only said you were not here. He hung up."

I drink and she works quietly, asking me if I want a glass or aspirin, wanting to take care of me in some way, and I shake my head. When she's finished we move to the bedroom and she starts the cassette player—classical strings and French horns waltzing—and we sit in the candlelight looking at each other, she on the bed with her robe tied and me in a wicker chair holding the friendly bottle. Coconut scent burning.

"You are not hungry," she says.

"No. Thank you."

"I want you to stay all night," she says, patting the bed, "sleeping here and making love."

"Alright. I'd like that."

She stands and opens the wardrobe and opens a drawer and tosses a vibrator on the bed. She smiles and reaches for the rum and takes a mouthful. She bends and kisses me, rum-coated tongue at the roof of my mouth, then straightens and pulls open the top of her robe, takes another mouthful and trickles liquor from her lips to her left nipple, alcohol cooling and rosy skin rising. She hands me back the bottle but I'm ingesting her performance. The pedestal candle twisted off its base and her breast put forward, coconut wax poured over the blushing tip, Sheila wincing, fist clenching as drops spill to the towel across my lap, her hand trembling above a stripe of solid encasement forming, the beginning of another skin, and it seems she wants to create a molded globe, a tender and malleable prize for me to peel and eat.

I settle the candle in its holder, a definite stirring occurring beneath my towel, reach past her for the vibrator, turn it on purring like a testing apparatus or a miniature V-2, beige plastic and smooth, a toy rocket missing its fins. And I'm slowly rolling it along her inner thigh, teasing it toward the launching pad when the phone rings again. Sheila freezes and straightens, pulls her robe closed and glances at the window though the curtains are drawn. I turn off the toy and the ringing continues, three, four times, the sound jarring, the classical strings still humming low around us in a mood diminishing.

"I'm not here," I say. "I checked out last week."

She catches it after the sixth ring. "Hello," she says. "No, he has gone. Don't call at night. No, he left last week. Goodbye." I hear the phone replaced, the door shutting.

"Same voice?"

"I think so, yes. Who is it?"

I stand with the bottle, carry it into the hallway and back as I pace. "No one knows I'm still here but you."

"What do you mean?" she says, tying the sash of her robe. "Did you make a news story about your departure? I saw you standing on the road. You were not invisible."

In the living room I peer out at the road from the edge of a curtain. "Do you have a gun?"

"What? What are you saying?" She's yelling now. "No, I have no gun. Why do you need a gun? Who is calling for you?"

I drop the towel and begin to dress, underwear, jeans pulled on, hopping on one clothed leg.

"What are you doing?" She grabs my arm and tugs. "It is better to stay. Tell me what is happening, Jacob."

I sit down to pull on my boots. "Someone's after me, Sheila. It's better for you if I'm not here."

She kneels in front of me. "You must talk to me. We are making love, for Gott's sake."

"Look! Some people might come here looking for me. If they see me here you won't be safe, even after I'm gone. You understand that?"

"Who is it?" She's holding my wadded shirt like a hostage.

"It's nobody you know. I barely know them myself."

She goes to the window and looks out, turns to look at me as I stand. "They want to kill you. Is this what you mean?" She says it with such sarcasm that it sounds ridiculous, so maybe she wants in on the joke, or wants to be included in a perilous possibility, the buildup of tension and the eventual release. Maybe she longs for an edge to her idyll. Romance and danger.

I shoulder my pack, go into the bedroom, unscrew the base of the vibrator and remove the batteries, put them in my pocket and pick up the rum for another slug while she watches. "This is not fair," she says, "taking my things, using me."

"It's only as fair as we can make it."

"You tell me shit!" she says. "This is something about Rita, is it not?" She throws the shirt at my head.

"I don't think she has any toys."

She slaps my face and the sting radiates into my head like a wake-up call. She stands holding her fingers, biting her bottom lip so that she looks angry and sad at once, and even with my face glowing I feel like holding her tenderly.

"It's got nothing to do with her. I insulted a guy and now I guess he's gone crazy. I wanted to stay with you but after that call I can't. I don't want you involved in this so I'm going, simple as that, okay? If you want to help me or help yourself, don't tell anyone you've seen me or know anything about me."

"So you will leave me here alone."

"I don't think anyone will bother you if I'm not here."

She sits suddenly on the bed, looking at the floor, still holding her hand, and I see a tear fall to the carpet and I know she's not going to look at me again and that I need to leave quickly. I set the bottle at her feet. I don't know what else to say so I leave the film I shot for her too, and then place my hand on the top of her head. I feel pretty bad as I leave, locking the door behind me.

Halfway up the driveway I remember the food for the dog, go back to the porch and untie the bag from the railing. It makes a thud as I set it down and I squat in the shadow of the porch to open it, even the palest starlight cast on the yard and gravel drive dangerous to me as I listen toward the road for anything approaching, the bag full of slop smelling like mashed excerpts from my last meal, a flat fold of paper found inside and slid from this an old and rust-coated, thin-bladed kitchen knife that feels like a useless tool, the cutting edge eight inches of nicked and dull steel that might make a decent letter opener if neither nail file nor pencil were handy. I slip it under my belt nonetheless, locate my flashlight in the pocket of my pack and substitute the fresher batteries for the dead ones, which I keep for wicked projectiles I might want to send spinning through the dark. Thus armed, I hop to the ground and move quickly up the drive into real dark, anxious for invisibility and solitude, for motion and progress, stopping at the hedge to peer long and hard into the black silence of the highway, and then I'm gone, trotting up the road and entering the night forest, my whereabouts unknown, intentions unclear, carrying a cache of smells that should attract every night-crawling carnivore within miles and feeling scared fairly shitless myself, wondering why I left my perfect throwing stones in the tent, grimacing skeptically at the plausibility of my own actions.

I don't use the flashlight until I'm off the road and into the trees. Even then I wish I didn't need it, but with only a star field scattered behind a mountain's clouds, I must see hints of the dense and shifting way before me. Once I'm inside, striding in clacks and knocks over the stony trail, pale pool of light jerking along ahead of me, I realize I would have to be carrying the brightness of a runway light to be spotted by anyone in the Red Ginger's vicinity or even at the trailhead.

Still, I stop to listen and flick my beam around every few minutes, tossing the precious light up the trail before me, bouncing it between the trunks of trees while I tilt my head to hear beyond the crickets and night-singers pausing at these sudden interludes of light disturbance, then playing on, then pausing, then resuming, while I strain to hear beyond my region for human sounds—machinery or voices—and from here and there in the distance, or from above, comes a hooting or a hiss, or a whistling undefined, and close by in the stillness the smells of the bag climb my neck and poke into my face and jam my nostrils and tie up this one sense so profoundly that the other protectors—sight and hearing—are over-stimulated and too imaginative in their reconnaissance.

I imagine there are three or four guys in a small car barreling up the mountain highway on a mission, all wild strength and murderous intent, thighs and biceps and muscular shoulders crammed together and moving restlessly, arms hanging out in the cool air, hands already reaching toward me, the easy prey.

So they arrive at the Red Ginger. It seems quite likely to

me that they have done so, or are en route at this moment. I imagine them on the incline approaching the drive, cutting the engine and the lights and easing close, parking roadside, creeping near the hedge to peer in on the property, to check things out.

Maybe a light is still on, maybe not. They are trying to figure out if I'm on the premises but there is no way to tell. They are muttering among themselves, discussing the possibilities. A basic search of the area, the cabins in particular, or else they consider going right to the woman, questioning her directly, peeking into her closet and under her bed. But suppose these men are not on this occasion acting rashly or thoughtlessly. They are passing a bottle but they are quiet, studying the building, the windows. Blandy puts a cigarette in his mouth—he thinks he doesn't give a fuck—and Rollo slaps it out before the match is struck. Rollo tells him once and it will not happen again. There is a gun among them. One is enough, to be used only at close range, maybe a matter of inches, when the outcome is no longer in doubt. It's not that the job is deemed so large, but it's easier in a group, like going to a sporting event, safer with the boys, getting up to no good but also taking serious matters into your own daring hands. A single crime in mind, or several; the line is faint between.

I'm hiking on leaves now, the beam at my feet or on the trail ahead. When I stop to listen and rest I cut the light to conserve its juice, and stand in the sound of my heavy breathing, an unilluminated denizen of the dark fearful night. Will they hurt Sheila? Rollo could rape her. Ask questions and tear the answers out. Will he kill her? No—she is local. It'll work in her favor, being white, European, won't it? Or it might be reason enough to slit her throat. If it becomes a spree. A rampage. If I've triggered a rampage.

The dog-bitten thumb beats like a heart at the brink of my body. As I walk I begin to worry about rabies. I begin to wonder if I'm not a little feverish. I spit white flecks at the ground, my mouth dry as dead leaves, and conjure up the foam that might be forthcoming. I remember myself as a boy at the movies, seeing *Old Yeller* going crazy with hydrophobia, gnashing his teeth and foaming savagely behind the woodshed door, no longer the valiant and loyal dog he had been, but a demon fit only to be destroyed, to be bullet-blasted from existence by the boy who was his best friend. It was tragedy beyond anyone's control and now, so many years later, I am likening myself somehow to the boy and his plight, though the boy was not bitten and my demon is human and not my friend and I do not possess a rifle.

I come to the stream and glance up and down the gurgling course, looking for drinking beasts, I suppose, my hearing impeded here at this noisy flow. I cross it in two steps and squat facing the trail I've ascended, my lively senses operating fully, my light on the rippling surface so I can inspect the water filling my canteen. When I'm finished drinking I stand and feel for the thin rusty blade at the small of my back.

More hiking and I hear the bamboo, the creaking and scraping of hollow poles, the wind-driven percussion of chambered pipes, and continue ahead, moving alongside the massive stands—impenetrable forests within the forest—inspecting them as I pass, looking between the individual stalks, their shadows in motion with the light, vertical bars rippling sideways, the forest moving as I am, or still if I stop, my beam catching a black rat as it disappears into the thicket. And I can feel the air now on the valley side, sense the open space like a vacuum amidst the tree-held peaks. Out there are the hunter owls, invisible shapes against a dark cloudy sky, dropping in silent plummets of feathered death, a shadow strike in a disturbance of ferns, rising with a faint rustle and prey lifted skyward. But nothing's going to attack me from above or fly me out of here either.

My tent is nearby but now I hesitate to go there. I've been gone all day, and it may be gone too, or ransacked. Wait. What was I thinking? My camp could've been found. Now I see the trap. What a nitwit. I'm walking directly into it. The place is staked out. They lie in wait, knowing the camper will return. The phone call helped. But what phone? Where? And how could they know? That call should've kept me away, kept me at Sheila's. Then wait a minute. Stop this shit. Stop the reversals, the second-fucking-guessing. How could anybody find me so fast? They're just fishing for clues. Get a grip on yourself. Get out your rusty shitty flexible brittle worn-out kitchen knife and go over and see for yourself if anybody is there.

But first get rid of this stinking bag of food. I bend a young stalk of bamboo down over my head and tie the bag to it, let it go, and it stays, swaying away from the bunch, hovering over the ground like bait, a summons to all the intelligent and agile rats of the neighborhood. Over here you shifty bastards, away from that camp.

I consider approaching the tent from behind, but what's the point? I'm off the trail now, my feet making a crackling racket as they come down, and I'm holding a light in one hand and this ridiculous blade in the other. Proceeding as planned a moment ago.

The blue tent, the covered pile of wood, an undisturbed camp it seems, and I appear to be alone. The beam rises into the trees above the camp. Bark. Leaves. Limbs. Down to the blue skin of my home away from home. Also a perfect hiding place. Standing there with the light on the door flap, the zipper closed like I left it. I slip off my daypack and set it on the ground, balance the light on top, beam cast across the flap. One hand on the zipper, knife gripped tight. This thin fabric like a shroud too, I'm thinking. Maybe a dead animal inside, maybe that hapless bitch Muttly. Zipper creeping up and I think I'll see Rita's head, her body, some horrible sight, or someone leaping through the opening as I fall back in terror, knife raised to impale whatever issues forth. Light poking inside and there is only what should be. Three stones retrieved. Hand shaking on the re-zip. I shut off the light, pocket my stones. Get a fucking grip! There's only you. Breeze and bamboo chimes. The everlasting insects. Piping frogs that sound like insects. Night lizards that sound like birds. A motherfreaking rat.

I grab my canteen and stand gulping water down the dry gorge of my throat. Sweat under my arms, my body hollow as bamboo, not as strong. Listening into the night. Breathe, man, just breathe. Calm and rational. I need to sleep, rest, and wake to the light of tomorrow. What day will that be? Wednesday, true? Market day in the big town. And all that goes with it. But first the night. Can I read? No, I have to save battery power. There are no luxuries here, just you and your head. Just—

Something is moving. I turn, hand on bark, upright and stable behind a solid trunk. There is something walking out there. I lean out to listen. Someone coming up the trail. I crane forward, holding my tree. No voices, no light, but someone moving. Flashlight and knife in my left hand, round rock in my right. Smooth hard stone rolling in my palm, very solid, very clean.

A gust of wind rustles everything above, tree debris falls around me, the sweep and rattle of leaf and limb covering all smaller sounds. I crouch at the base of my tree, twigs dropping like rain, waiting to hear approach or passing as the air travels overhead and blows away, leaving a sort of hollow silence in its wake. Then I hear a scampering and stand to determine its nearness, knife-fist braced against bark and throwing arm cocked, the sound crackling sideways or coming up the slope or receding in my ears, leaves and sticks crunching into the sounds of motion. I'm listening and looking about in the grainy space, eyes drawing upon all illumination filtered down, seeking movement among the dimmest shapes, seeing leaves as the merest mottled sheen, the charcoal poles of trees, the serrated mass of darkness everywhere.

A throat noise over there, but no more movement. It waits. Dog? Boar? Man? I hold the knife out with the flashlight and take aim. The beam hits the ground, finds a furry face flinching in the brightness. Muttly strained and snarling, squinting into a shaky light. Miss Huckleberry Hound, displaying her teeth.

A quick flash around to see that it's just us here. Hackles up, head lower than her rear, she watches the light, smells me but has a shortage of trust, an abundance of fear. "Muttly," I say. "Take it easy, girl."

The beam points out the tent, the camp, the way down to the trail, but she won't take her eyes off me. I pocket the rock. She growls, going wild pretty quickly. I look behind her again, listening down the trail. I stay where I am to let her readjust to me, see that I'm no threat. Now I see she's still got the twine, about six feet trailing from her neck. Lucky she's not caught up someplace. But then maybe she hasn't gone anyplace. I step around her and move down the slope and she follows me.

She watches me cut the bag loose, drop it open on the ground and step back. She waits, unsure. "Go on," I say, my light on the reeking sack. She glances back at me, takes a step, then another, her nose reaching forward. I squat, less threatening. Her head dips into the bag. Voracious hunger. She peers above the edge of the plastic, swallowing rashly, and keeps feeding. Rich human food. What a rank smell. Must be the dog too. I wipe my nose along my wrist, catch a trace of Sheila's soap.

The dog's going full bore, a couple of chicken bones gone cracking in short order. I leave her alone, go up to the tent and get the mess kit bowl and the water and bring them down. Put the water bowl next to her head. She looks up, licking the fur around her mouth, and after a few more nips and licks at the loose bag, sets herself to the water and laps it all up too. She stands cleaning her wet chops while I fill the bag with leaves and dirt and find a place for it back in the bamboo out of sight. Then I take the metal bowl back up to camp.

Save the light. Thoughts don't need light. I sit on the mat at the front edge of the tent. I'm not sleepy. I'm wishing for that rum I should have taken. No, I'm not. I need to be as alert as possible, even if I fall asleep at some point tonight. I'm thinking about being asleep in this tent and being a captive audience, a sitting duck for assault, trapped in nylon if and when the shit goes down. I can't get that scene from *Easy Rider* out of my mind, the one after the diner where they're camping uncovered in the woods, and those cretins from town sneak up with clubs and lay into the three sleepers and Nicholson's character takes a blow that stops his life from going any further.

I'm thinking I'll have to sleep elsewhere with the tent serving as a decoy. You can't take a chance if it means maybe getting beaten or cut to death in your sleep. Axe handles, bats or machetes, what does it matter? You're still dead as a fucking doornail. Who cares if the assailants are white, black, or mixed? They're men, aren't they? And you, the unprepared, caught-by-surprise, unlucky object of their hate, have become a mashed up, beaten-to-a-pulp, unrecognizable bloody sack of shit. You insult someone or they don't like the way you look or the way you think, that's enough right there. Is it simply the way it is, a fact about ourselves that's beyond our ken? Something so absolutely basic that we're unable to rise above it except in theory, a trait we can only conquer in our ideas and dreams, in our aspirations toward a better version of ourselves, toward greatness, even, if you can swallow that much dreaming.

The dog approaches me and smells my outstretched hand and I pat her wiry head, her matted back, pour a little more water in the bowl and she takes a few laps and then sits near my feet. I guess she likes the deal now. If she sticks around I'm hoping she'll wake me in time, before any trouble starts, barking with alarm or joy, I won't care which.

I drag out my mat and sleeping bag and zip the tent shut. With the light cupped at my side I start up the ridge, going someplace above the camp but not far away, and the dog follows. I have my daypack with canteen, camera, book, and toiletries. I wish I had a hammock but I don't, so that's that. Just lie down and go to sleep in the open with hostiles approaching from all sides in your frightened mind. Easier said than done.

Here's a spot. I don't expect to sleep much. Tramp it down some—so loud at night—look for insects running, hidden colonies in residence. Examine the area, the stalks and shoots protruding from ground cover. The mat goes down unevenly, the bag spread open in a large rippled square, my territory, and nearby I brush my teeth, spit at the base of a tree. I sit on my lumpy pallet listening to small sounds, the wind, a faint screech down toward the valley, frog whistles, the dog walking about the area. I lie back, stretch out tired, more tired than I realized, fully dressed, long sleeves buttoned, the air cool on my face, then sit up, put my jacket on, lie back down, arms crossed over my chest, one foot across the other, a folded shirt for a thin pillow, knife stuck in the ground behind me, the three stones under my pack, right beside me. The dog steps onto a corner of the pallet and settles there. Sleepy like me. Peaceful out here, really. I sit up to shine some light on my square. A big cricket has entered my zone but I suppose that's good luck. The dog is curled face to tail, eyes lifted at me. Alright, lights out.

A little later something's walking around but it's small. No worries. The dog is my alarm. We're breathing ourselves into sleep, Muttly. I smell her and she smells me. Thinking about Rita, hoping I can see her in a dream.

Sleep comes in sputters and flickers, like the uncertain light from a bulb about to burn out forever. I know that's a metaphor for death and I don't particularly like it, but it's on my mind and will not leave. It's an interesting subject, all will agree, but no matter how much you look at it and examine the idea of it, you cannot know it until you pass its gate, and by then it's too late to know anything else at all—probably. What's the purpose of thinking about an event so pervasively guaranteed and unalterable? You don't want to lose sleep over it, but you can't help it sometimes. I know it looks like I'm heading for a fatal confrontation, that I must have a death wish, but I don't. It's just this situation I'm in; it hasn't run its course.

I'm no crazier than anyone else. I love life the same as most people—what else have we got that's real? I like to take a good picture; I like to wake up in love; I like to read a good book; I like to travel without many plans; I like a shifting mix of the expected and the unexpected; I like to swim in rivers and oceans; I like to walk; I like to see sunlight coming through trees; I like old cities and snow and live music and all the kooky things I've been doing these last few days. All of it, the good and the bad and the stuff in between. I'm not saying I haven't made mistakes. I'm not saying I haven't been rude or cavalier or predictable. I'm only saying that if you asked me, I'd say, Yeah, I'm too young to die.

Muscles twitch; body shifts from back to side to back; a belch of basil; memory whistles down the wind; melodies of time and space: old TV theme song and *Shall We Gather at the River*. Black bike sinking in the sea. Am I lying in a meadow? Grass tips bending in a gentle wind. Ticklish situation. A blanket spread out. Who is this squirming girl? Faceless and eager, day or night I cannot tell. I cannot even see. But feel the nocturnal erection. Oh yes, I am alive. All systems are go, my ticklish friend. Hey, is someone here? HEY!

Frantic neck-slapping to get it off. Some thing! Scramble to my knees, hand flicking at my collar. Shit, what is it? Find the light, shine it across the sleep zone. Gray spider going over the synthetic edge into the land of leaves. Reach for the knife to stab at the ground, but then stop. At the side of my neck I feel a swelling welt, painful to the touch. Fuck! Am I poisoned now? Neck burning like a hot bulb. Dog standing to join my concern. "Goddamn it, Muttly, keep the animals off me!"

Walking around my area, to the tent and back, breathing hard and touching the bite on my neck. What next, land crabs? Taking a mental inventory of my first aid supplies, thinking, I already know I'm not going to do a goddamn thing except wait and see what happens. It's just a bite. I'm healthy and I have no allergies. I almost trip over the dog standing still and looking puzzled about what's going on here. Was I thinking aloud, I wonder. Does the dog wonder about my swearing? No, I'm fine, Muttly, go back to sleep. I'll wake you if anything's about to kill us, okay? You titmouse!

Feels like a lemon under my skin. Now my brain flashes an image of Rita's mother, Angela, a close-up of her neck problem, the evil-looking growth protruding there. What is that, a goiter? Rita said she was sick. She's overweight and she looks depressed and her neck is distracting to the viewer. Is it the big C? Is it a tumor? So common, more common than a spider bite. I'm sure her life hasn't been easy and I wish her well, I really do, but I care more about Rita's freedom to be with me. I think she wants me. Maybe she just wants a man, a relationship.

The baby, though, the family, the white picket fence and all that, no thanks. You have to hold the line somewhere. You have to stick to your guns, maintain your principles. I need to tell her the bottom line. Is that it? The baby or me, sweetheart. I'm sorry. Probably couldn't. Maybe I'd loosen up, let her make the decision and then live with it. Make the best of it.

Reroute my selfish road. It's possible. If Rita comes with me I might send Angela some money to see a doctor. You can't let a growth like that go unattended. Maybe she's trying to pray it away, a little bit every day. Maybe she would go to Guadeloupe and see a French specialist. I'll ask her if she'd like that. Of course, I'm assuming I'll see her again. I'm assuming this bite, this night or tomorrow, won't kill me. I'm assuming I'm invincible, the undying star of my own grand and perilous life. I don't have any money now but I'll make some more. I'll work harder. I'll do good works and make a difference, help someone else through their grand and perilous life.

What else is there to do? Life is a string of little things, acts and words and images, memories of what you did, who you are. I know it's totally pointless. I believe that more than anything. Still, you do the best you can. You live your life the best way you can. You live timid or brave, honest or cheating, afraid or outlandish, thoughtful or stupid. You eat, sleep and shelter yourself, collect a few items, work at something, watch TV, make love or make a pilgrimage if you're so inclined. You have a drink or a smoke, play cards, have a few laughs, watch the sunset and look at the stars, hold hands in awe of the common mysteries. You go to war, or prison, survive a bombing or a plane crash or a simple robbery gone wrong. Or you sit on a porch taking it easy, wondering how you've missed all the terrible stuff. You talk about the weather and the family and the latest fashions, the crazy activities that are only irritating or puzzling, and the ones that are dangerous for everyone. You talk toxins and traffic jams. You talk intolerance, politics, economic trends. You talk tornadoes and floods and locusts in the fields. You talk candlelight and fresh fish and a string quartet. You murmur in your hammock with a fire crackling low and an infant shivering with influenza and a doctor still forty miles away after daybreak. You talk about the tying run, welfare, soccer hooligans and heart attacks. You talk white caps and wind and highballs, winning yacht races. Keg parties and dates and washing your car with your best friend on the driveway under the oak tree. Fishing with your grandpa and eating cold watermelon cut open on the side of a road in some small town you've never seen before and never will again.

You talk lawmakers and lawbreakers and the similarities between them. Ammo and insurrection and glory to God. The birth of a nation, the death of a star. Dinosaurs and quarks and asteroids passing. Dante and da Vinci and Jesse Owens and Jimi Hendrix. George Washington and George Washington Carver. Joe Louis and Stonewall Jackson. Ho Chi Minh. Evonne Goolagong. Jesus H. Christ. Emma Bovary and Huck Finn. Black Elk and Buddha. Galileo. Sandino and Sancho Panza and Coltrane and Ralph in *Lord of the Flies*. Jackson Pollock and Hedy Lamarr and Angela Blanford and me.

I don't want to be a father. Have I made that clear? It's not the contribution I want to make. I don't want to add to the problem, the main problem facing us today. It's not some kind of obligation, is it? To leave your genes behind. Why? When you're gone, you are dead gone, you're not living on in someone else. I wouldn't want to be remembered that way: Oh yeah, he was another unnecessary procreator. Let's face it, almost any Tom, Dick or Harry can accomplish that little task. Fire a load into a fertile partner, let her bring it to term, see the little darling hatch, pop out, whatever. What miracle? Any turtle, bird or hamster can do the same. Try putting a little thought into it first.

And now it's sprinkling at the top of the forest. Feels like salvation when the moisture descends to my skin. A cool coating on my fiery neck, the airy, scattered drops like kisses from a caring sky. But as the wetness increases, so too does the noise, the smacking of leaves and the louder sounds of water streaming through trees and rattling away the fortress of silence. I collect my gear, shake out my pallet and drag it to the tent and stuff it inside, then stand holding a cool, damp stone against the lump on my neck, eyes shut and face lifted, relaxation seeping at last into this tired and anxious body. I crawl inside, smooth out the pallet, take off my jacket and stretch out under the pattering fabric. A minute later I sense the dog at the open flap and feel her entrance and smell her wet coat as she settles against my leg. She emits a shudder and then a sound like someone groaning in sleep, and I in my fatigue make-believe she is diligent at the door, my guardian, as I sink away and the sly night begins its actual passing.

Awake. Alive. Conscious of light and color and sound. Staring upward as drops hit the tent and roll but no rain falling. Sit up to a stab of neck pain, still local it seems, as my fingers gingerly caress the tender rise. Dog is gone. I peer outside into pale shades of gray and green, the light subtle and beautiful. Stand up and stretch, arms overhead, groaning into turns of the torso. Ah, the stiff spine. Body feels damp and moldy. Balls itch. Eyes feel puffy. Find the water bottle and take a long slug. Rub some in the eyes, the face. Step away for a pee. A scratch of the sweaty butt.

Grab the daypack, the stones, and walk down to the trail. Wind in the trees stirring and birdsongs sent across the misty chasm. A scratching somewhere, and when I glance toward the bamboo I see Muttly looking my way. Squatting she is, near the site of last night's rich feast, and here are the results. She looks pained, her back rounded, rump downward, a sickening stench signaling her condition. I give her a wide berth but her eyes follow me, their expression sheepish, her look one of apparent embarrassment.

I take one half-hearted shot of the valley—camera held high above my head—but it feels good anyway, the sound of the shutter working. When I return, the dog has moved a few feet but remains in the same excretory position. I stand nearby pretending not to notice, whistling and gazing about in other directions, but I'm thinking of taking her portrait. In my memory I see her on that first day, resting under Rollo's house, puzzled, then barking as the shouting started, she the reason I stopped to shoot, the indirect cause of the ensuing calamity. She finally regains her standing posture and takes a few shaky steps, stopping to flex her hindquarters, clench her flaming anus. I move forward and take up the trailing tether and lead her up the slope to a tree beside the tent and secure her there. She laps up the water remaining in the bowl and I refill it, and she drinks most of that too and my water is gone. I'll have to go down to the stream and come back up before the day's journey can begin.

I position myself for a picture: the dog, the tree, the tent, the woodpile, composed on a green slope. Camp dog. Then a tighter shot: dog face, tree bark, a blue field of background tent. She wears a smirk or a kind of smile perhaps, like the Mona Lisa. I pat her head.

I hustle down the trail with a stone in my hand, daypack swinging at my back. Kneel at the stream, wash my face and neck, remove my shirt, put a squirt of shampoo in my hair, wash the armpits too. Fill both canteens and start back up. The dog is standing and staring at my approach—no bark as she certainly smells me—and she looks like she's been sleeping. I fill the halves of the mess kit and take off again. Probably missing much of the early traffic. Probably missed Sheila as well, though of course she might have run me over.

Hot already and late. I should be in town by now. Instead, I'm hesitating to step into the clear, to leave the forest for the road, to venture forth where the crowds are gathering. Highway damp, sun hitting the high slopes. No engines heard. I step out of the brush and onto macadam, a man of the world once more, glancing forward and back, the road empty of man and machinery. Heart racing and rock within my grasp. Striding down the incline completely within my rights. Sheila's car is gone. The place looks peaceful.

I'm supposed to be gone and this is supposed to work in my favor. The trouble is, walking along so alone like this, my motives seem vague. I feel like some primitive down from the hills, unnerved on the road, exposed to any hassle that might come by. I stop to drink, open my book. Time clicks along like beetles in the trees. A vehicle descends. Black pickup. Man at the wheel motions me over as he slows. Truck bed full of banana boxes. Good day, sir. First transport yields a ride going all the way. Thank you very much. I'd do the same for you, I truly would. Say, buddy, you know my man Fred? Friedrich, I should say. He wrote this a hundred years ago. Went insane. Died paralyzed.

" 'Nothing is true, all is permitted': thus I spoke to myself. Into the coldest waters I plunged, with head and heart. Alas, how often have I stood there afterward, naked as a red crab! Alas, where has all that is good gone from me—and all shame, and all faith in those who are good? Alas, where is that mendacious innocence that I once possessed, the innocence of the good and their noble lies?"

Part 4

Traffic, vehicular and foot-wise, the surge of commerce, the market in full swing. You're like a hermit, nervous along the waterfront. Tables and crates and baskets and quilts arranged on the square, holding a heaped wealth of fruits of the soil. The sellers mainly overweight or elderly women under umbrellas and blue tarp-shade sitting with backs to the sea. Standing among them a few thin men, blue-hued and bored and out-of-place, while others toil within the adjacent meat shed, an orderly division of well-worn bins of fish and poultry and pig parts.

A seawall sign faces the market with an illustration of the government seal and the words of the island-state credo: After God The Land. And you're thinking instead: After The Land The Sea. Empty boats lined up, sea traffic offshore, and here on the streets of G-ville this Wednesday morning, all these people, all these market forces and faces, but no sign of friend or foe. Eighty thousand plus, living here on this one rock. Dis jungly rock, mahn, hardly place to grow a crop.

What was it Duchamp said? His epitaph, for the gravestone: *Anyway, it's always the others who die.* You see two old men playing checkers, not chess. And the bigger game swirls around theirs. Might be a photo there. Might be an imposition too. Just be considerate, within the job description. Problem is, you're not set up for long shots, for this candid stuff.

You take risks, play a beautiful game, make your favorite claim. Win at all costs, you say to yourself. He who laughs last, laughs best. Die young, leave a good-looking corpse. Whatever. There's one for every occasion. You can see other points of view. You can surely see Rita's, however it goes. You can see Sheila's easily enough. You can even see Rollo's. Sure, he's gone extreme, over the edge, but initially he had a point.

You see yourself at the edge of the market—still too busy for a man without money—a peripheral guy looking for compositions everywhere. In all this business, all this busyness. A hungry guy looking for bruised fruit, throw-away food. Looking to take a great picture with two rolls left. Trying to see things differently. Waiting for dark to accomplish things better unseen. Now wait a second! Hold it. Focus on the moment. Don't spread yourself too thin. Notice the elements in your field of vision.

This is a walk-by shot. Camera held at waist-level, aperture pre-set, focal length estimated before impact, small click of the shutter, no motor drive. Confident demeanor, bold but easygoing movement. People watch you coming to them as a potential customer. They see the camera and the white skin and the money and the leisure time to stroll. Okay, fair enough, easy mistake to make, three out of four ain't bad. Good day, ladies, with a nod or a tip of the cap, as hands are spread, fingers are pointed at lovely vegetables, flies are shooed with grace, straw hats tilting upward to reveal appraising eyes and plump cheeks, and you wish you could purchase a piece from every pile.

You cruise the entire locale, viewing all, as if you're the greatest comparison shopper this side of the Atlantic. Checking the light, the angles, looking for the best shots, for photos about to be born, but never looking through the lens. You're squinting and thirsty in this heat, working your way back down to the waterside, the checker-players under a beige umbrella, sepia-toned men smoking over a black and brown board with open light behind, and the mouth of the river gargling sunbursts into the sea. A pause, a click, and neither looks up. You gaze at the boats, readjust your focus, open up a stop, and on the return you stand nearer the game, lens board-level and the market as background, a blue and yellow striped umbrella the nearest, three women in a row beneath it, their wide tee-shirted backs white shapes sprouting dark heads and arms. A shot, a frame advanced, and another. One man looks up and you move on; you don't mean to break his concentration.

"You wanna take my picture too?"

You stop and look down. The woman is on a low stool, a grin in her eyes, a spread of freckles across the bridge of her nose, skin like rosewood and wrinkled about the neck as if she has suddenly lost weight, long silver earrings hanging and a white scarf covering her head. You squat to face her. "I do."

She indicates her tubers. "If you buy a dollar dasheen."

You glance at her mat, the brown pile. "That's all you have," you say. "How are you competing out here?"

"De best ones," she says, teeth showing a bit.

"No doubt," you say, rubbing your stubbled chin. "Your bargain seems fair to me. But I see two obstacles." You lean forward to your knees and dig into your pocket, pull out your few coins and put them on the mat. "There's one," you say, "the other being a lack of equipment to prepare these hard things for consumption. Like a grater, for instance."

She looks from the money to you, but her eyes are not meeting yours. She's looking at your neck, man.

"Spider bite," you tell her, touching the lump. "That's what I'm talking about. I'm sleeping in the forest. You can't stay in a hotel unless you have some money."

She laughs suddenly, makes a stack of your coins. "Why you tellin me dis tale? Juss for a click-click, dat right?"

"I'm telling you a true tale. A picture's something else. But listen, I've got my own idea of a bargain. If you get a picture of yourself, that's worth something, it costs money to get that print. So if I take your picture, then you owe me something, not the other way around." You smile. "Of course, you'd have to wait a while for your picture. You'd have to trust me to send it to you later. I'll gladly pay you Tuesday for a hamburger today," you say with a laugh, and seeing her look of incomprehension, hasten to add, "That's from an old cartoon we have in America. Popeye, you know? He always eats spinach, but Wimpy always eats—No?"

She's looking at your neck, man. She's looking at your camera.

"Not that I want a hamburger, dasheen would be fine, but cooked, a dasheen burger perhaps, with a bun, a little hot sauce."

She looks a little sad now, looking over at someone behind you.

"Yeah, I know what you're thinking. He's a tourist, he has a camera, he comes from America, the greatest consumer nation in the history of the world and all that, and yet, isn't it possible that he's just now a little down on his luck? So to speak. By choice, I might add. So how about it? A photo, your portrait, or any family member for a dasheen burger. I could even travel to your house if you envision your own yard as a suitable setting. Man, I'm getting thirsty. Or a piece of fruit. In fact, whatever you could trade one of these beauties for right now, anything edible on the spot, as we speak, because I'm a bit on the hungry side, all this bargaining. Or I could take the photo first if you like. How about right here?"

She's staring at you and your mouth is so dry now that a glass of water has moved up to the top of the list of things you need. And then—holy mackerel—you remember the canteens in the pack on your back. Slip it off and withdraw a bottle and raising it toward your mouth catch yourself and extend it to the woman first, holding it out uncapped as she decides, and you say simply, "It's water. Would you like some?"

She takes the canteen and drinks a sip and wipes the top and hands it back. And then you drink. You sigh and smile at her. "Best drink on Earth," you say.

"Whas your name?" she asks.

"Name? Oh, it's Vladimir."

She wrinkles her nose, freckles bunching. "Das Soviet."

"Well, what's in a name? Vlad is fine. What's yours?"

"Cornelia."

"Well, Cornelia, I guess I'll be moving along."

"You wait here a minute." She rises and steps away. You look around, not seeing her but seeing others who are looking at you, and you look down at your camera, not thinking anything.

She returns with a square of gray paper wrapping, stains like oil blotches bleeding through—you think you smell warm cheese—and sets it down with two bananas. "Breadfruit," she says, and sits, settles herself in her former position.

"Thanks," you say. "Can I take your picture now?"

"You may," she says, assuming a dignified countenance, hands crossed in her lap.

"How do I send it to you?"

"Cornelia Kensington, Granville Post. It will find me."

"Kensington. Like in Britain."

"Like dat, yes."

265

"We kicked their royal butts."

"You muss be very proud."

"Nah, it was a long time ago," you say, looking through the lens, making adjustments, watching her motionless face. She does not smile and you do not ask her to. There is a soft click and she seems to relax and you wind the film forward and take another, for insurance, for variety. So you'll have a choice. You put the food in your pack and take out your pen and notebook and write down what she told you, and then stand and lean forward to shake her hand. "I hope you like the picture."

"I will," she says, and you smile and take your leave.

You're having a bit of a wander, looking for a spot to eat, maybe sleep too. Last night wasn't the most restful you've ever had. Forget the jetty—too sunny, too exposed—and the adjacent waterfront lies in the market view. The park sounds better, and you walk beside the river, past the bakery, and here alongside the steep grassy bank you feel you're being followed, a breezy feeling at the back of your neck. Chances are it's nothing and you've half a mind to not even look back, but this is a game. In your paranoid and dodgy state you've no choice in the matter. The suspense could kill you. Hand like a spider in your pocket feeling for a stone. A glance back reveals several pedestrians, a few more steps, then a complete stop and you turn to survey. Scuffing along a half-block behind is the cardboard man. The toothless trash-picker, the strolling market troller, your old pal Estragon. Fair enough; you carry on. He's no doubt on some important mission of his own. Probably naps in the park. Does his calculations.

In the open space there's no bloody cricket, no bloody football, no bloody school kids. It's relatively quiet, the heat of a working day. No plethora of shade either. But you head for the far end, toward those few benches and trees, and you are ready to chow down. All the benches are in the sun so you pick a tree and a spot beneath, nothing unseemly in the grass where you settle, and who should you see approaching but Don fucking Quixote, man.

He sits on the nearest bench holding his bundle-bag, watching you looking at him, and he grins his gummy grin and says, "Heddy-ho, heddy-ho."

"Big Daddy-O, small world ain't it?"

"Oh ho, minny fon de park juss so."

"That's cool with me, Pappy, whatever you said."

He rubs his knee, then runs a finger under the edge of his warped and curling hat, scratching his scalp. "Dem markey pipple—" he begins, and makes a fist at you, "gif moshfoo fah Beg Deddy." He rubs his stomach, nods at you. "Beg Deddy."

"You hungry, Big Daddy? What'd you bring to the banquet?"

He stands and spits and ambles over and squats beside you. He wipes his beard with the back of his hand and proceeds to untie his bag and pull it open, revealing a dented soda can, a dirty towel, a ballpoint pen, a single flipflop, a chip of soap, a wad of string, some leaves, a split tomato and a soft runny soursop that smells rotten. "Soursop," he says, holding it up.

"Yeah, why don't you wait till it gets ripe."

He offers you the tomato but you shake your head and he shakes his too, and says, "No brid."

"That's true," you say, "but we have breadfruit instead." And you withdraw the wrapping and unfold the paper to display the bread-like slab and he reaches for it. "Hey, hold on," you say, pulling it away. "You'd think someone your age would've developed a little patience by now." You set the paper down and take out your knife and slice the piece in two, tear off some paper and put his half on it and hand it to him.

"Tanky," he says, and gums into his piece.

"You're welcome, Pappy."

It's thick and dense like French toast, a bit bland with a buttery, oily-fried taste, and Estragon gobbles it down while you cut yours into bites which you pop individually from the end of the knife blade into your mouth. Savory and filling, you're thinking, eating slowly. Meanwhile, the old man, watching you still eating, reexamines his tomato and eats that too, and finding you unfinished yet, rips open his soursop with both thumbs and dives into this fleshy mess as well. Which he is soon expelling from his mouth, juice and white bits and seeds, the fruit dropped and the spittle in his beard hanging as he hacks and spits on the grass.

"Jesus!" you say, "That's so appetizing. I can't even tell which is riper. No offence, Daddy, but it's bath time. None taken, right? We gotta dispense with the platitudes out here on the fringe. We gotta call it straight, don't we Daddy-O?"

He is scowling, forearms on his knees, dusty flaps of cardboard angled this way and that, his mouth open and the hairs around this hole wet and unkempt. Staring out across the field with eyes that seem traveled to a distant past, the man is like a vision of a lost forebear, a medieval nomad or a senior member of some straggling sideshow tribe.

You reach for your camera and he remains unchanged, hair in knots under his tilted hat, some sort of guru in a trance. You frame out the bench and there is only green grass and a background wall and this man impoverished who shuts his eyes as the shutter opens. Looks like he's crying but he is not.

"Here, Pop, have a banana." He takes it without a word and you peel one for yourself. "Cleanse the palate," you say.

Ants discover the soursop and you decide to read before your nap. Passersby stare at the two of you and there is a fairly steady stream of them. Sitting together on the grass you read to the old man. You feel insanely absurd but you don't blame the company. You don't blame anyone.

Flee, my friend, into your solitude! I see you dazed by the noise of the great men and stung all over by the stings of the little men. Woods and crags know how to keep a dignified

268

silence with you. Be like the tree that you love with its wide branches: silently listening, it hangs over the sea.

Where solitude ceases the market place begins; and where the market place begins the noise of the great actors and the buzzing of the poisonous flies begins too.

You look up to see Estragon watching you and listening, you assume, and when he extends his hand for the book you're impressed, thinking he probably reads better than he speaks and wants to take in a bit more of this stuff on his own. You hand it over and he holds the book open as he fingers a page to turn. With an unexpectedly deft move, one that appears well practiced, he rips the page out—"Hey Pops!" you say, reaching for the book as he leans away—then the next, and the next and the next, about eight or ten in all, while you sit stunned by his sacrilege, speechless on the verge of further objection, and finally figure he needs some reading to go.

He hands the book back and folds his pages in half and you're glad it isn't a novel. Still, he doesn't seem to be considering an apology.

"Glad to be of service," you say. "I hope you enjoy those passages and maybe the next reader will enjoy that random gap, Pappy."

He smiles and mumbles something, puts the pages in his bag and stands groaning, but does not straighten up entirely. He looks down with a grimace and nods toward town and then points that way but does not leave. He farts.

"Yeah, you're welcome. Take care."

"Jitty," he says, and takes a few steps. He stops and points again and seems to be willing to wait a moment in the event that you have a similar urge. "Down de jitty."

But you wave him away. "You go on down there and wipe your butt with Nietzsche's good work. I'll stay here, waiting for the sun to Godot down."

Maybe he thinks you stutter. He laughs and shuffles along

the path and stops again. He turns around and waves gleefully and calls rather loudly, "Beg Deddy."

You watch him go and reposition yourself, give the ants more room for their fruit party, take into account the apparent solar motion, the gradual shift of shade beneath the branches. You don't want to awaken stung or in the sun, in case you manage real sleep in this public place. You push and prod and poke your pack into some sort of pillow and somehow a deep warm sleep comes easily.

Your body jerks, arms thrashing up off the ground and you hear the remains of some audible dream-noise you have emitted. You sit up under the tree and glance around. Kids are running and shouting at the park's other end. A woman and two boys sit on the nearby bench watching you, your fidgeting sleep and turbulent return. You rub your face and breathe relief. No harm done. Coming out of your grogginess, you sit scratching like a mange-ridden mutt. Evening will fall before long.

You got lucky with the moon. Tonight there won't be one, or it'll be so new that you'll still have all the darkness you want. Because right now you're thinking two words: unlawful entry.

First thing on the agenda is to make certain the place is dogless, that no new animal has taken Muttly's old post under the house. As you approach the street you can see that Rollo's house is dark and the neighbors behind him have some lights on. The adjacent freight-related places are closed for the night. The few residences, mainly older, two-story houses that appear to be only partially occupied by families, are leaking sounds of evening home life, music and televised laughter, along with dramatic shouting, while the smells of cooking drift by like seductive whispers.

You walk down the empty lane and angle across the street, turn in behind the triple stucco place opposite your destination.

You wait here listening. One step at a time. Don't rush it. You feel your way down the space, the house in view just a dark box across the lane. You'll check the windows on either side and maybe the front and back too. You can hear snatches of conversation from the neighbors but there is no sign of a dog.

Walk straight across to the window you peeked in last time, reach up, pull at the center where the shutters meet. They give a bit but are definitely locked. Down toward the neighbors to the next one, the kitchen, presumably. Same story. Back to the front, around the corner past the front door steps to the other side. Stop and listen, flat against the house. You have to check the front window so you edge around the corner and stretch one hand up; this one is shut tight. Back to the side. Living room, closed, and down to the bedroom, also closed. Son of a bitch! You stand breathing sharply, then crouch and peer around this back corner at the neighbors. Light spilling pale from the screen door to the porch and the back of Rollo's. No movement though, just television. So what now? He gets his bike stolen and his dog goes missing so he locks the place up. With some kind of lever you could force these shutters. But where to get such a tool now? And imagine the sound of wrenching wood. You look up at the sky, the dark clear night above, and crane your neck to look at the backside of the house. And there—is it the bathroom?—you see the shutter angled away from the wall. You duck back into shadow. It's higher than the others but reachable. And risky with the neighbors so close. Okay, Mayfield, why not? Make a bold move, man.

You stare at the screen door for thirty seconds or so. The front, Hanover Street, still quiet. But the lane and the space between these two houses—all someone has to do is walk by and you can't see them coming from here. You have to move now or you never will. Step out under the window's single shutter. Legs jittery but you leap. Fingers lock on the sill, knees bump against the wall. One hand reaches the shutter and it swings open. You pull up into the space wondering if Rollo's asleep inside, and wiggle yourself over the sill, squeeze through and tumble down the wall into a tub, plastic bottles falling in clunks and spinning, rolling away, your pack flopping high on your neck and banging—the camera inside— on the lip of the tub. You lie breathless a moment, listening for movement in the house, the neighbor's screen door opening, footsteps or voices inquiring. But nothing comes. You are balled up like wire, your hands on the grit at the bottom of the tub, your luck holding.

This window is an exit, but small, and the tub is there. You should open another, a side window, not the lane side, but the other. You crawl out of the bathroom, away from the open view. Find your flashlight and cup it low at the floor. Hallway of sorts, bedroom door. You scoot forward, glance in the room, mattress on the floor, a fan and clothes, bureau with drawers open. Hot as hell in here. Stale and closed-up smelling. And what else? Some kind of oil, body oil or something too perfumy for your taste. Living room has space, some furniture, a toolbox against the wall. You stand up straight now, light straining out of your fist gripped over the beam. Wood floor, somewhat creaky, no rugs, tape player on a table between two chairs, cassettes scattered about. Couch against the front wall, sheet draped over it. Stool at one end, lamp and cup on it. Festival posters, calendar from a building supplier. You move to the side window, ease up the latches, let the shutters swing partly open. Ah, some air, but not much breeze tonight. Humid out. Take a look. No one in the yard. You squat by the toolbox, sweat running in lines down the skin of your torso. Pick up a hammer. They're all weapons.

Careful in the kitchen. The back door may open. Small table, two metal-frame chairs. Dishes in the sink, a bottle on the counter. Let's see. Rum. Half full. Care for a taste? Set the hammer down, uncap it, smell it, take a sip, then a swig. Here you are, drinking the man's rum. Have some more, make yourself at home. It's a home invasion and nobody's home. You got rocks in your pocket, rocks in your head.

Bag of dog food in the corner behind the door, pair of roaches holding steady, sensing vibrations down there. If you had room you'd take it for Muttly. If you had a car waiting down the block. If, if—c'mon man. You open a drawer. Utensils, no gun. And the next. String, nails, candles, junk. Try a cabinet, couple of cans you take down: baked beans, lima beans—

You freeze. Car coming! Which way? Up the fucking lane. Your forehead chills. Your muscles tighten. The car passes loudly, light glowing thin in the shutter cracks and vanishing in a reverberation of sound traveling. Turns right at Hanover and rumbles away, no stopping, no one getting out. You take a few steps, get a view through the front room window, see the tail lights moving. Fuck!

Gather the cans, put them and the bottle in your pack, feel the extra weight. Open the fridge. Light flies out all over the kitchen. Slam it shut. Pay attention, man! Crack it open, slip your arm inside, take an orange, bag of rolls, small bottle of hot sauce. Stuff them in your pack.

Take out your knife, slip it under your belt in back, swallow some rum. You could pour it around, light it and torch the place. But you can see the neighbors running from the flames, suffering for your tomfoolery. You can smell yourself, the sweat, the fear, the dirt and the jungle sleeping, and you wish you had time for a bath. If you knew he was out of town, up in the forest looking for you. If you were a cowboy with your gun under the suds. You shoulder the pack, grab the hammer and move to the bedroom. Scrape coins off the bureau, dump them in your pocket: coffee change. Top drawer has pens and papers, a light bulb, a letter from Australia addressed in a feminine hand to Rollo Joseph. A manual from a Defoe Loading Company. A magazine with a huge-breasted naked white woman on the cover. Fucking hypocrite. Check stubs from the Harbour Authority, but no cash, no bank statements, no personal checks. Two other drawers have socks, shorts, underwear, tee shirts. Clothes hanging in the closet and piled on the floor, work gloves on the shelf, several books about woodworking and leather craft. A bicycle tire tube, a pump, a soccer ball deflated. Beat-up pair of boots. Nothing worth stealing.

How long you been in here? Fifteen, twenty minutes? What are you doing? You should leave now. You have to take a leak, start to head to the bathroom, then stop. Are you such a polite guest? You drop the hammer on the mattress, unzip, piss all over the pillow. Ridiculous, the whole deal, standing in the dark peeing on the bed of the enemy.

What'd you expect to find? Are you gathering intelligence for some future meeting? You already knew more than enough. You think there'd be a written confession on the bureau?

A car pulls up in front, clatters at idle. One door slams and a few words are exchanged. You are in the hallway moving toward the escape window, the car rolling away and a key already scratching in the dark at the door. Your mind clicks into instinct, a dream-slowness that accelerates your body so much that reality slides and you can't be certain of the ensuing storm of events.

Even as the switch is flicked you feel the hammer leave your hand, and in the blast of light you see the man's surprise, his shock at the sight of you, the noise your throw is making, the heavy claw-head driven in tumbling revolutions of solid speed, an assault to the chest hard-stricken, the tool banging the floorboards as the body goes down. With you moving forward, dumbfounded, thinking of the man's identity, of making sure who this victim is, and the near-silence of the situation, the man moaning and struggling to breathe but not screaming or calling for help, one leg kicking to turn his body and propel himself in jerks out the open door.

You flip the wall switch and the light spilling outside is drawn back into the black hollow of the house. You see in your eyes the after-image of the yard and the street as your vision adjusts again to the darkness and the form of the man moving in the doorway. Your foot touches the hammer and you reach down for it, watching the man and thinking he should be beaten and kicked down the steps, but there are suddenly red lights in the picture, backing into the framed view from the doorway, the car not gone at all but returning as if the engine of time has reversed itself, motor grumbling; and indeed the hammer is back in your hand and the man down is outside once more. The car lurching to a stop as the red glow blinks off, door creaking open and left unclosed like a question, but no dome light casting its circle within, the other man calling out, "Rojo" and creeping cautiously around the front of the rattling car.

You stand aside, shielded by the wall, hammer-hand ready, and you can hear Rollo regaining his feet on the steps. You step out to hit him again, but lunging forward he grasps your arm and you both pitch to the floor. The tool bangs loose at impact, his elbow catches the side of your face and you hear the man's groans. Get to your knees quickly, lash out left-handed with your knife slicing air and you feel the brush of a missed swing. The palest shapes are seen in this hot box and the sounds are confusing, the squeaks of boards amid the scrambling for upright posture, a chair overturned as you move. Through the doorway the sound of the car masking the other's approach, so you are knocked from behind, pushed staggering further into the room, the bulk of your pack keeping the capturing arms loose, and you hear a voice cry, "Holdim bwoy!" as you bend at the waist and jab the knife up over your shoulder. The blade meets bone and bows, then snaps.

Released on your hands and knees, you scramble forward holding a dagger's half-blade as the stuck man howls, the metal piece in his head. The flesh of your dog-bitten thumb torn, blood follows and you switch hands on the slick handle, crouching and moving sideways to the sounds advancing. Scrape of wood, a rush of moving air, and you're struck hard, stool or chair knocking you down, ass on the floor, arm and leg in pain and blade slipped from your hand. You roll to reach it, arm sweeping, touching baseboard, touching steel. Just over your head a boot slams the wall, your arm bumped and then gripped, yanked upward. You stab horizontally and the blade imbeds easily as you are lifted in a roar and hurled into couch and wall, a crashing at your back and spasms of stars and fine flares of light in the blackness preceding an explosion of electric illumination that shows the position of all in a room rearranged, the wreckage scattered around damaged men, one leaning his bleeding head on the doorjamb, hand on the switch, Rollo bent over with a fist on the knife in his thigh and you slumping over the couch somewhat senseless, glimpsing his eyes and feeling in your gut the first stultifying rip of the talons of defeat.

You do not yet move, imagining for a moment the energy required, the reserve that must be summoned for retreat. That failing, you are meant to be killed here with these weapons. Rollo watching you as he extracts the blade, teeth pressed hard into a clump of hair, biting the mass as he grunts and pulls the blade free, eyes bloody too and pinching shut at the agony, and then he looks at the hammer on the floor. Because you are the one who entered and stole and attacked, and whose examined corpse could not even be considered the result of a murder. You look at the doorman and realize you've seen him here before. Your back feels strange but you can also feel the air drawing through the window you opened, and you mean to rise and dive through it to the ground before they can stop you. And with blood soaking his pants leg and making its way to the floor, Rollo takes a limping step and says, "Shut de door, Marcus."

Where are the neighbors? And then you believe one has arrived, seeing Marcus as he's reaching for the door, but then leaning back toward the steps. Someone speaks and he answers, "No problem, mahn."

And you think to yell out, demonstrate a lack of control, and maybe you do, rolling off the couch and into motion as Rollo advances toward you. There is a sudden thud by the door and a forced exhalation of air that brings with it a loss of light and unexpected movement, and in the darkness revisited there is the sense of a cyclone returning.

It seems that you are too slow to get your feet on the floor, to launch yourself through a window you can no longer see, and maybe the thought of hitting the wall causes you the barest hesitation, and by then the man has fallen upon you. The floor jars your skull, your face rattling as you try to rise, hearing a cry that is not yours and feeling a ripping pressure at your back. A blow to your head knocks you down and you roll and hit the wall. You hear a violent wind whistle so you know the window must be near, but the next gust ends with a thudding crack and a body falls beside you chattering gibberish. You cover your head and kick at the noise, and another whack rolls that body into yours. A club being swung in the darkness, the resistance of muscle and bone, maybe meant for you too, some demon in the room sent to kill all these fucking fools.

Then you are alone at the wall, Rollo somehow up and unkillable, and the punches and crashing furniture traveling in currents you are no longer caught in. You're on your knees and weaving even before you stand, already reaching your hands in search of the intended exit. You stagger to the opening, seeing the sky and blurry shapes on land as you lift a leg, climb into the frame to jump, then you're pushed and falling forward, your feet and hands hit the ground, a stick landing beside you and then the thud and grip of the man who is saying, "Let's go, bwoy," and when you start to run he pulls you by the pack, wheezing, "Dis way, to de car," and you know the voice but you can't quite put your finger on it.

Marcus has the passenger door open but the man tells him to get the fuck away and he backs off, you with a stone in your hand climbing in and Marcus protesting as the car is slammed into gear and jumps, scratching away from the house. Your door still open as the corner is rounded, then the next and the next and the car is pulled up behind a truck, ignition shut off and keys taken by the man as you both get out, and in the sallow light you are examining the raggedy beard and the face but you need to lie down so you clamber into the truck bed, get your pack off, and stretch out as the vehicle is started. It pulls away with you rolling dizzily until you steady yourself sideways off your burning back, and then the wind feels good and you're looking up at the long disk of stars, the spiral plane of the Milky Way, when you finally recognize the saving grace of Glenroy, and you laugh and say, "The Tasmanian Devil," and close your eyes to the vibrations and the night's cool air.

The truck stops somewhere on a dark cliffside, headlights shining on a guardrail above the sea, motor off and the surf-sound below better than music. Glenroy gets out and stands looking at you sitting up in the bed. "How you feelin, mahn?"

"Pretty fucking stunned. My back feels wet."

"Got a torch?"

You dig it out of your pocket and hand it over.

He takes a look. "Your back is cut," he says. "Bloody." He lifts your shirt. "Glass, mahn. Take it off."

You pull it painfully over your head, feeling your thumb aching too, and you wince when he plucks a sliver out. "Gotta wash dat back," he says. His right eye is swollen to a squint.

He shines the light on your pack and you see the wetness

and smell the rum, find the rips and blood spots on one side, the slash-cut in the front pocket. You unzip it and pull out the book and examine the cut and its depth in the wet pages, more than halfway through. "Look at this," you say. "Nietzsche stabbed." You unpack the camera, the cans, the bath kit and the canteens, the smashed rolls, the jacket and the extra tee shirt, toss the ruptured orange and shake out the remains of the bottle over the side of the truck.

Light glints off the railing ahead and your hear a car coming from the direction you're facing, headlights sweeping into view and you look out to sea, away from the beams as they pass over you and curve around the bend in a sound descending.

"Wheer you stayin now?"

"Camping on Morne Matin. Trail's near the Red Ginger."

"Better you go dere by mornin."

"I guess."

"You wanna sit in front now?"

"Yeah. You think anyone'll be looking for us? Police, I mean."

"Dey may be investigatin a disturbance but dose two dere, de injured parties, dey doan know me and dey woan speak much to police. Dey will tell some quick story and den look to patch demselves up." He grins lop-sided. "Quite surprised dey were, after all dat drinkin." He slaps the side panel. "Let's leave de roadside."

And you're off on a weaving roll up the west coast road, slowing through the villages, thinking the last time you saw these places was on the trip to the airport, going the opposite direction, Ambrose no doubt glad to see you go, and here you are heading back to Pagan Bay like a bad penny, leaning forward to keep your back free of the seat.

"What were you doing there?"

He squints over at you. "Followin de mahn home."

"I couldn't figure out what was going on, if you were a neighbor or what, but I appreciate your timing and presence of mind."

"I was quite surprised to find you dere," he says. "I start watchin de mahn two days ago at dat shop you told Ambrose about. Also seen him at de docks working like a stevedore, but I need to check de mahn's home. Today was a long time waitin by a bar in Hopetown, very boring."

"Were you planning to go in like that?"

"No, mahn, I was juss havin a look when all dat commotion start up. To my knowledge you were gone."

"I decided to stay a little longer."

"Workin on a suicide plan?"

"I was making my plan as I went along."

"More serious dan playin a chess game, mahn."

The dark unlighted outskirts of Pagan Bay, then one turn off the bayfront curve and you arrive at the first streetlight and then the blue shack, not as far out on this side of town as Ambrose is on the other, and no seaside living for G-Roy. He backs into a vacant lot beside the house. It's a shotgun shack, front and back doors aligned at either end of a square room, pallet bed along one side, shelves and chessboard, floor cushions on the other, counter and cabinets a divider for the kitchen space behind the bed, and in the opposite rear corner a bathroom walled off.

He puts a pot of water on the stove and you sit on the edge of the tub sipping a glass of no-label, its anesthetic qualities soon recalled. And with a soft brown sponge soaked in warm soapy water he washes your torn and tender back while you sit flinching, your eyes focused on a smooth gray stone squeezed and rolled in the palm of your hand.

You break out Rollo's rolls and hot sauce, Glenroy opens a can of tuna, heats up the baked beans. You sit on stools and eat and begin to loosen up. Some of the tension drains out of your neck and arms and you envision yourself sleeping on your stomach like a baby, a log, or a rock. You don't care where.

"I'm afraid those guys might fuck with Ambrose. You have to tell him what's happened first thing in the morning."

"I will, mahn. Definitely."

"I know he doesn't want anything to do with this, but maybe Rollo will think you were him, y'know, in the dark. Because he's probably never seen Brose either. We know he was over there at least once—That was what? Four nights ago—and no one was home except Smith. Let's not forget Blandy. He saw me and Brose at Pinder's that night. You know about that, right? He pulled a pistol on us outside the place."

"I got de whole story to dis point."

"I don't regret my actions, man, so I don't want to regret what follows."

"When you look at de world, do you believe you cahn love all?"

"No, I don't. But I don't want to end up in jail."

"Oh no, but you muss consider de options you yourself create. No chance except to get craftier and stronger and juss as bad as dose around you. In de end you muss adapt or die. Get your mind free of de rules."

"Are you speaking from experience?"

"No, mahn, I was de victim and my prison de forest, which is quite expansive, y'know. Solitary confinement witout walls, a beautiful place for healin pain. Das how—" Staring into the bottom of his glass he stops speaking, getting a bit too personal perhaps.

You stand and nod across the room at the pillows. "Is that the guest bed for any bloody guest?"

He sets his glass on the counter and stands too. "You need some bandage, mahn." Moving into the bathroom he rummages in a box mounted on the wall. You sit again on the tub edge and he blots your seeping wounds with a towel and drips no-label into the cuts while you spread your arms like wings and tense against the deep stings. There is some gauze, some expired antiseptic cream, but no tape, nothing to keep the cotton pads in place. So you shred your damaged shirt, tear and cut it into strips which are tied in pieces around your torso, and look ridiculous and feel uncomfortable as well. You brush your teeth and put on your other shirt, rum-scented but basically clean, and carry your discomfort—the pressure on the wounds amplifying their presence—to cushions arranged in a series of lumps upon the floor, and settle down muttering and then swearing to yourself and wondering what has happened to your previous fatigue.

You lie in the dark listening to the sleep-breaths of your host, you turn and scoot and stretch and curse every god you can name for the state of man. All your bruises and bothersome irritations begin to beat and itch and burn in concert until your entire body feels feverish and you think of walking the distance to the sea to submerge these sins of the flesh and suffer some sort of searing transformation in the surf. And you even think of walking through the night to the airport—you've got your ticket, don't you?—to catch the morning flight, forget the rest of your shit, and all the possible endings, and all the lives you've disrupted, finally disappearing like a regular tourist, crying in the air with pain and relief and sorrow, and the hope of finding in your new images the elements of life you'd rather see than touch. And at last this imaginary traveling pulls you away from your immediate self and you drift without knowing.

Stiff as a plank. Stiff as a tree bleeding sap. Daylight in the windows but no rays streaking over the mountains this early. You don't see G-Roy but you hear him out back. You smell coffee as you roll slowly away from the pillows and struggle to stand. Feels like you're wrapped in masking tape and someone's used a nail gun on you.

You pee and wash below the waist and brush your teeth.

Pour hot water through the coffee sock in the sink and drip it into a cup. Step out the back onto a small area of decking by the door, metal awning overhead, a wooden shed at one end, its door open and various tools revealed. G-Roy at his bench against the house, a short homemade speargun in a vise, in the process of attaching a stronger rubber strap to the slim wooden stock. You stand gazing absently into the vacant lot, chickens crossing into it through the hedge of a neighbor, a woman washing clothes in a tub behind the next house, pausing to wipe her brow and gazing across at you too.

When he's finished he fits a thin steel rod like a piece of barbed coat hanger into its groove, cocks the band back under the trigger and holds the thing like a long-barreled pistol as he looks about for a target that won't damage the point. You step inside and bring out the wounded Nietzsche and prop him against the shed door, and G-Roy takes aim at the cover portrait and fires. Puts the spear in the man's thick moustache and scoffs. "I miss de nose," he says, and opens the book to the point and pulls the shaft through.

"The man's been helpful," you say, "but he's taking a beating."

G-Roy loops the band around the wood and slides the spear underneath and holds the gun out. "Cahn you use it?"

"What do you usually shoot with it?"

"Crayfish. Only close range, y'know."

"I'd rather have a bazooka, but this might come in handy."

"Let's see if Ambrose is makin breakfast."

"We might surprise him."

"Believe he got some visitor stayin dere."

"I can't stay long anyway. I have to feed my dog."

"Your what?"

"I have a dog at my camp."

"What, mahn, a guard dog?"

"Sort of."

You're more of an invalid than you expected, your heart beating blood to injuries, the truck bouncing you along the bay road with the morning breeze, and when you open the gate and see the small sign—AMBROSE INN PARADISE—and the other one, the hog warning still posted, you feel nostalgic, walking around the side, ducking the vines, meeting the sweet stench of beached and heating seaweed floating in the air. And like a stab to your heart too, you miss the little black pig.

You hear some talking and low reggae as you and Glenroy step around the corner and startle two young women taking their seaside breakfast, watching you take the other table and sit grinning, nodding your silent pleasantries as you await the emergence of Ambrose.

They resume a conversation in French, casting wary eyes your way as you begin your appraisal. Both have long straight brown hair. One wears it braided, the other has it pinned up in haphazard fashion. They wear loose sleeveless shirts which expose bathing suits beneath, and baggy cotton pants of the sort one finds in India, a single wardrobe in soft browns, off-whites, and purple plum colors. Both adorned with beads and bangles, leather sandals on their feet and a silver ring around one middle toe. Excellent skin in evidence on tanned arms and shapely necks and smooth faces free of makeup. They've finished their food but for a corner of toast with a dab of jam, and the braided lass lights a cigarette, drops the match on her plate and watches smoke drifting to you as you regard the damp hair curled under her arm.

Brose walks out the back door holding a tray with coffee cups and this in itself is a funny sight, but even funnier is his pause, the faltering step and the way he tries to keep his face unconfounded at the sight of you roughhouse table-takers.

"The gentleman innkeeper," you say, and without response he delivers the coffee to his customers and answers them in French. Then he steps to your table holding the tray at his side, and looks down at you as if he were noticing mealworms. "Good work," you tell him. "Your clientele's improving."

"De airport close down?"

"No one's allowed to leave. We're under martial law at the moment."

"You bwoys doan look so good."

"Not as good as French hippie chicks."

"De beauty of liberation," Glenroy says.

"That stuff can backfire," you say. "Liberation all of a sudden becomes something beyond cooperation. Even a helpful man in complete agreement might be threatening."

"De two of you may scare any woman round de world," Ambrose says.

"G-Roy, I think this man's trying to score with clients."

The Frenchies are looking over but Ambrose is standing with his back to them. "What happen on your neck?" he says.

"Mine or his?"

Glenroy runs a thumb over his scar but the subject is dropped.

"A mahn should have a phone so visitors cahn call ahead," Ambrose says.

"He's got the scent so bad he wants to install more technology. I don't think we can save him, G-Roy."

"Too late, Jake. Now dey wavin for de mahn."

"Mr. Ambrose," you say in a falsetto voice, "can you apply more lotion please?"

"You bwoys should get some treatment for dose head injuries," Ambrose says, and then turns to attend the women.

When he returns to the kitchen Glenroy follows him inside, and in the next few minutes you half-expect to hear arguing. But you hear instead the waves lapping and a distant vessel's throbbing engine way down the bay, and the Frenchies conversing and then a chair pushed back and you see one of them going to their room—the Mayfield suite, you notice, the new room closest to the water, undoubtedly the first choice now—while her braided companion, the elder, you reckon, finishes her coffee without looking at you. When her friend comes out carrying a canvas bag, she rises too, and without a word or a smile they walk together through the gate, each holding a strap of the bag suspended between them.

Ambrose comes out with the tray and begins to stack their dishes on it. He glances at you unsmiling.

"We'll have whatever they had," you say.

"De mahn is makin it," he says, and looks over the fence in the direction the women have taken. He brushes crumbs off the table with his hand. "Din sit here too long lookin at you."

"That's right, brother. They didn't come here for no white boy American experience. They can't stand us, except for James Dean and he's been dead quite a while now. No, I'm afraid they'd sooner bear Glenroy's children than shake my hand."

"You misjudge dem," he says. "Dey harbor hate and love in equal parts."

"You mean if I walked over there right now, they might slap me and kiss me."

"Probably juss complain to de management."

"I don't have time to fool around here anyway, man. I have enough trouble already." You find yourself examining the concrete under the table, looking for blood stains. "I just came by to see if you want my dog, you know, after I leave."

"Shit, mahn, you always leavin. And now you wanna go home in a box."

"Nah. I wouldn't mind a narrow escape though."

"Already had dat. You playin a game wit your only life. True?" He nods at his own suggestion and you think he'll smile but he doesn't. "Which piece are you, bwoy?"

"I'm no queen. No king either, obviously. No bishop, no pawn. So, knight or rook? I'm not gallant or tricky enough to be the horse. That leaves the rook, straight ahead or to the side. But that castling for the king, getting sacrificed for the kingdom, I don't know about that. A rook's a cheat, a swindler, a corner piece. You tell me. I'm a man in a cul-de-sac of his own making. I try to look ahead but I can only see an hour, a day, or a night at the most. I'm so sore I can't even get up to make food or see what those two women are doing. Are they completely naked?"

He peers over the fence, taking his time, eyebrows moving upward, and emits a quizzical air-sucking sound that seems to signal his enjoyment or wonder or approval, or all of these, and says as if to himself, "Could be your last good time."

You struggle to your feet, skin and muscle pulling, body lifting painfully to its full height, and over the fence you see the women so far down the beach you can't tell if they're wearing mink coats or neckties in the nude, and you hear Ambrose chuckling his way inside.

The three of you having eggs and bread and chutney. Slurp of coffee heard and the wordless language of eating. The music provides a tuneful number about uprising and oppression and hope that sounds catchy and monotonous. G-Roy looks alternately happy and morose and seems a mirror to your own mood. Feeling anxious to leave, you keep glancing along the fence, between the sea grape leaves, at the water beyond the gate, imagining the immediate sting of the salt, the liquid healing and brief release from this shackling stiffness even as you scuttle the idea and look for another. No time for wet clothes and wounds rewrapped.

"We cahn expect dose two come looking for we two, or we cahn counter even before dem," G-Roy says. "Attack or wait defensive, hidin in de wilderness."

"Like bootleggers," you say, envisioning some B-movie car chase, getting cornered into a shootout using a speargun made for river crustaceans.

You dread the loss of momentum, getting caught off-guard, a lack of resolution and humor. Everything seems arbitrary and acceptable. G-Roy wants to dig up the pig for its sharp incisors, to make a weapon of ironic value. He swears he's serious and you welcome his fearless lunacy. A man who'll go whole hog.

While you crazy bastards plot war stategy and moves across the landscape, Ambrose remains the patient savant. "Some might say you reach a reasonable conclusion, true?" he says.

But you want aspirin, not advice. This place is no haven anymore. You need to keep moving. There seems to be a conflict between this moment-by-moment living and what lies just down the line, your unmade plans for the future, tomorrow or next year. This rushing here and there, doing this and that, life itself, somehow unsynchronized with the planet spinning and us hurtling headlong to our various finales like electrons breaking free. Ambrose might be something of an exception, calm and sagacious, but he can't tell you anything now. You need to get out of his sight, run like hell from the voice of reason with any excuse you can toss out. "Still haven't resolved this thing with Rita," you say.

The disparity is obvious. Call it what you like: the yin and the yang; the left brain versus the right. In the battle of the split brain, you stare across the hemispheric divide but cannot figure out which side you're on. The left side linear, rational, assertive, logical, masculine, the active yang in the universe. And the right side complementary, the place of patterns, tolerance, freedom, irrationality, the so-called feminine side, the passive yin in the universe. And each holding the other in its embrace. Sometimes, a stranglehold.

The road is already dust, a hot tunnel through a tight morning. You stop at the Cable office. Glenroy stays in the truck while you go in, look up the number, wait for a booth.

The place is busy and you stand sweating beside a metal fan, see your distorted reflection in the casing, hints of blood stain spotting your shirt, and as you twist, the bandage straps feel like snakes wound around your middle, fangs biting in back.

Deposit your coins, dial the number, stomach clenching, finger waiting to jump the cradle. Three rings, then a voice.

"Hello."

"Rita!"

"Jake? Is dat you?"

"I'm still here. I want to see you but there's been some trouble."

"But—"

"Is Blandy there?"

"No. He juss went out."

"Did he say anything?"

"Dere was a call dis mornin." She hesitates. "Jake, dey are lookin for you."

"I know."

"Why you wait so long to call, mahn?"

"I had to figure out what I was doing."

"Dey say you stayin at de Red Ginger. Dat true?"

"No, I'm moving around. I need to see you."

"Wheer?"

"I'm afraid your brother'll follow you."

Silence at the other end.

"You doan truss me?"

"The pig was killed a few nights ago."

Another pause, then, "Who did dat?"

"You know who."

Out of a long quiet hollow she whispers, "Jake?"

"What is it?"

"De blood test was positive."

You feel the heat in your ear radiating into your head. "It's alright," you say.

"I miss you," she says.

"I miss you too. Stay away from those guys. You hear me. I'll see you."

"Jake, what are you doin?"

"I couldn't leave you yet."

Click. Dead line humming. No time to get choked up, man.

Climbing up into green it's harder to breathe, gravity pushing you back against the seat, the air in your lungs full of hummingbirds and waterfalls, mountains pressing your chest. G-Roy should not be linked to you. He should remain anonymous for as long as possible. You slump lower on the seat, eyeline just above the dashboard, and duck at the passing of other vehicles. Keep this drab truck a secret too, if you can. Just another set of wheels running over the mountain highway. Everything here looks ordinary and expected—the land, the rising flank of Morne Matin, the unrolled ribbon of road, the sloping homesteads with woodbox houses and yards bush-cleared for hibiscus and heliconia—all familiar except you, man. You stand out like a leper.

And even as you curve into the downgrade approaching the Red Ginger, something goes amiss. The place has just entered your thoughts when a loud pop occurs at your window—your arm jerks from its restful edge and you flop down sideways across the seat—G-Roy fighting the wheel torque briefly, straightening the vehicle with a tug, and chuckling as he brakes and you sit up. The truck now listing to your side, the left in this left-hand-drive country, the blister blown on the left rear tire, limping toward the restaurant—whump, whump, whump—while you glance about, concluding that no one took a shot from the roadside weeds or the trailhead you call your own.

You look back through the rear window. "How's the spare?"

"Needs a patch too," he says, rolling past the driveway and stopping as a jeep comes grinding uphill and passes. Rental company name on the rear. White people waving.

You sit thinking, having already planned to disembark here after G-Roy had used the driveway for his turn-around and you'd had a chance to spot any suspicious persons or vehicles lurking in the vicinity. "You'll have to go to the Rocklee station."

"True, but you need to get out."

Looking down the drive at Sheila's red Toyota and two other parked and empty cars, you say, "Maybe I'll go down with you."

"Not necessary, mahn."

"I just remembered I need to get some dog food."

He stares at you for a long moment, pushing at his scar like it's some type of hugely annoying Congo leech, and says, "You are becomin a fairly constant amusement, mahn."

He takes his foot off the brake and the tires begin their roll and flop down the incline. "Load dat speargun," he says.

Even the best-laid plans. What can you say? Sometimes you let the rough end drag. Thumping down the road at a crawl. Easygoing Thursday morning in Rocklee, not much traffic, highway shops open, kids in school down the hill. A woman beating rugs with a stick, old men looking up from a game to catch the passing misfortune, a small event of note.

West Indies Petrol Station. One car at the pumps. Truck eases up to the garage door, the heavy kid in slapping sandals and cut-off overalls—his uniform, apparently—coming out to assess the situation. G-Roy goes around back to detach the spare and the kid focuses on you in your shades and low-pulled cap, coming around to your side to inspect the flat as you get out with your pack. You brush past him and walk to the road, an uninterested rider, speargun left loaded behind your seat. Look both ways and amble down the highway a hundred yards to the intersection—Granville to the south, Bambou to the east. At the fork of roads, a cafe-bar, a roti shop serving food by now. Window counter open, several men standing. The server a big woman in a white apron. You go to the screen door and step inside, eyes adjusting to an indistinct room, a half dozen dark patrons looking at you removing your shades. You stand there like you might have the wrong place, absorbing the greasy fry smell of chicken and onion and spices, studying the men's faces until you get a sense of equanimity, satisfied you are all strangers. And then notice two young women sitting at a table with soda bottles and straws. One stands and grins, making a motion toward you. She's short, in a tight tee shirt, sunglasses hanging by the earpiece from the V at the front of a plunging neckline. Sly feline eyes and a voluptuousness compressed to the point of bursting. And you know each other. A black cat and a white rat.

"Hey dere Jake," she says. "How it is?"

"Hey, Hotstuff. How's the Rocklee life?"

"Slow," she says, smiling. "Why you call me dat?"

"Oh, I don't know. Maybe that dance we had."

She purses her lips, pulls in a squeek of air. "You remember dat?"

"Are you kidding?"

"Hah! Come sit," she says, and gestures at her friend. "Dis is Glenda."

You pull up a chair and Glenda offers her hand. Janet reminds her of the event she missed a few weeks ago, and tells you about the next one, to be held a week from tomorrow night in a big seaside shed in the settlement of Bambou. She wishes to have another dance, or maybe a couple, and you tell her you hope to oblige.

She takes a long pull on her straw, watching you as she does, and lets it slide back into the bottle. "Rita give you up yet?" she asks, laughing.

You look at the big woman sweating behind the counter, cooking up some roti as she talks to a man leaning toward her. "She's giving me one more chance," you say, and both girls laugh. At least you're breaking up a dull morning.

"Wheer she at?"

"Probably at home," you say, and then lean back with a benign grin. "You seen her brother around?"

"Uh oh," she says, exchanging glances with Glenda, who makes a singsong hum. "Why you ask me dat?"

"Because I'm looking for that friend of his." You look from her to Glenda, then snap your fingers, glancing away, pretending the name is on the tip of your tongue. "The guy with the car."

"Stedman," Glenda says.

"Yeah, that's him. Anyway, we had a slight misunderstanding the other night and I was hoping to straighten things out, y'know. They were in Stedman's car. You know the one." You slide your fingers over the surface of the table. "Small Japanese car."

"Nissan."

"Right, that red Nissan."

She shakes her head. "White, mahn."

"White, you're right. It was dark out. Anyway, forget about that. My real problem is dog food. That's why I came in here. You think that sweet woman'll let me have some scraps for a hungry dog?"

"A touriss wit a dog!" Janet says, and they laugh again. "Gotta cat too?"

"That'd be funny, wouldn't it?" You stand, laughing also. "I'm just watching it for someone. The poor thing's so hungry I'm afraid it'll be dead if I don't get going."

"Buy some at de store."

"I can't. This dog only eats leftovers. Has an allergy to processed foods." You smile, extending a hand to each of them. "Love to see you in Bambou," you say winking, squeezing their fingers with some sincerity. "Take care now."

The woman watches you approach the corner of her counter. "Ma'am," you say, taking off your cap. She listens to you while she works, piling bits of meat and chunks of potato in square sheets of dough, rolling them up on a plate. A man on a stool beside you is listening too, and another man says something to the woman. You stop and wait, hat in hand, like some humble Depression-era tramp with a fictitious traveling companion.

She slides a can toward you with her leg and you bend and pick through it, the men murmuring, the girls giggling across the room as you make a mound of guts in your palm. You ask for a plastic bag and the man on the stool digs one out of his hip pocket and shakes it out and holds it open for you. You get all you can, then step without asking to the sink and wash your hands, pick up the bag and tie it closed, thank the man and to the big woman say, "Much obliged, ma'am," donning your cap and tipping it.

To your surprise, Janet and Glenda rise and follow you outside. A real novelty, dis mahn. Up the road on either side of you, Janet putting her shades on as soon as you do, the morning still holding its unclouded brightness. She moves like a cat, strutting her stuff, so bored she's dangerous, and looking like she might enjoy a wounded rat to play with.

"Wheer you goin?" she asks.

"Gas station."

"And den?"

"Pagan Bay, where the dog is."

"You come all dis way for slop can pig food?"

"I came from Granville."

"Not seein Rita?"

"What, are you writing a book? I'll see her later."

"Why you limpin dat way?"

You laugh. "I had an accident, you nosy little devil."

G-Roy is filling his tank, he and his truck looking ready to roll. As you approach, he replaces the nozzle and the gas cap, and pays Bigboy in the overalls, who's leaning against the pump.

"Well," you say, "gotta go, girls."

"Who your scuffy friend?" Janet asks.

"Just some guy I got a ride with." You open your door and set the bag on the floor. "If you see Rita give her a big kiss for me, okay."

"Gotta get one to give one."

"Use your imagination, Hotstuff."

She gives you a ferocious little smile. "You watch out now, bwoy."

As you pull out onto the road she's sitting with Glenda and Bigboy on the wall in front of the garage. She waves and you wave over the cab as you're rumbling smoothly up the highway.

"You know dem?" G-Roy asks.

"I've met Janet. The little sexy one."

"She know de story?"

"She knows something. The other girl mentioned a white Nissan that I think is cruising around trying to confirm my whereabouts. Guy named Stedman, with Blandy."

"She makin trouble?"

"No telling what she's making. I believe she'd be happy to see some action, no side taken."

The truck begins to climb the long curve below the Red Ginger. Now it's past eleven, lunch time. You see the hedges of the Red Ginger, the second story roof. There's no one behind you, and so far no one in view up ahead. You gather your bags, place the speargun at your feet. Ready to split up with the G-man. You've agreed to meet again later at the Red Ginger bar before dark. G-Roy can park there, maybe have a beer, then come up to the camp at dusk.

You don't bother to slouch; it hurts your back. The truck's in second gear, climbing, sun gleaming off the hood. You look down the slot between the hedgerows, see several cars, a white one facing the exit, a guy leaning on the driver's door, arms folded, watching you pass, checking you out. He springs off the car like the metal's suddenly hot, flings the door open as you leave his line of sight. G-Roy is looking past you through the passenger window.

"Okay," you say. "Here they come."

He downshifts and accelerates, the truck jumps forward—revolutions rising and engine howling—and he pushes it into second, gas petal on the floor, trying for a head start. You look back, see the Nissan turning out of the drive in pursuit.

The next three miles will involve more or less constant climbing along the spine of the island. No high speeds, just jungle walls, muddy cliffs, rocky drop-offs. Weaves and dips and steep ascents, no turnoffs except rutted red dirt drives and concrete tracks, eroding dead ends to sloping orchards and off-road homes. The car behind slowly gaining, two of them inside.

You can't outrun them but you can stay ahead. And when the grade changes, make your run to Pagan Bay. Or stop at the site of your choosing. They're maybe forty yards back and you can see their faces. Blandy, the passenger. What's he going to do, shoot out your tires? They're just following, to see where you go. If you stop, they stop. If you go home, they know where you live.

G-Roy is smiling to himself, eyes in the mirror. He's got his club behind the seat and you've got this speargun. Back there, Blandy's climbing over the seat, getting behind the driver. Of course, he can't shoot his little pistol left-handed.

A stretch of straightaway rising to a sharp turn. The Nissan makes a move, closing the gap, these boys wanting to ride your ass and maybe take a potshot. Blandy has you in his sights as he leans out, knit cap hugging his head, shirtsleeve flapping in the wind, his thumb and forefinger imitating a gun.

G-Roy with his foot flat on the floorboard. Nothing to say. Just watching the mirror and the road. Stedman's face dead serious, plain as pudding in this serious game. Engines running hot and loud on the incline. The Nissan edges up closer, as if it might bump you for fun, the sun flaring off the center of its windshield like a seam of heat. Behind the glass Stedman grins, his face pudgy and youthful and lacking control. A face from Pinder's, running up to you and Brose. You hear vehicles competing in sound, the car's whine against the truck's growling howl. You see Blandy lighting a cigarette. Takes a drag and blows it into the car. You see the green, yellow, and red colors of his cap. His left hand grips the front seat for support, cigarette sticking up like a point he wants to make—this is nothing but a relaxing sport—and he leans out with his gun this time and takes his wavering aim.

You lean into the corner of the cab, the truck weaving from side-to-side as G-Roy works the wheel, tires squealing, but he won't look back, doesn't look at you either, his eyes flicking from highway to mirror, ahead and behind, back and forth, his face as yet unseen by those trailing, you hope.

Out of the turn ahead a car swings into view, barreling down the grade. Then another. The Nissan fades, drops back quickly. Blandy's head and arm withdraw and he sinks from sight. The downhill cars blow by, local faces here and gone, flashing eyes in a wind of speed. Road and rock and tree and weed. Tires treading on a precipice edge.

Glenroy makes the turn, a sharp left—the Nissan gone from view—and stomps the brake as he pushes the clutch, worn tires holding while he's shifting into reverse. He turns and extends his arm across the seat back, looking around at last. "Hang on, mahn," he says.

297

The Nissan is upon you, braking, the driver's eyes surprised and Blandy leaning out, his body surging forward into the curve, hand grasping door beam, barrel-aim dropping to road surface as he grapples with balance. Stedman tries to turn his wheels away as the truck rams backward into his grill and locks the vehicles together with forces of mass and momentum. The truck a roaring beast mauling down the mountain, the Nissan unable to brake on the downhill slide, its tires crying and Stedman frantic at the wheel, head swinging around, looking over his shoulder into the curve and back to the looming tailgate, racing his engine and struggling to turn in a wasted effort to unhook his car rather than drive it backward. Glenroy keeping the pressure on him, the Nissan sliding right across the bend to the shallow stony fall, and Stedman realizing his mistake too late, slamming his car into reverse to accelerate out of the truck's grip, to separate and steer downhill.

Blandy fires—a smack of glass beside you and the shot repeats off mountain wall, cracks appearing in the pane like ice fractures, a small hole at their center formed—and the heaving truck catches a rattle in the cab.

Then the boy is fully inside the car, moving wildly, his door swinging open and closing again as the car follows partly the path of asphalt, right-side wheels edging into roadside rock and dirt, Blandy scrambling to the other side and jerking at the door as the car tilts sideways. The truck bucking forward for footing, wheels cut to angle at the Nissan's midsection, a rear door opening even as the truck returns, the metal bang and shock of impact felt as Glenroy brakes, kicks the emergency lever as well, tires sliding to a stop while the car teeters and then slips down the slope, someone hollering below the spray of dirt and dust as Glenroy finds first gear and the gas and springs the brake, and the truck jolts and lurches onto the surface of the road.

Crunch and crash of metal and glass meeting rock—

echoes of harsh sound suspended in a sudden stillness—but no other traffic traveling this stretch at the moment. You look at each other, his hand vibrating on the gear shift, waiting it seems for complete silence. The Nissan gone somewhere but no longer moving, you're sure, held in some mangled state down a rough ravine. You think of jumping out to see but you're looking up and down the highway instead and the truck's already rolling.

Hard turn left, a short back-up, wheel whipped downhill and you're coasting away from an accident unseen, a roadside patch disturbed, broken automotive pieces and tire marks left behind as you round the next bend and race on, wind whistling through the cab and a pellet rolling on the floor. You pick up the flattened slug, a small bullet spent, and hold it in your palm for Glenroy to see. Both of you inspecting the window hole too, a suspicious mark to say the least.

You put the bullet in the ashtray and gather your stuff, speargun disengaged. Coming down the grade, trailhead on your side. Glenroy will keep going nearly to Granville and turn up the coast road, take the long way home. The bullet rattling, and he says, "Two less rude bwoy on de road. Check?"

"Check. You think they're okay?"

"Dey are not dead, mahn."

He slows to a crawl and you open the door and hop out running into the bush.

Ground berries bursting in your mouth. The midday sun coming through the canopy like a welcome home party. The only problem is that you can't hike real well. A multitude of bruises running interference with your muscles, one of your hips not wanting to take these steep steps, and your back a battlefield of pits with the shifting pack pulling at wounds so that you're forced to carry it by hand. Just some quiet jungle rest needed, Beg Deddy.

You stop for water, somewhat dehydrated, and drink your

fill, wash your face and wet your neck, then move on, your stomach sloshing. No hurry. Take it easy.

Before you see the first stalk of bamboo, you hear the dog. Is it a bark of alarm, or one of recognition? She's playing her part, speaking canine code. "That's my girl," you say. So glad to hear you're not dead. Only twenty-eight hours alone without food. Times are hard, Muttly.

But don't take the situation for granted. You stop on the trail below the camp. Take a look around. She's yapping now, smelling the food. Better cock the speargun and have a rock in hand. Don't get lackadaisical when people mean to harm you. And see where this thinking leads: Is that really you, Muttly-girl?

It is. She's up on her hind legs and scratching the air with her front paws, tail wagging beneath the tether. Almost like she's learned a trick, a homecoming dance to impress you, which is fine, as long as she doesn't lapse into that Jekyll and Hyde number again. She licks your hand excitedly, dancing faster and yelping as you stroke her neck, pat her head. "Alright, alright," you say, "you're not abandoned." You loosen the leash and set her free. She prances like a puppy and runs a circle around you, throwing her nose at your bags in passing. Jumps at you and runs partway down the ridge, squats to pee, her eyes on the man returned, and scampers back to her bowl as you pour the water. You take the other bowl and tromp away from camp with the bag of slimy scraps. She follows at your legs and sits whimpering as you load the bowl above her head, put it down and stand clear. She licks at the pile— tendons and skin and gristle and entrails—and after it's met her approval, devours it without another thought, eyes glazed at the ground and a murmuring in her throat.

You shake out the sleeping bag and spread it outside and unzip both ends of the musty tent for ventilation. You sit by the door flap to inspect your wares. A can of beans, mashed bread, hot sauce, water and tamarind seeds. The dog roaming and you're alone, strange shivers like mild electrical buzzes running through your back and neck while you sit cross-legged chewing your seed pulp and gazing out between the trees toward the light of the valley. A crackle here and there and the hollow notes of woodsong whistlers, the midday heat settling among the trunks and your mind drifting away to the northwest with gauzy thoughts of home, but no end in sight. Your island days jumbled together, and you feel it's time to take a nap. You open Nietzsche for a look.

All good things approach their goal crookedly. Like cats, they arch their backs, they purr inwardly over their approaching happiness: all good things laugh.

A man's stride betrays whether he has found his own way: behold me walking! But whoever approaches his goal dances. And verily, I have not become a statue: I do not yet stand there, stiff, stupid, stony, a column: I love to run swiftly. And though there are swamps and thick melancholy on earth, whoever has light feet runs even over mud and dances as on swept ice.

You spit out a tamarind seed and lie back to rest.

You strap yourself in, somehow containing your elation as the propellers roar to life. In a moment you lift off over the coastal road, climbing above coconut palms and metal roofs. Over thin rivers and patchwork villages. Above orange blotches of flame trees in the wild green. Abreast of dense mountainsides. Pressed to the window, you search for a glimpse of a clear-water crater, but it's hidden somewhere among the hazy gray hollows and green crags slipping behind. You drone north over open water and the wide cleft slopes and sharp-thrown shadows blend together. The island shrinks to a few smooth ridges above the surrounding area, like a horseshoe crab settled into sand. Then the land becomes a single fading hump, no longer steep or green, but a plain low rock in a vast silvery sea, only slightly darker than the glimmering surface from which it rises. You veer northwest and the place vanishes into the past.

The engines drone. The plane vibrates with unhurried movement. Your head hums against the window and you think you may sleep as you squint into the bright air beyond the gleaming wing. The sea is a shifting mosaic of water and light. You dream of space pictures. From a vast height above the water you see a pinpoint of land. You sense yourself losing altitude against your will and you float without a plane. The land below looks attractive and you feel as though you should stop here awhile. You are glad to witness the presence of people, the wounds and scars on the rough landscape. You see a road to put down on. Someone is waving up at you. You want to end this long trip. But clouds seem to rise from the ground, and your view is obscured. The mist is like a mask over the land; there is nothing to see anymore. Then you're above the blue ocean again, flying on into clear sky. The weather is remarkable.

The light's gone gray. What time is it? Almost four. Your temporary dog is here, waking too, synchronized with the slapdash master. "I won't be long this time," you tell her. And you load your last roll, an omen, you hope. Sleeping bag stuffed inside, water bowl filled, the beast leashed. "Good dog," you say, and you're gone again.

The low clouds look stiff and textured and gray as pumice, settling close for the night, but with rays prying under the mass and firing over the orchard, a pair of birds in flippant loops of chase and play among the uppermost leaves. The porch windows are glazed in yellow streaks. Four cars are parked along the drive, plus Sheila's. No truck. One man in the bar and a few early diners bathed in the late brazen light.

As you step up on the porch a board creaks and the man at

the bar swings around so suddenly you halt in your tracks. But it's Glenroy, in long-sleeve shirt and vest, grinning at your expression, a sport bag at his feet.

"G-man, I didn't know it was you. Where's the truck?"

"Made a trade wit Sharon," he says. "De blue Peugeot."

"Cool," you say, glancing again at the vehicles. You pass the door and take a seat beside him, blocking yourself from the other room's view. "Nice place, huh."

"No service."

"She'll be here."

You both look up at the black boar's head, its glass eyes beady but all-seeing in appearance, forever clear now and dry, the stare tireless and dusty, the fur lost in spots along the snout and the nose like a mushroom cap curled and cracked. Glenroy's eyes meet yours but do not linger and no word is spoken.

Sheila strides in wearing dark green silk slacks and a blouse with matching cloth buttons held by loops, Japanese-style, tailored well and comfortable-looking, her hair pulled back and her suddenly unsmiling lips painted a deep red. She gives you a dubious look and stands before G-Roy. "Yes," she says.

"Beer," he says, and when she brings up a Heineken, he says "Two," and she places another beside it and then smiles and leaves the room. He slides one over to you. "So das de way it is," he says. "Close acquaintance."

"We had our ups and downs." You take a swallow. "It could have gone another way, in theory, but your life takes its one path. You can't live all of your choices. We always say next time. But there is no next time. We move on, and next time the situation is different."

"You cahn learn a better game, mahn."

"Sure you can, but it'll be a different game than the last time."

303

Lights flicker on around the dining room and the evening flutters to illumination as Vivaldi pours softly through the rooms. Far behind the open door the sky is mottled blue and gray and fading gold. You click on the bar lamp and take out Nietzsche and open the book to the inside back cover and poise your pen above this brown-stained but uncut blank page.

Dear Sheila:

It was great to meet you and spend some time in your beautiful retreat. You are a gracious hostess who went the extra kilometer to make this guest feel warm and welcome. I'm sure you spoiled me, for I feel doubtful of ever again finding the kind of treatment I received here. Thanks for the hospitality and personal attention to my comfort and well-being. Whenever I think of you I know I'll feel a powerful surge of fondness and a rampant desire for your exquisite food. And thanks too for the loan of this book. It's still mostly readable and maybe better if taken in small doses anyway. Farewell. Best wishes to you and the Red Ginger.

Yours truly,
Jacob Mayfield, Oct 22, 1987

You stand and return the book to its place on the shelf.

Glenroy goes through the adjoining door to locate the restroom. In a moment, Sheila reenters the bar.

"Ready to pay?" she asks, even though your beer is not finished.

"He's got the money."

She reaches under the bar for her cigarettes, lights one, flicks at an ashtray and sighs. "Must you annoy me this way?"

"It's not like that."

"What is it like?"

"It's a place to meet. Listen, I'm sorry about the other night. I was too nervous. If I had it to do over again, I'd be so happy to stay. I'm kicking myself now."

She scoffs. "You would never hurt yourself."

"You already called me a masochist once."

"Sure, for one moment, one day maybe."

"I'm not sadistic either. If I was an asshole, I'm sorry."

"What do you mean if?"

"Sheila, we were just having some fun. How'd it get so serious? I mean, if I'm so bad then why do you even care?"

She stubs the cigarette out. "Don't bring those bad men here," she says, and leaves the room as Glenroy returns.

Night falls completely and here you sit. Two more cars arrive, a party from Granville, you overhear. Glenroy watches through the door as Darlene passes back and forth, and all the activity puts you in the mood to act. "Back in a minute," you say, and slip off the stool and out to the porch carrying your pack. Snails on the rail and geckos on the wall. You step down to the path and head into darkness toward the generator, looking beyond to the black cabins. Passing the machine shed like you might be going to the lower bathrooms, as if the restaurant facilities are occupied and you can't wait.

You stop and listen—the engine overpowering within its main vibration radius—and glance back up the path. No one coming, no one in the surrounding gloom. Smells like it might rain and most likely it will. Smells like fuel burning as you move back up to the shed and try the door and quickly slip inside.

A closet of noxious bellows. Fumes and claustrophobic recoil. Like being in the lair of some snoring diesel beast. You cup your light and squat for some reason, because of the size of the place, or because you wish your actions to seem smaller. You survey the space, the chugging grease-stained machine, the black dust coating the concrete at its base; an open metal box beside it, wrenches in view; an exhaust pipe through the wall; a barrel drum at the back, a funnel on top; a small drum

305

and a gas can and paint cans stacked in a corner; jars and tins and oil on a rusted stand; a box of rags; a roll of wire, a rake, a shovel, a hacksaw, assorted lengths of plastic pipe and rubber hose; clamps and scattered screws. A skin of mold on the ceiling and walls.

You scuttle to the gas can, lift and shake it, unscrew the cap and smell it. Bingo. Remove your pack, pull out your Fanta bottle, set your light on the floor, beam blocked at the barrel. Grab the funnel, insert it into the bottle on the floor, and carefully fill it up. Cap and replace the can. Shake the funnel, put it back. You cut a piece of rubber hose, bend it double, wrap a strip of tee shirt around it as a seal, stuff it tightly into the bottle. You wedge the bottle upright in your pack, stand and move, cut the light. Fuel smell and loud sound forcing you out of this dank spot. A fire hazard, man. Crack the door on a world more discernable. Stick your head out. Breathe in the open night. Then you're clear, the door shut, and you're walking out among the frogs and lizards, the whole episode a simple series of saurian moves now behind you.

Glenroy has his money on the bar. He watches you sit and swallow the rest of your beer, then picks up his bag. You go down the porch steps into the drive and through the spilled light by the restaurant windows. He squats beside Sharon's car and reaches under it and retrieves his club, holds it like a walking stick as you continue to the road. You look up and down the dark highway and run together up the grade to the trail, leap into weeds and out of sight, your beam a puddle rolling over stones.

"Dat petrol I smell?"

"Weird, isn't it, how the whole world depends on it."

The dog barks and G-Roy chuckles his approval. Muttly, however, does not give hers so easily. There seems a two-fold question in her bark: Who is this intruder, and if he's got no meat, why bring him in?

You call to her as you crunch up the ridge. She bares her teeth in the light and growls at G-Roy. "Don't worry," you tell him, "she only bites me." You squat to pet her and she licks your hand, and G-Roy squats behind you and calls her name softly. You put the light on him and she leans forward with her nose working at him as you scratch her neck and tell her he's fine. "Alright girl, he's cool. Your friend and mine."

When you release her she walks a wide turn behind both of you and eases up to smell his boots, his bag, the stick he's holding, his workman's hand as he kneels motionless but for his mouth's issuance of mild and harmless sounds. She turns suddenly and walks away, apparently satisfied.

G-Roy has his own light and proceeds to inspect your uncleared camp. He withdraws his knife, a small machete, and begins to hack at saplings and shrub branches, tossing them aside until there is a sort of triangular definition to the area between the dog's tree and the tent and the woodpile, and you drag out your mat and sleeping bag and spread them there.

He sits sweating and you hand him the water. Insects are following the light, settling on the cloth like it's a landing pad. "Puts me in mind of my jungle time," he says.

You pick up the club-stick, smooth and solid and heavy, and slap it in your palm. "What kind of wood is this?"

He takes out his bottle of no-label and clicks off his light. "Ironwood," he says, and you hear him sipping in the dark. Then the bottle presses your arm and you grasp it well and take your turn. A series of sips and gasps and soon you are both blending into your invisible surroundings.

"How long did you stay outside?"

"Four months."

"Wasn't around here, was it?"

"To de south."

A bottle at rest between two men sitting in a dark wood, an occasional insect colliding with your warm-blooded forms, the

307

dog unheard for a while, nothing seen but the nearest elements of the camp, the evening beginning its slow stretch into night and the starlight in all apparent truth filtering like dust down into the deep spaces between the columns of the trees.

"You were stayin at de Ginger before Pagan Bay," he says.

"Actually, outside in my tent, except for one night in a cabin, getting acquainted with Sheila."

"Like dat," he says.

"Yeah, like that. I started seeing Rita and she got fired. Sheila was jealous and she has her rules."

A cacophony of cricket vibrations in the air—starting late, or maybe you're used to it—vacillating between loud and almost unheard, like some rattling soundtrack dependent upon the mind's attention or the pauses in human conversation or the actual vagaries of insect life.

"Anyway, I'm not really welcome down there now, not that I can afford it anymore. And with this plague of assaults following me, I thought it best to stay away from people."

You hear a sip taken. "A jealous woman a dangerous woman," he says.

The bottle finds your hand. You tilt it back and the liquid leaks into your brain. "I believe this stuff lets you see in the dark."

You cap the bottle, set it down. "This wouldn't be the start of your scar story, would it?"

There is a pause. "You heard it?"

"No, man, I only wondered if I ever would."

"Seems we got de time juss now."

"Absolutely."

He seems to be reaching for things. You hear his hands in his bag and then after a minute you hear a scraping of metal, a slow and chilling rasp of metal against metal, or rock, a steady cut of friction this way and that, and you finally figure he's working his knife along a whetstone, back and forth, and the sound is ominous in the darkness.

"Since de time I start callin myself a mahn, my life gone through periods of obsession. Dis tellin is about one of dem, my so-called fuck-phase."

You laugh, initially thinking he said fuck-face.

"I had passed de days of despisin every touriss and even turn round so much dat I take a job at a fine hotel, workin as a yardmahn at first. One day I see dis woman playin tennis. She look to me like someone from de pages of fantasy, or mythology, not actually albino, mahn, but de whitest of de white, a true beauty so tall and strong in a white dress, playin like de champion of de world. She and de boyfriend speakin a tongue I never hear before. I was rakin up some yard cuttin and watchin deir game, and every day for a week I find some reason to pass by de courts late afternoon time. I begin to think she is seein me too and I know I am catchin a serious affliction."

"What was it about her?"

"Everything, mahn. Her blond hair, her pretty face, her body, her motions, dose long athletic legs when she reach for de ball. Her friendly smile. She projected a certain jouissance. She seem to be a goddess who could change my entire life in one day, one minute even. I was not even dat close, mahn. My infatuation come from behind a chain fence.

"Soon my imagination start takin over. Me believin she eyein me by now, wishin we to meet. Dis yardmahn like a chicken, scratchin wit a rake."

"She just got in your head somehow."

"Mahn, I stand out in de dark after I finish workin, hidin in de bushes and watchin deir room. Dey come from de shower and my eyes are strainin so hard from dat distance, and I almost jump in de open to get closer but de mahn shut de curtain. I wait dere anyway, juss hopin for a good look at dis girl. I cahn't be in love, mahn, I never even met de lady. Bad enough slave yourself to pussy, but dis stuff I had never touched. Den I hear her cryin out, juss one time, but dat cry stay inside my ear even till now."

"What happened?"

"She walk out on de balcony and stand lookin straight at me in de bushes tryin to make myself smaller. She was breathin deep and givin me a full view of dat body so fine and light she seem to be hairless, mahn, a beautiful naked queen lookin ten feet tall."

"Did she wave or anything?"

"She turn and go back inside. Dey leave de next mornin."

"Did you get her name?"

"Eva Larsson, from Sweden."

"But she was gone."

"I took up de game of tennis anyway."

"You're really an optimistic sort."

"I began to appreciate my opportunities. I came to work early and left late, meetin more touriss women. I was chasin dat ball and chasin any foreign woman. My obsession start ragin me. In dose days of free love, lot of touriss girl wanna take home a holiday sex tale. I began to get a reputation, mahn, like a holiday gigolo, which was true. But also as a mahn puttin himself above his own people. Not true, but I took offense at de notion and when de season slow down I get myself a Granville girlfriend."

"I thought you nailed the Swede."

"Doan jump, mahn."

"Sorry. You go right ahead."

You hear the walking, the steps in the brush, and you both stop talking until you hear the lapping at the bowl, and then you call Muttly and she comes to the edge of the sitting area and puts her wet nose in your hand.

The man takes a drink too and goes on. "Soon we got a good thing goin, mahn. My girl pretty sweet, pretty sexy, and she enjoy plenty love-makin. But I know she start thinkin about de future, about us bein together. She doan say too much to me but she start tellin her friends she turn me around, bring me back from all dat foreign pussy. Den winter came around and I start dreamin of Eva because dat was de time she had arrived, December. So now three things happen. First, I move up to de kitchen, start wearin a white jacket and a paper hat. Yah mahn, I know dat create a funny sight in your mind. De second thing concern my girlfriend. She take a job in de office at de same hotel. The third thing, de most amazin part, cahn only be de return of Eva."

Muttly turns in circles at the edge of the mat, lies down and sighs, her dog-smell settling into your nose like roots. The air feels noticeably cooler now but these sips of raw rum are keeping your body warm. You hear the slow scraping, the man sharpening his blade further, as if he's putting an edge on his tale too, or needs to keep his hands busy while he talks.

"How cahn I say it, mahn? She look more beautiful de second time, better dan de memory I been carryin all year. And dis time she come wit a girlfriend so right away I see de message comin at me. First chance I go to de courts, start practicin my serve. Later dey come walkin by and I cahn see Eva observin my form. As dey pass she wave and I wave back and smile my friendly native smile and my next ball fly over de fence and lose himself in de shrubbery.

"De next thing I know she standin at de fence askin me, 'Weren't you here last year? You look familiar,' and I say I am thinkin the same thing. She say she is a player too and I say I remember dat. Den she say we should have a game sometime.

"From dis point I had only one true wish."

"I think I got it."

"By dis time I had become a special chef—meat cutter, omelet-maker, crab-stuffer—workin in de kitchen and out, a buffet-mahn at times, greetin de public and makin sure dey get what dey need. Eva and her friend start talkin and jokin wit me and pretty soon we got a tennis date, de three of us.

"No time now for other woman, not de girlfriend either. Eva only gonna stay a couple weeks. I keep wonderin if she saw me from dat balcony de first time, but we juss keep cool and friendly.

"Her friend doan play too well so when she sit out Eva and me play and she whip me hard, bwoy, but I make her work and sweat all de same. We begin speakin about goin somewheer else, about doin somethin off de property and it seems we both start understandin a new game.

"But de winter schedule was rough. I start lookin for any excuse to get off de job, lookin to make myself invisible. I had more concern wit de way she eat her fruits, de way she wipe her lips. I was livin in anticipation, extremely lost, mahn, my eyes followin her hips when she walk, her mouth when she speak. Meanwhile people speakin to my girl, and de manager speakin to me about quality control, about guests gettin de wrong omelet.

"Even de waitress tellin me my behavior too obscene for public standard, sayin she see me sniffin dat blond woman at de buffet. And I know dat, mahn. I was reckless but I din care. People could laugh in my face and I din care. My girlfriend came out to explain her embarrassment but she woan let me go.

"None of dis had any effect on me. My only wish was findin a place to fuck Eva. To me de dinin room was fine, de front desk, de lobby, de swimmin pool. I din care because I was expectin a religious conversion. How true dis prove to be I had no hint at de time. Eva was more original. Romantic too. She want to sneak into Fort Rodney at night and frolic among de cannons and such. Make new history in de colonial remains. She had seen dat big tree leanin on de wall since Jake pass by some two years before, but dat climb nothin most people would care for, even less to enter Rodney if he locked.

"I was opposed to complete nudity on government property but she doan care, standin like a ghost in de moonlight. Wantin to be seen, mahn. Enjoyin her nudity. De woman love to shed her clothes, love de feel of tropic air on her whole skin. Not shy, mahn, not at all. Actually a true nudist, ready to exhibit herself any chance she got. Quite comfortable in her skin. She was fearless, mahn."

"I'm with you so far."

"Y'know, mahn, sex is sex. We had a bench dere but after all dat buildup, things go pretty quick. But she was kind of loud, and de guard come around shinin his torch. Din bother her at all, seein dat old mahn's face when he get a look at her. She start laughin and scare de mahn. But some of dese security fella feel dey gotta force de law like police, so I take de mahn aside, tell him dis de only way she gives it, actin like a proper historian, conductin a cultural exchange, askin if he wanna mess up de touriss trade wit negative action. He doan answer so I tell him dat she and I are actually engaged dis evenin and he almost witness de consummation. He say we should be waitin till after de marriage. But mahn, I say, gettin to dis point was quite an achievement. And he very serious, explainin de rules and such. Take pity on dis pretty visitor, I tell him. My true love. But de mahn wanna make a speech about respect and morality, all dat stuff a bored old mahn workin alone at night like to speak about. Eva frighten de old fella. But we listen for a time and den I tell him we goin back over de wall, goodnight sir. He protest dat too, quite upset, askin us to exit proper and leadin us to de gate, unlockin us out dat way."

"That was decent of him."

"Yah, but someone see us leavin and report de transgression. De old mahn dismissed for allowin illegal activities, failin to report de violation of government property, failin to notify de authorities durin de act of trespassin so witnessed."

"What a shame."

"Dat fella start wanderin de street, mahn. No more job, no uniform, no home, no rules. A dirty fella now, walkin all across Granville. I see de mahn on occasion, dese days wearin cardboard—"

"I know that guy. Big Daddy, I call him."

"Wheer you get dat?"

"Just a nickname. We had lunch together in the park."

There is a pause, the scene possibly conjured in his mind's eye. "Worked in dat place many years, mahn. Some people even call him Sir Rodney, after de founder."

"You must've felt pretty bad."

"Din know all dat till half year later when I move back to Granville. Saw de mahn on de street. He ask about my wife, dat big spirit woman put wrong luck on him. I told him it was me, not her, and I din actually have a wife, my own fault too."

"You digress, man, leaping ahead to a new phase."

"True, true." He takes a drink, clears his throat. "Dat same night, too late to go home, so I go back to de hotel and sleep under a table. So tired, mahn, but Eva still wanna play. She knows my schedule, free time in de middle, and she wants me comin to her room even though we been sayin all along das a risky business. But of course, mahn, das de way it goes. Both of us wantin to get dat stuff while we cahn. Her friend gone to town and us fuckin wit de AC runnin loud and de maid comin in. She stop and step back but de harm already done. When I slip away, mahn, my girl standin down de hall, no word spoken.

"She got off at four while de kitchen staff preparin de dinner menu. Basically, mahn, I was half asleep on my feet, poundin meat wit a mallet. I hear a scream like somebody in a kung fu movie and she strike me wit a vegetable peeler. Next thing I see she on de floor wit my hand round her throat, mouth open but no sound escapin. My blood pourin over her face and

I got dat mallet raised up to break a head. At dat point, mahn, people yellin and chaos in de kitchen, someone grabbin my arm, and I start thinkin she already dead. So dizzy I was, and her face covered wit blood, I became confused. Den someone tyin a towel round my neck—Ever get a tourniquet on your neck? Picture dat, mahn—and a crowd walkin me outside, goin to hospital I suppose, and das when I start runnin. Hear dem shouts but I juss runnin, mahn, outa my head."

"You were probably in shock."

"Wake up on de forest ground, completely lost, wearin dat bloody white jacket."

"Why'd you run?"

"To my mind I had killed her."

"But it was you, man. That phase was dead."

You both take a drink and the pause spreads into the night.

"What came next?"

"A solitary celibate time."

"Sort of an extremist type, aren't you."

"Sure, mahn. Sittin here wit you, right? Dat solitary time was about gettin food from a place like dis. You hear dat owl cry while ago. Plenty meat here for us too."

"You couldn't have had much with you. How'd you survive?"

"Only my wallet and a gift from Eva in my pocket, a key chain souvenir. I wander for a couple weeks, eatin fruit and plantation food I snatch here and dere, but I need some tool, mahn, a cutlass, and fire too since I plan to stay a time, wantin to cook some meat. At last I walk down to a settlement, find a mahn workin in a shed. Must be I look like a bandit by now but de mahn doan comment, juss sell me a cutlass and a file and a lighter, and give me a sheet of plastic too. After dat I doan see many people."

His light clicks on, reveals his knife and two steel rods in his other hand. "Grab de speargun and wake dat huntin dog, mahn." The dog is curled in repose but an eye has opened and the ears are raised. "Let's find us a fat manicou for dinner."

"Manicou?"

"Dat night creature wit de rat tail and de belly pouch."

"Possum."

"Das de one," he says, standing.

You reach into the tent for the speargun, and stand and sling your pack over a shoulder. "Was that the last you saw of Eva?"

"De last, mahn. Four years ago."

"You still have the souvenir she gave you?"

"All used up, mahn."

"What do you mean? It was a key ring, you said."

"A silver dick."

"A silver dick. What, like a charm, a miniature good luck erection?"

"Yah, mahn. Das what she gave me. I doan know how many she got. Maybe a bagful. Maybe she gave one to all her lovers."

"Funny gift. A hard little dick on a key ring."

"Oh, de woman pretty funny. Pretty and funny. I never met a girl carryin round somethin like dat."

"What'd you do with it?"

"File it to a point and put it on a stick."

"No shit. A spear. Who'd you stick with it?"

"A pig."

"Smith's mother?"

"I din see de babies at first and I doan like to see dat happen anyway. Too much meat for one mahn. I could only catch one when dey scatter."

"But then you had your little companion."

"Dat bwoy was smart. But his mama, she learn de same hard lesson as me."

"Yeah, which one?"

316

"Dat dick cahn kill you."

"Ha. I know you enjoy that line."

He grips his light under his arm to load the gun, holds the other spear alongside the flashlight. "Let's go, mahn. Leave dat bottle. Bring de stick."

The dog takes off excitedly up the trail, perhaps sensing her mission, your motions coaxing her further into her feral self. She runs nose to the earth ahead of your lights, searching for signs, you hope, for scat, for intersecting paths to your shambling prey, the nocturnal scattered rambler at home on ground or limb, up or down, the furry pinball of the forest, leisurely careening here and there under the guidance of some untidy and highly private and erratic-seeming system of roaming and feeding and stumbling across night surprises, roads and cars and carnivorous foes.

You follow the barking up the ridge. It sounds urgent, an imperative bark. You arrive huffing, beams cutting through the space around the dog, who stands barking upward into that space, the beams climbing trees and peeking between leaves. Nothing. G-Roy examines the ground, then prods the dog with his foot and she moves on.

The man swinging ahead, his blade dinging through thin stems and vines. You wait and listen, moths crossing your beam. Turning your head, trying to hear in more detail, trying to catch any small sound out of the ordinary. You imagine yourself listening down the trail, your hearing better than humanly possible, as sharp as a deer's, ears turning like radar units to locate a cough, a sneeze, a groan, a foot falling on a brittle stick. There are many layers to penetrate, the unknown cries and calls, the songs of insects near and far, the mammals and the birds who stalk the jungle night. You keep walking, crunching after the light ahead, brain active and senses dull.

The dog is barking again, and you hustle to catch up. You find her relentless in her announcement, G-Roy with his beam pointing to the animal frozen on a limb, its eyes glaring back into the light, teeth shown and claws gripping. You touch the dog, trying to hush her, but she steps forward and continues her vocal confrontation. The possum is larger and whiter, its fur less gray than the North American variety you've seen so often alive and dead. But still, a sharp-faced goblin held immobile by the brightness.

G-Roy whispers, thinks he'll get a better shot if the animal moves farther out on the limb. He doesn't want to see his little spear stuck out of reach or vanish in the dark. Move him, he indicates, so you position yourself for the best broadside angle, holding your stone, your other hand extending the light while G-Roy sights along his torch and aims his rubber-powered gun two-handed.

Your throw hits the limb under the possum, clunks off and crashes in the brush, your light darting down to mark the spot as you palm another stone. The animal scuttling out and the limb bending. It stops, suddenly unsure, and then reaches behind itself to turn around and head back toward the trunk. The next stone knocks it loose and there is a hissing scramble to hang on, one forepaw clinging to wood as the body dangles and the smooth tail swings down like a pull cord out of reach.

The spear imbeds itself in the lower belly, the animal squeaks loudly and falls, Muttly howling like a jackal. Your light following a bundle of fur and G-Roy is on it with his stick—thump and hiss, a confusion of leaves, a crack to the skull—Muttly lunging close to the throes and sounds. And then it's over, the man carrying the furry mammal by its tail and you find one of your stones and leave the scene, this game like a trip to the fair with your dog growling at the dead prize won.

G-Roy beheads the animal, skins and guts it on the trail, Muttly left in bliss with the warm offal and the tail—a tube of fat around a meat and bone core—the hunting dog's reward. You build a fire, a splash of fuel and twigs flash into flame and burn, the camp dances in vivid orange light, the place crackling and lively, smoke aloft between the trunks. You wonder aloud how far firelight carries among trees, or the odor of smoke drifts on a calm night. And your companion says no one will come this late.

On a bamboo rack he chops the meat into limb and midsection pieces, bones included, cuts onions in a bamboo trough, tosses it all into his dented pot, adds water and hot sauce and salt. Possum stew.

Passing the bottle, poking the fire, squatting in the circle of heat and light. A tripod of split bamboo established over the flame, the pot hung, the dog lurking at the sweet savory edge of cooking meat. And you're thinking about phases and evolution.

"So you went from escort to hermit to handyman to chess fanatic. What now?"

He stirs the pot with his knife. "Change always comin."

"Let's go back to that foreign pussy phase, the hotel job. You said you had passed the point of hating—despising, you said—every tourist."

"Long time ago, mahn."

"We're just passing the time."

"Yah, dat was political. De angry young bwoy makin noise."

You both sit before the fire, its small flames throwing more light than necessary, flickering an area above and beyond the campsite with shifting licks and shadows. Glenroy stands and shields his eyes from the light and listens over the crackling of the burning wood. The dog watches him and looks off toward the trail too, her head aimed. He bends and looks into the bubbling pot and kneels again beside the fire. His black eyes molten in the light. "About dat time I feel some sympathy wit de Dreads," he says, watching you over the pot. "Who come from a movement, y'know, which form up outa black pride tricklin down from America."

"You mean before the rastas?"

"Yah, ideas movin slow from de north, whereas rasta come wit music, spreadin easy across de islands, Marley singin right from Jamaica and dem sound catch a breeze and everything sorta blend together after a time."

"Was everyone more or less unified by those ideas?"

"Din see too much unity, more like a fire burnin and people throwin different fuel to grow dat flame, some good, some bad. We get power and pride and so forth arrivin from de States, ideas washin up like shipwreck. But self-reliance, mahn, das something I learn from chess. Only *you* makin dose moves. No pretenders, no impersonators to blame. No team, no movement, no group mentality. Juss you, mahn, on your own. Doin de best you cahn. De trends from de States, de movements and changes tricklin down here some years after dey start—Black Power and free love—such a contrast, mahn. De flow of information like waves across de ocean. Of course for a time dese two mix, so sex wit white girl got political too, more like turnin de tables, flippin de colonials to see deir backside while you havin fun. A statement, y'know. But we been de majority here since Carib and Arawak time, even under French and English rules. Even in revolution against dem. Black power, das mostly American civil rights, but de concept help us become an independent nation. Juss ten years ago.

"Okay, true, we cahn feel kinship wit Africa too, we cahn see de value of unity witout killin white people on holiday. Dis small place actually start dependin on touriss, y'know, so some got a new resentment toward foreigners. But if you doan want dat outside money, doan take it. And if you do want it, shut de fuck up. Be cool, mahn. Cahn't have it two ways."

Glenroy sets the pot on parallel pieces of bamboo beside the fire. "Rain comin," he says, and instinctively you look overhead but see nothing of the sky. You sit and the dog sits next to you, and after a few minutes Glenroy spears a piece of meat and holds it up and blows on it. A one-note whimper bubbles from Muttly. The man passes the pot by its handle and you knife a chunk and smell it and wait, enjoying the moment, the presence and odor of fresh cooked meat weighed against a bothersome hunger, its alleviation imminent. And picking with hands and knife, you eat the meat dark and greasy sweet and tender enough, chewed off the bones and these delivered to the mutt, and there is a period of cracking and munching, and onion scraped by blade from the pot, and a hacking gag as the dog momentarily chokes. Bread and potatoes are sorely lacking but this is a meal. Thank you, Mister Marsupial.

Drops are falling before you've finished, infinitesimal sizzles upon the receding flame. G-Roy picking at the pot and holding his sheet of plastic over himself, the rain increasing as you gather the pallet and the bags and the speargun and the bottle, and push them ahead of you into the tent. The fire hissing and spitting as the dog licks the pot, and then G-Roy crawling inside too, the screen zipped and the dog left standing outside.

With the flame light dying and the tent skin drumming, you sit back in these close quarters as darkness returns, bellies full enough and bottle uncapped, settling down for the night, the dog nearby as your trusted alarm, the tang of woodsmoke hanging in the moist air and the magnificence of the midnight trees towering over you like silent breathing giants.

In your mind a song is playing. *Won't you help to sing, these songs of freedom, 'cause all I ever had. Redemption songs.*

"I saw Marley once," you say. "His voice blew me away. I knew he wasn't singing to me, but his sound was beautiful, like he felt something that he had to let out. Like he had no choice but to spread the word. His faith carried him, I guess, no matter what you think of it. It was easy to see how people could call him a prophet."

Glenroy clears his throat. "Now de mahn dead," he says, "prophet or not."

"I love his voice still. It lives on. But it was weird how he let that cancer go too late, thinking he'd get divine intervention."

"Thinkin Ras Tafari, thinkin Haile Selassie, also dead, gonna step down and help. I cahn't understand how dose Jamaican turn dat mahn into God."

"Me neither. It's incredible, labeling a living person that way. Or anyone. It's so random, so desperate. I mean, Garvey predicts an African king and his followers look at Selassie and say, there he is, the Messiah. And he lets them think whatever they want. He could've said: You're kidding me. I'm really Haile Unlikely. I don't know, maybe he declined and they wouldn't listen. He was already an emperor. Should be enough."

You hear the diminished dripping of the mountain shower and the dog walking, her nose breathing at the screen as she stands near these human voices in the damp dark.

"I don't care if someone wants to call this place Babylon and tomorrow's place Zion. Or heaven, or whatever. Just don't push it on me."

"Das all dreams, mahn. Mythology."

"I never understood that promised land business. I mean, who promised?"

"Me. I promise. Listen to dat rain fallin down on earth. Dis here is Zion, mahn. Rain fallin on Zion."

You're hearing the dog and the drips and the walking of wind through the leaves. The droplets blown and rolled and falling down around the dog on its guard.

"You think we'll get killed tonight?"

"If you doan kill me, I woan kill you."

"I can live with that." You laugh to yourself and shut your

eyes and the man belches and then sighs like a boar.

Soon you hear him snoring, not too loudly, and you figure you'll lie awake awhile under the rain and the night suffering some illusion of protection, trusting judgment and luck and a dog's keener senses. Surely by now she's developed some loyalty, some concern for you. And you picture her ideally, a noble and wiry little beast, sniffing the wind, turning the funnels of her diligent ears, and it seems in your drifting view that you're almost praying to Dog.

Outside, the dog paws at your knees while you stretch in the percolating dawn, the soft-formed scabs at your back pulling, unstitched rifts in the fabric of your skin. You itch all over and your face feels inflated, but you're smiling and your moaning utterance is like a song to the wood—the night survived—and you stand laughing, relief in your lungs like extra oxygen.

G-Roy crawls out and looks at you oddly. He rubs his face severely and seems surprised by his surroundings. You haul out his bag and yours and close the tent. He picks up his cooking pot and his stick, and you tie the dog to her tree and pour into her bowl what little water remains. As you stumble down toward the trail the colorless forms of trees are materializing in the middle distance as though whispered into existence.

After a while you've loosened up, arms are swinging and legs are moving well, though G-Roy has cautioned you about being too carefree, and you watch the way ahead as daylight reveals the details of the jungle.

Nearing the stream you startle an agouti who scampers away down the trail. Glenroy squats and drinks by hand as you fill the canteens, the water babbling in your ears and your eyes running along the path and through the surrounding wood.

"I'm thinking I'll break camp today or tomorrow, move along. Are you coming back up here later?"

"Before dark."

"That's great. By then I should know what I'm doing. Maybe I could crash at your place another night and get a lift to the airport."

"Of course, mahn."

"Can I ask you another favor?"

"Speak."

You tear a page out of your notebook and write Rita's number. "I'm thinking I should avoid the road today. I'm too easily recognized. Can you call Rita and tell her to come up here as soon as she can? She knows where." You look at his face and he nods. "Thanks." You're holding your pack, keeping the pressure off your wounds. He starts to move away. "Ask her to bring some food if she can."

He watches you a moment. "Keep awake, mahn." Then he heads on.

Bird calls high and low. A cooling mist rising and falling. The sun seems gone already. You need a bath but you drink and wash your face and neck and arms, and move along in the drab light of this waiting period. Waiting for Rita or Rollo or whoever else might show up. Or no one at all. In any case it's time to move on. This phase is ending one way or another. Walking up this familiar trail you look around from within your solitude and wonder what you're even doing here. What has happened to the freedom of indifference you once possessed?

Muttly speaks her mind. Wags her hindquarters upon seeing you and chokes herself against the leash. You set her loose and she thanks you with a tongue to the cheek and steps away to do her private business.

You consolidate your gear, pack stray clothes, then sit outside on your poncho cleaning your thumb wound, which looks pretty good. The bite on your neck is nothing but a bean-sized bump. You take a look at your passport, the entry stamp giving you thirty days here, and you add up the days and find that today is number twenty-five. You sit listening and all you hear is some vireo's persistent singing down around the bamboo thicket. The dog returns and you sit listening together.

You spend half an hour removing ticks from the dog's head and neck and ears, eliciting an occasional yelp but no nips, and popping the parasites on bamboo with the point of the awl on your knife, the bird singing all the while. Then you gather your daypack and the speargun and tether the dog for a walk down the trail.

Still overcast, a quarter past ten. The forest quiet and the dog also. You pick a vantage point above the trail that affords a long view of its curving circuit downward, tie the dog and sit beside her, sixteen shots in the camera, rain on the way.

You don't even have your departure tax. So there's more begging and borrowing to be done. You feel like you're not getting enough blood to your brain. Your throat feels tight and you know what it is. It's Rita. You're afraid she won't show, for whatever reason. That you'll be left here wondering what went wrong, that the constriction in your chest will continue to tighten and choke you. It makes you dizzy even as you sit, while nausea dances nearby, taking jabs at your stomach like some malevolent nymph. It's as if you've been thinking you've come out alright, triumphed over adversity for the most part, when you realize that the most important part is still unrealized. Otherwise, why are you waiting here, sitting on leaves? You could be home. You could be free.

You feel feverish. You passed up Glenroy's ride, an easy hop to the airport, and now you feel sick, rejected maybe, or powerless to bring Rita here. Perhaps it's simply hunger or a lack of coffee that could explain these sudden sensations. Maybe it's the cuts, infection setting in, your blood poisoned and weak and bringing you down. Because if she doesn't show up then what's the point, what's been accomplished here? Have you taught anyone a lesson?

Is it possible you missed her, that she's heading for the top of the mountain? Or something unpleasant happened to her. Or she's on the way right now. You should leave, break camp, give her another call, meet somewhere else. Go to her house despite the risk. Knock on the door and help her decide how she feels.

You feel sleepy and shake your head. Brush an ant off your boot. Take a sip of water. You shut your eyes and hear a rumble in the sky. You should go.

Your head hanging, bobbing now and again in a daydream sleep, the light sprinkle of moisture like waterfall mist. So pleasant to feel, and the smell a fleeting dream around you like fish in a rock pool at the top of the world. You have a poncho; all you have to do is get it out. But this reverie should not be broken. A rain falling on the back of your neck like the whisper-touch of a lover.

The dog growls.

Your head snaps up. She growls again, standing now. You see a movement way down between the trees, and in a moment you can see that it's someone walking. You lean forward and ease to your feet behind a trunk. How many? Looks like one person coming up. The dog barks! You squat and pull the leash and the dog into your arms, hushing her as she struggles to track the intruder. Yipping to break free as you spot the figure again and a bag carried and a yellow jacket withdrawn. Rita.

You lean on the tree for support. No one coming behind her. The dog under your arm scratching at wood. You put the animal down and she barks, and you see Rita stop and pull her hood back, look up toward the sound as you step to the trail. The dog barking as you start to trot, seeing the woman's face as she moves toward you, her smile reaching out through the tender rain.

Part 5

Witness love's sweet despair washed away by falling rain and flowing tears passed from her cheek to mine. Thunder above the trees and the dog barking at the threatening sound and the embrace of us humans excluding her. Strong arms pressing my back and the pain watering my eyes too. Then the wet kisses upon lip and nose and cheek and eye. Our giggling the music of possible joy, the clucking of waterbirds around the shore of a liquid reunion. Laughing and pecking in the rain.

"Rocklee," I say. "How nice to see you again."

"Blue Eyes," she says in my ear, squirming like a worm against my legs. "You are really still here."

"Hard to believe, isn't it?"

My gear gathered and my other girlfriend, the dog, meets the new female and halts her barking, even though she senses the excitement and remains excited herself, weaving among us as we walk, tripping us up with the leash until I loosen her to roam alone. I hold the poncho over our heads and try to answer the inquiries in regard to the animal and the weapon and how I've spent my days up here, but our meeting retains a dream quality and what is said is less important to either of us than the interchange itself. Being together in this ascendant fashion, climbing upward as we did before, and feeling again the breath and heat and heart of the other.

For the moment there is no mention of Blandy or Stedman or the condition of either man or the car I last saw them in. Or of Rollo, or the police, or any of the questions that have lately crossed my mind. That can all wait, I think. What is relevant now is only the fact that Rita and I are alone in the ripe and rainy physicality of the forest. All of the other stuff is lumped together into a category of potential problems to be examined later. Not now.

Rain continues to fall, the dog shaking herself every few minutes. The jungle somewhat dark for midday, no life seen, no vireos singing, only the sound of water splatting into pulpy plant matter and the wind above whistling and slapping at leaves. We move on up the soggy trail, playing under the poncho, laughing about the weather and our destination—she imagines it to be up on the shore of the high crater lake—and things repeated, finding comedy in our side-by-side situation, holding slippery hands, happiness informing the wonder of a stubborn pairing, suspending any threat against it.

Upon seeing my meager camp, she looks around in amazement, and the setting seems surreal to me too, as if I'm dreaming. Muttly shakes herself violently and attends her water bowl. Rita stands looking at the familiar tent and the cut stalks and the darkened ash pile and the tall sleek trees surrounding the small dog drinking and then the wild-eyed face of the man beside her, and she seems bewildered, as does he, as if all of their moments together have been somehow compressed, the elements of their mutual experience collected, and now lie unfathomable right before them. And I imagine us to be congruous, neither alone in this sweeping disorientation, but equally thrilled and frightened by the precarious presence of the other.

"I doan know why I feel completely crazy," she says.

"Me neither. Can I invite you inside?"

I unzip the door flap and put the bags in the corner and set the weapon on top, and we crawl in and remove our shoes. The dog attempts to join us but the screen is zipped shut and she stands looking in with water dripping from the fur at the sides of her nose.

Rita removes her jacket and I my shirt as we examine each other face-to-face in this small space, sitting on our heels, heads in the close air of the center peak. She makes a face at the strips of cloth wrapping my torso like string around butcher's meat, or some silly costume of minimal fashion, and we roll back like synchronized swimmers to peel off our jeans, and make layers of damp socks and underwear in this pale proximity, ready under the thin tapping tent to restate and reestablish our merger. Goosebumps raised on unclad flesh, the air cool through the nylon nest as we lean forward to touch, delicate as songbirds, as if something new is developing and we must be careful and sure, a rare egg to be hatched and we are inside it, blood and muscle moving, with the sound of the winsome rain and the dog turning at the door. We are nervous as squirrels, naked and caged and vulnerable to the world, forming a kiss demented, writhing in our spell. Without further thought or delay I am inside her and we are joined along our contours, our mouths molded as one, our chests pressed fast together, our parts linked hard and yet acting on their own, almost motionless, as if the simple connection is enough, and our mutual release feels miraculous and unavoidable at once.

Afterward we lie tingling and slick in the humid warmth, staring at the near blue roof, the rain still falling but the wind abated, our small domain humming with pulses and the raintree life growing slowly below and around us. I think of us like beetles in a woody burrow, snug and safe as long as we don't buzz or crawl or flutter out anywhere beyond our green and silent kingdom.

"What's in the bag?" I ask, my foot touching it.

"Food. Clothes and such."

"Going someplace?"

"Doan know what I'm doin."

"You mind if I put my film in there?"

She gives me a serious look. "I doan mind."

"I feel like an insect or a baby bird in here."

"I feel like a sleepy girl in de rain."

We try to nap a bit, lying there listening to the rain, but end up talking instead. The initial flush and blush of our reunion partially drains away, withdraws from the surface capillaries into the deeper regions of the body. I don't mean to suggest that the bloom is falling off the rose. Not at all. But the old thorny issues are certainly felt, and new questions and problems can't be ignored for long.

She can't seem to reconcile the fact that I've been here for days with the fact that I did not communicate this to her, at least not right away. "Juss one call," she says. "But I suppose you had more important things to do."

"I was concerned for your safety. It was like guerilla warfare or something. I was just planning it as I went along and I didn't see any place for you until it was over. Then I called."

"Are you tellin me das all finished now?"

"I don't know. In a way I feel like until I leave I'll still be waiting for Rollo."

"Because you messin wit dose guys. True?"

"Well, yes. I just felt like I had to stay and do something, if only to make a point: You can't go doing those things without some sort of reaction, some sort of retribution."

"What did you do?"

I give her a shorthand version of the week's activities, starting with my night at the guesthouse, and following Rollo and stealing his bike and then the dog, making this camp. I tell her I took some commercial pictures for the Red Ginger and got paid in food for myself and the dog. She doesn't interrupt and I go on, explaining how I went back to town, to the market, and went back to Rollo's and snuck inside and about the fight—confrontation is the word I use—without much detail except for saying that I stabbed him in the leg and got banged up myself, and would have fared worse but for Glenroy's appearance—like a guardian angel, I tell her—and moving on to our subsequent time together, the night at his place and another up here last night, waiting for trouble that never came. Then I add that Glenroy felt forced to push a car off the road yesterday that contained her brother and his pal Stedman. And that I also ran into Janet.

I sit up. "Is he alright?"

"Juss bruised. He say you try to kill dem."

"Did he mention shooting at us?"

"No."

"How's the other guy?"

"Smash up, like de car."

"Maybe he's out of the picture now. Any mention of the accident, or police?"

"No."

"How's Blandy treating you?"

"Askin questions, such as wheer you hidin. Angry all de time dese days."

"Thinking he needs to save you from me."

"He change alot dis year. Actin hard all de time. After you come along, I doan even know dat bwoy anymore. Makes me so sad." She pauses. "He was a cute one."

"He's what, a year younger?"

"One year, yes. Dillard. Das his real name."

"Dillard? No wonder he's mad. And now he has a personal cause, not just social theory. Wants to keep his family free of Caucasian influences. I wonder what he thinks about rape. Maybe that's okay if the perpetrator is the same color."

She sits up too and we begin to gather our clothes. There is a sort of frosty silence that the rain fills nicely.

"Did you pass any night at de Red Ginger?" she finally asks.

I turn to look at her. "No, I didn't," I say without hesitation, expecting further queries on the subject and thinking I'll tell her whatever she asks, but wishing for peace between us, hoping the topic will be dropped and telling myself it's behind me anyway, a closed door that might as well remain so. Wanting and admiring the truth, as most people do, even as they're lying.

After a minute, she says, "What now?"

I smile weakly. "A bite of food might do well. Also," I say, smelling myself, "I could truly use a bath."

"I din want to say," she says.

"I could break camp today. Stay at Glenroy's." I think of mentioning the airport, leaving for the second time. But I don't. "It might be better for us to leave sooner rather than later," I say, pulling on my damp pants. "What do you think?"

"We cahn eat now, wait for de rain to stop," she says, and wiggles into her pants.

"Alright. No rush, I guess."

She has brought dried fish and bread and rice cooked in cinnamon milk. We sit in the open door, the flap tied back and the dog standing at our feet at the threshold of our tiny dwelling.

I love this moment. This rain-fed wood and this ratty grungy mutt and being here with this fine young woman. But it's also the recognition of a time that seems so moribund, the end of something. Whether that means us, or the forest as it now stands, I don't know. I just don't think I'll be up here again after I step out onto that road. I don't think I'll ever see this place again.

She asks for the knife and proceeds to cut the knotted strips off my torso. An ugly back, she informs me. I dig out my first aid kit and hand it over and lie down on my stomach. There are three serious cuts, one of which has begun to collect pus, and several lesser lacerations. Into each of these she pours peroxide, which burns like hot coals on my back. She blots all the spots and applies small circular smears of ointment while I lie prone on my pallet, fists clenching cloth as her hands work to restore me on that side, the attentive nursing arousing me on the other. Band-aids are applied in Xs and asterisks, and when I'm allowed to roll over my frontal condition is obvious and I ask to have a look at her back as well.

Not exactly your back, I confess, as she stretches out belly-down. The general vicinity though, the same neighborhood, the next street down, the alley running south. I pull her pants down only as far as necessary, so the view is unobstructed, just her bottom exposed between shirttail and bunched up jeans. Her eyes are closed, face turned to the side, and I sit with my hand running slowly over these contours, feeling the smoothness and firm curvature, fingertips creeping into the deeper region, caressing the line and widening it, reaching in to probe her wet and welcoming center.

The funny thing is, disregarding the financial obstacle we face, I'd like her to go with me. And I intend to tell her this again, very soon, right after this next activity which I'm drawing out as long as I can. Because this is perfect, time suspended, seeing what is to be done right before you and not having to look any farther down the blind road of your life. Knowing it'll be extremely enjoyable but pausing in anticipation because you need to take time to contemplate the broader issues once in a while. Her pants are so high it'll be a real squeeze into place, now being a good time to move forward, even though it's a good moment to hold too, a slowing of time's inexorable march and the one-way drive of one's life. Then I'm in, we are joined again and speeding up. Rolling along without much contemplation, driving and reeling, running off the road, giving ourselves over to the rush, together in flight.

We lose sight of everything for a minute, happy to crash, then fall into sleep.

Startled into a waking sweat, I nudge Rita. "We have to move!" Pulling on my boots and scrambling unlaced outside, shirt in hand. Rain falling harder, the dog barking.

"What is it?" Rita asks, emerging.

"Someone's coming."

I grab her bag and my small pack and the speargun and the poncho, and zip the tent shut.

"Wheer we goin?"

"We'll have to hide someplace and let them pass. See who it is."

"What about de dog?"

"The dog's a problem. I'll have to let her go or tie her away from us somewhere."

"Let her go."

I untie the leash and the dog takes off. I wind up the twine and put it in my pocket as we head down the slope.

The dog stands in the trail, a small animal in a rainy haze glancing back at us. We hear a bark but it's muffled. Everything is muffled. A world fuzzy as mold, gray and darkening and indefinite. The taste in my mouth is like raw pasta. We don't have much time. We cross the trail quickly and move around the outer spikes of bamboo looking for an opening. I indicate a space away from the trail and we wedge ourselves single-file into the stand and extend the poncho to partially cover us as we crouch uncomfortably, Rita behind me and the speargun aimed like a defensive missile between the stalks that form the walls of our lair. Of course now we are unable to see the trail and whoever passes but we'll hear them and know when to start our way down.

We hear the dog again, closer, on the other side of our dense cover, announcing the presence of intruders, keeping her distance from them as she is forced upward in increments of olfactory contact, retreating to bark out the story of their progress.

I feel Rita move behind me. We snuggle deeper into our hole, buried under a brown drape of camouflage. Rain battering the crown of leaves, running in streams down the long jointed stalks. Hunkered down in a haven of spikes, unable to determine the dog's position. She could lead them to the camp easily enough, but that doesn't concern me anymore. What concerns me is getting out of here alive.

A voice suddenly shouts from the trail, so near that Rita jerks against me. "Das Rojo dog, mahn!"

From farther back. "Shut up, mahn. What I say bout yellin out?" Blandy speaking. A quiet minute passes and I can picture Marcus waiting until they are together to speak. Something is said that I can't make out, then the dog barks from somewhere, once, like a question, and I hear Marcus again, my thumb tickling the trigger of the speargun.

"We should catch up dat dog for Rojo."

"Fuck de dog." Blandy says. "Fuck dis rain too."

"No mahn, we kill de bitch and say we find her so. Irritate de mahn to extreme."

To this Blandy says nothing. Then I catch a whiff of tobacco and wonder how he's smoking in this rain, if he's got an umbrella or a piece of plastic over his head. They appear to be waiting, and so I wait for a third voice, thinking that Rollo must be moving slowly, hobbled by his injury. But after a short while they seem to have moved off, the smoke no longer reaching my nose, and I hear a cough some distance away uphill and begin to suspect that maybe only two men are on our trail.

"Who is de other bwoy?" Rita whispers.

I turn my head so she can see the finger at my lips. Listening through the rain for movement, wondering how far they'll go in the rain at this late hour. While having the dog as verification of my presence in the vicinity. And nothing to be heard but the falling water.

"That's Marcus, Rollo's other flunky," I say. "Let's run for it."

We extricate ourselves and stand cramped, stretching our legs behind the bamboo cover, the ashen air of the valley seen in speckles through the leaves and limbs waving apart in the rain before us.

Treading on a moist mat of bamboo matter we peer around the lower end of the great stand, seeing the trail clear downhill, and then creep out to look up-trail, not hearing the whereabouts of man or dog. I catch a glimpse of the open path, then scan what I can see of the ridge up toward the camp area. Hoping that Miss Muttly's leading them on a wild goose chase.

I slip the poncho over my head. "Ready to make tracks?"

"Let's go, mahn," she says, wiping water from her face.

Onto the muddy leaf-strewn trail we move, eager in our downhill tilt, leaping and slipping in our haste to travel this corridor to freedom. I take her hand but our disparate movements tear us apart, and I hear her laugh as I run flapping in the breeze of my own speed, plastic poncho tails whipping behind me. We seem like kids playing hide-and-seek, running down a mountain before anyone can find us. Running from her little brother, no less, so she must find the whole predicament ridiculous. Holding her bag like a child to her chest and mine swinging wildly across my back. The rain in our faces and everywhere the sound-cushion of water and wood.

A bark like a chirp and I look back to see Muttly galloping full speed down upon us, springing and bounding too fast, perhaps smelling us and misjudging our motion. Rita turns to see, staggering to stop, but her arms provide no balance as she sidesteps and the dog changes direction, leaves sprayed to the side as they collide, both of them startled into a spill. The dog tumbles like a toy and Rita pitches headlong down the trail, her bag dropped as she bumps the ground and slides through the mud and muck.

I move to help her up. She looks stunned but unhurt, the dog slinking over to join us, regarding Rita warily and moving somewhat sideways, her tail wagging hesitantly, as if she doesn't quite mean it.

The boys come barreling into view, one of them—Marcus, I'm sure—whooping and hollering victory calls, daring us to run it sounds like, which is just what I urge Rita to do as I start to move. But she stands staring at the approaching figures, gathering herself for a fight, unable to run from her little brother. "Let me speak to him," she mutters. I see the moment being lost, the chance to flee evaporating, and resign myself to whatever will happen, hopefully, or perhaps foolishly trusting a blood bond to outweigh a campaign of hate.

The boys are smug and swelling with success even as they arrive heavy and dripping, soggy assassins, the pistol dangling from Blandy's long arm, a piece of cold metal with rain running off the barrel. Neither man dressed for the weather and Marcus holding nothing but a wet stick.

They stand above us on the slope, Blandy scowling and Marcus smiling at me like he's remembering that rusty blade snapping off in his scalp, and wanting to thank me for having such a crappy knife. Rita rubbing her muddy hands together and the dog behind me as I brace myself, my poncho covering the speargun in my right hand and bulging out over my pack at the rear so that I resemble some one-armed and unhappy hunchback.

For a time it seems as though nothing happens, as if the next step might be insurmountable, the rain sticking us to the ground where we've stopped. But then I hear the dog growl and begin to worry that they'll kill her before I realize it must be Marcus making the noise, stepping down the trail and raising his stick as if he means to prod his prey into fight or flight. His head appears off-kilter, a patch of his pointy locks shorn to the scalp on the left side above the ear, no bandage, just a hole in the hair. He's close now, right in front of us now, and he angles his head to show me an insect of stitches in the center, all the while grinning, his tongue displayed like meanness, and in his eyes a disturbing bloodshot flatness reminiscent of his mentor. We have reached the crucial time. Statements must be made. Facts must come to light. Wounds must be reopened. Blandy has his pistol, but he also has his sibling.

Marcus speaks loudly, rain water sputtering off his lips. "Mayfuck, gotta blade for me head today?" He pokes me hard in the chest, forcing me to step back down the trail. "Under dat sheet?" He pokes again, harder this time, striking the edge of my breastbone, drawing a grunt from me and another step down. "Wheer your dark sneaky friend?" He grips his stick with both hands, jabs it at my face and laughs as I duck to the side. He nods at Rita. "Dis your friend? She all you got now?" He feigns a poke at her, then takes the swing at my head I've been expecting.

The stick lashes over me as I bend, and his follow-through puts him sideways to me. I straighten and lean forward lifting my poncho, my close-range crustacean-killer drawn as he braces for another swing, glimpsing me out of the corner of his eye as my arm extends toward his head. He comes around in reverse, his mouth open wide, my aim held on the flank of his face. The rubber pops with the release of tension. His stick

338

catches my arm and I drop to my knees as both weapons fall away. I look up to see Blandy with the pistol trained on my head, raindrops bursting off the barrel as I cradle my arm, and I hear Rita shouting, pleading in patois, and at the edge of my vision Marcus is squirming on his back.

I see the cuts and scratches across Blandy's brow and his eyes are two dark pits above the barrel's hole. Wait, boy! I want to shout. Isn't the man coming? I feel drops running like rain down my sides. Maybe it is rain.

Rita slaps at the gun, slaps at his arm with both hands, crying out unintelligibly, slapping at his face and head as he fends her off, blocking and pushing her hands away. "Dillard," she keeps saying, her voice high as a child's. The two of them playing slap-hands, a child's game, and he's holding a gun. Finally he lashes out with his free hand, smacks her face with force and shoves her away from him.

"Go home, girl," he says, and stepping forward kicks me sharply in the stomach as I raise my hands. Gasping for breath I notice the dog edging away, confused, her sad eyes cutting down the empty trail and back up to these calamitous humans. Marcus moaning and sitting up, his hands over his face and the shaft that punctured his cheek protruding between his fingers, blood seeping down his throat in watery streams and staining his white shirt rose across the neck.

Blandy scowls at his cohort. "Get up, fool!"

"Hook right trou," the boy cries.

"Pull it out you mouth, mahn." He wipes the water from his face in exasperation and looks like he's ready to shoot someone, anyone. He pulls off his sodden cap and starts to wring it out, twisting it with both hands, still holding the pistol.

A shot fires. Leaves leap off the trail between Marcus and me, all of us jumping at the noise, Rita flinging her arms up, and we all look to see the dog scampering away.

Marcus is drooling. "Rojo say no shoo."

339

"Shut up, fool. Who got de gun?"

Blandy smirks at me. I remain on my knees holding my arm, non-threatening, and I glance at Rita who's feeling her bottom lip with her teeth as she looks at me.

"What you lookin at?" he shouts, and lifts the gun at me. Neither of us answers and he sighs loudly. "I say go home now, dirty girl."

"I goin nowheer," she says.

He seems upset by this lack of compliance and says to me, "Take off dat cape, freak!"

I lift it, yanking at a corner caught beneath my knee, and when it's over my head I hear him move and I tense for the kick, another one to the midsection, and slump forward as he rips the poncho away from me and flings it behind him, saying to Rita, "Better for him you go."

But she just stands there staring hard at him, daring him perhaps, and he leans over me and grabs my pack by one strap and brings the weight of the gun to bear upon the base of my skull. One arm is yanked behind and then the other strap slides loose and I fall into the mud and roll onto my back to face whatever is coming, my jangled brain interested in the wavering paths of falling drops, memory harkening back to my first days in this forest, the views taken skyward into trees, the mingling leaves and the trunks standing in contemplation. Blandy's head enters the picture, leering over mine. The pistol is pointed and no one forgets who is winning.

I'm not sure what to say. At first I think of calling for Rita but I realize I must say something to him. I blink away the drops and watch his eyes far beyond the gun. "Are you an assassin, Dillard?"

There is a long silence. I hear a clipped laugh, and see his teeth in a frozen smile that's upside-down, like a frown. Then he looks away.

I turn my head too. See Marcus looking down at me

between the peaks of his knees as he sits clutching the spike in his cheek. He angles the shaft back toward his ear so the point can be directed outside the hole of his mouth. A two-handed task, fingers reaching in to grasp the barbed tip while the metal is slowly pushed through the entry wound, the cheek sunken while the pressure is on, the elastic tissue concave and reluctant as the spear slides. It looks as if we are witnessing some sort of ritual scarification, a boy becoming a man, pulling a giant needle through his face while his eyes water and squeeze shut and he copes nearly silently with the pain. Or maybe someone doing a circus trick, except for the blood spilling out over the rim of his mouth.

He pulls the spear free, spits a mouthful of scarlet between his legs and presses a hand to the wound. "Futt you," he says, and spits again. His dribbling tongue looks swollen and dark, like a piece of liver. "You deay, Mayfutt," he says.

"Take me to your leader," I say.

We are all drenched. Rita looks dazed. She keeps looking at her brother but he hardly glances her way. She sees me looking at her and makes a slight motion with her head and I sit up.

"I doan even know you now," she says.

Blandy says nothing, watching my movements. She turns around and picks up her bag and he says nothing still, maybe hoping she'll finally leave. He tosses my pack to Marcus. "Maybe you wanna go home, bwoy," he says, digging a plastic bag out of his back pocket. Holds it upside-down and fingers a smoke out of the pack inside, withdraws a lighter—keeping an eye on me all the time—puffs aggressively at the flame as it sizzles, stuffs the bag away, then cups the cigarette and squats, his gun hand dangling over one knee.

Marcus stares at him a moment, then starts to rummage through my things, taking out my shirt and setting it on his knee. Unzips the toiletries and finds the peroxide and pours the contents down the side of his face and blots it with the dry shirt. Pulls out the camera and shows it to Blandy. Then the bottle of fuel, which he sniffs. Sunglasses, hat, jacket, swimsuit. Spare spear. He points it at me and shuts one eye like he's sighting a shot. Then puts everything back except the spear, zips the bag shut and stands. He spits blood in my direction but without enough force to reach me. I stand too. In a plastic bag in my pocket I have my passport and air ticket.

"How you get down dis evil way?" Rita says.

Blandy stands but ignores his sister altogether.

Marcus leans over, picks up the speargun, stands looking at Rita. "De bag," he says, extending his hand.

"Nothin for you, bwoy."

He glances at his companion who is silently pulling smoke from his cupped hand, studiously maintaining his brooding demeanor.

Marcus slots a spear and cocks the band. Gestures at Rita's belly with the loaded weapon and reaches for the bag again. She looks at me and I shrug, thinking of my film, and then suddenly of Cornelia Kensington and my promise to her.

Rita shrugs too and takes a tentative step forward, sliding the bag off her shoulder. He reaches for it and she punches him in the face. He staggers back holding his nose, his eyes watering and blinking spasmodically. He raises the weapon at her and she holds her bag lengthwise in front of her, blocking her body from chin to waist.

"Back up, bwoy!" Blandy shouts. He flicks his cigarette at the boy's head but misses. "She no part of dis."

Marcus is nearly crying now, his face screwed up in pain and frustration. "Who you wif, fuckah?"

"Watch dat crazy freak," Blandy says, motioning with his pistol. "I take care me sistah."

Marcus is wrinkling his nose like a rabbit and trembling with rage. He looks at me and I'm ready to move if he shoots.

"Rojo woan be happy wif dis," he says.

"Shut up, bwoy. You always talkin too much."

Rita turns and starts to walk.

I stand watching the other two, waiting for instructions.

Blandy points at me. "Let's go, rain-dog," he says, and I fall in behind Rita heading down the trail, Marcus following me and Blandy at the rear.

After a while the rain lessens but the forest seems prematurely dark. It feels good to be moving, though having Marcus behind me feels bad. Rita looks back often but doesn't talk or wait for me to catch up. She must like the fact that we're moving too, trying to think of something to say or do. Like I am. Some way to exploit the dissension in the ranks.

My clothes feel heavy with dirt and my skin is cold, my legs clumsy in their downhill locomotion. I hear Marcus close behind but I'm afraid if I look around I'll draw a shot to the eye. He steps on my heel and I say over my shoulder, "Hey, thanks for carrying my stuff. I appreciate that." Then I try to move ahead but he jabs me in the back with the loaded speargun he's holding. A sharp stab that just misses a cut and sends me leaping involuntarily.

"Mah stuff," he says, and spits. "You doan need nuffin now."

A minute later he sticks me again. I try to ignore it but I realize he's found a game. "Wheer you frien?"

"Are you talking to me?"

He jabs savagely into a wound. I spring ahead, choking on pain, gritting my teeth against nerves on fire. Thinking madly of planting a stone in his forehead. "I didn't fucking understand you," I say. Rita is looking back at us.

He gets close again. "You frien," he says. "You frien!"

"Oh, my friend. He's around here someplace."

I hear footfalls and duck and cover my head. A hand on my shoulder spins me around and Blandy steps back, gun waving. "De mahn wit de truck," he says. "Who is dat?"

"Beowulf."

He aims his pistol. "Doan juke me, white bwoy!"

"Hey!" I raise my hands. "I can't help what the man calls himself. I can't change his name for you. It's Beowulf."

"Wheer is he?"

"I don't know. He's a jungle man. Last night he shot a possum, a manicou, and we fucking ate it, I swear to God."

Both of them start to look around more carefully. Rita is standing down-trail, hands on hips, anxiously looking up at us. With her bag and her yellow jacket with its hood up, she looks like a schoolgirl out for a walk in the woods. Maybe out picking berries or wild spices for the family dinner. Or looking for a lost dog or just taking some time alone to think things over. We are all three looking at her as if she doesn't belong here, as if she's lost her way. Blandy saying earlier she has no part in this. But knowing she does. I know it. She knows it. And Rollo knows it, looming somewhere down there. And though it may be an illusion, she seems to be the complete innocent, someone you'd like to accompany on her walk, someone shy you'd enjoy talking to, and after a while and a few smiles maybe, you'd brush a little kiss across her full lips and she'd shut her eyes and. . . .

My face catches a backhand slap—a stinging impression of fingers and knuckles—and Blandy's voice follows the impact. "Why you fuck her, mahn?" A rhetorical question, but still, like he's read my mind. His expression belies any pretended puzzlement, his clear intention simple admonishment, as if he is reaching back to find the one true cause of his familial predicament.

Marcus holds the speargun inches from my throat. "He pith Rojo bed too."

My windpipe shrinking as I try to speak. "We're planning to get married."

Blandy stares at me now with what appears to be genuine consternation, then looks at Rita like she's the poster girl for traitors everywhere. For a split second I consider jumping for the pistol but it's still pointed at my gut and beneath me is mud and poor footing so this seems like a bad bet. I keep my eyes on him, feeling that Marcus is only a hair's breadth from shooting me and knowing he won't be satisfied until he does.

"Hey boss," I say, and Blandy turns back to me. "Don't let this guy puncture your future brother-in-law." I picture myself throwing my arms open as if to embrace him.

"Not if you deay," Marcus says. "Woan be no weddin."

Blandy glances at him, then me, as his sister heads up to join us. She pulls her hood down and Marcus trains his weapon on her now.

"Dis bwoy pointin me belly," she says as she rubs it. "He like to kill dis baby, kill de nephew you got growin dere."

Blandy scoffs. "You two playin—"

"No!" she shouts. "Listen me, bwoy. You check de clinic. Dey got de test. I got a true baby growin in me."

He seems possessed of an anger inarticulate, his mouth moving like he's trying to force something viscous out of it.

She shrugs. "You wanna dead de daddy? Let dis fool shoot de baby too? Will dat please you? Think it over, brothah. But doan leave me alone, bwoy. Doan leave me here witout de papa and baby. Keep de family together and juss dead all three."

"No baby dere," Marcus shouts. "She vex you deep. Dat sly bitch twistin you, mahn. Dis fuckah gotta girl protectin him."

"I tell you true," she says.

Blandy gives me a cold stare. "You conjure up dis baby?"

"No boss, I believe it's real."

"He not de boss, fuckah." Marcus spits. "Rojo woan hear dis shit."

345

"Keep still, cunt. All you nerves comin loose."

"All dis shit mushin you head soft," Marcus says. "Rojo, he finish dis mess up."

Blandy whirls, his gun arm striking like a snake at the head of Marcus, who lifts the speargun feebly between them as he flinches before the pistol and sinks to his knees with the barrel pressed into his injured cheek. He cries out, his other hand waving helplessly.

"Irri-tate me, bwoy!" Blandy pushes him farther, makes him bend to the ground, pushes his face to the earth. "Look your face, smart ass. Dat de face de mahn in charge? Huh? Das de bloody fuckin face a bwoy prayin he sur-vive." He stands stiff-armed over the boy, pinning him down, his hand trembling with tension.

Marcus croaks into leaves and mud, his eyes watering but his voice plainly heard. "You woan be no survivah, bwoy."

Blandy looks over his shoulder at us, sees Rita covering her ears, the horror in her face, and nimbly leaps away from his pitiful companion, crouching and swinging his gun in every direction, an island swashbuckler striking a reckless pose, loose-limbed and dangerous.

"Fuck on home, Rita!" he shouts, brandishing his weapon at the surrounding trees. "You hear de poor bwoy. I woan even be no survivah."

"I slave to no mahn, little brothah."

"No, he's right, Rita," I say. "This won't have a happy ending."

She gives me a mean squint. "You hear what I juss say."

"Dillard," I say, "is the way clear for her?"

He scowls at me a moment, turns to watch Marcus dragging himself off the ground, spitting and wiping his dirty mouth.

"Dat big bad mahn waitin for me?" Rita asks. "Gotta another job for me?"

346

Blandy doesn't look at her. "Not you, sistah."

I cannot help my sarcasm. "Women and children straight to safety."

"Shut up, mahn!"

"You think he's just going to let her waltz out of here?"

"He beat me once," Rita says.

Blandy grimaces like he's in pain, jaw muscles bunched, and shows me the open end of the barrel. "Das your story, not mine." He leans down toward Marcus. "Let's go, bwoy. You ain't hurt bad."

Marcus hoists the pack but seems out of words. He points down the trail with his weapon, spitting blood and showing me the way. Blandy gives me a sharp push and Rita and I start walking together. For a second I think she's reaching for my hand, but no, we're better off as strangers now. The rain continuing, cold drops running down my neck, and I feel the trenchant reach of desperation.

Rita moves on ahead of me. I don't know what her brother believes, but I don't look back and neither does she. We march on, wet and pathetic in a slippery world, a miscarried cadre of doomed soldiers on the downward path to apocalypse.

Ah, my old pal Fred, I think of you now. I know your words and I hear the passion and pain in your worthy voice.

I do not spare you; I love you thoroughly, my brothers in war!

Rita builds up a lead on us. I picture her as a scout, looking ahead for signs of trouble, for surprises. We find her waiting by the stream. I glance at my watch—four fifty-five and gloomy, in every sense of the word—and kneel to drink.

"Take dat off," Marcus says.

I unfasten my watch and toss it over my shoulder. Cupping a hand of water to my lips, slurping the first cool taste, I am struck sharply at the back of the head, a focused, driven wallop that feels like a ball-peen hammer strike and knocks my face into the water, left eye socket banging on a stone. Some sort of sputtering noise I make, a startled sound, the pain partly nerve shock, and before I can figure out what hit me I feel the spear back there quivering with my head's motion. And I hear garbled laughter from half a mouth. He feels better now—that's nice. I reach back to remove the wobbling rod, grasping it where it parts the hair, thinking the point is into bone but too shallow for the barb to catch, but not thinking fast enough. The spear is yanked loose, pulled through my hand, and the barb rips my index finger. I plunge my hand in the stream and crab-crawl across, face my attacker from the other side. Marcus wears a one-sided smile like a stroke victim and he reloads while I cup water to the back of my head. Blandy just watching and Rita already leaving. I feel a phantom shaft still in place when I turn my head. Feels like a cavity the size of a dime, the opening of a hole going down through layers of headache and torsion, a cranial mineshaft sunk into the worry regions and the thought-strata of a brain growing darker. Just let me get my fucking drink. Like an animal at a waterhole, eyes up as the mouth goes down.

The rain has gently quit but one would hardly know it. Everything is moist and muffled and dim. Yet we are thirsty. At least I am, constantly. Forgetful too. I've left my canteens behind. Somewhere in the vast blue tent of my past. Oh, for a thicket of ferns in which to lie and disappear.

I know this trail. Know every ambush curve. When Rita screams, I shudder, a cool wind rippling over my scalp, down my back. Do what has to be done, man. Give it free rein. "Dillard," I call, "get your sister out alive." Then I run.

There is a man sitting sideways on the trail like some stone lion, his hair a huge dark mane around his head and shoulders, his sloping throne an old lawn chair, the staff across his lap a hefty stick, and his noble beast, the royal mascot Muttly, at his feet. I am halted by this strange sight but my eyes dart down the trail, my heart leaping at the thought of Rita's swift passage. I don't expect to see her. I expect her to have gotten through, sailed on down to the road not far away, and I hope she's getting help of some kind. But even as the boys gather round and I shift my feet and adjust to their restless presence, I know that I am being stupidly hopeful, that Rollo only appears to be relaxing in the forest.

He sits immobile, a dark form seemingly forged from volcanic rock and dressed in human attire, some pseudo-recreant in sandals and tanktop and torn shorts, a wide gauze strip of stained bandage across one damaged thigh. Stone face lurking behind coils of beard, eyes small-bore and half-hidden beneath a tangled canopy of compressed matter, a wildly grown organic enclosure that adorns and enlarges his head.

Rita moans, reveals herself facedown in the leaves and tendrils a few yards from the invalid and his comforting pet. I glance back at the boys, their energies unfocused between Rollo and me, and I go to her, tearing through the brush. She must've been slugged by stick or fist and I start to roll her over—examining back and neck and head for injury—when I notice a drop of blood in her ear. Her eye twitches, or maybe she gives me a little wink, and I leave her alone.

Blandy appears anxious and perplexed while Marcus sidles over to his lord and master and presents the captured weapon. Rollo reaches up and turns the boy's chin to see his bloody cheek. The dog watches me from under the chair.

"Gettin concerned down here, thinkin you did meet de devil heself. Now I see de pale demon alive and thrivin among we. Das why he doan run now." He appears to be talking to the speargun, emphasizing syllables of certain words, amplifying their meaning or encoding them, his voice so deep it seems as if it's being called up from a fissure in the ground.

"I'm here to get your picture. You look good in that old chair, like a tribal chief, not just a common lowlife."

"Oh we know dat devil insane, so why he remind us so?"

"What happen to her, Rojo?" Blandy asks.

Rollo cocks his head at the boy. "She stumble, bwoy, runnin too fast in her careless desire to cross dat road, make extreme pronouncements to save de transgressor."

"That's bullshit, Blandy," I say. "Why don't you ask her. See if she can speak."

The chair creaks and leans down the grade as Rollo moves to rise, bearing down on the metal frame, stick and speargun falling to the ground as the dog scampers a few feet away and Marcus steadies the standing man. He gives him his stick and keeps the speargun himself, and follows the man limping off the trail toward Rita and me.

"Dis leg cut bad," Rollo says, "de nation too, devil mixin poison in de black race all trou oppression history. Crafty structure and domination spreadin all direction to desecrate de first mahn, bloodfuck de true people, dis devil corruptin a young girl wit evil seed." He leans on his staff above her, lifts his hand toward me. "Dis demon fella fill de little girl head wit fanciful story, eh Blandy?" He looks over his shoulder at Blandy standing mute, arms long at his sides, the pistol like an ornament hanging from a useless limb.

Rollo looks at me and Marcus points his weapon at my head in case I have an urge to speak. With the prostrate form of Rita separating us, I cannot look down. My muscles want to fly in all directions or collapse en masse upon my spine. Fear and anger, my brothers in war. Rollo clears his throat and works his mouth and spits on her back. "Das a Babylon whore, bwoy."

"She goin home, mahn," Blandy says. "De girl sick."

"Yah, true. Quite ill. Sufferin serious impurity."

"But Rojo." He starts toward us. "We got Mayfuck."

Marcus leers at me. "Any last requess, Mayfuck?"

"Yeah. I'd like to take your picture, all three of you."

Marcus snorts, looks at the boss. "Cahn he, Rojo?"

"Doan be stupid, bwoy. You want your soul cursed by dat fool touriss?"

Blandy comes over beside Marcus and looks down miserably at his sister, her stained and spit-marked shirt, pieces of leaf in her hair. "Sistah," he says, his hand tapping the pistol against his leg. "Rita. Rita Blanford."

The fingertips of her right hand move a fraction but there is nothing more.

"Rita," he says, "wake up."

"She juss restin, mahn," Rollo says.

"You hear me, sistah?"

"She stumble directly into my club, mahn."

Marcus laughs. The three of them are facing me across her body, Blandy bending over her while the other two are looking at me. Marcus leaning closer, waiting for the word, the speargun hovering around my face, Rollo leaning on his stick, breathing audibly, liquid seeping through his bandage.

"Come now, Blandy. Execute dis demon freak."

"I didn't knock her down," I say.

"He waitin so patient to forfeit he grievous existence."

"I didn't beat her the first time."

"Fulfill de obligation you carry in your blood, mahn."

"He wants you to kill your own sister, man."

Blandy aims the gun at my heart. "You bring her here."

Marcus is fascinated. "Do it, mahn. Do it."

"He wants you to kill both of us."

Rita struggles to rise, supporting herself with both arms, her head swaying from side-to-side, one side of her face drawn in lines of forest debris.

Marcus steps back as she vomits and gags, drooling on leaves. Blandy looks sick as well, his mouth slack in sympathy, the gun drifting toward my groin.

Rita rises to her knees, wiping her mouth and reaching up toward her brother as if she wants his help, as if she needs him to comfort her, as if by touching him she might somehow recapture the bond of childhood playmates. And as he extends his hand toward hers they appear for a moment to be children again.

She whirls and throws herself at Rollo's injured leg, grabbing it in the crook of her arm and pounding his wound with her small hard fist. He tries to knock her off with one hand, using his stick for balance, hopping on his other leg, his hair flapping in long pieces.

Marcus and I reach for her and Blandy starts swinging the gun around, covering everyone, hollering at us to stop, and we freeze in place, watching Rollo knock at the girl's head with his fist until a solid blow, or the accumulation of blows, jars her loose and she slips off his bleeding leg. With sweat dripping from his anguished face he lifts his stick like an ax over a stump and I rush forward to block the strike.

Blandy fires a shot over the man's head, maybe aiming for the stick itself, and Rollo checks himself, holding the staff high, biceps flexed, his eyes on the boy as the gun lines up with his head and he stares down the barrel and into the boy's terrified face.

There is a quick movement from Marcus, a guttural curse uttered, and a spear springs straight into Blandy's neck, a sliver of metal imbedded. Remarkably, he does not shoot Rollo. He turns his head mechanically, his downward eyes searching absurdly for the rod extending from his body, and he touches its entry point as his gun hand searches for Marcus. He starts to gasp and fires wildly as Marcus dives below the barrel.

Flinging the stick before him, Rollo steps awkwardly over the dazed girl, the wood catching Blandy across the chest and arms as he is set upon by the stronger man, big arms entangling thin ones in a rapid grappling for the gun. Blandy trying to find his aim as the gun is engulfed by a huge hand, his gangly arm bending the wrong way, his sickened eyes finding mine as I'm digging a stone from my pocket, crouching to take Rita's arm. With Marcus on all fours watching the pistol turn inward, the pop of the report so small, the third little clap in a row, like the Black Cat firecrackers I played with as a kid, when nobody ever got hurt too bad.

The boy drops from Rollo's grasp, sits down in the brush holding his stomach with both hands, his knit cap drooping to the side, snagged on the rod in his neck, a failed executioner watching his sister's slow movements toward him. He manages a small shrug while his mouth looks for words in the silence following, the expression on his face boyish and earnest and full of realization, as if he has now remembered something he's meant to tell her for quite some time.

Rollo takes a step away, limping, his chest heaving. Marcus regains his feet, stands looking down at the other boy's pitiful weakness. Rita has pushed away my tugging hand, awakened as if from a dream, and I'm thinking we've missed another chance to flee.

"Blandy, he catch a great confusion," Rollo says. He trains the gun on me and I scramble backward, trying to get my legs to lift me upright as he steps closer. He's got me sighted so I roll to the side and hear the trigger pulled. Click. And again. Click. I look up at him. Click. He leans forward and slings his hair down and brings it back up over his head in a torrent. He sights again and pulls the trigger. Click. Click. Click. The empty magazine will not produce any more cartridges. I get to my feet.

"Muthafuck," he says, and kicks Rita in the stomach.

Blandy cries out like it was he who received the blow. "Doan, Rojo," he says. "She got a baby in dere."

"Dat so?" he says, looking over his shoulder at Marcus. "Gimme dat stick. Check de bwoy pocket for bullet."

Marcus lifts the stick to Rollo's hand, then squats beside Blandy, pushes him flat on his back and feels his front pockets. Then turns him partway over and rips the plastic bag from a back pocket. "Juss smokes," he says.

"Get away, homo," Blandy says.

"You in no position, bwoy."

"Baby," Rollo says, and kicks her belly again, grimacing through a short, swift kick that barely allows him to keep his balance. "Maybe she got a dead baby in dere."

"Rojo!" Marcus cries.

Rollo turns, but I am already in motion. He braces to meet me as my thrown stone cracks hard above his eyes.

The stick and the stone fall to the ground and there is a moment of stunning silence in this place as if the man has drawn every sound of the forest into his head. Then he looks upward and claps his hands over his face and roars like a beast wounded. He staggers about in a tight circle around his bad leg as if he is chained to a stake, making horrible noises through his hands that seem to frighten Marcus.

"Get up, Rita," I say. "Get up."

She lies on her side with her knees up, like she has cramps, a pained expression on her face. "Blandy," she says.

"We'll come back for him. Stand up."

Rollo falls quietly upon us and instinctively I lean away. His body lands face-down across Rita and she screams under his weight. Dead weight, it seems, as I push his shoulder trying to roll him away. No good. I grab his arm and lift, glancing over at Marcus, who appears to be paralyzed on his feet. But Rollo is heavy and slick with sweat and my hands slip repeatedly. Rita is trying to push herself out from under him without success, and I look at his hair and then gather as much as I can in my hands and pull his head up, leaning back to put my weight into it, lifting his shoulders so that Rita can push against his chest, his head as it angles upward dripping blood on her but the effort working, my position like someone holding the rope in a tug-of-war.

He rolls too easily and I sit down with a bump, banging into a tree, losing my grip as he reaches for me, his head split open and his face resembling a dark red rubber mask, the frightening visage of some monster I mistakenly brought back to life. I get to my knees and he is on his, grabbing for my head, my neck, my arms, anything to pull me into his grip, and I am swinging, nothing solid, just a frenzy. We hit each other's hands and arms but he's half-blind and I'm trying to find his head and knock him senseless again. His hands are covered with blood and my arms are slick too. It's sloppy, like a mud fight.

Marcus appears on my left side, and I raise my left hand between us as he fires. The spear strikes my palm and dangles, and my other hand takes the rod and tears the hook loose. Rollo grabs the hand holding the spear and pulls it toward him, and I hear my name shouted and try to duck as the club is swinging. It catches the side of my head—my left eye sees something like a solar flare—and I pitch over on the leafy ground.

I hear more shouting and realize it is the voice of Blandy. *De Wuf. De Wuf. Baywuf.*

The feathered arms of tree ferns are blurry in my sight, and I hear the rush of wings and the shouts of lunatics, idiots down in the village, banging into one another like hobbled rams. For some reason they cannot kill me. They didn't bring enough ammo. They did not reckon on Rita. Blandy is sitting up and calling for something. I hear the gurgling throb of my brain but I am spared, alone on the ground and wrapped in ferns. Vireos are singing again, proclaiming the end of the rain, the end of the day.

There is the sound of absorption, the forest drinking, nothing more. The light is almost gone but if I squint I can see protozoans all over the place.

Rita is sitting beside her brother, touching his shoulder. The boy is lying in a small swamp of blood and he requests a cigarette. I search around on hands and knees, looking with one eye, feeling for the bag. My hand dripping, I sit the boy up.

You frien here.

Yeah, the dervish returns.

Find the smokes. Put one between the kid's trembling lips. Move the flame around to hit the target. Left eye's gone fuzzy, makes me feel sick. Distances are distorted. Perception off. The boy draws on his smoke, leaves it in his mouth, not using his sticky hole-plugging hands. Talks around the filter. Watching the standoff.

Dey fraid him, Mayfeel.

Everyone's afraid of the Tasmanian Devil.

The boy laughs a little. *You lucky mahn, frien like dat.* His head slumps down, his words grow fainter. *Helpin you. Dis crazy shit.*

Smoke is trailing up the side of his face, leaking out of his nose. *Thirsty, mahn.*

Drip a few leaf drops onto the cupped bag and roll them into the boy's mouth.

Rita stands almost upright. I lift her arm over my shoulder and we huddle together, preparing to walk. I have her bag and I reach down for mine. A short way down the trail Marcus stands touching his head, his stitches split open and the wound running anew. Rollo leans against a tree rubbing his eyes. He is shirtless and has a piece of cloth tied around his head. Between them and us G-Roy holds his ironwood stick like a cricket bat. We take a few steps and Rita looks back. Blandy lies swallowed by plants, mumbling to the sky or to the trees or to himself and I turn his sister away. Our adversaries watch us pass beside them without words, our group of three leaving,

Rita and I shuffling like an old couple, G-Roy guarding the rear. Blandy is cast off worse than a stranger to lie alone in the forest while his life seeps away into the dark. He put on a show and his part is over, left behind like roadkill.

Rollo and Marcus dog us down the mountain, G-Roy keeping them at bay. Near the rocky bottom, trail stones rain down around us with clonks and knocks and rattling rolls. I had started feeling that the road would mean freedom but now it is night and these tragic agitators are still with us. Rita walks poorly, cramping at her center, and I can't claim to be much help, wrapping dirty twine around my palm's raw cavity. A rock rips through fronds beside us and I hear G-Roy cursing behind me.

The trees cast us into the open, the sky purple and clear to my one clear eye. We crash through roadside grass, fall from the ditch to touch mottled macadam, a placid strip of highway gliding serenely down the curve. And there at the roadside is a bronze Mazda waiting to trundle our tormenters away. A rock falls close and breaks open like peanut brittle and we race so slowly toward a paper cloud, a wizard's kite hovering improbably over the car and the road and the hills standing to the east. Music floats up with the fumes of fish. Trombones and frogs and fruits of the sea. Classical strings and crickets in their intricate static. Friday night, and at the familiar drive the gatekeeper is a dog standing still and ghostly as soapstone. She hears our spongy feet and slips between the hedges toward the sounds of a house.

G-Roy bounds upon the road and then the other two are cast out from the rustling brush. We crouch behind the car and wait for the G-man to join us, looking across the road toward the driveway of the Red Ginger, which promises to be, after all that this day has delivered, the pathway to civilization and order and genuine safety.

Marcus comes jogging down and Rollo follows, favoring

one leg and flapping his arms as a means to help his hobbling, huffing descent. But Marcus slows down as he approaches his car, out of weapons altogether and facing a new situation as he watches our group moving across the road.

The three of us stand on the premises of an active establishment—several cars in the lot, drinkers in the bar, doors open to the porch, diners witnessed through well-lit windows—with G-Roy holding his club like a barrier to further entry, his own vehicle parked nearby. The boy is waiting for Rollo, who stands alone in the middle of the dark highway. Looks like they'll have to leave and we'll go to the party, an unkempt and bleeding trio sure to be granted service, to be admitted among the guests as curious miscreants, harmless and needy vagrants. I stand watching Rollo while Rita tries to tell me something about her brother.

A car comes around the curve below, raking its lights across the driveway and back to the road, lighting the Mazda and the boy beside it and climbing on toward the man up ahead who does not yet move. He stands frightfully certain of his position, staring into the beams, the horn hollering at this insanity, this dangerous shape of man lit up in full view, his awareness apparent, no complaint or fury able to move him.

The car passes, the two men inside expressing their negative opinions of this highway reprobate, street menace and public lunatic. Rollo is pointing at us, his arm aimed in accusation, as if we're the reasons for all this and his behavior is somehow sound, the simple effect of a cause he wishes to extinguish.

The Mazda cranks up and lights up in reversal, backing up the hill to meet the man. He who is waving me over, motioning me toward him with open arms as if he wants to say goodbye, bury the hatchet before he goes, inviting me once more to settle my accounts. And for one crazy second I imagine this last communication to be something else, if not an apology then a truce he's asking me to join.

Behind me are the fuzzy lights, the laughs, the fine smells and musical offerings, the culture of centuries. I take Rita's hand and head down that way, wearing my woodsy little pack and holding her bag to my chest like some lumpy stuffed animal I won at a fair, wanting to vanish in the property, clean up in the cold river, rest awhile on the steps of a cabin. Then Glenroy can take us all someplace else, and I hope no one calls the cops.

Two white people are leaning on the rail outside the bar, watching us approach. I don't look at them, don't encourage a discourse or contact of any kind. We may appear to be a pair of wretched backpackers or victims of a mugging returning silently to our cabin to suffer in private. I catch a flash of movement in the orchard, the blink of a firefly or a bat's wing, and as we enter the zone of the thumping generator I glance back into the wash of light from the dining room and glimpse the tables and the people behind the bright panes, the serving girl in motion, and I can hear faint strains of Schubert, violin and piano floating above the bass of the diesel machine. I notice the porch people looking toward the road, and see Glenroy still back by the cars.

I look at Rita. Her face is puffy and carries a layer of bitter distaste, her eyes drifting and wet. I can feel the generator beating at her pains and mine, an external rhythm hammering us into a state of exhaustion, and it seems as we near the shed that the surrounding drone is creating a vacuum in which we are cut off from the world. Even in the long sloping yard the feeling is claustrophobic, as if we are convicts ambling down into a factory pit. Within this capsule of sound and smell even the stars lose their power, twinkling like illusory spots. The frogs are vanquished, the night-blooming fragrances overrun by a noxious, invisibly billowing exhaust. We are fragile mammals on a path to the river and this pounding, spewing assault makes us queasy and weaker, crippling Rita. She grips her belly, stumbles to her knees. I crouch beside her, feeling skittish without my full hearing, the engine house just ahead and a feeling coming to me like a distant echo. I look back and see G-Roy moving down the drive and waving at us, the Mazda turning in behind him.

I pull her toward the shed, thinking vaguely of taking shelter inside or behind the small building. She pulls the other way, repelled by the pounding sounds and leaning toward the brush below the orchard. I let her go. She staggers and falls across the path into the grass and weeds. At the door I pause, suddenly thinking: Fire Hazard; thinking: Fire. Hazard. I pull my pack around, my hand digging inside, touching the cool glass of the Fanta bottle at the bottom. The Mazda running lightless down the drive and picking up speed as G-Roy runs alongside it, his mouth opening in usurped yells and more people drawn out to the porch. I shake the bottle, pull out the rubber hose and stuff the soaked scrap of rag back in, the car jouncing down the path, two tires in the grass, two figures inside, and in the ambient light from the restaurant I can see the hair behind the wheel. G-Roy still a steady threat, the car swerving at him, taking a swipe that veers him off-track, the whole scene like one from a silent movie, grave and comedic at once. I cradle the bottle in my clumsy bound hand, fire the lighter with my right, touch the fuse and flame blossoms like a lethal flower. I step onto the path, waving in my hand a bright marker for the driver, and I mean to get back behind the building before the car knocks me down to the cabins.

I see the car swimming and weaving like a mudfish through the ripples of my watery vision. G-Roy falling away slings his stick at the driver. The grill and the hood look like armor, even the windshield is curved for deflection. I change my mind, take my aim wide to the side, hurl my diesel cocktail sidearmed at the window, the car turning at me and the bottle missile a streak of light between us, a wobbly fiber trail in the pallor and noise and bedlam of the moment. The bottle shatters on the side mirror, liquid fire spews in the window, the car jerks side-to-side without slowing as flames splash across the interior. The sudden flash of light a silent explosion within the Mazda's high howling, voices inside a part of that noise, the generator drumming deeply as the car crashes through the building's corner, cinder blocks broken and thrown, collapsing on hood and windshield and roof, glass cracking, metal rending and the shed door splintering. The car burrowing further into a chaos of sound, its motor running with clank and squeal, and as the machines collide there is the boom of steel concussion and the beginning of an engine symphony blowing apart.

The horn blares an awful whine—a warning, a half-ass Klaxon—and quits, signaling a change in sound, a change in the night which now surrounds this fire, the distant light of the establishment flickering to extinction as the generator thumps its death beat, chugs to a stop amid the crumble of its housing, the void left by its loss swiftly filled with shouts of exclamation and panic drifting like dream calls into the fire zone. The fire itself a flamboyant genie granting its own wish, popping and expanding out of the car and into the shed, crawling up the walls to the rusting roof, licking all materials for sustenance as its impact-scattered offspring run like fiery tadpoles over the grime and petrol-taste of the opened room. The car now a chamber of flame, its engine stalled too, and the boy's piercing scream suddenly rupturing these strange motorless moments before the boom.

The driver's door swings open and Rollo staggers out wearing a wreath of flame about his shoulders, slapping at the fire rising, his beard and hair burning as he claws at his head, emitting a terrible gargling sound, twisting his torso in a macabre fit of energy as he weaves across the path toward me.

On the passenger side the car is wedged into the shed and

the door is hard against block as the boy hollers. Through the flames I see G-Roy moving to that side, approaching the blaze with an arm before his face, his other arm whipping his shirt at the heat as he tries to penetrate, to reach the boy in the window, a writhing crying figure caught in a funnel of flame breathing through that hole. But there's no hope for Marcus, the boy being consumed by fire while the diners lining the rail obey the orders of someone's logic or their common knowledge and begin to edge back inside, G-Roy fading back too, the car engulfed, its combustible state promising certain peril.

With a foulness of burning hair and branded skin, Rollo surges past me like a zealot flailing himself, spots of pink melted open on his arms and neck, lurching drunkenly down the slope but keeping his feet, running from hell toward the river. I turn and run too, through the grass where Rita went, following my shadow over weeds seen in fire glow and watching the man—shocked and crying out in pure torment, his dark skin revealing its innerside in lurid glimpses of the body's palette, the clump-strings of his hair swinging about in gestures of cinder and smoke. A vision of man ambling damaged through a fiery night and screaming at his fate, howling at what he understands and all he cannot, at the trap he constructs by his own deeds.

Then the explosion shudders the air and lights the clouds and I am on the ground covering my head, face pressed into wet roots and earth. Scraps of metal falling and more blasts spawned, flammable cans like rockets streaking, the machines waging a small war with whistles and a shrill pissing upon the land, the ping and clang of the generator's parts; gas tank, pipe and pan blown away and concrete lumps like gravel thrown. A rain of industrial rubble and shards of glass. Roofs bang as pieces fall. The fire crackles and wheezes and eats what it can. Patches of grass are burning and the smell of solvents drifts in the air. A smoky haze hangs over the weeds like a battlefield finished.

A rustling approaches and I picture the dog's head nosing through the grass to find me. But this scenario dissolves and I have a sense that Rollo has circled back to confront me again. There are legs beside me and I see a hand reaching. A feeling of disembodiment claims me in a convulsion and I think I still hear screaming.

"Jake," Rita says, her voice breaking, "cahn you move?"

"Did you see him?"

She kneels beside me, touches my face. "Let's go, mahn."

"Go where?"

"Find Glenroy," she says. "Get away from here."

"I killed that boy."

"Doan be sayin dat." She pulls me by the arm and we stand into the poisoned light of the fire.

We help each other walk to the path. The shed is a bunker blown apart, smoldering block and metal wreckage, twisted tools and scattered parts, the Mazda a black shell of a car nursing a burn of plastic and stuffing and rubber and the corpse of Marcus, none of it clear to my squinting watery eyes. The acrid smell of the fire provokes a dreadful urge to puke, the smoke like mustard gas or some debilitating stench working on the lungs and skin. I feel it on my arms and in my mouth, but I stop and look back at the bathhouse and cabins visible in the firelight, an empty outpost standing against the darkness beyond. Rita pulls me on.

Amid the debris along the path we come across her bag. Here and there objects lay smoking in the grass, and people are coming down the porch steps and wandering into the yard like zombies. We are too sick and thirsty to speak.

A flashlight beam darts around inside the restaurant. A few voices can be heard and table candles are flickering. A car starts. It backs up into the drive and throws its brights at us and the carnage beyond. We move toward the porch, shielding our eyes, and the engine shuts off. Several people approach us asking questions but we don't answer and some keep walking, going closer to see for themselves. Others watch us from a safer distance.

Glenroy comes down the steps with a napkin draped over his arm and a pitcher of water in his hand. "Table for two?" he says.

While Rita drinks, he squeezes my shoulders gingerly, probably afraid he might hurt me, looking me in the eye, examining me and maybe expecting me to speak. Finally he just nods toward the road. I take the water and shut my aching eye, wanting only to slake this gruesome thirst.

We hear a car and then it turns into the drive, another set of lights pulling up beside the first. Glenroy looks to see if he's blocked, starts walking, and Rita follows. The new arrivals sit in their vehicle a moment, taking in this unusual scene, then a man who looks local steps out and stands staring at the fire, maybe wondering if he's chanced upon a special cookout. He looks over at me and I hear Sheila, a tone of instruction in her voice, talking to a confused customer who'd like to finish her meal. Others are heading for their cars. Down at the wreckage someone stifles a scream.

Sheila spies me eyeing her and comes right down the steps, puts her flashlight on my face and runs it down the length of me. Her lips are pursed, as if she's about to spit, and her eyes have their own fire. Then she suddenly looks as though she might laugh. "Was du machen?" she asks.

"It was a freak accident, a bad driver."

"Scheisse!"

"I'm sorry about the damage."

She looks around, takes a deep breath, her glare perhaps keeping others at bay. "I am sorry for you, Jacob."

"Thank you."

She looks at my face again. "Go to the hospital."

"I can't close my hand," I say. Mister Ludicrous.

"The Polizei are coming." She shines her light over the cars, picks out Rita and Glenroy beside his truck.

"She lost her brother," I say, maybe to compare their losses.

She smiles sardonically at her good fortune. "We have lamps. We will continue our business."

"More romantic than ever."

"How lucky for me. Maybe I will fall in love one day."

"I hope we understand each other, Sheila."

She coughs, shakes her head. The man standing by his car is trying to get our attention but she is looking down toward the fire. "You choose the difficult way."

"Didn't you?"

She shrugs. "The Police will ask many questions."

"Try to tell a simple story, Lady Sheila. A tourist and a local were attacked on the road as they returned from a walk. A man in a truck came to their aid. They were walking down to the bathhouse to clean up when these criminals tried to run them down. The result is plain to see. The ringleader went to the river. The owner of the vehicle is still in it. There is another boy a short distance up the trail across the road. The victims have gone to Granville to seek medical attention."

Someone is calling her. Darlene comes to the door and stands looking at me and I turn and walk away. I hear Sheila speaking to someone but I'm sure it isn't me.

I slip into the truck next to Rita and Glenroy turns out onto the highway toward Granville, plain for all to see. We suffer through the twisting route, then take the turnoff to the coastal road north and drive the long way home.

There is blood on the seat under Rita and her pants are wet. A waxing crescent, a cool hangnail moon is sinking into the dark waters of Pagan Bay, taking a trip around the world.

We stop at a house in Glenroy's neighborhood. He goes inside for a moment, then returns and ushers us in to meet Miss Cleo, a wizened and knotty old woman who studies us in her kitchen light and seems to know in two minutes everything that might be worth knowing about us. A young girl in a long white dress pours us fruit juice and puts on a kettle to boil. Miss Cleo takes Rita into another room and then we hear the sound of running water.

I step outside with G-Roy while he cleans the mud off his truck tags, the dark paste he used to cover the numbers. He mentions a boat that's leaving tonight, in about two hours, from here, from Pagan Bay. He says he spoke to the captain this morning and brokered the idea of a passenger or two traveling with the cargo. There will be a fee.

"Where's he going?"

"Saint Lucia."

"Wrong direction."

"Any direction tonight de right one."

"That's right. How much does he want?"

"Two hundred. For two."

"Why so much?"

"I had to tell de mahn somethin." He leans against the tailgate and looks up and down the street. "I speak about de need for privacy and he ask me straight if you are a fugitive. So I say no, not yet. He laugh and say he gotta meet you first. But I know dis mahn long time. He will do me a favor but not free. He puttin himself at risk too."

"Sure. Okay. I'll ask Rita."

"Will she wanna go?"

"I have no idea."

We stand there under a black, by now moonless, sky. The few streetlights are so dim they only illuminate themselves.

"I can't see any investigation going too far up that trail. Can you? My tent has a few holes in the floor but it still works.

My pack's in there, with another camera. Take whatever you can use."

A man comes clanking by on a bike, mutters goodnight as he passes. G-Roy responds in kind. He steps to the cab and produces a bottle of no-label. The first sip makes me gag but the second levels me out some. The bottle is passed a couple more times, then the front door opens and the girl beckons us inside.

Rita lies on a couch in the front room, as if asleep, wearing a dress I don't recognize. In the kitchen the girl gives us mugs of tea and Miss Cleo directs me to a back room that adjoins the bathroom. She sees me eyeing the tub through the door. "You would enjoy a bath," she says, English-sounding. "A clean voyage." She smiles, not requiring an answer. She sits me on a stool opposite hers and takes another look at me.

"How's Rita?"

She puts on her glasses, light blue cat-eye frames that look thirty years old, and pats her close-cropped mat of gray hair. She touches my chin, turns my head gently one way, then the other. "Dat baby all gone away now." She seems to grin at me, lacking several of her teeth, watching my reaction, but I don't know if I have one.

"But how's Rita?"

"Very tender," she says, indicating her middle region. "Three day rest she need."

She takes my left hand in her small dry fingers and begins to unwind the dog-twine fused there in crusted blood and dirt. She drops the twine on the floor and frowns at my palm, the deep grimy cut and ragged skin, and the reopened bite at the thumb. She sets the hand on my knee, steps into the bathroom and runs water into a basin. I pick up the twine and stuff it into my pocket.

There is a reading chair in one corner, a lamp beside it and a wooden tray balanced on a foot stool. Boxes of books and magazines along the wall. A cot with blankets and a pillow. Some shelves with bottles and bags of dried plants. An old gray metal cabinet. Pictures of wild horses on one wall, a duckbill platypus on another.

She moves the foot stool over for the basin and while my hand is soaking I sip the tea, which tastes basically like cinnamon.

"Dat hand not gonna work for a time," she says, and I nod. "How you feel it?"

"It hurts and it feels numb."

"Nerve damage," she says, and I nod again. "You catch a knife?"

"A crayfish spear."

"And de older wound?"

"Dog bite."

"Gracious. Mahn and beast."

She opens her cabinet and removes a tray of surgical implements. She injects my hand and cleans and sutures the wounds as I sit with eyes closed, almost napping. Then she runs the bath and helps me out of my clothes and I sit washing my feet with one hand, keeping the other dry, while she washes my back and my hair. She gives me a few minutes to myself and afterward I dry off and she treats and dresses my back wounds. I get back into the same clothes, which are all I have except for a swimsuit, a tee shirt stained with Marcus' blood, and a jacket. I take some pleasure in brushing my teeth, and then Miss Cleo fashions a patch for my eye with a piece of yellow felt and a rubber band, and tells me to leave it for a week.

"Then what?"

"Den you see."

I accept this ambiguous prediction and stand to leave. "You saved us a great deal of suffering," I say, hesitating, thinking: What can I possibly give you?

"Free clinic," she says.

"Really? All the time?"

"Sometime."

I stand looking at her eyes for a moment and she removes her glasses. "People love you," I say.

She smiles. "Some do."

I smile too. "What about the platypus?"

She laughs. "My favorite."

"Frankenstein's pet," I say. "Ever see a real one?"

"No."

"Me neither. If I ever do though, I'll take a picture and send it to you."

"If I am still here."

"You plan to move?"

"No plan called for," she says.

At Glenroy's place there's a pot of rice and beans in the fridge and he puts it on the stove. Rita sits on the cushions by the chessboard and leans against the wall. The time has come again to talk about leaving so I sit next to her.

"Are you looking at my patch?"

"You should color it black."

"Like a pirate?"

"Yes, like a pirate."

I slide a little closer, so that our arms are touching and I can feel her skin against mine. "I'd like to hug you," I say, "but I'm afraid someone would get hurt."

She smiles a little half-smile and puts her arm around me and I put mine behind her, and we manage a docile embrace. We remain that way for a time, holding each other against the pressure of the other and feeling a warmth and a soft lightness after all the day's hardship and brutality. We don't speak and I close my eyes and it seems our surfaces together are slowly forming a membrane. In the background are Glenroy's

369

comforting movements about his house and I seem to be floating when I feel her quiet sobs against me. And as she cries I begin to feel lighter and my pains seem to be something like clouds moving across the sky.

Glenroy announces that he has rum, bread and beans ready for consumption.

"Not exactly the Red Ginger," I say.

"But somewhat safer," he says.

I get to my feet, offer her my good hand. "Can you eat something?"

"No," she says, standing beside me.

"Can you travel?"

She looks at me with wet eyes. "Whas de meanin?"

"Our good friend here has made preliminary arrangements for us to ship out on a little freighter going to Saint Lucia tonight, real soon in fact."

She wrinkles her runny nose. "Saint Lucia?"

"That's where the boat's going."

We move to the counter and I have to assume she's considering the adventure. I mention the short notice as usual, and the fact that the timing couldn't be better for me, for her too if she doesn't want to be hauled in for questioning. It could go much worse for me, of course, and I've been saying we should take off anyway. She began the day with the thought of a journey, she tells me, though she could not see how it would happen. Her problem now is that she needs to tell her mother something about Blandy.

Glenroy offers his help, even though she would be the one to corroborate his story when the time comes to tell it, when the authorities insist that he come down to the station and fill in the blanks, when they hassle him and threaten to press charges for leaving the scene, for complicity in the deaths, for whatever they feel like hanging on him, depending on how large a case it becomes, when he may find himself sitting in a stinking cell awaiting his clearance while she floats away to freedom with an injured and penniless and wayward traveler.

Admitting she has her money and passport, that she has a bag packed at home and that her mother will not be completely shocked about her leaving but will become hysterical at the news of her dead child, she stands at the counter beside us, silent in her thoughts, and for some reason I know she is shedding a skin. Glenroy and I sit without words during this time, and after a few minutes she examines us and takes a sip of my rum and goes to the bathroom. We hear the splashing in the sink and her nose being blown, and when she rejoins us she sits and asks for paper and pen.

"Do it in the truck."

"No one will be able to read it."

"I mean after we get there. We can't miss the boat."

She looks at us both with a sick expression. "I doan even know what to say."

"Say that Blandy got involved with the wrong people and you're sorry you couldn't help him. That you have to go away right now. Just don't say where or how. And that you love her very much."

Captain Copeland looks about sixty, though he is probably younger. His vessel, the *Lucy Gallante*, is a typical island trader, about forty feet of well-worn wood that looks to be green or blue in the scanty light at the end of the dock. His young mate and two other men are loading boxes along the gunwale of the bow. The captain is robust and clear-eyed with the wrinkles of a seaman and the grip of a freight-hauler.

"Been fightin?" he asks.

"Yes. A long feud reached its zenith today."

"How de other fella fare?"

"Worse."

He nods, glances at G-Roy. "Anybody followin you?"

"I don't think so," I say. "Not after we're gone."

He looks over at Rita sitting in the truck's pale cab.

"She's writing a letter to her mother," I say, thinking this sounds pretty decent.

"You folks travelin light. You have documents?"

"We have passports but we'd rather go in unannounced and rest for a few days without any questions."

"I'll be goin in to Castries Market. I could drop you before town."

"That'd be fine, Captain."

"Dis a cash ride. He told you?"

"He did. We have enough."

He looks at Glenroy, standing by as a silent character witness, then looks back at me and says, "Welcome aboard."

What can I say to Glenroy Oliver Davis that's not too trite or foolish at this moment along the quiet shoreline? I know that time and distance have a way of turning even the most heartfelt, face-to-face sincerities into memories of old exploits with interesting characters who can never be loved as much in remembrance.

I take his hand and hold it with both of mine. "You are the truest of friends, Glenroy. Wherever I am, anytime, my door will always be open to you. You don't have to rush because that offer will stand as long as I'm alive on this planet."

He laughs. Then adds his other hand to mine. "Not such a longtime offer de way you goin lately." He looks over at the boat, the men bustling about. He releases my hands and then shakes my shoulders lightly, looking at me as if he is memorizing this moment.

"Dis time was good for me. I got some profit by it, juss knowin you." He smiles.

I have to laugh at that. "Man, I have no reason to disbelieve anything you tell me."

There are demons within us all. They reside nowhere else. You may subdue or contain or control them if you're lucky or talented or perceptive enough, but you will not slay them or ever be rid of them. I don't know why this is. They might manifest as cancer or murder or addiction or arrogance or bitterness and loathing as you're lying in bed late at night. It's the way of the world, part of it anyway, the only world we know. The bad with the good and all that. I mean, right and wrong, they're interchangeable at times.

We say the end justifies the means. Maybe. But that might sum us up too easily. I don't know if I can justify what's happened to Rita. She may want to return home after she collects her wits. It wouldn't surprise me.

After the fare, we have a spot on deck and a hundred and seventy-four dollars left. We're ready for a sea cruise to an island neither of us has seen. Captain Copeland is in the wheelhouse and we're standing beside it. His mate, a friendly fellow named Kent, brings us a blanket and two oranges.

The boat pulls away from the dock and we are watching Glenroy, a lone figure on the shoreline. He waves and rubs his raggedy beard as we rumble away into the darkness. Rita starts to cry but I know she's looking beyond the man and into the land itself.

*****

About the Author

Michael Jarvis was born on an air force base and traveled regularly, living as a child in Guam, Georgia, and England. He graduated from Florida International University and lives in Miami, scouting locations for various film projects and writing fiction.

His short story, *American Kestrel*,was published in *The Secret of Salt: An Indigenous Journal* (Key West) in 2008.

CPSIA information can be obtained at www.ICGtesting.com
Printed in the USA
LVOW082334310313

326826LV00002B/9/P